W9-BHN-432

Untamed Love

Stone lunged toward her and grabbed her by her slender waist with sinewy strong hands and yanked her back down in the sweet-smelling hay. Her breathing was ragged from the force Stone had executed on her and by his nearness.

"You are confusing me. Before you came, I was never confused," Kristianna said. "I knew who I was and what I wanted to be. And now you have me thinking strange things all the time. I do not like it."

"Believe it or not, I've been a little confused myself," Stone admitted.

"I . . . I find myself thinking about you. Wanting to . . . to touch you." Hot shame burned on her cheeks.

Her honest admission sent fire to his loins.

"I know it is wrong and sinful of me, but I cannot help it." She cast her eyes down, unable to meet his stare.

"Then don't help it," he commanded in a sensual whisper. He cupped her chin in his calloused hand and gently tilted it up. "Touch me."

FIREFLY

STEF ANN HOLM

LEISURE BOOKS　　NEW YORK CITY

To my husband,
Barent Jerome Holm,
who has given me the support
to pursue my dream.
I love you truly.

A LEISURE BOOK ®

August 1990

Published by

Dorchester Publishing Co., Inc.
276 Fifth Avenue
New York, NY 10001

Printed in the United States of America.

ACKNOWLEDGEMENTS

Writing this novel has been an exploration of my roots. My ancestors on my mother's side were Swedish farmers and in creating Kristianna Bergendahl, I hope I have conveyed a little of how my family lived. I like to hope that somewhere back then, there was a young girl, who despite the vast differences between them, met and married a trapper.

As in all creative endeavors, I cannot take full credit and I'd like to give special thanks to my mother, Gloria, for her help with all of my Swedish translations. My father, Frank, for his historical eye. My grandma, Agnes Blomquist, who gave me insight into Minnesota farm life and Swedish customs. My cousin, Kathy, thanks for the loan of the Swedish books. Also, Paul Douglas, the weatherman at KARA, Minnesota, for helping with the northern lights information.

And most importantly, my best friend in writing, Barbara Joel. Your comments and gentle, but forceful, nudges even when I didn't quite see it the same way as you at the time (and you were right) have been my inspiration and my motivation. Thank you so very much.

To Lawrence Taliaferro, Jean Nicollet, Fronchet, and George Catlin. I tried to place you where you were when you were alive. Thanks for your contributions to all of us today.

Lastly, a special thanks to my Uncle Artie who showed me what a firefly ring was. Your little trick has stuck with me throughout the years.

· PROLOGUE ·

1827
Buffalo Village
Erie County, New York

Stone Alexandre Boucher stood on the plush landing, transfixed by the tall clock outside his father's closed study doors. The clock's pedestal, constructed in rich mahogany with gilded inlay, was solid and firm just like the old man himself. Gold, spear-shaped hands met over the Roman numeral twelve, and rather than the baritone "gong" one would expect from such a stately clock, a soprano "ting-ting" chirped from behind the fretwork. The clock may have been a reflection of his father, Alexandre Baptiste Boucher, but it had the soul of his stepmother, Solange.

Taking a deep breath, Stone headed determinedly for the closed doors and rapped twice with his knuckles.

"*Oui?*" The heavy wood muffled Alexandre's resonant voice, and the sixteen-year-old Stone

1

could never figure out how the man could make the word yes sound ominous.

"I'd like to have a word with you, sir."

"Then what the hell are you doing standing out in the vestibule, boy?" his father bellowed, his speech lightly inflected with a French accent. "Come in. Come in for Christ's sake."

Stone pushed the doors open and immediately closed them behind him. It took a moment for his eyes to adjust to the dim light of his father's lair. Alexandre's passion for earth tones was reflected in the velvet, sable-colored draperies, the darkly stained floorboards, the cherrywood-paneled walls, and the dun ceiling. Shelves of musty leather-bound volumes lined the southern walls, leaving the northern walls open for his father's prized oil paintings and collection of wooden, cigar-store figurines displayed in glass cabinets. A floor-to-ceiling window on the eastern wall created a picture frame for the distant harbor below the bluff on which the grand house was built.

"What is it, Stone?" Alexandre stood tall next to a wide, unlit fireplace trimmed on both sides with mule-deer and elk antlers. His fine, white lawn shirt was open at the base of his throat, the lacy ruffles a striking contrast against his burnt-honey skin and smooth chest. The sleeves were rolled to his elbows, and he rested a strong arm on the mantle, his long fingers dangling a tumbler of yellow-gold brandy. Rich emerald trousers sheathed his well-toned legs as well as ebony, leather boots that fit snugly over his calves. Thick, umber hair was brushed away from his forehead which was creased in expectation. Stone couldn't help thinking the old man looked powerfully male, and secretly hoped to look as fit when he was forty-four. Some said, they were carbon copies now.

"I have some business to discuss with you, sir."

"I'm waiting," the older man said, gazing pointedly at his son.

Stone seethed inside. The old cuss could sure be hardhearted without even trying. For years, it seemed they'd been angry with one another, and what he was about to say would not bridge the growing distance between them. "I'd like to discuss West Point."

"Then discuss it. Hesitation will never advance you from cadet."

"It won't make any difference what rank you want me to advance to, sir. I've decided not to go."

Alexandre stared hard for a moment, then turned from the hearth and moved to his writing desk. Lifting the heavy lid of an ornate tobacco box, he selected a fleshy, aromatic cigar and slid it between his lips. "I hope I didn't hear you correctly."

"You did." The newly formed planes of manhood on Stone's face set into a firm resolve.

Their eyes locked—a collision of teal-blue. Each saw himself in the other's unflinching face, reflections of what was to come and what had been. Jaws clenched resolutely; dark eyebrows spired over hooded eyelids. And while one chin was rough from years of a razor blade, the other was shadowed with the promise of a beard. Though still in his teens, Stone was extremely tall like his father. But Stone topped his father's six-foot height by two inches.

After what seemed an eternity, his father moved to light his cigar, as if taking command of the situation. Alexandre snapped the cigar lid closed and took a seat in his New England wing chair. He drained his tumbler and set it on a cherrywood tea table. Steepling his fingertips, he settled back to enjoy his smoke.

It was Stone who shattered the tense silence. "You'll not make me change my mind, sir."

Alexandre crossed his legs at the calves. "Are you proposing to come into business with me at an earlier date than we've discussed?"

Stone stared thoughtfully out the window for a moment. Through the verdant boughs of tall trees he could see sunlit Lake Erie not more than a mile away and the top masts of ships at anchor. Though hidden from his view, he knew each dockside building, weathered and unpainted. He could picture the spume and refuse in the black eddies of the wharves. As the sails moved slowly from view, Stone wished he were riding the wind with them, and with that image, he pulled from within him the strength to fight his father. Straightening himself to his full height, he balled his lean fingers into hard fists. This time, his father would not win. "Not in the way we discussed, no."

Alexandre raised a brow. "You've had a better offer than the New York Fur Company can give you?" he asked with doubtful sarcasm.

4

"No, but your concept of running a business and mine differ. You're content to stay behind a glass window and reap your rewards. I want to see what is beyond the horizon." Stone waited to see if the old man would interrupt him, and when he didn't, Stone continued without restraint. "I want to see for myself what lies on the banks of the Great Lakes, to see the beaver on their own ground, not skinned and tied in bundles. I want to learn the language of the Indians. I want to know how to walk in the forest like a woodsman, to be a man of my own means where the seasons tell the time, not finely crafted clocks. I want to trap the beaver for you, sir, not sit back and watch someone else bring them to us." He had rehearsed his speech in his mind many times and was glad to finally have said it. Excitement flushed his face as he anticipated his father's answer.

Alexandre rolled his cigar between his fingertips, his stare thoughtful. "And who will teach you to walk like a trapper? The beaver, *non*? And a man has to pack provisions. I've seen you enjoying good brandy and cigars. And what of your gambling friends? *Oui*, don't look so surprised, Stone. I've found many of your discarded New York Consolidated Lottery tickets. So then, I ask again, who will teach you to walk like a trapper?"

Stone didn't let the slap of words break his spirit. "Sir, Jemmy Paquer—"

"Jemmy Paquer!" Alexandre's temper snapped like a dry twig in autumn. "*Sacré bleu*! That half-breed Seneca Indian who smells like the

5

goddamned hides he packs. He works for you and me!"

"He works for the frontier."

"The frontier is it? Do you want to have your vitals cut off by some redskin? Have your scalp hanging from a victory lance? I *pay* other men to take that risk."

"Sir, I—"

"The damn Indians are sure as hell going to cut you first chance they get—Jemmy Paquer or not! You lie down with dogs you get fleas!" Alexandre slammed his fist on the tea table with such force, the empty tumbler toppled to the floor and shattered.

"I fail to see—"

"You're damn right you fail to see. You're not a man yet and you want a man's job." Alexandre pointed his smoldering cigar at Stone. "You'll go to West Point, boy, and learn *how* to be a man."

Stone stood still; he was so angry, he was afraid to move for fear he'd lunge at the old man's throat. "No, sir," he tried to say, but no sound escaped his lips. "*Non, Monsieur,*" he repeated, this time, his words were loud and firm. He turned on his heels and headed for the doors. Flinging them open, he was met by Solange, who was visibly startled.

She had been about to enter the room and fairly trembled from the surprise Stone had given her. She clutched onto a pair of shears and a straw basket of freshly cut flowers from her garden. Her black hair was drawn tightly to her head and anchored at her nape with a tortoise-shell comb. Her plain, ecru gown was gathered under her bosom. Her eyes as blue as the north-eastern lakes, her skin as white as magnolias and her high cheekbones lightly dusted with rose-colored powder, made Stone think of a fine porcelain doll.

"Madame," he curtly acknowledged before brushing past her and striding purposefully out of the house, leaving the mouse to the lion's large paws.

Stone crossed over the charcoal-gray veranda and down the clean steps. His stare was intent on the white picket fence ahead of him and his freedom. How could he have thought his father would understand? He wanted no part of the old man's world or his fancy house on Delaware Street. It was the only one on the backwoods road and his father had mocked the natural setting with his elaborate edifice and well-constructed grounds.

The Terrace, as Alexandre Boucher called it, was a stately Georgian mansion rooted on a solid foundation of terra-cotta brick near the front of Delaware Street surrounded by high, white pick-et fences. A lush carpet of manicured grass and lilac-headed clovers was overshadowed by wide, spreading sycamore trees. A part of the grounds was used as a special park where elk and deer grazed; and in the rear, a beautiful grove of handsome trees shaded a pond fed by springs and stocked with fish.

The old man was a goddamn backyard hunter! Stone snorted as he slammed the slatted gate behind him, but it swung open as quickly as it was closed. Turning, he snatched a palm-sized rock that was in the gate's path and slammed it again. This time, the jolt reverberated down both sides of the fence as the lock caught.

"Damn your soul, you old cuss," Stone gritted between his clenched teeth. He squeezed the rock as he walked down the broad country road, green with native trees and chestnut groves. He knew where he was going without even thinking.

Squirrels and flocks of geese crossed his path, while cattle grazed along the roadside and pigs roamed at their own will. The pungent smell of cut pine and sap came to him as he passed one of the many lumberyards closer to the village. Yes, the frontier was being gobbled up before he had a chance to taste it. He veered to Main Street, his decision firmly made. He would go with Jemmy Paquer this season, just as they discussed. He *was* a man, regardless of what his father thought.

The musty scent of the Buffalo River and Lake Erie alerted his sense of belonging as he hastened his steps. Buffalo was not legally a city yet, but rather a booming village, whose port was the exit and entrance to the Erie Canal. And depending on which way a person traveled, it was the gateway to the civilized cities of the East or the challenging wilderness of the expanding West. Wide banners adorned many of the shipping office's rooftops, boasting of great passages and fares in both directions.

Stone passed the Eagle Tavern, a place where he had lately found solace, and gave a mock salute to the brass wingspread eagle above the doorway.

"Not today, old boy," he muttered, and con-

tinued on toward the smell of oily fish and steam
and the sound of bells and whistles and the cries
of harbor masters.

Almost from the opening day of the canal, the
waterfront was noisy and colorful, and crowded
with newly arrived Yankees, immigrants, and the
usual contingent of camp followers. Seneca Indians strolled the streets wearing moccasins and
blankets to cover their nakedness, while children
rolled hoops down the slight hills of dirt streets
and the gently arching bridges over the canal
waterways. At the shoreline, buildings had been
constructed of cut stone to withstand the strong
breezes of the lake, which often struck unexpectedly.

Perched on the riverbank was Front Street
where new arrivals mingled with merchants and
dock hands, sailors and ship captains, travelers
rich and poor, and confidence men who preyed
on them all. Stone headed for the New York Fur
Company, located between Main Street and
Commercial Slip, hoping to find Jemmy Paquer
on the Central Wharf.

"Hallooo!" a raspy, woman's voice called out.

Stone turned and saw the fishmonger's wife
beckoning him for a chat. Her wiry gray hair was
covered with a soiled mobcap, and she waved a
fat mackerel at him.

"Good day, Madame Cleary," he returned. "I
have not the time today." He liked the old lady,
and had spent many an afternoon listening to her
rambling tales of her colored youth.

"A fish for ye supper then?"

"Send a barracuda to my old man," he tossed

9

back and under his breath added, "they're a fine pair."

"Right-o, dearie!" she cackled.

Stepping up onto the boardwalk, Stone randomly glanced at the wooden signs hanging above his head. Each held some symbol of the profession practiced within the shops—two folio volumes on the map makers'; a powder horn and musket on the gunsmiths'; brick and mortar on the masons' and stone cutters'; and then there was the New York Fur Company's. The sign was not made of wood, rather the monogram of a stretched beaver hide was etched into a fine plate of gleaming brass. Naturally Alexandre Boucher had to be the best, Stone thought sourly.

His fingers tightened on the rock he had carried ever since leaving The Terrace. On an impulse, he drew back his arm and in his fury, threw the rock.

The door opened, and Jemmy Paquer ducked as the rock slammed into the sign and came showering down in pieces. "Hey! You trying to kill me, Boucher?"

"I'm going with you tomorrow. To the West."

· 1 ·

Stone took a quick leap to his left in order to avoid colliding with two brawling trappers in his path. He side-stepped a puddle of fresh mud created by a melted patch of snow and continued on, paying no heed to the men, as all around him, hell broke loose. Rendezvous brought out the best in a man, he thought, filling his lungs with cool, crisp mountain air. He headed toward the sloping riverbanks on which Fort Snelling was built at the fork of the Mississippi and Minnesota Rivers. Pitched on the embankments were the different Indian villages—the bleached, rawhide tepees of the Dakotas, a band of the Sioux nation, and the birchbark wigwams of the Chippewa. A few dozen lean-tos of the free trappers were disbursed in a less orderly fashion, and on a solitary canvas tent a weathered wooden sign

11

hung precariously with childish writing spelling WHISKEY. It was illegal to sell alcohol to the Indians, but after a long winter, the ban didn't hold up. The firewater made all men, red and white, forget they hated each other for a few weeks until the rendezvous was over. Then it would be every man for himself again.

Smoke from cook fires mottled the clear, powder-blue sky, and mingled with the grayish puffs from fired rifles. Throughout the camp, fiddles played to the sound of encouraging claps, dogs barked chasing after horses and riders, and old friends renewed acquaintances and told wilderness tales. This was what he'd been born for, Stone reflected. He was alive in this country; he thrived in it.

Squaws bedecked with tinkling hawk bells ran after him, giggling behind their bronzed hands. He waved them off with a rewarding smile and a promise. During the past nine years, he'd grown four inches and now stood at six feet six. His height couldn't help but draw attention to him. With his winter beard and mustache and his umber hair hanging way past his wide shoulders, he resembled nothing of the boy from Buffalo, New York. Not an ounce of extra flesh covered his body, and he filled out his buckskin trousers like a second skin. Since the last day in May had warmed up sufficiently to melt the ice left on the ground, he wore his calcutta rendezvous shirt with the lacing down the front, and had rolled up the sleeves to let the sun color his arms a rich burnt-honey. The barrel of a J & S Hawken rifle rested on his right shoulder, the butt firmly secured in his large, well-worked hands, and calloused fingertips.

"Boucher!"

Stone tilted the low crown on his felt hat farther up his head to view the mountain man who called him. He was pleasantly surprised to see the familiar red cap of the French-Canadian voyager, *Monsieur* Red. "*Bonjour, mon ami!*" Stone greeted and heartily shook the man's hand.

"*Bonjour*! Eet has been a long time, *oui*? Two season, eef my mem'ry serves me right. What are you doing poaching in my backyard, eh? Last time I see you was at Pierre's Hole rawn-da-voo."

"Paquer and I wintered just west of here."

"Paquer? He ees not dead yet, that Seneca of yours?"

"He's up at the fort, buying supplies. You want to come with me?"

"*Non*," the Canadian laughed deeply. "Zee wheeskey down here ees as smooth as a whore's kiss, and I doubt I could walk up the heell weethout falling, *n'est-ce pas*?"

"*Oui*." Stone nodded in good humor.

"What have you been trapping all year, *mon ami*?"

"Coons, marten, beaver. Not so many beaver now."

"Beaver are at Pierre's Hole rawn-da-voo. Who has zee best price on pelts?"

"We're trading with Farribault at Land's End."

"What he geeve you for beaver, eh?"

"Four dollars for beaver; thirty for coons; one twenty-five for marten."

"Zhen I weell trade weeth Farribault myself,

13

though I have seen Sibley, zee skunk for Astor's American Fur Company, and Heacock zee agent for zee New York Fur Company."

With the mention of the latter, Stone felt the muscles in his fingers tighten. His teal-blue eyes grew dark and stormy. No one on the frontier except Jemmy knew Stone was connected by blood to the New York Fur Company. And blood was where the connection stopped. Stone hadn't seen his father in nine years and as far as he was concerned, he could draw his last breath without ever seeing the old man again.

"Weell, I see you and Paquer before you leave zee rawn-da-voo, *mon ami*?"

"*Oui*. We're camped a mile down by the Minnesota."

"*Au revoir*, then my friend."

Stone grasped the man's hand firmly. "*Au revoir*." Then he continued on toward the fort.

The American flag billowed lightly from its pole on the round tower as Stone entered the large diamond-shaped fort. Though he'd never been at Fort Snelling before, it reminded him of others he had seen. The wide interior was surrounded by brick barracks, a commissary, hospital, guardhouses, and the other buildings that made up a military post. Through the knot of horses, supply wagons, and blue-and-gold uniformed men on foot, Stone spotted Jemmy Paquer in front of the Sutler's Store. As he made his way past the blacksmith shop, the echoing ring of hammer against anvil followed him.

Jemmy sat back on his heels, paring his nails, carving a wicked point in the left forefinger. He

14

was a notorious barehanded fighter, and the point was a valuable weapon. When he saw Stone, he stood to his full height and put his Green River knife away in the red girdle about his blue tunic. He wore blue leggings and very neat moccasins, and fancy silver earrings hung from tiny holes in his copper-toned lobes. On his red jacket, he'd anchored a silver brooch that looked like a heart with a crown on top of it. Though seven years older than Stone, Jemmy concealed his age well.

"What took you so long?" Jemmy asked, brushing back his long, jet hair. "I cut all ten." He held up his hands.

"You missed one."

"I feel like starting a fight."

"Quit boasting."

"It's not boasting when you can back it up."

"You're full of wind, Jem."

"Better that than nonsense."

Stone pushed his partner's shoulder playfully, then leaned against the awning post of the store. He reached into the parfleche at his waist and drew out his cigarette makings. Deftly, he rolled a smoke and brought it to his lips then lit the end. He scanned the interior of the fort and the men who occupied the vast space. One man in particular caught his eye. He sat on an old crate with a pad of paper in his lap. Occasionally, he looked up at a Sioux warrior in full dress and paint, then would lower his head again and scratch on the paper.

"Who's the greenhorn?" Stone asked Jem.

"He does look like a greenhorn at that, don't

he? But I hear he's been down to Fort Pierre and all over the damn countryside painting Indians and the like. Name's Catlin, I think. George Catlin."

Stone studied the man a moment longer, then spoke, "I saw Canadian Red down on the slope."

"Yeah?" A light of surprise veiled Jemmy's tanned face. "What's *Monsieur* Red doing in this part?"

"Same as us. Staying one step ahead of the Blackfeet, I reckon."

"He's well?"

"The same old cuss," Stone replied, taking a drag on his cigarette, the smoke curling above his head. "You have any trouble getting the supplies? Astor's boy, Henry Sibley, is down there passing rotgut for four dollars a pint and thirty dollars for half a dozen traps. Damn varmint ought to have his legs caught."

"Bidwell is high, but accommodating. He's filling the order now. I did get him to give me this while we wait." Jemmy reached down by his foot and picked up an amber-hued bottle. "Liquor. Taos lightning." He took a slug and offered it to Stone who declined.

"You know what they put in that stuff? Gunpowder. It smells like goddamn sulphur."

"Bull, it smells like the apron pocket of a serving wench in a Mexican cantina." He grinned at his wry wit and took another gulp.

"Where do you concoct these statements? You've never been to Mexico."

"Paquer!" Erastus Bidwell called from the threshold of the Sutler's Store. "I got yore gear put up."

16

"Let's go," Stone told Jemmy, pulling at the Seneca's tunic sleeve. "While you're imbibing your cantina wench's pocket, I'm going to be making some wagers on my expert shooting ability."

"Expert? Hell, I can outshoot your ass any day—" Jemmy's words were cut off by a woman's scream of terror. Then a gunshot echoed across the sky and all was quiet. Even the dogs stopped barking.

Kristianna Bergendahl wished she owned a pair of driving gloves. The leather reins woven between her long, tapered fingers were stiff in her hands. Each rut and valley the buckboard's large wheels dipped into caused the team of oxen to jerk their harness yokes and cut the grainy rawhide into her sweating palms. If she were a man, she'd have a fine pair crafted from the best hides. But she was a woman of sixteen, a fact she was reminded of when a fine wisp of long white-blonde hair fell free from her black velvet cap. Her braid never seemed to hold together, and she momentarily transferred the reins to one hand in order to push the wayward strands under the waxy, black lace on the brim of her hat. If she were a man, she would not have such a fine hat, but that was one consolation about being a woman. This was her favorite and best hat, which she'd made herself, each stitch finely sewn with black lace that spilled a frothy web over her forehead.

Tiny shafts of sunlight pierced through the emerald-foliaged canopy, the dappled rays dancing on Kristianna's gracefully sloping nose and high, angular cheekbones that were a natural, carnation-pink. Her profile was set in what appeared to be a frown, but was really deep concentration, with her slightly pointed chin held high. She would not let the animals get the best of her.

Glancing over her shoulder, she smiled faintly with full, dusty-rose lips at her mother, Ulla, and her sister, Noelle, who were in the wagon's bed, silently assuring them that she was capable of handling the team though she'd never done so before. The ride from their small farm seemed longer than usual, but then Papa had always driven the ten-mile distance to Fort Snelling. Kristianna missed having him there, telling her stories of the old country. Her pale iris-blue eyes would focus on his face with unflinching attention and she never realized just how long it took to get to the fort; it seemed they were always there too soon. Since they had received no word from him, she hoped he was faring well in Saint Louis and that he would be home soon. He'd left them to find work in the city having had no choice since he had to raise the money to buy the new plow they greatly needed.

Kristianna inhaled deeply, tasting the scent of wild clover and strawberries that were abundant in the spring forest. The tree branches seemed to whisper at each other as the wagon passed below, and the sweet grass that grew alongside the country road waved and danced in its wake. She arched her back, trying to stretch some of the tension from her muscles. As she straightened, it was evident that she was an extremely tall young woman. Even while sitting, she appeared taller than most men. When she stood, she was five feet eleven inches. Her shoulders were slender and square, enveloped by a white blouse with puffed sleeves and a worsted shawl. Her dress was made of soft linen in a narrow striped pattern of prairie-brown and black. White ribbon was threaded through the eyelets in her bodice, which outlined her full, rounded breasts. Tied about her narrow waist was a crisp white apron, and on her feet were neatly carved wooden shoes.

The front wagon wheel lurched into a rut, and Kristianna automatically grabbed for the four-foot long Kentucky rifle on her lap. She transferred the reins to one hand once again, and ran her fingertips along the smooth maple wood butt, then the ornate brass design on the stock. The gun was loaded, and she gave it the respect it was due. Knowing how to use a firearm was imperative in the wild open land of Minnesota Country, and at a young age she had been taught its importance. Against Mama's will, Papa had shown her how to load and fire the weapon, and she knew the range of its accuracy was over one hundred yards.

Though Papa often taught her things that only a man should know, he cautioned her not to show that she knew them, especially to her husband-to-be, Gunnar Thorson, whose pride would be insulted.

A clutch of prairie chickens hurriedly crossed the wagon's path, as the males called "ooo-loo-woo" but before Kristianna had a chance to enjoy their courtship song, a rifle shot echoed from the distance ahead. She knew its origin and did not pick up the Kentucky. Instead, she raised up on tiptoe to better cradle the weapon in her lap.

As the wagon rounded the last corner, they were greeted by the flowing water of the Mississippi River which paralleled the road. Not more than a mile away, the hill of the military outpost was dotted with tepees and canvas tents. Just as she thought, the shot had come from Fort Snelling and the spring rendezvous.

Another discharge sprang forth, the boom sounding like thunder, then another, until the air was peppered with clouds of spent powder. Kristianna hoped none of the lead balls would go astray and strike them dead in their tracks. How wasteful and foolish these mountain men and Indians were. Bullets were for survival, not for playing games.

The closer they came, the more obvious it was that nearly all the grizzled trappers and painted Indians were drunk and that worried Kristianna. The oxen seemed to sense her discomfort and slowed their steps. Kristianna hated to use the whip Papa kept under the springboard seat, but she certainly didn't want to stop in the middle of hundreds of drunken men. She struck each animal smartly on its ginger-colored rump.

"Get on, Jake! Tony!" she called in a firm voice that was laced with a Swedish accent.

The oxen strained in their harnesses and reluctantly continued to climb up the hill.

"I see the shoe!" Noelle cried from her perch in the buckboard.

Keeping her eyes ahead, Kristianna was glad

that Noelle was trying to distract them from the rendezvous by playing the game they always played when they came to the fort. She corrected her sister, as she always did. "It is called the Sloo, Noelle." Kristianna prided herself in knowing the correct English word for what Mr. Bidwell had told her was the tall, circular tower five stories high pierced by tiny holes for gun barrels to peek out of.

"Take the turn easy, Kristianna," Ulla Bergendahl cautioned her daughter. "Remember the eggs and pies." There was an undeniable tension in the older woman's voice. Ulla sat ramrod straight, with a white cap framing her plain face and the ribbons resting on the collar of her homespun blouse. While usually talkative on the ride to the fort, today she had kept quiet so as not to distract her daughter.

"*Ja*, Mama," Kristianna answered, feeling a slight trickle of perspiration roll between her breasts, and her thin chemise cling to her damp, skin. How could her body be hot when her nose was cold? "Get on, Jake! Tony!"

Kristianna pulled the reins to the left, urging the brawny beasts up the gently sloping incline. She kept her eyes focused on the narrow road, trying to shut out all the disturbing factors around her as they passed through the heart of the rendezvous. She willed herself to ignore the numerous trappers and melee of Indian war cries, but to no avail. A shiver ran through her. The Chippewa and Dakota had caused the settlers trouble in the past by uprooting spring gardens and stealing valued stock.

A thundering bang broke over her head, causing Kristianna to jump. "Easy!" she exclaimed to the animals, and the oxen stopped dead in their tracks.

"Whoa there, gal," roared a rough-looking trapper, his voice heavy with the slur of alcohol. He glared at her through watery blue eyes with pupils so small they looked like pinheads. The front of his buckskins were smeared with food grease, and around his neck was a string of leather with a turquoise nugget tied to it. In one of his dirty hands, he clutched haphazardly an old, scratched, flintlock trading rifle. The other hand had snaked its way into the wooden yoke around Jake's neck. "What's yore hurry, petticoat?"

Kristianna lowered the reins to rest in her lap while she fingered the smooth trigger of the Kentucky. "Let us pass," she commanded with a calmness that she forced herself to reflect in her face and in her tone. Controlling her anger, she waited for him to do as she bade.

The trapper cocked his bushy brow at her and spat, "What did you say, sugar?"

Kristianna heard Ulla gasp with fear, but did not dare turn her head away from the trapper to calm her mother. "Let us pass," she repeated in a firmer tone, raising the rifle's barrel a fraction.

A small group of the trapper's drinking partners, some of who were Dakota Indians, gathered around him, waiting to see what would happen next.

"Now I don't know if I want to do that yet, clodbuster. You think yore so high and mighty coming in here and busting up the land. Well, I'll tell you somethin', little gal, all yore doing is ruining it for us by scratching at the soil."

That statement brought on encouragement from the crowd, some even went as far as to yell, "Yellowheads" and "Wooden Shoe People."

"There ain't no beaver now, on account of you—"

Kristianna didn't let him finish. She raised the Kentucky and aimed it at the trapper. "You let go of that animal."

"Yumpin' Yiminy, boys, she's gonna shoot me!" The trapper laughed with mock fright and inched toward her.

Kristianna touched the barrel of his gun with her own, screamed for him to leave them alone, then she squeezed the trigger. The impact sent the trapper to the ground, knocking the trading rifle from his hands. The Kentucky's recoil slammed the butt into her shoulder, and she steadied herself on the seat.

The crowd grew ominously quiet, waiting for the trapper's reaction. He shook the numbness out of his hand as a look of disbelief washed over his face. He quickly checked to see if any of his now powder-blackened fingers were missing. After finding all five intact, he spat, "God A'mighty, you little alley cat, you done shot up my flint-lock." He moved stealthily toward the buckboard. "I'm going to kill you for that. No little piece of yard goods is making a booby out of me."

Kristianna's heart hammered in her chest. There was no time to reload the Kentucky so she dropped the useless piece to the buckboard floor and vigorously slapped the reins, hoping against hope the oxen would move fast enough to elude the trapper. But even she knew there was no chance of that as he lunged toward her with a murderous glare in his eyes.

Kristianna screamed with fright as the trapper's iron grip circled her wrist. Ulla rose in an attempt to help her daughter, but she was pushed down into the buckboard's bed by one of the Indians. Clutching Noelle close to her bosom, she bit her lower lip from crying out.

Kristianna pushed at the trapper's grimy chest with all her strength. She was raised off the seat by his aggressive force just as a shot rang through the crisp air, so close to her ear that she actually heard the lead ball whiz by. The proximity of the ball was enough to halt the trapper momentarily.

The onlookers jerked their heads away from Kristianna as a giant of a man and a Seneca Indian pushed their way through the throng. The tall man, with the barrel of his Hawken raised to the cloudless blue sky, and the butt on the ground, was already getting his powder bag from his waist. "Next time I won't be aiming at heaven's belly, Newt," he called to the trapper.

"This ain't got nothing to do with you, Boucher," Newt Fraeb ground out. He kept his fingers shackled around Kristianna's slender wrist.

Stone pushed up the brim of his low-crowned felt hat, his blue eyes hard as flints and filled with rage. "Seems it hasn't got to do with you either, Newt. Let her go."

"You ain't the law around here." Newt didn't back down. His foot remained firmly on the wagon's hub.

"This piece of iron makes me anything I say."

Newt scanned the faces of his cronies and when he realized they wouldn't come to his aid, he tried to make light of the situation. "I didn't mean no harm," he stammered. "She's a sod-buster. We can have us some fun—"

The greasy trapper's words were cut short as Stone tossed his rifle to Jemmy, then took one step forward, one step that would have been a leap for a man of average height. The distance between them was cut short enough for Stone to land a solid punch on Newt's craggy face before Newt even knew what had happened. He let go of Kristianna and staggered back.

Newt rubbed at his sore cheek. "You damn son-of-a—"

This time it was Jemmy Paquer who cut him short with another blow to Newt's unshaven chin. Jemmy took a moment to give Stone a grin and toss him back his rifle. "I told you I was in the mood for a bare-hand. Get her out of here while I have some fun."

Newt came back at the Seneca and in no time, the pair was rolling in the dirt. The crowd followed them, egging them on. It didn't matter that Kristianna had been let go. A fight was a fight.

Kristianna retrieved the Kentucky from the wagon's floor, and aimed it at Stone.

"Don't point that at me, honey, even though it's not primed. I'm the one who just saved your tail from that snake." And with that, he put a hard-soled, moccasined foot on the step, and swung his weight into the seat next to Kristianna. "You and the child all right, ma'am?" he inquired over his shoulder to Ulla.

Ulla, too scared to answer him, merely nodded.

"Let's go then." He picked up the reins and slapped the oxen's rumps.

Finding her voice, Kristianna gasped, "You just wait a minute, Mister!" She was so flustered, her words were thickened by her Swedish accent. "We have no need of your assistance now. The man is gone."

"Well, you got it, like it or not. Sit back and catch your breath. He hurt your wrist bad?"

Kristianna glanced down at the reddened skin on her hand and gingerly rubbed it. She was a little surprised that a mountain man would bother to inquire. After all, they were all alike just like that Newt. But this one's deep, gravelly voice held a certain uniqueness that she'd never heard before.

"I am fine," she answered curtly, then turned to reassure her mother and sister, talking in Swedish.

Stone admonished, "You know, if you're going to be dumb enough to pull a gun on a man, you'd better be smart enough to know how to use it."

Aghast by his observation that she had shot at Newt's gun instead of Newt, Kristianna stared back at his profile, her lips parted in disbelief. "I do know how to use it. I—I just did not want to kill him. I wanted to frighten him."

"Well, you'd better think twice next time."

Kristianna hoped there wouldn't be a next time. Why was he taking the time to give her advice? she wondered. She'd come across other frontier men and, before today, they had ignored her except for an occasional stare. Pondering that thought, she took a moment to collect herself and study the man next to her. To her surprise, she realized that for the first time in her life, she had to look up to see a man's face properly. He was by far the biggest man she had ever seen, with a full beard and mustache that covered his mouth and the bottom half of his finely planed cheeks. Over his long umber hair, he wore a hat so low on his forehead that she couldn't see his eyes. Before she could assess him further, he glanced her way. Flustered by his startling teal-blue eyes, she snapped her head away and looked at her wrist again.

"You picked a poor day to come to Snelling," he commented while guiding the oxen through the fort's entrance.

"I did not choose it," Kristianna reflected. Coming to Fort Snelling to buy and trade wares was usually a fun outing, but today they were there to post a bill asking for a hired man. Having to admit that she wasn't able to handle all of the chores herself cut into her pride, making her feel weak and feminine. She was sorely reminded of that when all of her strength had nearly been sapped by harnessing Tony and Jake that morning. She had finally agreed with her mother that they take on extra help while Papa was gone. The money Mr. Bidwell gave them for pies and eggs would just be enough to pay the man.

"Well, you best watch yourselves. There's more than one man around here with opinions like Newt Fraeb. I can't say I don't agree with him," Stone said matter-of-factly as he stopped the rig in front of the Sutler's Store. "Woodsmen don't take kindly to settlers. They have a saying: 'Woodsmen use the forests, settlers conquer them.'" He wrapped the reins securely around the brake handle and swung himself over the side. "You need any help getting down, miss?" he called with mock courtesy to Kristianna as he fetched his Hawken.

She raised her chin toward him and grandly declined his offer. "'Keep your tokens for the rebels,' Mister."

When Stone didn't answer, Kristianna adjusted the stiff lace brim of her hat to rest on her delicate, light eyebrows. "It is from the Old Testament of the Bible. You know the Good Book, do you not?"

"I know what it is. I don't read it." There was that gravelly voice again.

"Maybe you should," Kristianna concluded, and for the first time, looked him straight in the eyes.

What she saw staring back at her nearly made her shiver. He eyed her so intensely that she wondered if he was going to grab her.

"Is—is something wrong?" she managed to choke out.

He was quiet for a moment before saying, "Your eyes . . ."

Then it dawned on her what was wrong. Sometimes the unusual color of her eyes bothered people. They were such a pale blue, they looked like winter ice. She had never liked them. Slightly embarrassed and indignant that he was rude in pointing out her flaw, she kept her gaze level. "Yes, I have two eyes. Now, we have no further reason to talk to each other. Good day, Mister."

She turned away from him, not at all liking the way he was acting. For all she knew, he would turn on her, too, like the other trapper. She tried to make light of the fact that he was still standing there as she alit from the wagon. She ignored him and went about her business, checking the insides of the baskets in the wagon bed for damage, but not really seeing what was inside them at all.

He finally moved away, crossing the fort yard, only to lean against an awning post and continue his vigil. She pretended not to notice him, but the fine hairs on the back of her neck tingled as if he were close enough to breathe on her. Only after she entered the store did she truly feel she was rid of him.

·2·

Kristianna loved the smell of Mr. Bidwell's Sutler's Store. Though she sometimes had a hard time understanding his rough interpretation of the English language, the bald-headed bachelor was rather soft-hearted for a frontier man. Kristianna thought that it was a shame that the short, stout storekeeper had never married since he seemed to know what a woman liked. Mr. Bidwell believed in pleasing a woman's sense of smell with enticing fragrances by placing a sheaf of clover or pressed wildflowers between the many folds of fabrics on the notions table. He hung cloved apples from the tobacco shelf, and mixed the aroma of coffee beans with the sweet scent of cinnamon. It was a good store, Kristianna thought, and it helped her to put the giant of a man from her mind.

Ulla set the baskets on the counter and lifted the gingham napkins over the tops. "No broken eggs. A blessing. And only a small piece of crust on the apple pie was torn off. *Ja*, it is good." She'd regained her dignity and was ready to take charge.

Kristianna surveyed the contents of the baskets she had put on Mr. Bidwell's counter, and noted that they, too, were undamaged.

The store was nearly filled to the rafters with mountain men and Indians trading goods and buying supplies. While waiting for Mr. Bidwell to finish with his customer, Kristianna took Noelle's tiny hand and went to explore the wonderful items. She ignored the rugged men, wishing that it were the soldiers who filled the store, for the military men had grown accustomed to their visits. She took Noelle to the side where the leather smell of boots and saddles and belts were strongest and where a hoop of tangy cheese was sitting on its turntable, waiting for a customer to raise the hinged knife and slice a wedge.

"Oh, Kristianna! May I have some cheese?" Noelle asked, her face upturned in expectation.

Kristianna straightened the child's disheveled skullcap and poked the wheat-colored hair back under it. "A small piece. I will cut it for you." She pushed the knife into the golden cheese.

"*Tack*." Noelle thanked her, then she sank her straight pearl-white teeth into the slice.

Seeing the contentment on her sister's face made Kristianna decide not to let anything spoil their visit to the store. It was a rare treat to see all of the fancy goods and she wasn't about to miss any of it. She took Noelle's hand again, and they walked to the cotton bags full of sugar and flour. From the rafters above them hung hams, slabs of sidemeat, and pots and pans.

"Kristianna, I made a flower," Noelle declared. Kristianna looked down to see a small five-petaled flower finger-printed onto the dusty counterside that housed the flour bags.

"How lovely." She smiled fondly at the upturned face. She was pleased Noelle had forgotten about Newt Fraeb, too.

"May we look at the dresses, Kristianna?"

"If you do not touch." She was secretly glad Noelle asked, for the dresses were her favorite part of the Sutler's Store.

"I promise."

They made their way to the women's section where Mr. Bidwell kept a small glass case of handkerchiefs, stockings, and lace collars, and where several dresses hung from a wooden dowel. There was a serviceable dove-gray traveling suit; a muslin day dress printed with a flowing floral pattern in pinks, blue, green, and mauve; and a creamy-white silk tea dress with crimson roses and tiny matching buttons trailing down the back.

Noelle looked up to Kristianna who was deep in her own admiration of the dresses, then she tentatively stretched out her hand to feel the fine silk-covered crimson buttons.

"No, Noelle!" Kristianna admonished, and lightly slapped the child's hand away. "Never touch the buttons. They are evil."

"Why are they evil?"

"Because Mama says they are. And Mama knows." All of their garments were fastened with hooks and eyes because they were acceptably plain and that was the way it always had been.

"I do not understand."

Flustered at not having a reasonable explanation for the girl, Kristianna gently ordered her to check on Mama to see if it was their turn with Mr. Bidwell.

Secretly, Kristianna wondered what the buttons felt like, but she was too old to be as curious as the five-year-old Noelle. And yet, though she had been told many, many times that red was an evil color except when Papa wore a piece of red cloth on his shirt to show he worked his own farm, she was always drawn to the dusty, scarlet parasol propped up in the corner. It rested on its point, the faded silk tassels tumbling upside down over the flaming, folded web. She'd often wondered why no one had purchased it. If she were allowed such a frivolity, she would have bought it long ago.

Carefully Kristianna glanced to see if her mother was looking in her direction, then slowly held out her hand, her fingertips gently testing the tassels to see if they were as soft as they looked.

"And who will slap your hand?"

Kristianna turned with a start and looked up into the face of the giant mountain man. He had followed her into the store! He seemed much taller now with the top of his hat nearly touching the rafters. Under the brim, she noted that his

rich brown, almost black, eyebrows were his
most unique feature. A darker shade than his
hair, they were full near his nose then smoothed
out into a pronounced arch that tapered thinly
past his teal-blue eyes. The effect made him look
like he was scowling. Now, without the distraction of the rendezvous, she noticed that he
smelled like Bay Balm, the same scent Mr.
Bidwell kept on his counter. That surprised her,
as all of the other trappers she had come in close
proximity to smelled like bear grease, old food,
or body odor.

"You have been watching me?" she accused,
knowing full well he had been for some time if he
saw her with Noelle.

"I won't tell, if that's what's bothering you."
His shoulders were as wide as a barn door and
when he took a step toward her, she backed away.
He made no effort to hide his study of her eyes,
and it galled her to the bone. Why couldn't he
leave her alone?

"*You* are bothering me," she said crossly under
her breath, hoping not to call any attention to
them. "If you do not leave me alone, the . . ."
She grasped for the right words and found that
the ones he had spoken earlier were the best
weapon to throw at him. "The next time I will
not fire at heaven's stomach! I will fire at yours!"
She hastily turned away and headed for the
counter, not giving him the opportunity to respond to her threat.

Who *was* this man who stared at her so? Did he
expect something from her for having rescued

her from Newt Fraeb? If he did, he would have to wait a long time. Though grateful for his interference, she didn't owe him anything but her thanks, and she had withheld even that because of his cockiness toward her shooting ability. She didn't like being chastised by him. Normally in command of her emotions, it rattled her that he had made her blush. Of all things to catch her at—touching the parasol!

"Kristianna." Noelle's voice brought her out of the thoughts that fogged her mind. "Kristianna."

"*Ja*?" she answered vaguely.

"Mama bought us each a peppermint stick." The child handed Kristianna her candy. "I am going to bite into mine and I know how you will eat yours. You will suck on it until there is nothing left! I could never do that." Her words were followed by a loud crunch as she did indeed take a bite from the swirling red-and-white candy stick.

Mr. Bidwell made several notations into his book and looked up at Ulla Bergendahl. "Ma'am, ya gots purdy clos' t' five-dollar credit in this hyar book. Ya wants the coin or carry o'er?"

"I should like the dollars, please," Ulla answered in her soft voice, though there was an underlining confidence to their meaning. The money would pay for the handy man.

Reaching behind his counter, Mr. Bidwell withdrew a black strongbox and proceeded to count out the proper amount. As he calculated, he inquired, "Ya takin' care whilst yore mist'r is in San' Louie? Keep an eye out af'er them Sioux. They's shore as put an arra in yore back shore as night an' day."

"We have posted a notice for a hired man," Ulla informed him, and looked at Kristianna to confirm that it had been done.

"*Nej*, Mama." Kristianna dug into the pocket of her apron and produced the piece of paper. "I forgot."

"Post it now then." Ulla accepted the money from Mr. Bidwell and secured it in the bottom of one of the empty baskets, placing the neatly folded gingham napkins on top of the coins.

"Ya best post that notice where it kin be read. I don' rightly think ya should be alone out thar, ma'am. M'be ya could take on a room at this hyar fort 'til ya find yoreself an able man t' help wid them chores."

"We can manage, Mr. Bidwell, thank you," Kristianna answered. "We have neighbors not far from our farm." Oh, if only she didn't have to post the notice at all! What a waste of good money when she could do most of the tasks herself.

Mr. Bidwell was moving on to the next customer, and left them with a farewell. "I kin keep m'eyes wide fer ya an' make shore he ain't no skunk that pick off that notice."

"That would be most kind, Mr. Bidwell," Ulla answered, and ushered her daughters toward the door. "Let us post the notice and be on our way, girls. I want to get home before dark."

Though it wasn't spoken aloud, Kristianna

knew that Ulla meant to be out of the rendezvous as soon as possible.

"Let me post the notice," Noelle cried.

Kristianna granted her request and pressed the paper into her sister's small hands. She wished she were at home now, instead of having to deal with the oxen again—and maybe another Newt Fraeb. She looked up to see that the bearded man had not left the store and was still standing at the counter. He didn't even pretend to have business with Mr. Bidwell. He was more interested in *her* business. His stare pestered her like a gnat and it was all she could do to keep from swinging out at the air.

Noelle stuck her candy in her mouth to free her hands for her task. She took the paper and looked at the board for a clear space. The Wilderness Call, as Mr. Bidwell named it, was for trappers and mountain men to trade news and information, as well as list things to sell and buy.

Feeling very important, Noelle's tiny fingers worked a nail into the paper and then the fleshy wood. "Is it high enough for a big man to read?"

Kristianna felt her gaze involuntarily turn to the biggest man in the room and once more assessed his mammoth height. "*Ja,*" she answered in a regretful tone. "Let us go home."

Stone waited until the family had departed before making his way to the wall board. Pushing the brim of his hat off his forehead, he was about to read the paper Noelle had pinned up, when the notice above it caught his attention. His face was

37

an emotionless mask as he scanned the bold writing on crisp parchment paper. He tugged it from the wall, not bothering to remove the pin before doing so. Then, as if he just remembered what had drawn him to The Wilderness Call, he read the Bergendahl ad.

Smoothing down his full beard, he shrugged before yanking it down. He stuffed both pieces of paper into his pocket, turned on his heel, and strode out the door.

·3·

"What the hell does he want with me after nine years?" Stone's words barreled from his chest like a ball from a .40 caliber Kentucky rifle.

Dawn cracked open the night sky, promising the first day of June would be warm once the light fog that drifted from the Mississippi River lifted. The hazy wisps snaked through the rendezvous camp, carrying the scent of strong coffee from various cook fires.

"Don't know, partner." Jemmy was hunkered down on his heels, adding kindling to their campfire. "Who is this Samuel Granger?"

"My old man's solicitor."

"You don't think Alexandre is—"

"Dead? That cuss. He'll outlive me just so he can see me buried in the marble orchard first."

Stone bent his head to better view the under part of his chin in the crude mirror he'd nailed to the tree that held up his and Jemmy's diamond-shaped lean-to. He'd just finished shaving off his winter beard and mustache. "I don't like this. I don't like people tracking me." Satisfied he'd done a smooth job, he put his razor back into its leather pouch, then brushed the remnants of beard trimmings from his bare, broad chest.

"What you going to do about it?"

Slipping into a blue calico shirt, Stone tucked the tails inside his buckskin britches. "I'm going to find out what he wants before he finds me."

"How you aim to do that?"

"You"—Stone pointed to his partner—"are going to help me. Granger knows what I look like. He doesn't know you."

Moving around the camp, Stone gathered his various personal affects. He laid open a large split cowhide and arranged his buckskins, black powder arms, faded red, long underwear and a wool Mackinaw blanket. He tied the bundle together with the leather thongs that were sewn on it. "Flush him out and pump him for information. You can't miss him. He'll stick out like a sore thumb. Tall, thin, round wire spectacles. Most likely he'll hang around Heacock thinking he knows where I am."

"Where you going?"

"I'm seeking other accommodations. That immigrant family we ran shotgun for yesterday needs a hired man."

Jemmy looked up with astonishment. "You don't mean . . . They're dirt farmers."

"No one would ever think to look for me there."

"You're making a big mistake, Boucher. You don't know anything about farming. They're our enemy, them settlers."

Stone strapped on his sheathed Green River utility knife. "I'm not going to plow their fields."

"You sure you're going there just to dodge Granger? That piece of petticoat was fine-looking, even in that stupid hat. You afraid Newt Fraeb will get to her first?"

"I oughta give it to you in the meat basket for that, Jem." He hated to admit it but part of what Jemmy had said was true. He did want to see her again. He'd thought about her all night while trying to decide what to do about his father's watchdog. She was the most damnable, beautiful woman he'd ever seen and the most all-fired dead set on taking care of her own. Maybe he was a little intrigued by her. "Newt's too stupid to go looking for her."

Jemmy held his tanned hands out in front of him, warming them by the small flames that danced from the burning logs. "What the hell am I supposed to do while you're gone? And just how long you going to be gone? Rendezvous is over in a month. I thought we were going West to check out possibilities."

"We are," Stone assured his friend. He moved to fill his possibles pouch which kept his personal things: razor, measure, bullet starter, rifle oil, harmonica, and a flat piece of obsidian that he used as a whetstone. "I'll be gone as long as it takes you to find out what Granger wants. Meanwhile, take our pelts to Farribault and watch he doesn't add lead to the weights."

Jemmy rose from his perch near the fire and pushed back his silky, black hair. "I ain't no detective, Boucher."

"And my old man doesn't give up until he gets what he wants. And he's wanted me to run the New York Fur Company since the day the doctor slapped my behind." Stone moved to where their animals were hobbled. Stroking the nose of his mule, he turned to Jemmy. "Take care of Uncle Mary for me, will you."

Jemmy nodded. "How the hell am I supposed to find you?"

"I'll be shy of ten miles up the Mississip, west side of the river."

Stone then lifted a saddle onto his horse's snow-white back and kneed the animal in the ribs to make him exhale so he could secure the girth. After attaching all of his gear, he was ready to leave.

"Don't go get yourself in too many fights," Stone warned his friend in a playful tone, trying to make light of the situation. He noted earlier that Jemmy sported a small cut on his angular cheek from yesterday's scuffle with Newt.

"Don't lecture me. You'll burn out your tonsils. I'll fight when I want to," the Seneca grumbled, and took his place next to the fire again. "You take care of that horse. Don't stable him with cows when you feed him. Cows run spit out of their mouths when they eat. You never seen a horse cutting grain with no cows . . ." He stirred the bubbling pot of coffee with a green twig. "We ain't playing this game for longer than one month, brother." He didn't look at Stone when he said it.

Stone swung himself into his saddle, the leather stretching and squeaking under his weight. He took up the reins and stared at his partner's broad back. "*Swa-ne-dock*," he said in Seneca. *One month.*

Then he turned his horse to the north and nudged it forward.

·4·

A light chill in the dark, early-morning air made Kristianna hope that spring was finally going to let summer come. From her lantern, a beeswax candle burned evenly, sprinkling light through the snowflake-like holes in the metal encasement. Tightening the worsted shawl about her shoulders, she hurriedly followed the short path to the barn, taking heed of the ominous tree stumps on either side of her. After unlatching the gate to the corral, she opened it with a heavy push as the hinge always stuck. She quickly closed it behind her then swung one of the barn's tall, wide doors open.

"Here, boss," she called to the cow.

Familiar shadows greeted her as she hung the lantern on a nail in one of the rafters. She cupped her hands together and blew a puff of warm breath on her fingertips; Dearie didn't appreciate cold hands. Kristianna eased her fingers straight, favoring the several blisters that marked her palms, a reminder from yesterday that she did not have riding gloves.

Kristianna found the cow waiting patiently in her milking spot. "Good morning, Dearie," she greeted with a trace of sleepiness in her voice. She stroked the soft, copper hair above the cow's wet nose. "You smell the carrot? You are a smart boss." Reaching into her apron, she pulled out a pale yellow carrot that was soft and flexible. "Soon your carrots will be firm and crunchy, not wilted from being stored in sand barrels. It will be garden time soon." The easy chomping of the cow brought a beautiful smile to Kristianna's lips. "Oh, you like that, *ja*?"

Positioning the three-legged stool, Kristianna sat down and spread her skirt over her ankles. She reached for the whitewood bucket and placed it under Dearie's full udder. The Jersey was a warm companion, and Kristianna snuggled closer, resting her forehead on the side of the cow's rounded belly. She grasped two teats, and in a rippling motion, she gently pulled.

Steam rose from the warm, rich milk as the bucket filled, and the barn was quiet except for the sloshing milk.

This was the time of day Kristianna liked best. She could lose herself in thought without any disturbances. She thought of a variety of things, mostly American women and Gunnar Thorson. Though she had been in America for ten years, she never considered herself American, for she was not allowed to wear Yankee clothing. But it didn't stop her from wondering about the military wives. She wondered how they got their hair to curl in such tight rings. She wanted to touch one of those springy curls to see if it would bounce from her fingertips. She wondered what it would feel like to have silk and taffeta next to her skin. Maybe, someday, when she was married to Gunnar, he would allow her one taffeta dress.

She closed her eyes and willed his face to appear in her mind. His reddish-blond hair was as fine as corn silk, and his smile revealed straight, white teeth and a glimpse of his upper gum. His long, thin nose was pleasing to look at, and his cheeks were slightly concave, but not so much so as to make him look unhealthy. His eyes were teal-blue and . . .

Kristianna snapped her eyelids open, the thick lashes making a grand sweep. Gunnar did not have teal-blue eyes! The mountain man did. Now how did he get in her head? Or maybe he had been lurking there since yesterday, waiting to creep into her thoughts. She had been more interested in him than she cared to admit. Cloudy visions of him had haunted her dreams, his face towering above hers when he caught her with the parasol. He had an oddly stirring effect on her, but she brushed it off to her gratitude for his intervention with Newt Fraeb. He was too arrogant for his own good. She wondered what he looked like without all that hair on his face and head. For a moment, she was tempted to conjure his face as she imagined it would look clean shaven, but quickly discarded the notion. There was no sense in dwelling on him. She was sure she'd seen the last of him and that was fine with her.

The notes of songsters flitting from the leafing hazel bushes broke her reverie. The roosters crowed; the oxen lapped water noisily from the troughs in the corral.

Kristianna had filled two buckets. She stood and stroked the coarse hair between Dearie's large ears. "Thank you, boss. You are a good girl, *ja*." The cow fussed, not wanting affection once her milking was finished. She backed up and headed out the open door and to the wide fresh space of the corral.

Balancing the milk buckets in her hands, Kristianna secured them in a yoke and fit it over her shoulders and followed the cow out of the barn.

A faint apricot light dusted the silhouettes of tall trees surrounding the farmstead and she could see a thin swirl of smoke rising from the cabin's smooth rock chimney.

The roosters crowed again, and the hens clucked, fluttering about the coop. Tiny, white down feathers scattered over the powdery, scratched earth. Kristianna frowned and entered the cabin.

It was nice and warm inside. A cheery fire snapped from the hearth where her mother stirred mush in a large black pot hanging from an iron rod and Noelle . . . Noelle was nowhere to be seen.

"Mama," Kristianna began, setting the buckets on the whitewood board table top, as white as hands and ashes could scour it, "if Noelle does not gather the eggs soon, we shall have more chickens. I fear we shall sprout feathers if we have to eat them all."

Ulla placed a hand on her hip and looked about the small room. "Noelle!" she called, not seeing the child. "Noelle, you gather those eggs this minute. Mr. Bidwell does not pay us for chickens, he pays for the eggs."

From the loft above and behind the wide chimney that rose through the roof came two cherubic hands which clutched onto the wood railing. A white skullcap appeared, then a pair of green eyes, a small button nose, a pouting pink mouth, and finally a jutting chin.

"And do not dare cry about it," Ulla warned.

Noelle positioned herself on the straight ladder and backed down. Her legs were covered with black stockings, with a tiny hole at the knee, and her short linen skirt trailed on the step above her, revealing her white underdrawers. She reached the bottom rung, reluctant to let go.

"Noelle." Ulla's tone was stern. "Get the basket."

"But, Mama," she cried, large tears threatening to spill, "they peck at me! It hurts."

"All hens are bad-tempered. Collect from the white ones first, then the brown. The white are more agreeable to giving up their eggs, and once the brown ones see they have no choice, they will follow suit."

Kristianna waited for Noelle to collect the basket and when the child made no move, she said, "Do not be a baby, Noelle. And what were you doing up that ladder? You are too young to climb to my room." She was genuinely concerned for her little sister. She was a blessing child for her mother who had conceived her late in life.

"You be quiet!" Noelle sassed her, and reached out to pinch her sister.

"*Veckan har sju dagar. Damerna är inte här i dag,*" Ulla declared without raising her voice.

Kristianna and Noelle stopped their bickering, knowing that their mother had just said: "There are seven days in the week. The ladies are not here today."

"Now"—Ulla crossed her arms over her bosom and looked pointedly at Noelle—"will you gather those eggs, miss, or must I get out the hickory switch?" She waited for an answer.

Noelle couldn't speak. Her throat closed up, and stinging tears filled her eyes, flooding over the rims. The plain and simple truth was that she was afraid of chickens.

Kristianna sighed heavily and grabbed the basket from the wall hook by the door. "I will do it—just this once, Noelle." She swung the door open with the intention of getting the job over and done with as soon as possible, but she hadn't taken a single step when she dropped the basket and screamed.

Stone Boucher bent down and retrieved the straw basket and held it out to Kristianna. "You dropped this," he said in a restrained polite tone of voice, then doffed his hat.

Kristianna trembled, barely able to take the basket from him. His long fingers brushed hers with bold familiarity as she grasped the wicker handle, a familiarity he had no right to, but all the same sent a flighty tingle up her arm. Her earlier musings of his face without facial hair were now a vivid picture right before her. He had indeed shaved his mustache and beard, the planes and lines of his cheekbones angular and well defined. He'd brushed and tied his long, umber hair back into a glossy tail with a leather thong. His shoulders, encased in a greenish-blue calico shirt which mirrored the color of his eyes, filled the narrow doorway. His legs, slightly spread apart, were sheathed in fawn buckskin trousers that afforded not the slightest inch between his hardened skin and the fine leather. His confident manner unnerved her, and she slowly gave an inconspicuous glance to the heavy beam above the door and the hooks which held two very long—and loaded—rifles.

"May I help you?" Ulla asked, stepping forward next to Kristianna. Noelle stayed back, openly gawking.

"I came about the notice you put up at Bidwell's." His voice was deep, and he cleared his throat as he reached into the pocket of his buckskins. He handed the paper to Ulla. Kristianna leaned over her mother to see if it was indeed their notice. Regretfully, it was; she'd printed it herself.

"*Ja*, this is our paper. You have hired man experience on a farm?"

"Yes, ma'am, I do." The lie rolled off his

tongue as smooth as the finest brandy.

"Come in then, please, Mister—?"

"Stone Boucher, ma'am."

Kristianna could do nothing but stand back and stare as he entered. He was so tall, he had to slightly bend his sinewy torso and duck under the doorway in order not to brush the top of his head on the frame. He filled the room with the scent of tobacco, wood smoke and . . . Bay Balm. The Bay Balm was so distinct, she wondered if it hadn't been clinging to her from the day before and she hadn't realized it until now. Just what was he doing here? Hadn't he forced himself on her enough?

"Kristianna, Mr. Boucher needs a chair," Ulla said, wiping her hands on her embroidered apron.

Kristianna reached behind her and pulled down one of the four chairs hanging on individual pegs on the cabin walls. Biting her tongue, she kept her eyes from Stone's as she put the slat-backed chair next to the table.

"May I offer you some coffee, Mr. Boucher?" Ulla asked.

"Thank you, ma'am." He remained standing. "I'll wait until you and the girls sit, too."

Girls! Kristianna nearly choked, but checked herself by clasping her hands tightly together. She was no more a girl than her mother! Girls indeed! The rooster crowed again, and she gave Noelle a nasty look. If they hadn't been bickering, she would have heard Stone Boucher's arrival and would have had ample time to prepare herself for his invasion or at least headed him off before he

51

had the chance to come in! Well, she'd see that he was gone before his coffee cup was cool. They had no need to hire *him*.

"Forgive my manners, Mr. Boucher. These are my daughters, Noelle and Kristianna."

Stone gave Noelle an easy smile which she returned with candor, no longer wary. He turned to Kristianna and nodded ever so slightly, as if testing her mood. Her reception could have frosted the sun.

Noelle quickly took in Stone's attire, noting the deadly knife at his thigh. It was not often they saw a trapper up close. She took no notice of her sister's discomfort as she struggled to say his name, "S–Staw–St—" then gave up trying to pronounce it with an English accent and resorted to her own Swedish pronunciation. "S–Steurn, do you know many Indians?"

"Noelle," Ulla chastised, "he is Mr. Boucher, and do not ask him of his personal affairs."

"That's all right, ma'am. She's got the freedom of innocence on her side." He gave the child a disarming smile.

Happily, Noelle asked the question again, "Steurn, do you know many Indians?"

"I know a few. My best friend is a Seneca Indian."

Kristianna's attention perked up. There were no Seneca Indians in Minnesota Country. Was he hiding something? If he was lying to Mama, she certainly couldn't hire him. Pressing him further on the issue, she cast him a confident glare. "Mr. Boucher, I was not aware of any Seneca Indians in Minnesota Country. Could you be mistaken and that your friend is a Sioux?"

"Not likely," Stone replied to her challenge, his naturally honey-tanned face showing no discomfort at all by her interrogation. "Jemmy's a Seneca. Half-breed. From Buffalo, New York."

"New York!" Noelle breathed in awe. "Mama and Papa and Kristianna came from Sweden on a big ship to New York and rode a wagon across a sea of grass. That's what Papa called it. I never saw it. That was before I was born."

"Noelle," Ulla quietly, but firmly said, "that will be enough talk for now."

"*Ja*, Mama."

Ulla turned to the hearth. "Mr. Boucher, have you had breakfast? We were just about to have ours."

"Don't go to any trouble. I usually just have coffee and hardtack." He was still standing.

"Please, Mr. Boucher, sit down." Ulla took charge. "Kristianna, bowls and cups, please. And the white sugar."

White sugar? Mama reserved the store-bought, white sugar, actually a slight tan color, for special guests and holidays. It cost two dollars and ten cents a pint! For everyday, they used brown sugar Papa made during the winter from maple sap. Not wanting to disobey her mother, she dutifully collected the Delft earthenware cup with its missing handle and chipped lid which contained the white sugar, and set it on the table in front of him. He relaxed comfortably in the chair as if he planned on staying awhile. His being at ease didn't go past Kristianna, and it galled her even more. She gathered four tin cups, each a different size, and four wooden bowls. She arranged the cups on the table and brought the bowls to Ulla to fill with the mush. For the time being, she willed him from the room and pretended he wasn't there.

While Ulla Bergendahl spooned large helpings of oatmeal into the bowls, Stone took in Kristianna's shapely figure. She provided him with a tempting view of her backside that, even though hidden in many layers of petticoats and a skirt, he had no doubt was firm. She was the most exotic woman he had ever seen. He was now ready to admit that her eyes had captured him the day before like none other had. They were so unique he could barely believe they were real. The irises were dark and fathomless, the surrounding color violet. And ringing the circles was a darker blue, deep as twilight. The lashes that framed her beautiful eyes were lush and sweeping, and undeniably feminine. Her cheekbones were high and tinged a sweet carnation-pink. Her rose-tinted lips, full and inviting, had barbed and baited him since his arrival.

As tempting, inviting, and feminine, as she was, he was not here for her, but for a place to hide a while. They were two totally opposites with not a single thing in common, and it was best he study the inanimate surroundings rather than her. He examined the house with a quick perusal. It was sturdy and well thought out, and he was sure Mr. Bergendahl was a sound man with a logical head on his shoulders, but not so smart to leave three women alone. He wondered, not for the first time, why the man would venture off, entrusting them to fend for themselves.

The center of the room was broken by the large hearth that served to warm both the living area in front of it and the sleeping area behind it. He could see into the back room with its patchwork curtain parted that it was the sleeping area for Mr. and Mrs. Bergendahl as well as Noelle, for there was a trundle bed under the master one. The large, polished wood-frame bed was covered with a calico coverlet of rosebuds and roses and little birds on green vines that looked painstakingly real. He wondered if Kristianna had made it.

Kristianna. The name was interesting. Kris, if he shortened it, sounded soft and sweet. Where did she sleep? Then he glanced at the straight ladder and the loft. He stole a quick look at her, backing down from his resolve. She seemed out of place here as much as he. She was extremely tall for a woman, yet not gauche. She moved very gracefully on her long legs as she took the bowls from her mother.

Stone finished his examination of the cabin, noting the cupboard was filled with dishes, mostly blue and white or wooden, but on the top shelf were several mismatched pieces that he had called "golden-edged" dishes when he was younger. A butter churn graced the corner along with a water bucket and dipper and straight ahead was a canvas covering an opening the size of a doorway in the log structure that someone had cut out.

Kristianna placed the steaming bowl in front of him and took a seat before he could thank her.

Then Noelle resumed her questions. "Do you have a horse?"

"Yes, I do."

"What is his name?"

"*Hogh–gee–Nug–qua.* It's Seneca. Want to know what it means?"

Noelle nodded her head, her wheat-colored curls bouncing from underneath her rail cap.

"It means Brother Moon. You know why? Because my horse is as white as the moon on a still night."

Completely captivated, Noelle continued, "Is he like your brother, Steurn?"

"I guess you could say so. He's as reliable as my partner, and that's saying a lot."

"Tell me, Mr. Boucher," Kristianna asked, apparently not at all affected by what he was hoping was pure charm. "Why would a trapper want to take on farming responsibilities? Did I not hear you correctly yesterday when you said you did not like farmers?"

Stone paused with his spoon in mid-air. "My partner and I won't be trapping until fall sets in. I could use the income." It was a bold-faced lie. The money that Farribault would pay them for their pelts would be enough to last all summer and then some.

"I see." She gripped the handle of her spoon with anger. "Farmers are of use to you when you can make money off them, *ja*?"

"Kristianna!" Ulla nearly choked on her coffee.

"That's all right," Stone bounded back. "She's

got a right to her opinion. I did state mine yesterday."

"And boldly so," Kristianna added hotly. "If this is about yesterday, Mr. Boucher, I'll thank you now for having come to our aid. You owe us nothing more."

"I just thought you'd rather it be me here than Newt Fraeb." He narrowed his eyes in her direction.

The statement cracked across the table like the tail end of a whip. Kristianna hadn't thought of that. Newt Fraeb could easily have picked up their notice or someone worse than him. But who was to say this Stone Boucher was different? He did seem genuine and he did look pleasant. Actually handsome. But those were not reasons to trust him.

"Your opinion of us has changed overnight then, Mr. Boucher?" Kristianna asked curtly. "We are still the 'sodbusters' as some call us. We have to cut down the trees to survive. Not everyone makes their living like you do. As much as you may want to, you cannot roll people out like biscuit dough, all round, all the same. We are not dough, Mr. Boucher." She suddenly stopped short, realizing she'd gone too far.

Stone arched his dark brows in an uncanny manner. "I've never had it explained to me quite like that before, Miss Bergendahl."

Kristianna wasn't sure if he was teasing her or not. Given the warning glare from her mama, she kept quiet and put her attention into eating her oatmeal.

Noelle didn't like the turn the conversation had taken at all and resorted again to talking about animals. "We do not have horses, only oxen. They are named Jake and Tony. English names," she said with pride.

Kristianna paid little mind to Noelle's chatter, but instead took in Stone Boucher's every move. She watched with pent-up anger as he scooped generous amounts of the white sugar and cinnamon on his oatmeal, then he poured milk over the entire mound. He ate the mush as if he hadn't eaten in a month. He wasn't rude about it, but he sure had a healthy appetite. If he only knew how much they treasured that sugar . . .

Noelle watched the mountain man studiously and ate her oatmeal with as much vigor. When Stone drained the milk from his tin cup without his upper lip or teeth touching the creamy liquid, she did likewise.

"Noelle! You are spilling your milk," Ulla declared, and was quickly at the table with a damp cloth to wipe up the mess.

Noelle removed the white beard from her chin with a quick backhanded swipe. "Sorry, Mama," she mumbled not taking her eyes off of Stone.

Kristianna pushed her barely touched bowl away. Why was Noelle taking such a shine to the mountain man? She wasn't that attentive toward Gunnar.

"Mr. Boucher, may I bring you more to eat?" Ulla asked, wringing out the towel in the water bucket she kept in the house to do her dishes in.

"No, ma'am. This was very good. I appreciate it. I'm a fair cook, but nothing compared to you.

Now, maybe you can tell me what your husband needs done. That is, if I have the job."

"Oh, *ja*. It is yours."

Kristianna's squared shoulders slightly slumped. There was no time to forestall her mother's decision, short of screaming, "Mama, do not do it! I can take care of things for you!"

"First," Ulla began, "let me tell you my husband went to Saint Louis to find work so he could replace our plow. When he was plowing the west field, he broke the plow on a nest of roots. As you can see, we are surrounded by trees. Sixten had thought he would be home by now, or he would not have left us." Ulla felt the need to explain her husband's misfortune so he would not appear foolish in the eyes of the stranger. "I cannot offer you much in the way of wages, Mr. Boucher, but I can offer you room and board."

"That would be fine, ma'am."

"My husband was planning on adding to our house." She pointed to the canvas covering.

"Papa was going to buy us a real stove," Noelle supplied.

"I can fix that hole." That was the truth. He and Jemmy had built a cabin two years back. "Did he have a kitchen in mind?"

"*Ja*, with a real stove," Ulla said, a look of pride in her soft, green eyes. "Mr. Boucher, I do not know how long my husband will be gone. He will write us letters and send them to Fort Snelling. Would it be possible for you to build a split-rail fence for the garden? Can you tend to the barn, clean and rake the stalls of the oxen and cow if need be?"

"I reckon so." Hell, what he didn't know, he could figure out. What could be so hard about taking care of oxen? They couldn't be much different than horses.

"Then, Mr. Boucher, we have an agreement, *ja*?" Ulla gave him a hesitant smile.

"I would say so."

Kristianna let out a huff that didn't go unnoticed by Stone.

"You will sleep in the barn. There is a good bed of hay in the haymow."

"I will show him, Mama," Noelle offered, and nearly leapt from her chair. She ran to Stone and took his large hand in hers which swallowed her small fingers, the contrast in skin tones quite sharp. "Come with me, Steurn."

"Thank you for the breakfast, Mrs. Bergendahl." He set his hat on his head and nodded toward Kristianna. "Thank you for the cup and bowl."

"You are welcome," she briskly replied, and proceeded to clear the table, but not before she noted how Noelle's hand fit into his lean, tanned fingers. Noelle never held Gunnar's hand.

The pair were halfway out the door when Kristianna heard Noelle ask, "Do you like chickens, Steurn?"

Then the rooster crowed—again, and she knew in the days to follow that outlaw hens would emerge from their hideouts brazenly leading broods of fluffy chicks and it would be all Noelle's fault!

She hoped Stone Boucher liked chickens. Let *him* eat them all!

·5·

Later that afternoon, Kristianna looked out the window to see Stone bent over the hinge on the corral gate. He had rolled up the sleeves on his blue calico shirt, revealing his well-worked muscles, and was diligently rubbing some kind of grease over the gate's joints. His corded back tightened the material of his shirt with his movements. Bent at the knee, his thighs strained against his buckskins.

Dropping the gingham curtain back in place, Kristianna sighed. She would have to face him sooner or later. The thought of him as her audience while she did her chores was not a welcomed one, but she couldn't wait much longer. The kettle was surely ready.

As if she could read Kristianna's thoughts, Ulla announced from the table where she was peeling potatoes for the evening's supper, "The kettle will be boiled out before you get to washing, Kristianna."

Kristianna turned around and grudgingly grabbed the basket of dirty clothes and a pannikin of lye soap. "*Ja*, Mama." Before she went out the door, she faced her mother. "Do you think Papa would approve of Mr. Boucher being here?"

Ulla dropped another ribbon of russet peel to her pile, then brushed back her fine, brown hair with her wrist. "I think Papa would want me to do what is best for us. And that is what I have done. Now get on to the wash so it can dry before sundown."

"*Ja*, Mama." Kristianna strode out the door and purposefully averted her eyes from Stone Boucher. She took brisk steps toward the side of the house. The pleasant scent of a split-wood fire filled the air as embers crackled and sputtered under a large, black kettle. Resting on a long, wide bench was a half barrel filled with cool creek water. Doing her best to ignore Stone's presence, Kristianna submerged part of the laundry in the barrel and scooped up a handful of the pale, thick soap. Smoothing it over the washboard, she started scrubbing. Normally, she would think of married life and having a house of her own while she repeatedly swept the dirty clothes over the rippling board. Today, she kept all her attention on the task at hand.

After scrubbing the clothes, she dipped them into the boiling pot. Removing them with a long, wooden fork, she rested them on the bench to cool before squeezing them out.

Stone was diverted from his work by the strong pungency of lye soap. He finished working on the hinge and stood to observe her washing process with interest. Leaning against the closed gate, he reached into the pouch around his waist and drew out his cigarette makings. He'd done his own laundry for years, but he'd done it like the trappers and the Indians. He used the creek banks where smooth rocks were plenty, and then he'd lay out his clothes and soap and beat them with a stick until they were clean. It didn't matter if you had hot water or not. And as for his buckskins, all they needed were to be brushed with a rounded piece of sandstone inside and out.

He lit his smoke as Kristianna bent over the tub again, her white-blonde braid swaying with her fluid motions. She had twisted her hair into one long, thick rope and topped her head with a silly five-pleated cap. Feathery wisps of hair framed her oval face, her complexion a satiny cream color. Those unusual eyes that had caught his attention looked down in deep concentration. Her blouse was a plain buff muslin and her brown skirt was too short. The lack of yardage offered him a view of her shapely ankles which brought an easy smile to his lips. She wore heavy wooden clogs on her feet that looked extremely uncomfortable. He couldn't begin to imagine what his feet would feel like in hunks of wood, having worn Seneca moccasins for numerous years. He wondered what she would think of fine skins around her toes and hugging her calves.

A breeze fanned her fire and a melodious sound floated to him. The strains were so mesmerizing, he left the corral to track them down. Taking giant steps, he rounded the back of the house, where all along the eaves hung chimes, dozens of them made from discarded relics. Old rusted scissors, cow and farm bells, pieces of broken farm implements, hinges, horseshoes, barrel rims, and even pieces of broken china. He ran his index finger across an assembly of rusted nails; they sounded like shattering icicles. His eyes filled with admiration for the craftsman.

"My papa made them."

Stone turned, surprised to see Kristianna standing behind him holding the clothes basket. Her cheeks were flushed from standing over the hot kettle, and there was a fine bead of perspiration on her full, upper lip. He forced his attention from her mouth to her iris-colored eyes. "They're unusual. I like them."

She didn't acknowledge him again. The only reason she had spoken at all was to stop him from touching the chimes. They were Papa's. She walked away from him, intent on hanging the laundry. To her dismay, he followed.

"Where did he get the pieces?"

"He picked most of them up on the prairie," she answered as she spread the linens on a dried grapevine, using the thorns as pins.

There was an awkward tension before Stone spoke again. "I fixed the corral gate. It was sticking."

"I liked it the way it was."

Stone took a deep pull on his cigarette before

commenting, "You don't like me much, do you?"

"No, I do not." Kristianna didn't mince words and continued to fasten the clothes to the vines.

"Might I be privy to why not?"

"I do not trust you. You may have convinced my mama you are honorable, but I find something about you that is not sincere. You may look like a fine piece of pine, but you have knots in your inside."

"Do you always voice your opinions so eloquently? Pine knots and biscuit dough?"

"I know no other way," was all she said, continuing on with her task. Then she abruptly stopped as blue-gray smoke curled around her nose. "Mr. Boucher, if I had wanted my laundry smoked, I would have put it in the smokehouse." She waved at the smoke which filtered through the grapevine.

Stone was a little taken aback. Nevertheless, he dropped the cigarette and ground it out in the dirt with his heel. "Most women enjoy the smell of good tobacco."

"I am not most women."

"I can see that."

For a brief moment, neither spoke, but merely accepted the other's presence. Life slowed down for a minute. The sun seemed to stand still, and the shadows seemed not to change at all.

Stone broke the silence. "I'll start on the kitchen walls tomorrow."

She didn't answer him. In her haste to complete her chore, she dropped her underpinnings in the dirt. Stone got to them before she did. He held them out to her, and she blushed as red as the geraniums Mama kept in her flower box. She reached for them, noting how soft and light the white cotton looked in his tanned and calloused hands. He could easily crush the fabric with those powerful fingers, instead, he gently handed them to her. To her surprise, he didn't make light of the situation as she brushed the smudges of dirt from the legs.

"We're not that different you know." Stone folded his arms across his chest. "I live off the land. You live off the land. I could show you some things. You could show me some things. Maybe we would understand each other then."

"But you would still say we conquer the forest."

"I've got nothing against your farming, Miss Bergendahl. I just don't approve of where you do it, that's all."

"Where would you have us farm?"

"I've come across many prairies that—"

"*Ja*, whose earth is tough with the wire roots of bluestems and prairie clovers that do not give against the blade of the plow. You need six yokes of oxen to clear a small parcel of land. There are hidden bees' nests, and never-ending mice. The prairies do not offer proper drainage. There are uncontrollable fires. And what of the Indians? A family is out in the open to be slaughtered, Mr. Boucher." Kristianna felt frustrated at not being able to better convey her feelings in English. Ramming her blouse into the thorns, she pricked her finger. She immediately brought it to her lips to draw out the dot of blood.

"You all right?"

"I cannot find the right words to tell you how much this land means to us." She ignored his concern. If there were only some way she could get across to him the importance of the timbered area they had settled in. Though she was doubtful he would understand her reason, she had to try. "Come with me."

He watched her go to the copse of butternut trees that edged the back of the barn. Her skirt swished with determination, her stride smooth, and any doubts he'd had about her being comfortable in those awkward shoes vanished. Looking over her shoulder, she called to him where he was still standing at the spot she'd just vacated. "Come on. I want to show you something."

A little bewildered, Stone headed toward her. He followed her through a grove of dense black walnut and pine trees. The massive trunks towered above him almost farther than he could see. Small shafts of light filtered down on Kristianna's head, splashing her braid in golden spears as she walked. He stepped over rocks covered with ruffled, gray-green lichens which gave off a musty smell. The crunching of dead leaves and needles under Kristianna's heavy shoes broke the serenity. She'd starve as a trapper, Stone thought, who out of habit, walked soundlessly.

Kristianna came to the edge of the forest and stopped.

There were numerous felled trees and burnt-out stumps lining a large expanse of cleared land. The earth was dark as coffee and just as rich. Half of the lot was combed into neat, smooth rows, the other half was marred with thistle and rag-weeds, and the leftover brown clippings of winter wheat. In the middle, dividing the contrasting plots, was a solitary shovel plow. Even from a distance, it was obvious the cast-iron share was cracked. A blue dragonfly hovered around the hardwood handle, pausing briefly to sun itself, then flew off.

Kristianna dropped to her knees, and with loving familiarity, scooped up a handful of the black earth and let it run through her fingers. "It has just the right amount of moisture for early planting. You cannot find soil like this in the prairie, Mr. Boucher."

Stone crouched down next to her.

"Feel it," she commanded softly.

He dug his hand into the earth, stretching his fingers wide into the warm, loose soil. When no revelation hit him, he withdrew, his fingernails filled with the dirt. "It's just dirt to me. Nothing to topple the trees for. Trees hold everything together, Miss Bergendahl. The branches hold the sky, and the roots hold the earth."

" 'Take also of the tree of life, and eat, and live forever.' "

"The Good Book again?"

"It is from Genesis. About the garden of Eden."

"Eden wasn't filled with beaver, coons, and marten to trap. Eden wasn't destroyed. Adam and Eve were."

As each contemplated the other's reasons to be right, a grasshopper landed on the ground in front of them. Stone crept his hand forward and captured the insect by the wings. "Want to see something?" He snipped off a blade of grass between his fingers and held it out to the grasshopper. "If you hold him easy and gently poke the grass into his jaws, he'll nibble it fast."

In an instant, the juicy green spear was devoured.

"I think that's sort of a wonderment, don't you?" Stone asked.

Kristianna reached for the grasshopper, not sharing the same admiration for the creature as Stone. "Do you see the little yellow dot by its leg?" She touched it with her fingertip and the leg popped off. "*That* is a wonderment, Mr. Boucher." She stood and dropped the grasshopper, then crushed it under her clog.

Stone rose next to her. "Damn, I guess we don't agree on grasshoppers either, do we, Miss Bergendahl? I left it in one piece."

"And I could not let it live to eat our summer corn. Supper is just after sunset if you are still intent on staying." Leaving him to ponder their situation, Kristianna headed back to the cabin.

To Kristianna's chagrin, Stone Boucher was at the table for supper, but there was no mention of their earlier conversation. Noelle's chatter filled any uncomfortable silence, and Ulla didn't seem to notice her eldest daughter's reserve.

After the meal was finished, Stone bid them good night, and Kristianna climbed the ladder to her loft room. Normally, she would light a lantern to get ready for bed. This night, she undressed by the pale light of the moon. There were no curtains on her window; there had never been the need for them. First thing tomorrow, she would search Mama's rag bag for remnants.

Kristianna removed her rail cap and placed it on her pine bureau, gingerly resting the ribbons on top of the folds. She unfastened the hooks on her blouse and skirt, dropping them to the planked floor. Retrieving them, she hung them on the wooden rods along the ceiling. Quickly shedding her *särken*, a thinly strapped chemise, and pantalets, she slipped on her nightgown, slightly self-conscious of her inordinate height even to view her own body in the small, round mirror above the bureau.

Kneeling on her bed, which was below the window, Kristianna gazed at the stars. A full moon shone down through the opening in the trees. She saw Stone's shadow cross the path toward the barn. He entered, then there was a faint light glowing from the haymow. He opened the weathered shutters and was silhouetted by the flicker of a lantern.

She was drawn to watching him. His movements were fluid and easy as he made himself a bed of hay. He pulled off his moccasins, and his felt hat followed. Instead of extinguishing the lantern, he rested his back against the shutter jamb with one knee bent. For a long while, he sat like that, giving her the opportunity to view him without being detected from her dark room.

Finally, he reached into the pouch around his waist, then put his hands to his mouth. A melody, sharp and wavering at the same time, floated to her ears. How could he do that? Make music

70

with his hands? She observed him for quite some time, trying to figure out how he made the music. When exhaustion overtook her, she crawled under the covers.

The music, soft and haunting, was a contrast to the hard-muscled man who was creating it. It was not at all like the lively woods tunes Gunnar played on his fiddle. But oddly, the notes lulled her into a peaceful sleep.

·6·

Nearly a week later, Kristianna stood at the table with the flatiron in her hand. The heat from the coals made the crooks of her fingers perspire as she ran the iron back and forth over her mother's apron. Ironing was one thing she hated in the summer. She had opened all of the windows, but no breeze stirred the air today. It promised to be as hot as a *krum kaker* griddle.

Outside, she could hear Stone with a hammer and wedges, splitting the wood that would be the walls for the new kitchen. He'd already put up the framing, making the lean-to a perfect square skeleton. Noelle's voice buzzed over the scrape of his plane, and for a moment, Kristianna felt sorry for him having Noelle as his shadow. The child meant well, but she sometimes was a bother. She supposed Noelle was very lonely, not often having children her own age to play with. Many times, she spent hours talking to her rag dolls in the shade of the full boughs, using acorns and leaves for cups and saucers, creating her own private tea party.

Half the ironing done, Kristianna arched her back, then wiped her damp brow with the back of her wrist. Though she wore a white, cotton blouse and a thin, wide-pleated black skirt, she was still hot in the small room. She glanced to the noon mark on the window sill, noting that it was not as late as she thought. Not even near noon yet. She picked up one of Noelle's homespun dresses to press out the wrinkles. The iron whisked across the skirt, then bodice, before Kristianna jerked her hand away. The hook, having been heated by the iron's heavy plate, burned her thumb.

Hot and disgusted, she put the iron on its rest and grabbed two small tin buckets. Before leaving the house, she snatched her *klut*, a cinnamon-colored coverchief, from the peg by the door. Lifting the leather latch string, she left the dreaded ironing behind.

Ulla was crouched over the garden, weeding and making ready the earth for summer planting.

"I am going to pick blackberries, Mama."

Ulla looked up. Her face was encircled by a headband, her brown braids anchored in a crown on the top of her head. "Did you finish the ironing so soon?"

"Most of it. It is too hot."

"*Ja*, you say that every year." Her mother

smiled with fond remembrance. "Take Noelle with you. I fear the child has worn Mr. Boucher out."

"I was going to."

Kristianna crossed to the side of the house where Stone was busy laying the freshly cut logs next to each other. He wore the same white calcutta, laced-up shirt he'd worn the first time she saw him. His movements were strong and sure as he checked the lengths of each puncheon. Tiny beads of sweet sap oozed from the timber, filling the air with a woodsy fragrance. Noelle sat in the midst of everything with wood shavings over her ears.

"Kristianna! Look, I have earrings!"

"Noelle, do not bother Mr. Boucher while he works."

Stone turned, not hearing Kristianna's approach. He took a brief moment to admire her overwhelming beauty before speaking. Her unique eyes drew his gaze to her face. Her lashes were so thick that her eyes seemed to be outlined by kohl, and her full, alluring lips made him want to run his fingertip over them to test their softness. She was completely oblivious to her beauty, which enhanced it all the more. "I don't mind. She's been telling me stories."

Kristianna inclined her head toward her younger sister. "Have you now?"

"Oh, *ja*. Steurn is my best friend."

Surprise filled Kristianna. Just what kind of stories did Noelle know? "I am going blackberry picking. Come with me, Noelle."

"And Steurn, too." She stood up and brushed

the wood remnants from her skirt.

He caught Kristianna off guard with his reply of, "Why not?"

She couldn't rally quick enough to protest.

"I'll set some rabbit traps and bag a wild turkey for your mother. I heard some gobbling early this morning."

"I am sure she would appreciate that," Kristianna replied politely, deciding it was best to accept the fact that he would accompany them. She could at least be civil. "We have not had fresh meat in some time."

Not long after, the three walked down a natural path. Stone carried his traps and possibles pouch as well as his rifle, which was covered in a soft hide. Kristianna's and Noelle's empty tins rattled in their hands. Kristianna was acutely aware of Stone's presence. His steps were longer and stronger, and she had to put a little bounce in her stride to keep up with him. Occasionally, she'd peek at his rigid profile, studying his straight forehead, dark slashing eyebrow, hooded eyelid, aquiline nose, sensual mouth and the shadow of a beard on his jaw. She knew now why he'd sported a beard. No doubt, he had to shave twice a day to keep a smooth face. She wondered why he'd shaved it off.

Deep in her assessment of Stone, Kristianna nearly tripped over a pebble in the path. She mentally scolded herself and diverted her eyes from his masculine appeal.

A sudden change took place in June, when all nature was robed in cheerful color. The woods were full of violets, buttercups, thimble flowers, and tiny starry grass flowers. White summer moths flitted around with a regal air. Verdant leaves sprung forth from the saplings of cottonwoods, birches, and elms.

They walked along a small tributary where tamaracks lined the easy-flowing water. Stone reached into his parfleche and took out a bleached piece of bone.

"What is that, Steurn?" Noelle asked, looking up at him.

"My turkey call. I made it from the hollow bone of a turkey's wing." Stone held it in the end of his hand and sucked on it. A noise similar to a turkey's call emitted from the bone.

"That is funny, Steurn." Noelle laughed.

Kristianna kept her eyes straight and her tread brisk. "Papa can call for turkeys using his hands."

"I reckon I could, too, if I had the need for it."

"You would like our Papa. He is . . . Look! Kristianna, a rabbit!"

A gray rabbit, with its nose wiggling, stood frozen on a grassy patch. Rosy sunlight filtered through its long ears with their delicate veins and the softest short fur on the outsides. Kristianna liked rabbits and, of course, ate them. But it was different when Papa brought them home already dead. When they were living, she wanted to reach out and touch the thick fur on their backs. In a flash, the rabbit disappeared into the brush.

Kristianna dashed to the newly vacated spot and placed her hand on the flattened grass. "It is still warm," she said joyfully.

"Let me feel it," Noelle insisted. "*Ja*, it is! Come, Steurn. You feel it, too!"

He felt a little foolish bending down to feel the crushed grass, but did so nonetheless. If Jemmy ever knew he'd done it, he'd never hear the end of it. Rabbits were good for nothing but pelts and meat, and here he was feeling how warm their behinds left meadow grass!

The delicate flush on Kristianna's face didn't go unnoticed by Stone. For a moment, she had let her guard down and actually smiled. She looked up. Catching him staring at her, her expression dimmed to casual indifference.

The moment broken, Stone opened his pouch and withdrew a trap. "Warm behind or not, he'll make a fine stew." Taking a feather, he dipped it in bear grease and rubbed it on the hinges of the jaws and springs of the pans. Setting the trap open, he covered it with the grass. "Mind you be careful of that, Noelle," he cautioned. "It can take your finger off."

And the rabbit's leg, Kristianna thought, the image of the furry creature still etched in her mind.

"Come along, Noelle," Kristianna said, almost crossly. "We have dallied long enough."

Just a little further was a patch of blackberries, the fruit a deep, dark purple. The leaves were spiked and the thorns intimidating, but the rewards outweighed being pricked.

Noelle gingerly plucked a berry, staining her cherubic hand. She popped it into her mouth and bit it, and the juice ran down her chin.

"You need not stay here, Mr. Boucher. We can manage." Kristianna skillfully reached through the leaves.

"Believe it or not, Miss Bergendahl, but I have picked a blackberry or two in my life," he said sarcastically. "I won't be but a holler away, *if* you need me." He strode off with his rifle across his shoulder.

Kristianna wished she had the good grace to call after him and apologize for her behavior. Why was it he always brought out the worst in her?

What was supposed to be fun turned into a mechanical task. Noelle soon tired of the picking, having eaten most of what she took off the vines. She moved away to settle by some jack-in-the-pulpits. Pulling one of the herbs from the base of their long stalks, she proceeded to use it as a makeshift sword. Kristianna peeked into her sister's bucket to see five measly berries. Not even enough to make a tart!

Kristianna lost track of time, moving through the brambles. She had filled her tin and was nearly halfway finished with Noelle's when she realized she couldn't hear her sister's play talk.

"Noelle?"

Silence.

"Noelle? Where are you?"

Silence. Stillness.

Kristianna dropped the tin and moved from the shrubs. The jack-in-the-pulpit spear lay on the ground, discarded. A chilling panic worked its way up her spine. Indians . . . The Sioux were nearby for the rendezvous.

"Noelle!" This time she screamed sharply. "Come out!"

She bunched her skirt in her hand, and in a near run, blindly backtracked the way they had come. Her eyes scanned the trees and flowers for movement but found nothing. She stumbled and fell. Tiny pebbles cut into the flesh on her palms as she tried to cushion her fall. Her elbows bruised, she winced with pain. Pushing herself up with her hands, she saw small, leaping tracks in the earth. The rabbit's.

Noelle was inquisitive enough to . . . Dear God, no!

It seemed forever to reach the spot where Stone had set the trap. Once there, she dropped to her knees, her breath coming in ragged gasps. The deathly jaws were still hidden under the grass, untouched. She allowed herself only the smallest sigh of relief before calling again.

"Noelle!"

A whimpering scream answered back.

Turning to where the sound came, Kristianna pushed through the underbrush. Branches slapped at her face, scratching her cheeks and pulling at her *klut* until finally it was snatched from her head. Wisps of hair gave way as the budding twigs snagged her silken braid.

"Noelle!"

Soft childlike cries came to her ears.

Kristianna entered a clearing, her heart hammering in her chest.

Noelle was standing in a ravine with three sharply sloping walls enclosing her. Her tiny face was smudged with dirt and tears. Her black stockings had holes in them and her dress was torn.

"Noelle, how did you—"

A loud snort broke the girl's sobs, and Kristianna saw that the only exit was blocked by a thistle digger. A wild hog. Long-legged and long-snouted, its large bones protruded from its gaunt body. Its ears were flat and its back arched with erect bristles from head to tail.

"Do not move, Noelle," Kristianna ordered in a tone she hoped sounded calm.

Cautiously, she inched forward. The hog trembled, readying to charge. Her breath caught in her throat, but she took another step. A dead and dry twig crunched under her clog and it seemed the crack echoed louder than any thunder. The razorback turned its head toward the rise Kristianna stood on. It lifted its snout, its nostrils quivering as it calculated the foreign scent.

The hog decided the little girl was the easiest prey. It lunged forward at the same time Kristianna did, but Kristianna was pulled sharply back by a sinewy hand.

Suddenly, Stone was there. He pulled the cover from his rifle, holding the stock with one hand while the other yanked the cover free with a quick jerk on the muzzle fringe. He aimed his gun, then there was a bright flash in the pan, an enormous flash from its barrel, and the hollow, thudding explosion of coarse black powder. Kristianna was momentarily blinded by the light, but heard the hog squeal. Rubbing her eyes, she saw it topple. The ball had been put up high between its shoulder for a swift kill.

Struggling to her feet, Kristianna was instantly sliding down the embankment. Noelle sat huddled in a tight ball, her small body racked with painful sobs. Falling to her knees, Kristianna embraced her fiercely, clutching the child tightly to her breasts.

"Are you hurt? Do not *ever* leave me again, Noelle! Ever!"

Noelle's cries continued.

"What were you doing down here?" Kristianna choked.

"I—I was looking for my ch–charger and I slipped down the hill."

"Oh, Noelle." Kristianna stroked the girl's disheveled hair under her askewed rail cap. "You do not have a horse."

Stone reached them and helped them up. "Varmint's dead now." His voice was thick and unsteady.

"Steurn, you are my knight. You saved me." Noelle's words were shaky, and she left Kristianna's arms to wrap herself around the body of the giant mountain man who had come to her aid.

As Noelle clung to Stone, her tears dampening his shirt, an unknown feeling breathed its way into the recesses of his heart. This child . . . this wooden shoe girl pulled at the deepest parts within him and he suddenly felt the loss of never having had any siblings. He'd never much considered what his life would have been like with a little sister. There had been happy times at The Terrace, but after his mother Elaine's death at an early age, Alexandre had thrust himself into his business, giving no regard to the small boy who followed his every move. And when Alexandre married Solange, there was never any hope for a tightly knit family, as Solange was only five years older than Stone. Looking down on Noelle's disheveled curls, he wondered if she had the power to make him care, or had his heart hardened too much over the years? He had never cared about anyone before, much less loved someone. He respected Jemmy. He had been fond of his mother and accepted Solange. And his father . . . his father was nothing to him.

A little afraid of the possibility that he could get attached to Noelle, Stone gently eased her small arms from his waist. "You best do what your sister tells you next time, Noelle." His voice was rough, masking his true feelings.

"Do not tell Mama I wandered, Steurn." Noelle wiped her face with the hem of her dirty apron.

Stone looked to Kristianna with a question in his eyes, as if to say, "It's okay with me, if it's okay with you."

"I will not," she answered Stone's silent question.

"We'll tell your mother that you fell in the blackberry patch and Kristianna came in after you. And I had to drag you both out."

Noelle grinned from ear to ear. "*Ja!*"

"Come on. I reckon we can't take this prairie shark home for supper then. We'll have to waste him. And I was fairly tasting a ham. It's a good thing I got us a gobbler."

"Oh, I love turkey!" Noelle cried gleefully.

"Are you not glad Mama hired him, Kristianna?"

She didn't reply. At this moment, she was certainly glad, and this day, she had gained a little respect for the trapper, if not a little trust. "Mr. Boucher," she addressed him, "twice now, you have come to our aid and I have given you nothing but bad manners in return. I apologize and I want to thank you for all you have done." Not knowing what sort of good-will gesture a woman should make toward a man, Kristianna extended her hand for him to shake like Papa would have done.

Stone hesitated at the offering, then conceded and wrapped his browned fingers around her fine, white hand. His palm was calloused, lean, and strong, and she recalled the first time she'd noticed his hand when Noelle had held it. Now, it was her turn. Their thumbs were nearly the same length, and she was almost tempted to see if their fingertips matched evenly. His grip was firm and confident, and as she drew her hand away, he gave it a little squeeze, then brushed her knuckles with his thumb. Confusion churned inside her at the loss of her hand in his. Why hadn't she ever been reluctant to leave Gunnar's clasp?

Stone cleared his throat. "We better head back before your mother wonders what happened to us." He reached down and scooped Noelle in his arms and carried her to the top of the embankment. Putting her down, he looked her squarely in the eyes. "Next time you get the notion to go finding yourself a horse, you come to me. I'll saddle up Brother Moon for you."

"Kristianna, did you hear?"

Kristianna started up the steep hill and smiled. "I heard."

Stone skimmed down the rise, sending tiny rocks and dirt tumbling. "Now it's your turn, big sister."

Before she could protest, Stone swept her off her feet with a quicksilver motion. Her first reaction was to voice her protest, but the words never formed. She became conscious of where his warm flesh touched hers and an awakening glow, new and untried, radiated from the top of her head, to the tips of her toes, and across her skin. Never had she been so affected by a man. Leather and tobacco filled her lungs as she breathed his scent in, aware of everything about his nearness. It was wrong to be in his arms. Oh, but it felt so right! Even as she denied her attraction, she fought against dropping her chin against his wide, strong chest.

Kristianna, the farmer's daughter, would not have allowed him such an intimacy; but Kristianna, the girl on the brink of womanhood, wanted nothing more than to be in the woodsman's embrace.

· 7 ·

The next several days the atmosphere on the farm was as mellow and as pleasant as the weather. During the day, the women busied themselves with running the household— mending; baking; cleaning; tending the cow and oxen; weeding and planting the garden. Stone labored over the kitchen lean-to and put up all of the planks, sealing the room off from the outside. He'd filled the chinks in the walls with oakum and cut all of the roofing shingles. Kristianna felt safer with the house whole again.

Saturday greeted them with a warm, northwest wind. Feathery, white clouds wisped across the cerulean sky all morning. By late afternoon, they turned into vague dark smudges, dragging their shadows over the woods, turning into rolling thunderheads. With no chance of finishing the roof before the rain came, Stone was forced to cover his unfinished work with a tarp and continue the kitchen from inside.

The air was full of electricity, and the humidity made Stone's shirt cling to his back. He wondered if Jemmy had found out anything from Samuel Granger. He'd been here for nearly a week and hadn't had the opportunity to go into Fort Snelling. The work had been good for him, though. It took his mind off Granger's note, and Kristianna was a lot better to look at than Jemmy.

The thought of spending the afternoon with her in the house created an erratic beating of his heart. He wasn't immune to her and that somewhat disturbed him. There was no future for them, since there was no room in his life for any woman. He'd been wandering too long to settle down. And yet, every time they shared a meal, or any other domestic chore, the closeness was pleasant to him. He pushed the thoughts from his mind. If he kept up with that line of thinking, he'd find himself married to her.

Before entering the house, he walked across the yard to the half barrel filled with creek water. He dipped a hollowed gourd into the water, brought the gourd to his lips, and drank deeply. Then he unbuttoned his shirt and pulled it down over his shoulders so it hung by his waistband. Scooping the cool water in his large hands, he splashed his face and neck, and the clear liquid dripped down his naked chest. He took off his wide-brimmed hat and smoothed back his dark brown hair, but an unruly lock settled right back on his tanned forehead. Feeling somewhat refreshed, he slipped into his shirt again and replaced his hat.

He turned, surprised to see Kristianna standing in front of the barn, a yoke across her shoulders with two full milk buckets dangling at her knees. There was a guilty flush on her face as she started toward him.

"Dearie gives twice the milk in the summer." Her voice was light and casual, concealing the torrent of emotions that were erupting inside her. She had no business looking at him the way she had. She should have made her presence known, but she was so caught by the sight of him that she could not. She had never seen a man without a shirt before. Not even Papa. Her reaction shocked her to the core. She wanted to reach out to him and press her palms on the hard ridges of his ribs to see if they were indeed as strong as they appeared. Then to her horror, she found that she wouldn't have wanted to stop there, but continue and follow the lines of his chest, and run her fingertips through the curling dark hair there and then up to his smooth, muscular shoulders.

"That brown-eyed critter doesn't happen to give cold ale?"

Snatched from her thoughts, she realized he was speaking to her. "*Nej*," she replied, not taking him seriously. "But Mama and I made some cold tea."

"I'll drink it inside. Rain'll be here before supper."

To her surprise, he took the heavy yoke off her shoulders. As if he'd done it before, he expertly balanced the frame in one hand, holding it high enough not to drag the full buckets on the ground. They reached the front door together. Stone stood aside so she could enter first, and as Kristianna brushed around him, her arm came in contact with his. A warm tingle spread through her with the intimate graze that vanished all too quickly when he moved to set the buckets on the table. Self-consciously, she took down a tin cup from the cupboard and filled it with the tea, then measured a spoon of white sugar from the Delft earthenware cup, and stirred it into the beverage. She gave it to him before she had time to analyze why she had willingly added in the store-bought sugar.

Standing at the hearth, Ulla looked up, with a smile radiating her face. She was sifting yellow cornmeal through her fingers into a kettle of salted, boiling water. "Mr. Boucher, you have done fine work on the kitchen. My husband will be pleased. Thank you."

"It's not finished yet. I'll end the day in here since I can't nail down the roof."

"*Ja*, Steurn." Noelle spoke up from the corner where she was looking over a McGuffey reader. "You can tell us Indian stories."

"Noelle, must you always pester Mr. Boucher?" Ulla used a big wooden spoon to stir the thick, yellow bubbling mass. "Let him work in peace. And you, my *dotter*, should be looking over your English lessons. Papa bought that book new so you would not be behind."

"But, Mama, stories are lessons, too." Noelle pouted.

"I don't mind," Stone assured Ulla. "It's a sad day when I can't work and talk at the same time."

"Then you stitch your sampler, Noelle, while you listen."

"*Ja*, Mama."

Kristianna hastily moved the churn into the center of the room to afford her ample view of Stone as he worked. She skimmed the cream from the milk and took down a chair from the wall, setting the churn between her legs. She was just as interested in Stone's stories as Noelle was.

"Who are the meanest Indians you have ever met?" Noelle asked, plopping her embroidery on her lap. Her eyes were round as she leaned forward waiting for his answer.

Stone moved into the kitchen. In the heat, sticky pine juice dripped down the new walls, and in places, drops dried to hard, yellow beads. He stood a puncheon on its end and picked up his plane. Before sliding the sharp tool down the plank, he replied, "Flatheads, beyond a doubt. Meaner than griz. They'll take out your heart and eat it for a victory dinner after they've done you in."

"Mr. Boucher!" Kristianna sputtered. "I do not think such a story is fitting for a child. And surely, it's not the truth."

"It is."

Ulla set the kettle on a spider off the main fire so the hasty pudding could simmer. "I think Mr. Boucher should tell us about the Indians so that we can be prepared if the need arises."

And so the next hour passed with wild talk of Indians and the escapades Jemmy and Stone had

had over the years. The house was animated with Noelle's interjections and occasional yelps from sticking herself with her needle; the sloshing of whipping cream being churned by Kristianna; dishes making cheerful little sounds as Ulla washed them.

"Tell us about your Seneca, Steurn." Noelle was trying to untangle the mass of knots her red thread had created on the letter *C*.

Stone removed a nail from his mouth and hammered it in the broad, rough-timbered floor. "He's the best trapper I've come across. He catches more beaver in his traps than anyone else. He swears and coins more queer and awful oaths than anyone has a right to."

He paused and reached for another nail, hammering and talking at the same time. "He drinks more liquor than anyone I know, and goes in pursuit of game into the neighborhood of hostile Indians without a second thought. His gun was fired so much one time, it was too hot to hold. And he claims he can shoot higher and deeper, wider and closer, straighter and crookeder and rounder and more of any way than I can; but, he's more winded than a zephyr."

Noelle was fairly breathless at such a colorful description. "He sounds just like you, Steurn."

He threw his handsome head back and roared with laughter. Kristianna was so surprised at his sudden show of emotion that she stopped the dasher in mid-motion.

"I always wanted to be like him, ever since I was sixteen." Stone chuckled. "And now, I'll be damned if I haven't taken on all his bad habits."

"Do you go around assaulting people, too, Mr. Boucher?" Kristianna asked, resuming her churning. "That was your friend, this Jemmy Paquer who threw himself on Newt Fraeb?"

"I do, if there's a call for it." He was a little agitated at her tone toward Jem, as if he were nothing more than one of the trappers she didn't like.

"And where is Jemmy Paquer now?" Ulla queried.

"More than likely dead drunk, or in a fist fight at the rendezvous."

Ulla wiped the dishes with a clean, cotton towel. "You should invite him for supper sometime, Mr. Boucher. It is not right that a man should have to live so . . . so boisterous. I am sure he is lonely and does those things only to pass the time."

Stone quirked a dark, slashed brow. *Jemmy lonely*? No, Jemmy was never without some embroiled battle or cause. Besides, Jemmy would probably say he didn't cut meat with settlers.

"Tell us more," Noelle urged.

Kristianna watched Stone move with graceful strength and easy movements as he continued to awe Noelle with his tales. And herself. She wondered if half of what he said was true. No man could live through all that. She found herself more and more caught up in the way he moved than the stories he told. He seemed to be made of iron as he effortlessly swung the hammer. His forearms were like steel, bulging with muscles at each whack of the nailhead. There was a forbidden magnetism to him that she couldn't quite explain.

Deciding it was best if she did not dwell on him, she slowed her churning as the cream began to form butter islands. Lifting the lid, she removed the bits and hunks of golden butter with a wooden paddle and put them into a wooden bowl. She washed the butter many times in cold water, turning it over and over, working it with the paddle until the water ran clear. Then she salted it. She turned her attention to Stone's voice again as she put the butter into a mold with a carved image of a strawberry with two strawberry leaves.

"There's been many times that food was so scarce, we could hardly wait to cook it. I've eaten more pemmican than I care to."

"What is that?" Noelle inquired.

"It's Indian fare. Dried beef and fat."

"Well, I have been made to eat more lutefisk than I care to," Noelle added, pulling the red thread so hard that it snapped and frayed in her fingers.

"Lutefisk? You'll have to enlighten me."

Noelle wrinkled her nose in disgust. "It is white fish put into barrels with lye and it smells so bad that Mr. Degermark's dogs lift their legs on the barrels!"

"Noelle!" Ulla and Kristianna parroted at the same time.

Stone leaned in the doorway and crossed his arms over his chest. A generous smile danced on his lips. "I don't think I'd want to eat anything a dog lifted its leg on either."

"That is what I tell Mama."

"Enough talk, Noelle," Ulla hastened in a scold. "Have you finished the *C*?"

"No, I broke the thread."

Ulla left her post at the table to help her daughter re-thread her needle. Kristianna waited for Stone to return to his work, and when he didn't, her heart fluttered. His gaze was unflinchingly leveled at her. She tried to ignore him, aiming her concentration on cleaning the table's wood grain. But to no avail. When she could stand his gaze on her back no longer, she faced him, a nervous edge to her voice. "Do you drink buttermilk, Mr. Boucher? I saved some from the butter-making."

He remained poised under the kitchen frame. She found herself extremely conscious of his virile appeal, noting the light sprinkling of tanned hair over his large forearms as they remained crossed over his wide chest. Why couldn't she just look at him without thinking anything?

"I do," he replied in a resonant tone. "How could I turn it down after all the trouble you went to to churn it? You know, one year at Pierre's Hole rendezvous, an old woman put her dog on a treadmill and when he ran, he turned a little wheel that was attached to her barrel churn. In no time at all, we were drinking cold buttermilk without a drop of sweat being lost. Now, that, Miss Bergendahl, is a wonderment."

She wasn't sure whether to believe him. Before he moved back into the kitchen, he handed her his empty tea glass, leaving her to ponder his words. If she wasn't careful, she could become just as mesmerized by Stone as Noelle.

Shortly before supper was ready, Stone left the house and headed to the barn. He returned a brief time later in a faded red shirt and lightweight denim trousers tucked into his calf-high moccasins. His long hair hung past his wide shoulders in a gentle tumble, the ends damp from being washed. He'd combed it neatly back and left his hat in the haymow.

The deepening purple of evening was graced by filaments of lightning that danced above the treetops. Low rumblings of thunder sounded in the distance like kettledrums being whacked by high spirits. The weathercock on the barn's roof twirled under the beginnings of an opaque moon surrounded by a hazy ring.

They were all seated at the table when the warm rain fell. The droplets tapped on the rooftop in a merry chorus as they ate cold potato sausage, biscuits with fresh butter, and buttermilk.

Ulla had left the front door open, but put down the summer netting. Every so often, a june bug would fly into the deceptive opening and land on the dampening ground outside with a thud.

Kristianna looked to the place where Papa usually sat which was now occupied by Stone who seemed to dwarf the table. A pang of longing filled her, and she hoped Papa would return home soon before she grew accustomed to seeing Stone in his place.

After a few moments of companionable silence, Stone pushed his plate away. "I'm stuffed as a Christmas goose, Mrs. Bergendahl. I keep eating like this, I'll be plump as Bidwell."

Noelle and Kristianna giggled.

Soon after the dishes were cleared and washed, Ulla took her seat under the lantern to work on her knitting. Bits of firelight came through the seams of the etched chimney and twinkled on her steel knitting needles. Stone reached into his shirt pocket and kept his hand closed around a tiny object.

Kristianna leaned forward with interest, catching a glimpse of something shiny before Stone brought his hands to his mouth and musical notes sprouted through his fingers. She momentarily forgot herself and lapsed into Swedish, awe-struck. "*Titta, Mama, han kan göra sin hander sjunga!* Look, Mama, he can make his hands sing!"

The three women stared at Stone as he played the light melody of an old trapper's song. When he was finished, all three robustly applauded in wonder.

For a moment, Stone wasn't sure why they were so appreciative. He was a fair player, but not that good. Then it dawned on him.

"You thought I was—" He stopped and held out the harmonica for them to see. "It's a mouth organ."

Noelle practically stuck her nose in it. "Oh, Steurn, it is beautiful." She ran her finger across the fine wood and the shining metal cover.

"I have never seen anything to compare to it," Kristianna said exuberantly. "Can you play something else?"

He brought the reed to his lips and began a lively tune. Noelle took Kristianna's hands and they danced in a circle, while Ulla clapped her hands to the beat.

Stone observed Kristianna with more than casual interest. Her long braid slapped her back, and tiny wisps came free and framed her flushed face. Her eyes were clear and bright, her cheeks stained a fine shade of pink. As she danced, her skirt and apron whirled around her trim ankles. He didn't want to see her stop, so he continued playing, improvising the notes as he went.

She was beautiful, so beautiful, it brought a quiet ache in him. He battled the urge to cup her flushed face in his hands, to stroke her fine cheekbones with his thumb. Her lips were so lush, they begged him to reach out to her and crush his mouth on hers.

The clopping of her wooden shoes on the puncheoned floor was a harsh reminder to him who she was. He forced himself to remember that they were from two different worlds. She believed in everything he didn't. She stood for everything he and Jemmy fought against. Clodbuster. Forest-toppler.

He abruptly stopped playing.

"More, Steurn."

Ulla looked up from her yarns. "It is late, Noelle. Time for bed."

"Oh, Mama." She stamped her tiny, clogged foot in frustration. "Good night, Steurn," she sighed in resignation as she passed him on her way to the patchwork curtain and her bed.

"Good night," he answered, his voice gravelly and deep.

Kristianna smoothed back her hair and apron, a little embarrassed for losing herself in the music. She had always enjoyed Gunnar's fiddle, but Stone played with much more ease. She didn't want him to go yet. "Would you like something to drink? More buttermilk, Mr. Boucher?"

"No. If you don't mind, I'm going out for a smoke. I'll see you in the morning." He shoved his harmonica in his pocket and strode to the door.

"Good night, Mr. Boucher," Kristianna called after him, but she wasn't sure he heard her at all.

Kristianna lay in bed wide awake as the rain flitted and bounced off the rooftop. What was usually a soothing concert became a nerve-wracking march. Light flashed outside her window, then the rumbling followed. She stared at the rafters waiting for the next flash.

Stone Boucher. Why did his name fly around in her head like the white moths that gathered at the porch? Why did she find herself thinking about his long, tanned fingers? Or the way he effortlessly took the milk buckets from her? Or how snugly she fit against his chest that day on the hill? He was strong and aggressive as well as sensitive and thoughtful. Gunnar would never have taken the yoke from her, as it was woman's work. Gunnar. How could she betray him with thoughts of someone else? Was she so weak that in only six days she'd forgotten everything she stood for? She was a farmer's daughter. She lived to reap, to sow, then to reap again. Stone was a trapper and he condemned her.

She rolled onto her side and tucked the sheet under her chin. There was no denying he was handsome. Maybe she was attracted to him because of his height. It made her feel like a woman when she was able to look up into his eyes, rather than gaze at him at the same level as she did Gunnar.

The torrential rain filled the small loft with humidity, and suddenly Kristianna sat up.

The rain barrel!

Kicking off the covers, she snatched her cambric wrapper from the wall peg and tossed it over her shoulders. Making her way soundlessly down the ladder, she padded to the hearth where she'd left her clogs. After slipping them on, she moved to the door and pulled on the latch string.

The tepid rain splashed on her face as she dashed across the yard, and her white nightgown rippled behind her. She reached the barrel and unceremoniously dropped the lid to the ground and turned around to race back to the house before she was drenched.

She stopped short of the porch, seeing the glow of a cigarette.

Stone.

"You taking a Saturday-evening bath, Miss Bergendahl?" A flash lit the sky and she could make out his silhouette in the porch swing.

"I . . ." She was at a loss of words, startled to see him there.

"Come on over before I have to wring you out."

Stone's eyes never left her as she ran the remaining distance and stood by the front door. Her long hair hung free to her waist like a silken curtain, the crown wet from the rain. The thin wrapper had done little to protect her from the downpour. Her lawn nightdress clung revealingly to her tall, delicate frame. Even in the dim light, the outline her firm breasts made in the bodice was nearly more than he could stand. He'd stayed out in the rain to cool his burning thoughts of her, now he fought to control the river of heat flowing to his loins.

She offered him an explanation. "I . . . I forgot to take the lid off my rain barrel."

"Must've been pretty important to go getting wet for." He combatted his desires, keeping one hand clenched at his side, the other almost snapping his cigarette in two.

"*Ja.* It is my special hair-washing water." It wasn't easy for her to admit she allowed herself some feminine vanity.

"Looks like you just washed it without the rain barrel." He exhaled a swirling cloud of smoke that mingled in the air with the scent of damp earth, minerals, and trees. "Sit down," he said in a low voice.

"But I am not properly dressed," she protested.

"You're proper enough." If he had his way, he

would have gotten rid of the wrapper and gown all together.

A voice inside her head told her to go back inside, but her legs had a mind of their own as they propelled her forward. She sat down next to him. The seat was narrow, their thighs but a whisper apart. She could feel his warmth seeping through her nightgown and it jolted her to frank awareness. It was scandalous for her to be sitting here with him in just her night clothes. But the danger was a thrill she welcomed after the thoughts that had left her sleepless in her bed. He still smelled of fresh pine from the kitchen wood and when she closed her eyes, he smelled like the land she cherished, crisp and clean.

"You asleep, Miss Bergendahl?"

Her eyelids snapped open like a window shade. "No. I was just smelling the rain."

Under the spell of the moon, the clouds were outlined as they crawled across the deep, midnight blue sky. The heavens were zapped by fingers of light, the glare almost painful to the eye.

"It's like a magic lantern show," Stone commented as he tossed his cigarette out into the yard. The ember sizzled a moment, then was quickly extinguished. They sat there quietly for a moment, like an old married couple enjoying nature's display. There was an occasional creak from the swing's ropes as Stone pushed them with the strength of his foot.

Kristianna was certain he could hear the blood pounding to her heart. The very proximity of him was completely unnerving. She had sat on this very swing many times with Gunnar, but she never got into a frantic tizzy. As if to quell her wayward perceptions, she broached a safe subject. "I very much enjoyed your playing, Mr. Boucher."

"You call me 'Mr. Boucher' one more time and I'll feel like my old man."

"I would not find it comfortable calling you by your Christian name."

"Try it sometime." He stretched out his muscled leg and rested his heel on the porch post. "You want to play my harmonica?"

"I have no talent for music."

"You ever play an instrument?"

"No."

"Then how can you say you have no talent for it?" He dug into his shirt pocket and handed her the harmonica. "You've blown off some fine euphemisms at me, just blow into the piece this time."

Though Kristianna had no idea what "euphemisms" meant, she took the small reed into her delicate fingers; it was warm to the touch from having been next to his chest. In the very dim light, she could just barely make out about a dozen or so small, square-cut holes. Like a blind man, she ran her fingertip over the shining cover, noting the raised portion that must be a decorative design. Tentatively, she raised it to her lips. There was something extremely wicked about putting her mouth on it when he had just done so not an hour ago. She inhaled slightly and brought her lips to it, then exhaled into the harmonica. A single note emerged, wavered, and died as she lost her air into the musical chamber. "Oh, my!" was all she said, then repeated the process. This time, she struck a different note.

"You run your mouth down it and it'll ripple with music."

She did so, then gentle laughter rose from her throat. "I did it."

"I didn't doubt you could."

Their knuckles lightly met when Kristianna handed him back his harmonica. That undefinable surge struck her again, and she immediately withdrew and folded her hands in her lap. "You may not believe it, but I admire your ability to seek adventure."

"Don't tell me you've thought of seeking a little adventure of your own?" He dropped the harmonica back into his pocket, but not before he slowly ran his fingertip over the holes where she'd had her mouth.

"My life is here."

"But the world outside the big trees has a red parasol calling your name."

"I. . . . That was not fair to bring up, Mr. Boucher."

"Fair or not, you're human. Don't deny it."

The rain let up to a slow drizzle. The light northwest wind stirred the wind chimes on the side of the house, their various strains playing out nature's recital. A firefly ventured out into the storm, its lighting signal flickering. Stone sat forward and captured the beetle in his fist.

"Hold out your hand," he told Kristianna and she hesitantly did. "No, put your palm down." She did.

In an act that would have caused any city girl to swoon, he took the glowing bulb from the lightning bug and placed it on Kristianna's finger.

"It's an old trick. Now you have a glowing ring."

She looked down at her hand. On the finger that would someday hold Gunnar's wedding band was a glowing luminescent dot. Confusion welled up inside her, so strong it threatened to devour all her common sense. How could such a simple gesture affect her so? "Why did you come here?"

"I don't know. I'm beginning to think it was a bad idea."

"You hate us that much?"

"Quite the opposite."

"I cannot change who I am."

Stone stared pensively into the darkness. "You'll never find out who you can be, if you don't get away from who you are."

There was an underlying wisdom to his words that made her want to confide her innermost secrets to him. He was right about the parasol. She wanted desperately to feel it, to have it, but it was forbidden to her. Instead of answering the way she wanted to, she said what Papa would have wanted her to say. "I want to be a good Swedish wife. A farmer's wife."

She felt him tense beside her. His hard thigh pressed against hers as he turned to face her. The

103

sky was bathed in a startling flash of light, and she saw the determined set to his square jaw. He pulled her to him, his fingers digging into her shoulders, the contact a searing brand through her thin nightgown. His mouth was inches from hers, his breath caressing her trembling lips. "I think you're a little confused, Miss Bergendahl. Let me set you straight."

He was going to kiss her.

She leaned into his embrace, closed her eyes, and waited breathlessly. She had never been kissed, and at the moment, it seemed so right that he be the first one to do it.

The kiss never came.

She slowly lifted her lids to gaze at the fire in his teal-blue eyes. They were expressionless, as if he didn't understand why he'd held her in the first place.

"What is wrong?" she whispered, the pulsating thrum of her heartbeat clear in the night air.

"Everything. This." He removed his hands from her and stood. Driving his fists into his pockets, he spoke in that gravelly tone that sent shivers up her spine. "I keep forgetting you don't like me much. I'll still be the same person tomorrow. No kiss is going to change that." He spun away from her and was gone in a quick stride.

Kristianna was too stunned to move. What had she done? Almost done? The startling reality struck her like a slap in the face. He was right. She did want him to kiss her and she didn't care about anything else. How could she be so foolish? So easily swayed?

She hugged the rail of the swing, the wood cool and rough against her burning cheek.

Tomorrow was Sunday.

Tomorrow she would pray for God's forgiveness.

Tomorrow, Gunnar was coming.

·8·

Streams of bright sunlight broke through the tiny cracks and crevices between the barn wall timbers. Stone stretched out on the haymow in his faded, red long johns that were cinched at his tapered waist. The top half of the underwear had been cut off for summer use. His elbows were bent, his head resting on his meshed fingers. He rubbed off a piece of hay on the toe of his woolen sock with the heel of his other foot. The movement caused a flutter of dust motes to dance in the bright rays.

He had passed the night in a state of fitful dozing and uneasy sleep.

Earlier that morning, while the sky had still been dark, he had heard Kristianna come in to milk the cow. Normally, he'd have been up and gone from the barn, but today, he'd lain there, quietly listening to her. Her voice, sweet and soft, purred an assurance to the cow in a language he didn't understand, but she spoke it with such feeling, that he could define the meaning of her words. He heard the soft swishing sound of her skirt and petticoats, and the light way she moved around in her heavy, wooden clogs. She was as unique a person as her iris-blue eyes. Maybe that was what drew him to her. She was not only beautiful, but sensitive, courageous, and daring. He remembered the way she was ready to take on the wild hog herself in an effort to save Noelle. Nor had she cowered from Newt's attack. And she'd given him a talking down more than once, never holding back her true thoughts and emotions. But for all her boldness, there was an innocence in her, allowing her to be awed by the rabbit's warmth in the flattened grass, and harmonicas.

Things were changing between them, but he couldn't be sure when that had happened. Though he still did not agree with her beliefs, nor she with his, there was no denying there was a raw force pulling them to each other. When their skin had met on the porch swing, they'd had their own electrical show.

That night she had wanted to know what his mouth would have felt like on hers, and he had no doubt that it would have been her first kiss. He began to think his being there was a mistake. His kissing her would definitely have been a mistake. She was greener than prairie sod.

He'd had his share of women, too many. Though not all professionals, they were quite skilled at their craft, knowing which words a man wanted to hear—or at least the ones they thought he wanted to hear. He was beginning to tire of that sort, and he tried to understand why he was so attracted to Kristianna. She was everything he'd always shied away from. Putting aside the fact that she was a farmer's daughter, no decent lady wanted to get involved with a man who moved across the plains with the seasons. But it was her innocence and vulnerability that drew him to her. The easy, open way she laughed about simple things, her unspoiled freshness and genuine candor. There were no artful flirtations from her, only naïve curiosity that drove him crazier than if she'd played the coquette. She was like a ripe plum ready to fall and he wasn't sure how much longer he could stay around without plucking her from the tree.

Stone sat up and shoved his feet into his moccasins. His idea of hiding out at the Bergendahls' was not going as he planned. He needed to get out of here. If not for good, at least for the day. He'd go into Snelling. He was hopeful Jemmy had tracked down Samuel Granger and had found out what the hell his old man wanted.

But an inner voice taunted, *Face it, Boucher, you're running scared. She's getting to you.*

He balked at that thought. No female had ever gotten to Stone Boucher. He was a man of the woods, a trapper. He lived off the land, going where he wanted, when he wanted. He owed nothing to no one.

Kristianna sat in front of the rounded mirror on her bureau, carefully brushing her long hair until it gleamed. She'd washed it with the rain water and her special shampoo of cinnamon and bergamot, a type of mint. After the ends were dry, she artfully plaited it against her head. The braid hung down her back, reaching her hips, in a thick, glossy rope.

Wearing her plain, cotton shift, she moved to the bed and picked up her best batiste blouse and slipped her arms into the lightweight fabric. She skillfully fastened the tiny hooks up the form-fitting bodice. Carefully sewn seams ran down each front panel and over each breast, emphasizing their fullness. The cuffs were trimmed with thin, crocheted navy cords, ending in tassels. When she tied them, the sleeves were full and puffy. She stepped into a goffered skirt, the same deep navy color as the tassels. Then she put on her best leather clogs, polished to softness with tallow.

What had happened with Stone last night, or nearly had happened, had been buzzing around in her head like a yellow jacket and with it a dull headache grew. How could she have been so enamored? Even if she had not been engaged to Gunnar, there was absolutely no possible future for them. He would not be accepted by the small circle of Swedish immigrants, nor would she be accepted by his fellow woodsmen. There was no in between. She had to force herself to stop thinking about him, to stop imagining . . . but it was so hard! Even now, she was hoping he would approve of her best Sunday dress.

Checking her appearance once more in the mirror, she bent down to a small pot of dusting powder. Using the end of a weasel's tail as a powder puff, she dipped it into the pot and lightly dusted her face. Her complexion was as smooth as cream, and the powder enhanced her skin tone. She pinched her cheeks to a soft pink before gingerly easing her waxy, black lace hat on her head.

She was barely down the ladder when she heard the jingling of harness tack and Noelle calling from the yard.

"Gunnar is coming!"

The house was empty as Ulla had gone out earlier with Noelle to wait for Gunnar. Taking a deep breath, Kristianna ran her moist hands down her ankle-length skirt and checked for any lint. She had dressed for Gunnar, she repeated firmly in her mind, making sure it sunk in. Then why was she so nervous about seeing Stone? How could she face him after last night? What would she say? What could she do? To make things worse, she would have to confront him in Gunnar's presence. Would Stone care that she was to marry Gunnar? Why should he? It was none of his concern. Stone Boucher was the hired man. He would be gone soon and she would stay there where she belonged. There was no room for him in her life, and he didn't want to be in her life.

"*Ja*. It is done," she said, to assure herself as

she walked outside to meet her fiancé.

Gunnar Thorson guided the reins of two stocky, flaxen-colored horses with ivory manes and tails. Their coats gleamed, and it was obvious he cared more for his animals than his rig, as the old four-wheeled cart he pulled was in bad need of fresh paint.

Kristianna moved toward him, glad for the time being, Stone was not in the yard. As Gunnar rolled to a stop in front of the house, she reached out to one of the horses and rubbed her hand along its nose which was prickled with a few stiff hairs, but soft as velvet. "Hello, Gunnar," she greeted, smoothing the short fine hair on the horse's forehead.

"*God morgon*, Kristianna," he said, showing a full array of teeth, then jumped down from the cart and removed his visored cap called a *kaskett*. "*God morgon, fru Bergendahl. Noelle.*"

Noelle was hovering over the garden tossing stray worms back into the soil that had washed up from the rain. "*Hej*, Gunnar." Concentrating on the wiggling creatures, she didn't look up at him.

"Noelle, get away from that garden. I do not want you soiling your Sunday dress."

"*Ja*, Mama." The child trudged over to Gunnar, to see his horses.

Kristianna felt as if her insides were being churned by a dasher. Gunnar had no idea what she had almost done last night. Why was she so skittish around him? It wasn't as if she'd actually kissed Stone Boucher. Oh, but she had wanted to! She clutched her hands together, trying to stop them from shaking. "How is Liv? Your brother must be anxious."

"Her time is any day now. Olaf strung a cowbell to the porch so that she can call him in from the fields when the baby is ready."

Noelle stroked the horses's shining coats. "I like Flicka and Fredrick, Gunnar, but I think I like Brother Moon better."

Gunnar half-raised an eyebrow so pale, it was barely visible. "Brother Moon?"

"*Ja*, Steurn's horse. Want to see him?"

Gunnar looked at Kristianna, puzzled. All attempts to control the battle raging inside her made her flounder for an explanation. Nothing came to her lips.

Ulla cast a questioning glance at her daughter, then spoke, "He is the man I hired to help out until Sixten returns."

A faintly bewildered look etched its way on Gunnar's face. "There is none of our kind with that name. How did you meet this Steurn?"

"Stone," Kristianna squeaked, correcting Noelle's pronunciation. "Stone Boucher," she said again, her voice regaining its strength. "We posted a notice on The Wilderness Call at the Sutler's Store."

"The Wilderness Call?" Gunnar's eyes widened in astonishment. "Forgive my impudence, *fru Bergendahl*, but that is for the ruffians and mountain men who terrorize our land. Do not tell me you have gone and hired a trapper?"

Kristianna interjected, feeling she needed to stand up for Stone. "I did not want to at first, but he has done a good job on the kitchen and I—"

Gunnar cut her off. "Where is this Stone Boucher now?"

As if on cue, Stone strode across the yard with such intimidating steps the chickens scattered in different directions and ran for cover. He was like a hulking giant, with that deep-set scowl on his face that looked worse because of the dark eyebrows that slashed over his teal-blue eyes. Kristianna drank in his appearance, noting the obvious dissimilarities between the two men. Where Gunnar's clothes—a gray homespun jacket with the red strip, gray stockings, and goat skin breeches—were loose and billowing, Stone's buckskins fit him like a second skin, leaving very little to the imagination. There was a maturity to Stone that was lacking in Gunnar. She could see it in the slight creases at the corners of his eyes, and she knew that any physical confrontation between the two would be no match.

Stone ignored Kristianna as if she weren't even standing there, and pushed up the brim of his hat to better view the stranger. "I'm Boucher. Who are you?"

"I am Gunnar Thorson." Gunnar neither backed down nor moved forward with an extended hand. In all his days, he'd never seen a taller, brawnier man. Glaring at Stone with fierce resentment, he hoped his false bravado was not unnoticed by Kristianna. Seeing he was no match for the man's size, he capitalized on a fact he was sure the mountain man didn't know. He had not been so blind as to not notice the possessive way Stone had looked at Kristianna. It was with a great deal of pleasure he said, "I am Kristianna's intended." The flash of surprise on the trapper's face confirmed he hadn't known.

Stone glowered sharply at Kristianna, whose cheeks had blushed a deep crimson that flooded to the roots of her hairline, before turning his attention back to Gunnar. "I didn't know she had an *intended*."

"I . . ." Kristianna began, the tension between the two men tugging at her like an invisible cord. "We will be late to church." She made a move toward the cart.

"Mr. Boucher, would you care to join us for services?" Ulla asked. "We have a picnic afterward. We do not work on Sundays."

"No," he answered, simple and flat, his eyes leveled on Gunnar.

"Are you not out of your element, Mr. Boucher? Or do you normally go around answering farmers' bills?" Gunnar quizzed, his mouth a thin-lipped sneer.

"I don't think my history is any of your concern, Gutter."

"Gunnar," he tossed back sharply, visibly agitated at the obvious insult.

Stone didn't know why he was so riled. Maybe it was because Kristianna had kept her betrothal a secret. Maybe it was because she was willing to kiss him when she was engaged to someone else. Maybe it was because this Gunnar was a damn farmer, too. If the man cared at all about Kristianna, why the hell wasn't he here instead of Stone?

"Mrs. Bergendahl, I'm going in to Snelling for

114

the afternoon," Stone said tightly. "You need anything?"

Kristianna momentarily forgot her discomfort. "Mr. Boucher, could you check for a letter from my father?"

He nodded slightly, his eyes unwavering on her face. He wanted to throttle her for not telling him about Gunnar but he had no right to. She could do whatever she wanted, yet a vision of her in Gunnar's embrace made him want to flatten the man into the ground. He refused to admit to being jealous. His anger stemmed from the fact that the man was a clodbuster.

Gunnar looked from Kristianna to Stone, noting the easy flush on her face when she said his name. He roughly pushed on his *kaskett* and possessively put Kristianna's hand into the crook of his arm. "As you said, Kristianna, we will be late for church." He scooted her to the side of the cart, then mounted the seat without offering her assistance.

Noelle climbed into the cart's bed filled with straw. Ulla followed, depositing two wicker baskets covered with delicate linen napkins. Kristianna turned to step in as well, when she felt a strong hand at the base of her back. Her heart drummed in her chest at Stone's contact. His fingers splayed her narrow waist as he gently applied pressure to lift her up. He lingered over her ribs with his hands, before slowly sliding them down her narrow waist.

It seemed as if his face were only inches from hers when she heard him whisper, "I see you made use of your rain water, Kris." His resonant

115

voice played havoc with her senses. "Your hair smells like sweet Indian grass."

She met his daring eyes. He was slowly and seductively gazing at her, as if he meant to undress her right there! Dear God, why was he doing this to her after he pushed her away last night? She was fairly dizzy from that look in his smoldering eyes. It took every ounce of self-control for her not to lean forward for his kiss. What kind of woman was she that she would forget all she stood for just to have his lips touch hers, and in front of her mama—and Gunnar!

Stone inched away and broke the spell. She fell back, as if released from some invisible force. "Afternoon, ladies." He touched the brim of his hat and turned, not extending a farewell to Gunnar who most likely wouldn't have heard it anyway, for he had put the horses into motion.

Kristianna held onto the side of the cart for support as it jostled over the holes in the narrow, crooked road. She let out her breath as she watched the tiny house in the woods disappear. At least her careful toilette had not gone unnoticed. The trouble was, it had been noticed by the wrong man.

Or was he?

There were seven Swedish families settled near the Bergendahl homestead, and at present, there was no church. Services were usually held during the summer and fall when the weather permitted in a small clearing in the forest, using the felled and split maple trees as benches. The space was lined with wildflowers and butterflies and was pretty enough to rival any stained-glass windowed church. Mr. Degermark and his son had crafted a crude pulpit and each of the men in the families took turns preaching every Sunday. Today, it was Gunnar's father's turn. He was nearly a carbon copy of Gunnar, with the exception of a fine streak of gray at his temples.

"God morgon, fru Bergendahl, och fröken Bergendahl. Hur står det till?" Karl Thorson greeted in Swedish. He spoke very little English and asked how Ulla and her daughters were in his native tongue.

The respective responses were exchanged and services began. Kristianna's thoughts wandered, unable to concentrate on Mr. Thorson's lessons from the Old Testament. From under the cover of her lacy hat, she peeked at Gunnar sitting beside her. Comparing him to Stone, he dimmed like the last sputters in a candle before the wax consumed what was left of the wick. Then again, why should she compare him to Stone at all? It wasn't fair to Gunnar.

Maybe they had waited long enough and should marry now. That would solve everything. Once she was in her own house with children to raise, she would forget about parasols and military wives . . . and trappers. Having no doubt Gunnar would agree, she felt as if a weight had been lifted from her shoulders. She decided to speak with Gunnar after church when they were alone on their picnic.

It wasn't too long before Karl Thorson said his closing blessing and outfitted in their Sunday finery, the families milled around exchanging weekly news. The conversation flitted from Mr. Degermark's dog Nellie's having a litter to the Nilsson's planting their corn early to the Lundbergs' relatives coming from Sweden and to Olaf and Liv Thorson's remaining at home, still awaiting the arrival of their first child.

Noelle played with the other small children, and Ulla talked to several of the women about quilting patterns and about the few young people of marriageable age. Margit Mellgren was twelve years old, Anders Qvist was fifteen, and seventeen-year-old Hanna Lind who was hopelessly smitten with Gunnar Thorson.

Kristianna moved to Gunnar who was in conversation with Johan Andersson.

"*Nej*, you have to burn the dead grass," Johan advised Gunnar. "Do not till it under and you will have less weeds in the spring."

Kristianna lightly touched Gunnar's sleeve. "I have a picnic for us. I thought we could take it to Sky Lake."

"*Ja*, in a moment," Gunnar replied, brushing off her suggestion as if it were her fingertips on his sleeve. He never even looked at her. "But I am turning a half acre a day. What with chopping and girdling trees, burning stumps and splitting rails, I do not have time for grass burning."

"Trust me, Gunnar, you will not have near the work in spring."

"Your pardon, *herr Andersson*, but I must speak with Gunnar."

Gunnar turned, visibly agitated. Though he enjoyed his Sunday time with Kristianna, it wasn't every day he could talk to another farmer other than his father. "*Ja*, Kristianna, what is it that is so important?"

She tried to hide her hurt at his disinterest. "I need to speak to you privately."

Johan smiled politely. "Go on, lad. Your fiancée's attention is more important than mine."

"All right, then," Gunnar said as he took the small basket that Kristianna had been holding. "Where would you like to go?"

"I thought Sky Lake would be nice," she repeated.

"Very well."

They had barely crossed the small clearing when Hanna Lind caught up to them. A plain girl, with a light sprinkling of freckles over her nose, and plain, brown hair, Kristianna thought Hanna looked like a field mouse. "*God dag*, Gunnar. Kristianna. Are you going on a picnic?"

"*Ja*, would you like to come?" Gunnar invited.

Before Hanna had a chance to reply, Kristianna intervened. "I only have enough for two," she lied. "Come along, Gunnar." She linked her arm through his and pulled him along.

"Gunnar," Hanna called after them, "my father has a copy of the *Farmers Register*. The May edition. Edmund Ruffin says that wheat will bring one dollar, nine and a half cents per bushel; and corn will bring two dollars, ninety-three and a half cents per barrel." She smiled boldly at Kristianna as if to say, "Can you top that one?"

Gunnar stopped in his tracks. "The May edition, you say?"

Hanna nodded confidently.

"Gunnar," Kristianna said firmly, "I must

speak with you. You can see the register later."
Feeling as if she were fighting a losing battle, she
pressed her arm closer in his and leaned slightly
into his body. She was no expert at seduction, but
she had liked it when Stone had done it to her. It
won Gunnar over.

"I will look at it later, Hanna. You tell your
papa not to leave until I have spoken to him."

Disappointment was clearly etched in Hanna's
large, hazel eyes. "I will do that, Gunnar." She
frowned.

Kristianna and Gunnar made their way
through the thinly dispersed trees to a small hill
and down the other side where on the shallow
valley floor was the lake named by the Swedes. It
was so clear and blue, it mirrored the sky as fine
as any cheval glass from the East. As if it truly
were a mirror, it was framed by budding birch
and maple trees. Along the bank were asters
nearly three feet tall and ruby red phlox with
feathery heads.

Kristianna spread out a piece of canvas by the
lake as Gunnar moved to a cottonwood. He
reached into his vest and pulled out a small
pocketknife. Notching the tree, he watched the
sap run out. "It is going to be an Indian summer.
The sap is slow."

Kristianna didn't care if it was going to be an
Indian summer. For once, she wanted to talk to
Gunnar about something other than farming.
"Come and sit," she bade in a pleasant voice. "I
have cheese, crisp bread, white fish, and rice
porridge with syrup. And Mama gave me a small
flask of raspberry cordial."

He broke off the twig and took it with him, feeling the sap with his calloused fingers. They ate in silence as Kristianna wanted his hunger appeased before she brought up any talk of marriage.

The sky was clear, with a few puffy white clouds moving slowly. For the moment, she was content to nibble her cheese and watch the patterns the clouds made on the smooth water.

When they were finished, she poured Gunnar another glass of cordial and packed away the picnic. He took off his hat and shed his jacket. After removing the bands at the cuffs of his shirt, he rolled up his sleeves.

He reached out and took Kristianna's hand in his. She had always been pleased to have her hand in Gunnar's, but somehow, the intimacy didn't compare to Stone's strong fingers. Gunnar's were lean, with his flesh just covering the bones and joints. There was no tingling, no revelation. "About this Stone Boucher, Kristianna."

She dreaded the interrogation she knew was coming. How could she explain Stone to him, when she couldn't explain her feelings to herself?

"I do not think it wise to have him on your place. Sixten would not approve."

"My papa would approve of any course my mama thought wise. And Mama thinks Mr. Boucher is needed." She suddenly had the impulse to pull free of his hand, but stopped herself.

"I do not like him."

"That was obvious."

Gunnar gave her hand a slight, damp squeeze.

"I can trust you, Kristianna. I do not trust the trapper. He has eyes for you."

Kristianna's face brightened at the suggestion. Did he? "*Nej*, you are wrong. He hates settlers."

"Then why did he take the job?"

"He wanted to protect us from the other trappers. When we went into the fort last Sunday, there was a mountain man who—"

Gunnar did not listen. "I think you are too easily fooled, Kristianna. Beware of him."

"We would have no need of his services if you could help out until Papa returned," Kristianna said hopefully. "I can do most everything but the plowing, and now that the kitchen is nearly finished—"

"You know that is impossible. I have barley, corn, and oats to plant. Not to mention the new corn cribs I have to put up."

"I only thought . . ."

"I cannot. Just beware, Kristianna. I do not like this situation at all."

Then do something! Kristianna screamed at him, but the words remained implanted on her tongue.

He released her hand, lay down on the canvas, and closed his eyes. Kristianna studied him a moment—his blond hair, parted in the middle; his straight sideburns a shade darker; his long, slightly sloped nose—and realized that he hadn't a care to what she wanted. It was as if she were not his intended at all.

"If I can plant forty bushels to one acre of wheat," he said with his eyes still shut, "that would be . . ." His voice trailed off as he was figuring.

"Gunnar," Kristianna began, interrupting his train of thought. "When are we going to be married?"

He raised himself on his elbow. "You know that is not possible until I get a good start."

"How much longer?"

"I do not know. I do not have a decent house for you. I want to build you a fine cabin."

"I do not want a fine cabin. I would be happy to share your lean-to."

"*Nej.* My lean-to is not fit for you. I spend most of my time sleeping at my papa's. That is not how I want it for you."

"But I want it."

He frowned at her and she was sorry she had said it. Papa had warned her not to speak up to Gunnar.

"You are a woman, Kristianna. You do not understand what it is like. You have to keep at the land with the grubbing hoe. Those sprouts get waist high around the stumps in the wheat field. A man just has to keep everlastingly at it or the woods will take back the place."

A feeling of helplessness and humiliation washed over her. Was she that ignorant of what Gunnar and her father went through to sow a harvest?

"I am sorry," she mumbled. "We will wait until you are ready."

"It is best that way, Kristianna."

"*Ja,*" Her voice was a mere whisper across the lake. "It is best."

He leaned over and pressed a dry peck on her smooth cheek. He would never dare to go further until after they were married. The gesture was not the slightest bit stimulating to her, and she tried to imagine what it would be like to have him kiss her breathlessly on the lips. Somehow, she doubted he could and for the first time, she had her doubts about marrying him.

"Anyone seen Jemmy Paquer?" Stone queried from his mount to a group of buckskin-clad frontiersmen. He loosened his hold on the reins of his horse and crossed his forearms over the saddle horn. Brother Moon, having been to numerous rendezvous, was indifferent to the gun blasts and shouts.

"Last I seen, he was jawin' with Lawrence Toliver."

"Taliaferro?" Stone corrected the mispronunciation. "The Indian agent?"

"That how you say it? What a god-awful name to spit off your tongue." The statement brought guffaws from the circle.

Stone moved back his hat a little and put his weight on the stirrups. "Wonder what he wants with him?"

"Don't know, but they was with two chiefs. One was a Dakota, Rising Sun. Other, Chippewa, Hole in the Day."

"Jemmy?" Stone asked incredulously. "Was he beating up on them?"

"Hell, no. He was talking politics."

Stone looked around at the melee of trappers and confusion just as thick as it had been opening day. Powder smoke stung his eyes and dusted the air in hazy clouds. "Where are they now?"

"Up to the battery, last I seen."

"Obliged." Stone nudged Brother Moon up the congested hill to the fort. He'd stable his horse first, then stop by Bidwell's.

Bidwell told him there was no letter from Sixten Bergendahl, and that bothered Stone. Where was this farmer, anyway? Didn't he realize that leaving his wife and children alone was an open invitation to disaster?

He crossed the courtyard, and took notice of the man Jemmy had called George Catlin. He was painting another Indian in full regalia. The artist looked up at Stone as he passed, and Stone touched the brim of his hat. He continued on, more curious about Jemmy than a view of the painting.

The battery was a semicircular tower in which sentries noted all those who traveled on the Mississippi and Minnesota Rivers. Stone could see Jemmy's gleaming black hair taking in the sunlight, his back turned away from him. He was garbed in his Seneca costume of a red tunic, his Green River knife at his thigh. He laughed at something Major Lawrence Taliaferro said, the fancy silver earrings at his lobes swinging with his movement. The two chiefs were gone.

"What in the hell you been up to, Jem?" Stone's deep voice caused his friend to pivot.

"Boucher, you dog!" Jemmy greeted him, and firmly clasped his partner's hand and forearm. "You here for good?"

"Could be, if you've seen our friend," Stone

returned casually, directing his attention to the officer in dress blue. "Don't believe we've met, Major. Stone Boucher."

Lawrence Taliaferro extended his large hand. Tall and dark-complected with high cheekbones and dark brown eyes, his mouth was full, his Roman nose long with slightly flared nostrils. "Boucher. I've heard much about you. Paquer's filled me in." He spoke in a Virginian drawl, but he was of Italian descent.

"Don't believe a word he says. He's winded."

"Hell if I ain't," Jemmy denied. "I've never ventured from the truth in all my life."

"Which life, partner? You've had more than a cat."

Their comradery and respect for each other easily surfaced and showed in their banter.

"You want to enlighten me as to what you've been up to? A few of Sublette's boys said you were cavorting with chiefs."

"That's a fact," Jemmy confirmed. "Hole in the Day and Rising Sun."

"How did you manage to get them together? You pass out some of your Taos lightning? Get 'em drunk?"

The major stepped in. "No. I've been talking to Paquer about the Bureau of Indian Affairs."

"Sounds interesting."

"I'll let Paquer fill you in. I've got a matter to attend to." He shook Stone's hand again. "Pleasure meeting you, Boucher. Hope we can do business."

A little confused, Stone nodded. When the

major had gone, Stone turned to Jemmy. "What's this 'business' he's talking about?"

Jemmy smoothed back his hair with his copper-tanned fingers. "Let's talk about it over a bottle."

"Last time you said that, we were at Pierre's Hole and ended up searching beaver claws for lead. As I recall the trappers that weighed their pelts down for the extra cash didn't like us much."

"Trust me on this one, partner."

Stone stroked the day-old stubble on his chin. "I know I'm not going to like this. You find Samuel Granger?"

"Nope. I came close, but I just missed him. He left for Prairie du Chien two days ago."

"Why the hell would he go to Fort Garrison looking for me?"

"Don't know. He'll be back, though. He left some stuff with Heacock at the New York Fur Company's tent."

Stone rubbed his temple. "Damn, that means he'll be back before sunset. I can't chance him spotting me."

"Why don't you just confront him? Get this mess straightened out. I'm sure he knows you're around this neck of the woods. Hell, you stick out, being as you're tall as a pine tree."

"You don't remember my father very well, do you, Jem? He'd have no qualms about shackling me and forcing me back to Buffalo if needs be. I'll see Granger dead before I get my legs caught."

"Since you're already in a foul temper, did you

see Newt Fraeb on the way up?"

"Newt?" Stone said the name with distaste. "No."

"He's looking for you and that yellowhead family. Been asking all around where their farm is."

"Goddamn," Stone mumbled under his breath. "I reckon he's not as stupid as I thought."

"I don't think he knows you're out there."

Stone drew out his cigarette makings and deftly rolled a smoke. He lit it and exhaled while he talked. "How'd you get that gash through your eyebrow?"

Jem raised his hand to his forehead. "This? I was 'restling with *Monsieur* Red. It's a scratch." He shrugged it off with false concern. "You got a couple hours 'til sundown. Come with me and I'll buy you a drink. I got me an appointment with Miss Cameo Starr. Now ain't that a name? She's got hair oranger than sassafras. No doubt from a bottle. But a bottle I'd like to drink from. Come on, once she sees your pretty face, you'll have her."

"You buy me that drink and I'll think about it."

"Sure, Boucher. Let's go see the whiskey man."

"Tell me about this Indian Affairs deal of yours on the way."

Before he turned to go, Stone stared out over the Mississippi River, and looked north over the treetops. Somewhere under the cover of those sprawling trees was a little farmstead.

And Kristianna.

And with her, that oaf Gunnar.

128

·9·

Kristianna put her foot on the shovel and pressed down, grinding the blade into the dirt. Tightening her grip on the handle, she turned over the soil and broke it up. Moving down five inches, she repeated the process. At least the ground was soft from the rain two days ago.

The afternoon was airless and hot. She'd wrapped her hair in a *hilka*, a white hood, and covered it with a braided straw hat to keep the sun from her face. It did little good. Perspiration dampened her hairline, and she could feel her cheeks and the tip of her nose pinkening under the hot rays every time she looked up to see how much she'd accomplished. It was a slow process without the help of the plow and oxen, but she had no choice.

Yesterday's talk with Gunnar had, if anything, opened her eyes. It was thoughtless of her to expect him to marry her now. After all, he was securing their future. What honor would he have without his land cleared and lush with corn, barley, and wheat? Their land. And as for him kissing her, well, she never should have expected more. Gunnar was a gentleman. Gentlemen didn't go around kissing girls just because they caught their fancy.

She attacked the dirt once again, imagining the shovel was slicing Stone's heart in two. How dare he toy with her? Pretend he was going to kiss her, then cast her off as if she were nothing more than an old shirt. And then, to taunt her and flirt with her openly in front of Gunnar and Mama! She wouldn't have it. She'd been momentarily blinded by Stone Boucher and his wild tales of adventure but no more. She was going to prove him wrong. She belonged on this land and this was her life.

How foolish she must have appeared that night on the porch swing, melting in his embrace, naïve as a newborn calf. Why, she was no better than Hanna Lind chasing after Gunnar! She had been smitten with the trapper, but that was behind her. Now, she would prove to Gunnar and Papa that she was just as capable of running a farm as they were. All along, she'd said she could look after things. Maybe Mama would dismiss Stone once she saw how capable Kristianna was.

She dug into the ground once more, this time catching the bottom of her black skirt. There was a tug, then a tear. She looked down to see a split in the weave of the dirt-smudged fabric. It could be repaired, but noticeably so. Dropping the shovel, she looped the hem of her skirt into the waistband of her apron, exposing her stocking-covered legs just below her thighs. She didn't care. It was better than ruining the rest of the skirt.

She resumed her cultivation of the vast field. The rain had pushed up small green stalks of turkeyfoot grass in the area her papa had already plowed. It was as if no work had been done at all. If only she could fix the plow! Working behind the oxen would be hard, but definitely more rewarding than this. If Stone could see her now, he would surely laugh at her and tell her she was crazy.

He had come back late yesterday, long after the sun had gone down. For a while, Kristianna had thought he wouldn't return at all, and when he did, she was a little disappointed, and maybe a little glad, too. He'd been drinking, but was not drunk. She wondered who he'd been drinking with. She had seen what type of women were camp followers at the rendezvous and a fleeting picture of him with a robust woman on his lap, and his enjoying it, had made her madder than a bear with a beehive out of its reach.

He had said there was no letter from Papa, but he was sure there would be one soon; and he brought back a picture window for the kitchen. He had already cut out the hole the day before so her mother would have the best, unobstructed view possible when she did the dishes. His thoughtfulness surprised Kristianna. She didn't think a man took notice of those sorts of things. Papa had planned on a sashed window, not being able to afford one solid piece of glass. Her mama was overwhelmed by Stone's generosity and Noelle, too, was once again completely taken with the mountain man.

This morning's breakfast had passed politely. Noelle chattered about her loose tooth, and Ulla talked of putting up bean poles. Kristianna had remained silent most of the time, adding to the conversation only when spoken to. Stone had not talked directly to her since Gunnar had come to fetch them for church. She wondered if he was waiting for an explanation about Gunnar then brushed the thought off. She owed him nothing. The best thing to do was let the matter drop. With luck, he'd be gone soon and that would be the end of it.

Small blisters began to form on her palms, and she stopped her digging to gently press the swollen, reddened skin.

"How long you aim to keep this up?" Stone's gravelly voice startled her from her musings and she jerked her head around in his direction.

As always, the sight of him made her pulse race, and her resolve to be indifferent to him melted away in tiny drops. She had to hold onto the shovel's handle to keep from running into his arms. She masked her emotions with a cocky tone. "Why do you always sneak up on me? Lucky for you, I do not keep a gun at my side, or you would be long dead."

"Maybe you should keep a gun with you," he answered, quite seriously.

He swaggered toward her, wearing a worn, red calico tunic and form-fitting buckskin trousers. His long, rich brown hair gleamed under the scrutiny of the sun, the top part covered by the low crown of his hat. Resting on his broad shoulder was his Hawken.

"Your mother said you were out here. She doesn't like it, and I don't, either."

Kristianna turned away from him. Clutching the shovel handle, she stabbed the earth. "Well, I do not see how it is any of your worry, Mr. Boucher. You were not hired for your advice."

"You being off like this is an open target for stray dogs. And I don't mean the four-legged kind." He thought of Newt Fraeb. Then he was inclined to add himself to the list as well. Looking at her now only confirmed what he fought to deny. He wanted her.

Dirt-streaked, and with the touch of a sunburn on her high cheekbones, she was still the most enchanting woman he'd ever seen. With her skirt hiked up, it offered him a tantalizing view of her legs. He wanted to rip off her garters and roll down her ridiculous dark stockings to see for himself how soft and creamy her long slender legs were. Did she know how appealing she was? Her eyes were set with such determination, it made him want to pick up a shovel and help her, but he would not. He could not.

"I do not need an audience." She continued with her work, trying her best to ignore him.

"You've got a long piece to go." His hooded eyes glanced over the large field. "Why doesn't that intended of yours help you?"

133

Kristianna sucked in her breath. He had finally said what she knew was coming. She had been embarrassed that Gunnar had not offered his assistance. But after Gunnar had explained his duties, she felt he was right about working his land while her papa was away. "Gunnar is none of your concern."

"The man's a fool. You don't know him at all, and I'll bet he doesn't know you from apples, either."

She swung her head around. "My family has known him for a good two years. He is honest, kind, hardworking, and respectable. And he has been a good friend and will be a good husband—"

"What about love? You forgot to mention that. I can tell you about him in one minute. He's a self-centered man with no regard for anyone except himself. He doesn't know about your dreams and wants, and even if you told him, he wouldn't listen. Given the choice, he'd choose his fancy trots over you or anyone in your family. He's going to scratch at the dirt all his life and never have a single parlor grace. If he had any backbone at all, he would have run me off the place yesterday."

Kristianna's mouth dropped open. She had never been given such a talking down! "Now let me tell you something, Mister!" She heaved the shovel down with vented rage and it landed inches from Stone's feet with a soft thud. Putting her hands on her hips, she glared at him. "Gunnar Thorson is the man I am going to marry, and

I will not have you or anyone else insulting him! He would help us, but he is plowing the fields that will one day be mine, too!" Her bosom rose and fell with pronounced anger. "You can just get off our land now. I do not want you here anymore. You take your highfalutin talk with you, Mister." Without realizing it, she had cut the distance between them and was nearly nose to nose with him.

Stone gazed heatedly into her eyes that he once compared to melting snow. At the moment that shade of blue had turned into a frosty blizzard, with fragments of ice. He was inclined to reach out and shake her until she saw things clearly. He held himself back, balling his hands into hard, tight fists. "If he's so goddamn righteous—"

"Do not take the Lord's name in vain," she interrupted hotly.

"Why the hell doesn't he hire someone to plow the fields for you?"

"It costs eight to twelve dollars an acre to till under. Now who is being a fool? You do not seem to understand. I admit I was momentarily swayed with your fancy tales, but now I know what is important. Corn and wheat and barley and"—she bent down to grab a handful of dirt—"earth are important, Mr. Boucher. Not butter barrels that dogs churn, or grasshoppers, or parasols."

"Why are you bullwhipping me? Is this about that kiss—or the lack of it?"

Shocked that he would have the indecency to even mention it, she returned peevishly, "No

135

respectable man would bring that matter up."

"My kissing you would just be a matter? Did you need something to compare that Gunnar of yours to?"

Her face reddened like a ripe apple. He'd come too close to the truth. She gave him a feeble laugh, trying to hide the fact that his arrow had hit the target dead center. "Go away and leave me alone. You cannot seem to get it through your head that"—she let the small grains of dirt run through her fingers—"this is what I am."

Stone rested the barrel of his gun on the ground and leaned his weight on one leg. "Only if you want to be."

"'There is no wrong in mine hands,'" she said.

"I thought we were beyond the Bible quotes."

"For a man who holds God in such a low esteem, you know His Book well."

"Well enough to know better."

She backed away from him. She couldn't think straight when he was so close.

There was a long pause between them, each trying to gather their wits.

Stone stared out at the useless plow in the middle of the field. "You know I can't help you with this."

"I did not ask you."

Stone knew it was useless to talk her out of it. The thought of her out there alone each day bothered him more than he cared to admit. It only took one stray Chippewa or Sioux . . . or one Newt Fraeb. Unprotected, she was at their mercy. "Listen, if you're so all-fired set on this venture, at least keep that old piece of iron you call a rifle with you. You did say you knew how to tote it?"

"*Ja*, I did say that," she agreed, some of her anger abating.

"Then prove it to me." Stone gazed over the field. "Use mine to shoot into that hollowed stump over there." He pointed to the western grove of trees that bordered the plot.

Kristianna raised her hand to the brim of her hat. She figured the target to be a little over seventy-five yards. Papa had told her that the accuracy range his old rifle had was about one hundred yards, and that was considered a long shot. Papa had a hard time hitting a deer at that range. He'd taught her well enough to know the stump would be no challenge.

She reached for Stone's rifle and in that instant, when they both held onto the gun, their eyes locked, then he relinquished his hold.

The weapon was strange to her, being lighter than Papa's. She put all her muscle into cocking it, then raised the barrel. Peering down the shaft, she focused on the stump in the sight. Confidently, she squeezed the trigger. Unknown to her, the gun was much more powerful than her father's. The metal cap of explosives struck the hammer. Fire flashed down the tube and ignited the main powder charge in the barrel, speeding the ball on its way.

The mighty kick threw her back against Stone's massive chest. He steadied her with his strong hands on her quaking shoulders.

"I—I told you I could do it," she said shakily. The raw strength of the smoking J & S Hawken surprised her. She lowered the gun and twisted in his embrace. His hands slipped down her arms and pulled her to him.

His closeness was tearing at the barrier she had erected against him. The rifle fell from her grasp. She was helpless to draw away from him.

"I never doubted you." His face was so close to hers when he spoke that she could smell wild mint on his breath. She had always thought his eyes a greenish blue, but up close, she could see tiny flecks of gold in them. He had not shaved from the day before, and there was dark stubble around his mouth. She was inclined to reach out and touch the roughness of his beard, then run her fingertips over the fullness of his lower lip.

Stone took Kristianna's face in his hands and held her, easing his calloused fingers over her temples. She was silk to his touch. She closed her eyes and allowed him to stroke her. He moved down, feeling every angle and curve of her light brown eyebrows, eyelids, and sweeping lashes, high cheekbones, nose, and finally, her dusky-rose mouth. She parted her lips as he continued to trace her jaw and long, slim neck.

He moved up her throat to her lips again. She involuntarily pressed a feather-light kiss on his thumb, tasting his scent of leather and tobacco. Feeling completely feminine in his arms, she melted into him as he removed her hat and pulled down her hood. Her mane of hair tumbled down her back, and he pressed his fingers into the fullness of the light tresses. Pulling her face closer, he brought his wide mouth down on hers. He kissed her slowly and skillfully, sapping any common sense she might have had to pull away. There was a strong hardness to his lips as he blended his warm moistness with hers. She was shocked by her own eager response, kissing him back, shadowing his movements. She was slightly startled when he forced her teeth to part, his tongue invading the velvet recesses of her mouth. The contact made her dizzy, and she tightened her grip on his back. She worked her hands up his spine and shoulders, feeling the thick cords of his neck. It was as if her blood had turned to fire, fueling some hidden desire she never knew she possessed.

"Kristianna!"

Ulla Bergendahl's voice came to them from out of the copse of trees that divided the field from the house.

Breathless, Kristianna broke free. It took a brief moment to compose herself and get her bearings. Without looking away from Stone's passion-filled face, she staggered back out of his grasp. Her cheeks were flushed a guilty pink. Stumbling, she hastily bent down to pick up the discarded shovel.

"Kristianna?" Ulla was now walking swiftly across the open expanse. "I heard a gunshot. I got scared."

As visibly shaken over the kiss as Kristianna was, Stone pulled his hat down over his forehead. Stooping, he retrieved his gun. After clearing his throat, he reassured Ulla, who had reached his side. "I was only seeing if your daughter could shoot, Mrs. Bergendahl."

"I thought there were savages in the area. I

139

thought—Oh, Kristianna, are you going to give up this nonsense? You cannot possibly hope to turn all this over. Wait until your papa gets home."

"*Nej*, Mama." She dug the blade into the earth, her movement unsteady, her senses not yet returned. She inhaled deeply, cooling her burning lungs. "I have to try."

Ulla looked up to Stone. "Can you not talk to her, Mr. Boucher?"

"I'd rather do something else with my mouth."

He turned and strode away, leaving Ulla to wonder what he meant, and Kristianna to hide her agitation and embarrassment at his suggesting insinuation.

And yet, the truth be known, she'd rather be doing that something with his mouth, too.

·10·

There were plenty of hours in the next few days for Kristianna to rid Stone Boucher from her thoughts. But no matter what she did, she couldn't stop thinking about him, or that kiss. Try as she might, her brain acted of its own free will and he snuck into her mind constantly, whether she was washing, ironing, soap-making, or cleaning. His lean, rugged image danced about her as if it were the man himself. Occasionally, she would press her fingertips to her lips, remembering his mouth on hers. She could almost feel his soft shirt and the hard, muscular shoulders underneath. The silky strands of hair that fell gently into her hand when she'd tangled her fingers in the umber locks. Would she ever be free of him? Even after he was gone? And, certainly, he would be gone soon. After all, Papa would be back in a matter of days; a week at most, she hoped.

Though her mornings were filled with domestic duties, being near him at breakfast was torture. After a hasty lunch, she went to the field where she was making marginal progress. By supper time, she was too exhausted to dwell on his presence. It was all she could do to finish her meal and drag herself up the ladder to the loft. Each night, she collapsed into bed and fell into a deep sleep. Before sunrise, she began all over, starting with Dearie.

Though she had encountered him during the last several days, she hadn't really had to face Stone alone. He'd been busy with mending the split-rail fence attached to the side of the barn. Jake, the ox, had turned over a section of the corral fence. It took Stone the greater part of one day to repair it, and the next two days were spent reinforcing the other rails and posts.

Today, however, with the job completed he was able to work on the kitchen again. He strode easily in and out of the small cabin, each time, causing a fluttering distraction to Kristianna. He was installing the picture window, the job requiring him to nail both sides, set the sash, then caulk the perimeters.

Kristianna sat at the table with her mending in her lap. Holding her sewing needle between her thumb and forefinger, she favored her palm. The blisters she'd developed from using the shovel were nearly healed. But it was not her sore fingers that caused her hand to shake every time Stone sliced his way through the room. She looked up to catch a glimpse of the back of his calcutta shirt, the thin, white material pulled taut against his muscled back. It was different now to look at him. Now she knew how sinewy those muscles were. Now she knew just how lush and thick his long, glossy hair was.

And every time he moved to go out the door again to secure the outside of the window, she could see his face, her eyes focusing on his full and pleasant mouth. Those lips had covered hers so sweetly, beyond anything she could have ever imagined. She wanted to reach out to him, to slide her fingers up his chest, to feel the warm pulse at his throat. To kiss him again to see if it would be the same sweet harmony. She wondered if he was thinking the same things? Or had he kissed so many women that she was merely one more on the list?

It was with great effort, and out of necessity lest she jump up from her chair and kiss him right in front of Mama, she willed such thoughts away! She pushed the needle into her black skirt and pulled out the thread, then pricked the fabric again. Thoughts of kissing would be reserved for Gunnar. Oh, but his lips had never intrigued her!

Since the weather was slightly cooler than it had been, Ulla was catching up on her baking. She bent over the hearth, brushing the coals off the cast cover of her flat, low kettle. The rim was turned up an inch so it could hold the coals and serve as an oven. Once the embers were removed, she picked up the pot by its four foot long handle and brought it to the table, placing it on a cooling pad. The aroma of freshly baked rhubarb pie pleasantly filled the tiny room, diverting some of Kristianna's brazen thoughts to food.

Noelle, who was supposed to be helping with the mending, had complained earlier of a stomachache. Kristianna had watched her mother pour some gooey peppermint essence in a wooden spoon, knowing it was a waste of medicine. The child had no talent for needle and thread and would say anything to release herself from the chore.

Noelle leaned forward as her mother lifted the lid to remove the pie with long, heavy tongs. "It is a good one, Mama. Are the pie crust cookies finished?"

Ulla turned around, and using a hook, pulled out a cast-iron frying pan. It was filled with the remnant odd shapes of dough sprinkled with cinnamon and maple sugar. "*Ja*, they are finished, but none for you."

"Please, Mama." The child pouted. Her curly, wheat-colored hair peeked out from her three-pleated skullcap. "I feel much better now."

"Now that the mending is finished," Kristianna supplied, anchoring a knot in her skirt and cutting the thread with a quick snip of her scissors.

Stone's heavy steps crossed the threshold. He'd rolled up his sleeves to expose his bulging forearms, and loosened the lacings at his throat to reveal a small triangle of hair. A fine sheen of perspiration covered his brow, and he'd tied a leather thong around his forehead to catch any moisture from running down his face. He paused at the table to admire Ulla's pie. Leaning over,

144

the front of his shirt gaped, offering Kristianna a view of the dark, curly hair that trailed down his abdomen and disappeared into the waistband of his tight buckskins.

"Fine-looking pie, Mrs. Bergendahl. You're cooking more than one man can eat."

The smell of leather and Bay Balm floated around Kristianna, enveloping the pie's sweet aroma and replacing it with the masculine scent of one, Stone Boucher. It was more than she could bear. She abruptly stood, spilling the contents of her sewing basket. Hooks and eyes, and various cards of earth-toned threads scattered in all directions with a flurry. "*Ja*, much more," she choked, her voice battling to combat the jagged emotions ripping through her. "I think we should bring a pie to Olaf. I am sure Liv has not been up to cooking a large meal, since her time is so near."

"What a wonderful idea. I would like to see how she is doing," Ulla said, already taking her wicker hamper from the wall peg. She set it on the table and was fetching a gingham napkin to place over the pies to keep them hot, when she stopped short and looked at Noelle. "We cannot go. Noelle is sick. I would not want her near Liv."

Noelle's green eyes opened wide. "But, Mama, I feel much better now."

Kristianna's short-lived spirits sank, and so did her shoulders in a visible sign of defeat. But she was not one to give up so easily. She had to get away, away from Stone and anything that reminded her of him. At least for a while so she could clear her head.

"Maybe Mr. Boucher would find it agreeable to watch Noelle?" She hadn't really given much thought to the idea before she spoke it. But once said, she didn't see anything wrong with the notion. Noelle doted on the mountain man. Certainly, she would be safe with him.

Stone stood back from the table, slight amusement in his eyes. So, she was that desperate to vacate the premises, was she? Well, it hadn't been one big picnic for him either, strutting in and out of the house, seeing her appraise him like a side of buffalo every time he came under her perusal. But it had an oddly stirring effect on him. Due to his generous height, he was used to being stared at and it was something he had accepted. But when Kristianna cast those violet eyes at him, he felt his pulse quicken. Thoughts of their kiss, of her sweet body pressed against his, had plagued him the entire morning, nearly rendering his arm useless with the hammer and nails. Getting her out of the house would be as much a godsend for him as it would be for her. And it would allow him to finish the window without the possibility of him turning into a blathering idiot and shattering the glass to smithereens.

"You go. I'll watch her."

Noelle turned her face toward Stone's. Olaf and Liv Thorson's house suddenly dimmed at the chance of having Stone all to herself. "*Ja*, my stomach is feeling bad."

Ulla gave her eldest daughter a chiding stare before speaking to Stone. "It would be an inconvenience for you, Mr. Boucher. Kristianna never should have asked." She resumed her baking, removing the crust cookies and setting them on a cooling grid.

"I wouldn't do it if I didn't want to."

"Let him, Mama," Kristianna blurted, looking up, as she retrieved the sewing notions from the planked floor. Hastily, she deposited the tangled mess of threads and hooks back into the sewing basket. She snapped down the lid with such force, it threatened to topple again.

"I would like to see Liv . . ." Ulla contemplated the situation aloud.

"And I am sure she would like to see you, Mama," Kristianna added with hopeful urgency.

"Mr. Boucher, Noelle can be such an adventurous child. I would hate for her to cause you trouble."

"He likes adventure." Kristianna had begun to fill the wicker hamper with freshly baked bread and rhubarb tarts, knowing she was on the brink of success.

Stone moved toward the door. "I'll hitch up your wagon. Don't give it another thought, Mrs. Bergendahl." He hadn't given much consideration to the trade off he'd made to get Kristianna from the house. Then it hit him like a speeding lead ball that he'd be in sole charge of a five-year-old. More to assure himself than Ulla Bergendahl, he said over his shoulder, "Don't worry. What bother could a pint-sized girl be?"

One hour later, his words would come back to haunt him.

The time away did Kristianna good. It renewed her sense of priority, her heritage. Seeing Liv's

147

house decorated with fine embroidery, laces, china, and trinkets from Sweden filled her head with visions of her own home. Someday, she would share a house with Gunnar and she would display the wedding presents Mama would give her.

Olaf had built a sturdy rocking chair for Liv, lovingly carving the spindles and arms. He said that the chair would get many hours of use, as Liv's rocking in it would comfort the baby. Kristianna silently envied the woman who would one day be her sister-in-law. Liv was so content, without any reservations toward her husband. They were in love and she wondered if the feelings she felt toward Gunnar were love. Stone had said they were not. But what did he know? He never confessed any undying love for her, either. Maybe love came after a man and woman were married. After all, Mama and Papa loved each other, and they were married.

The three women talked over herbal tea and the rhubarb tarts, and before they knew it, Olaf came in, stomping the dirt off his boots, looking for supper. Kristianna and Ulla bid them farewell, and made the six-mile journey back home.

Kristianna guided the team of oxen through the trees. There was a little over an hour of sunlight left, and the humidity had risen. Feeling sticky, she thought of nothing but a cool bath. Normally she bathed in the barn, but since Stone's arrival, she'd dragged the old half barrel to the side of the house and cleaned up after she saw his lantern light fill the haymow.

"I hope Noelle had the good sense to give Mr.

Boucher something to eat," Ulla mused from her perch in the bench seat next to Kristianna.

"I am sure she did."

Kristianna rounded the final corner to the farmstead and turned Jake and Tony toward the barn.

The glowing orange sun bathed the treetops in a fiery hue, making them shadow the house with spired forms. For a moment, it was hard for Kristianna to see Stone on the roof of the kitchen, nailing down the remaining shingles. But when he moved, there was no doubt the rugged silhouette was his. Something next to his leg moved and Kristianna shielded her line of vision with her slender hand. There, next to him was Noelle. On the roof!

Kristianna barely set the brake handle before she hopped down from the springy seat and dashed to the side of the house. Stone faced her, a nail between his straight, white teeth. She shaded her eyes with her hand again and stared up at him. With a nervous, angry edge to her voice, she called, "Mr. Boucher! What is my little sister doing up there? She could fall and break her leg!"

Ulla raced to Kristianna's side. "Noelle! Come down!"

"I cannot, Mama. Steurn tied me to the chimney." She lifted up her white apron to expose a piece of hemp rope securely anchored around her tiny waist with a five-foot lead; the other end was tied to the chimney stones.

"Why in heaven's name did you do that, Mr. Boucher?" Kristianna inquired hotly.

He stood, an unwavering giant on the rooftop,

his tanned and brawny arms akimbo. "Because she was a lot safer up here with me than on the ground. She kept disappearing."

Noelle cast her eyes guiltily to the bag of nails in her lap. It wasn't as much fun as she thought it would be having Stone all to herself. He didn't want to play make-believe. He wanted to finish the kitchen and he didn't take too kindly to her playing hide-and-seek.

"Noelle, I told you to mind your manners with Mr. Boucher," Ulla scolded. "Did you at least have the sense to feed him supper?"

Stone squatted next to Noelle and untied the rope around the chimney. "She made me biscuits and blackberry jam."

"Biscuits?" Ulla echoed. "Noelle does not know how to make biscuits."

"I found that out. I cleaned up most of the flour."

Ulla was fairly in a tizzy. "*Uffda*! I wish Sixten were here! He would place the hickory switch on your bottom, little one. Come down right now!"

"But Steurn said if I handed him the nails, he would take me fishing."

"I am sure Mr. Boucher has had enough of you today."

Stone grabbed Noelle by the waist and hurdled her over his shoulder as if she were nothing more than a sack of oats. He slowly backed down the ladder and when he reached the ground, he unfastened the rope from her middle. Coiling the rough hemp, he put his arm through it and rested it on his shoulder. "I promised her, Mrs. Bergendahl. And I hate to say it, but I'm starved." He slapped his flat belly, the sound taut as a kettledrum. "Fresh fish sounds mighty fine. Sundown is the best time to go at it."

Ulla looked to Kristianna, doubt etched in her fine features. "I suppose you could take her, Mr. Boucher. Only if Kristianna goes with you to discipline Noelle."

Kristianna's eyes met Stone's over the top of Noelle's capped head. Her outing had done nothing to dim her view of him. He still was, and would always be, the most handsome man she had ever seen. She was also aware that she was extremely attracted to him. But in the wake of the time she'd been gone, she did remember her roots and her impending marriage to Gunnar. With that, she felt a little safer from her traitorous heart in his company. And to look down at Noelle's upturned face, veiled in eager anticipation, she hadn't the heart to say no. "Very well," she finally replied, saying the words more to Stone than to her sister.

"I will get Papa's fishing box." Noelle skipped across the yard to the barn.

Ulla removed the empty hamper from the wagon and headed toward the house, shaking her head in wonder as to what kind of disaster lay ahead of her in the kitchen.

Alone, Stone caressed Kristianna with his smoldering gaze. "You have a nice visit?"

"Very," she practically whispered. His voice was like honey and it made her body feel just as golden and syrupy.

"We missed you." He moved a step closer to her, the distance between them mere inches.

Kristianna's breath caught in her throat, and for a moment, she thought he was going to brush her cheek with the back of his hand. But before he had a chance to do what she hoped for, Noelle came bounding back to them. Rattling in her hands were two willow poles and lines, a tackle box, and an old milk pan to put the fish in.

"I am ready, Steurn." Her pale, round face fairly beamed.

Stone backed away from Kristianna and grabbed the rods and box. "Let's go then and get us a whopper." His tone masked any amorous feelings he might have been about to display.

Sighing, Kristianna trudged behind them. Fishing was not one of her favorite things, but if it afforded her a little time with Stone Boucher, she'd tolerate it, as long as she didn't have to bait the hook.

There was a wide creek that flowed just past the edge of the Bergendahls' farm. It was fed from a tributary of the mighty Mississippi River. Bubbling and gurgling, and dusted with yellow pollen and fallen leaves, the water was a soothing sound over the sunbleached rocks. It emptied into a deep pool that Sixten used as a fishing hole, and Kristianna occasionally used as a bathing spot. The water in the pool deepened to a midnight blue, then it picked up speed again and traveled north following a crooked pattern. Silky meadow grass lined the edge of the stream, as well as grand rocks in various sizes, shapes, and hues of gray.

"Right here, Steurn." Noelle unceremoniously

dropped the milk pan and began digging for worms with a small tin scoop. "Papa always catches a catfish here."

The sun was beginning to deepen its twilight descent, and the feathery limbs of cottonwoods and tamarack were cast in different hues of red and magenta. Kristianna sat under the cover of a verdant cedar bough and watched Stone remove the coiled rope from his shoulder. Putting numerous hooks on a line, his fingers moved very agilely, as if he'd threaded fish hooks thousands of times.

Absorbed in his task, he momentarily forgot she was there. She felt a slight loss from his lack of attention and thought of a reason to make him notice her.

"It only takes one hook to catch a fish," she intoned, leaning back against the tree. She bent her knees up under her skirt and fanned the thin, nutmeg-colored skirt around her.

Stone lifted his head. The late glow of day was trapped in her hair, making it a radiant golden, rather than white-blonde. Sitting there with the shimmering sun behind her, she looked like an angel. She hugged her knees to her well-proportioned chest, and the pointed tips of her wooden shoes peeked out from the hem of her plain brown skirt. Her eyes were a pale iris, her face faintly tanned, her slightly upturned nose a little pink. She was a vision beyond compare. For a moment, he envied George Catlin's ability to re-create images on canvas, for if he were a painter, he would capture her face in oils forever. Instead, he sketched it in his memory.

"Five hooks, one baited," he finally explained. "You catch five fish for the price of one. They don't know any better."

"An old trick?" she queried, remembering what he had said about the lightning bug ring.

An irresistible grin overtook his rugged features. "I reckon so."

Noelle came forward with an old spice tin filled with several, plump and squirming black worms. "We will get a big one with these, Steurn."

"Big as a beaver."

There were numerous rings in the pool where fish were nipping at evening insects. Stone baited one of the shining hooks with the wiggling creature and drew back his long arm. Kristianna watched in fascination as he smoothly aimed into the center of the deepest part and cast the line. It seemed as if the bait barely touched the water when there was a tug on his pole.

Noelle excitedly jumped up and down, her skirt and snow-white petticoats twirling around her pudgy legs. "You got one! A big cat! Bring him in."

Caught in the excitement of it all, Kristianna rose to her feet and sprinted across the sandy beach. When Stone pulled up the line, she stifled a laugh. "A sunfish! Look, it is only five fingers long!" The yellow-and-blue sunfish wiggled and danced in the air, trying to free itself from the deadly hook. "Where are the other four, Mr. Boucher?" The even whiteness of her smile was dazzling.

Stone took the fish off the line and tossed it

sharply back. "Well, then Miss Know-It-All, you catch us some."

"Kristianna is afraid of worms." Noelle taunted her with the tin.

Kristianna took a step back. "I am not."

"*Ja*, you are." She dug into the can and pulled out a fleshy, brown worm that was akin to one of the fat cigars Mr. Bidwell kept in a humidor at the Sutler's Store. It squirmed in Noelle's cherubic fingers, fighting for freedom. She extended her arm and waved it in front of Kristianna's horrified face.

"Get it away, Noelle!" Kristianna spun around and darted for the cedar tree. Noelle raced after her, chasing her around the wide, thickly barked trunk.

Stone threw his head back in laughter as Kristianna raced passed him, her apron flying as she headed toward the creek. "Noelle, stop it!"

"Worm! Worm! Wor—"

Then there was a shallow splash.

Noelle landed in the middle of the pool, the hem of her dress ballooning around her small shoulders. Her rail cap was stuck to her wet hair, and her eyes were open wide in surprise. Reacting swiftly, Stone dove in after her. In an easy stroke, he was at her side and hooked an arm around her waist. She did not struggle as he swam with her to the sandy shore. Gripping her shoulders, he pulled her to her feet. She looked a little bewildered standing in her black-stockinged feet. Her clogs, having fallen off, were floating nearby. Stone reached over to get them before they were drawn away by the current.

Kristianna looked at Noelle, then at Stone, who was wringing wet. His shirt was plastered to him like a second skin, the water making the white material almost transparent. The buckskins that covered his long legs were already beginning to stretch, offering her a further view of his flat belly. Drops fell from his curly hair that trailed slightly down his back and over his chiseled face. He looked more surprised than Noelle did.

Kristianna put a hand over her mouth and fought the peels of laughter that began to bubble from her throat. It was a futile attempt, for not soon after, they shook her uncontrollably and she released them with a flourish.

Noelle joined in with her own giggles.

Stone drew his prominent brows down in a frown. "What's so damn funny?"

"Noelle knows how to swim, Mr. Boucher!" Racking with deep chuckles, she held her side. "Your pants are going to fall off!"

Looking down, Stone saw that the leather hide was expanding and drooping. A part of his red, long underwear began to show under the transparency of his calcutta shirt. "Well, isn't this a flash in the pan! Why didn't you tell me she could swim?"

"You did not give me the chance," Kristianna returned, trying to keep a straight face.

"I see." His tanned face was alight with playfulness. "Then I'll take the chance that you know how to swim, too, since we scared all the fish away anyway!" He took one step forward and her laughter came to a halting squeak. She was quickly caught in his powerful arms, no match for his steel-like grip. Hoisting her effortlessly into his embrace, he deposited her over his shoulder and turned toward the creek.

"Mr. Boucher!" Her laughter died and was resurrected by a pleading scream. "Mr. Boucher! Put me down!"

"Dump her in, Steurn!"

Stone climbed effortlessly onto a high, round boulder. She scissored her feet, thrashing and kicking off her clogs. He gave her slender and curving waist a light squeeze, then heaved her over his chest. She cried out at the top of her voice as she hit the cool water, the contact sending a series of waves onto the bank. Surfacing, she brushed back the tendrils of wet hair on her forehead, and waded in the middle of the pool, waving her hands over the water. In spite of her effort not to, a tentative smile found its way to her lips. "I will repay you for this one, Stone."

He crouched down by the water's edge, not missing the fact that she had called him by his Christian name. "I hope you do." The underlying meaning to his words were not lost on Kristianna. Her eyes locked with his, but the spell was quickly broken as Noelle knelt next to Stone.

"Can I go swimming, Kristianna?"

"It can do no harm since we are already wet and sure to be scolded by Mama anyway."

Noelle rolled down her stockings, dropped them in a wet heap, and jumped in.

Kristianna swam to the shore and got out. Her clothing did little to hide the feminine curves underneath. The thin, eggshell linen blouse was plastered to her chemise, offering a near-perfect view of the shoulder-strapped undergarment. The skirt molded her perfect legs. Her petticoat was wadded between her thighs and she was almost tempted to take it off—almost.

Picking up Noelle's sodden socks, she draped them over a rock. Trying to wring some of the moisture from her skirt, she looked up to see Stone deftly unlacing the front of his shirt. "What are you doing?" Her words were a pitch higher than normal and a little shaky.

He pulled the material over his head, shrugging out of the sleeves. To see his chest peeking down an open shirt was one thing, but to see him without the shirt was something else indeed. Muscles rippled over his smooth, broad shoulders with an easy grace, his skin tanned a rich honey. His chest was covered with a dark tuft of curly brown hair that straightened down to a thin line, disappearing into his drooping waistband. "I'm going swimming, too."

He sat down next to her and shucked off his moccasins. Without his socks on, she was able to study his feet. Once again, she found herself seeing a part of a man's anatomy completely bared for the first time. A chest, now feet. She had never dreamed it wouldn't be Gunnar's chest and feet. Stone's feet were long and flat, the skin darker than her own, but for obvious reasons, not tanned like his arms. There was a light sprinkling of hair on his ankles and even a little over his big toes. Such a simple show of skin sent a dizzying current through her.

When he stood and adjusted the waistband of his buckskins, she sucked in her breath. "You—you are not going to remove your trousers?"

He gave her a flirtatious stare under his hooded eyelids. "No. Can't let leather dry off your limbs or it will never shrink back right to fit."

"Oh . . ." Her rosy lips slightly quivered.

"Disappointed?"

"Certainly not," she shot back a little quicker than she had intended.

He moved stealthily to the ground where he had laid the rope he used to tie Noelle to the chimney. With a snap of his wrist, he swung the end over the cedar bough and secured it with a large knot.

"What are you doing, Steurn?" Noelle floated to the water's edge and gripped a piece of a tree's root that had been exposed by the flow of the creek.

"I'm going swimming," he supplied matter-of-factly, then clutched onto the hemp and ran while he held it. When he was at the shore, he pushed his feet away from the sandy beach and swung into the air. Once over the inviting water, he released his hold and fell with a grand splash that rained on Noelle.

She fairly beamed at the ingenious method. "Me, too!" Scrambling to her feet, she ran to hold the rope. In seconds, she copied Stone's flight and was in the pool.

"You, too, Kristianna! It is fun."

Kristianna looked hesitantly toward Stone. The water did look awfully inviting and the mosquitoes that buzzed around her head were beginning to annoy her. What better way to get rid of them? Stone bobbed up and down in the middle, offering tempting views of his bare chest. What was the harm? Noelle was there, too.

Kristianna turned her back and lifted the hem of her wet skirt to her thighs. After rolling down the garter that held up her black, knit stockings, she pushed them down and slid them off.

Very conscious of her naked feet, she made her way toward the rope. Not even Gunnar had seen her bare feet and here she was parading them in front of a stranger. Well, not exactly a stranger, but a man who was not her intended.

She stepped on a broken butternut shell, the edge sharp from being nibbled on by a squirrel. Wincing, she bent down and brushed the sharp hull from her heel without a second thought.

"Are you scared, Kristianna?" Noelle called.

"*Nej*," she tossed back, then clutched the rope. It was stiff and coarse in her hands. Her palms were moist and she momentarily let go to wipe them on her damp skirt. Little good that did. She retook her hold and followed Stone's example. Putting her weight into her movement, she padded on the soft ground littered with downy leaves and pine needles.

"Here I come," she said, and squeezed her eyes shut as she swung out over the water. With a giddy cry, she let go and bounded into the pool with an easy splash. She surfaced to find Stone a breath away, his arms reaching toward her. He captured her waist with his large, splayed fingers and gave her a slight embrace. The contact was like fire on her skin, burning through the material of her blouse and chemise, regardless of the fact that the water was many degrees cooler. She sorely missed the heat when he released her seconds later.

Noelle waded to them and playfully raked the water with her hands, sending a spray showering on Kristianna. "Noelle!" She laughed and proceeded to douse her sister in return.

Stone caught the good humor and skipped his arm across the sparkling liquid sending a big wave crashing down on them both. In a sea of splashing and spraying and raining creek water, they were blind to the approaching figure.

Gunnar's father, Karl Thorson, quickened his steps upon hearing the abandoned laughter of voices, one of which was distinctly baritone. His high-cheekboned face was set in grim determination. His distinguishing blond hair, streaked with gray, sprouted from the sides of his handwoven straw hat. Though he was a reed of a man, his booted footsteps pounded into the ground with growing anger. He stopped abruptly, as if he'd run into a glass wall.

His hands on his hips, he bellowed, "*Vad har ni att säger*? What have you to say?" he repeated in the best English he could for Stone's sake.

The water was instantly calm. All playing ceased and the trio turned toward the man on the bank.

Kristianna's heart jumped to her throat. "Mr. Thorson," she gasped. "What brings you to our parts?"

"What indeed, *fröken Bergendahl*. I was at

161

Fort Snelling buying supplies and thought to stop in on my way back home to make sure you were faring properly."

"We·—we are fine." She shivered, but not from the water now turning cold with the onslaught of evening.

"My son told me you hired a man of the traps to help while Sixten is away. Is this your idea of help? Swimming and frolicking! And with an innocent child like Noelle, too," he reprimanded harshly.

Stone stared hard at the thin man before him. His expression was stoical, save for the tightening of a muscle in his square jaw. Effortlessly, he made his way to the shore with long, easy strokes. He rose from the creek and retrieved his shirt. Water glistened off his bare, upper torso, the ever-fading golden light catching in the tiny drops. Without much regard for the pair of deep-set blue eyes on him, he proceeded to rub himself dry.

"You have a problem with swimming?" Stone asked stiffly.

Aghast with such an obvious insult, Karl plodded toward Stone. "Listen here, you man of traps. I will not have your kind talking down to me. You are nothing but dung. Do you hear? Several years back my barn was burned down by woodsmen and savages—you are one in the same. You do not want us here any more than we want you here. Why Ulla was *tokig*—crazy— enough to hire you is a beyond my ken." He looked to the creek where Kristianna and Noelle were silently wading. "Out of there!" he ordered.

Stone cut the distance between him and Karl Thorson, towering over the farmer by at least a foot. He pointed a heavy finger at Karl and poked it against his lean chest. "I never burned down anybody's barn. I think you better go home before I do something I wouldn't regret."

Jag skall gå hem, då jag är färdig. I shall go home, when I am ready."

"Well, I think you're ready because I sure as hell don't like you coming here and barking orders."

Kristianna sprang from the water, Noelle in tow, and was instantly by Stone's side. Without thinking, she slid her arm into Stone's in an effort to stop him from baiting her future father-in-law.

His eyes narrowing, Karl took in her appearance and the gesture with clear disapproval on his stern face. "Ah! You have no shoes on. Have you no shame? And you expect my Gunnar to wed a woman with no decency?"

Stone's fists hardened to granite. "You just wait a minute old man—"

He was cut off by pressure on his upper arm from Kristianna's fingers. "Stone, please. He is right." Her words were so soft, at first, he thought he didn't hear her correctly.

"He is right," she repeated sorrowfully.

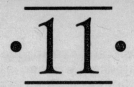

·11·

Glowing yellow light from the tin lantern's holes was stenciled onto the oval frame of Kristianna's tambour embroidery work, as she passed the hooked needle under and then up in a smooth motion, making a chain of blue floss. The hour was late; her mother and Noelle had gone to bed long ago.

Sleep eluded her and she thought her stitchery would tire her. So far, it had done nothing more than further her pattern along.

As the tallow grew low, the candle's wick sputtered and wavered in the hot pool of wax. The house was quiet, save for Noelle's occasional sighs and rustling in her trundle bed. If only Kristianna could sleep, too.

Somewhere outside, an owl hooted. The room in near darkness now, Kristianna was forced to either get a fresh candle or abandon her stitching. While deciding, there was one last flicker then a soft sizzling sound as darkness surrounded her.

She sat there for a long moment, her hands still holding the embroidery hook. It was as if time had stopped, giving her the chance to sort out her thoughts and feelings. But hadn't that been what she'd been doing all evening ever since Gunnar's papa had found them at the creek?

Stone had been ready to fight for her honor, but she had restrained him. She had felt the tenseness in his arms, the tightening of his muscles at her admission of shame. It had been wrong for her and Noelle to go swimming with him. It had been wrong for her to remove her stockings. Her bare feet were for her husband's eyes only, and she'd not given that to Gunnar, but to Stone. Stone, who didn't realize what wrong she'd done, who was now angry with her, and maybe even a little confused. He did not know about their traditions, their customs. He was not Swedish, but an outsider, a man of the traps.

He was like a wisp of smoke and soon would be gone.

Then why did her heart ache with the thought of his leaving? She should hate him. She should feel the things for him Gunnar and his papa felt for him. But they hated what Stone stood for, not the man he was. In reflection, Stone was an extremely generous man. More so than Gunnar would ever be. For Stone, though masculine and rugged, knew what a woman wanted without asking. He knew that Ulla wanted a picture window above her sink. He understood Noelle's make-believe world and played along, and he knew that Kristianna wanted him to kiss her.

After that day in the field, that was all she wanted—and more. Though what more went with kissing, she wasn't sure. Only that when he had kissed her, she felt a stirring in the deepest part of her being that was like a warm glow, melting her to the core. Had her mother not come when she did . . . A blush heated its way to her face.

Why were things so difficult? Why did he have to be a mountain man? So headstrong. In the agitated state he was in, he'd not returned to the house with them, but stomped to the barn. Karl Thorson had left soon after, wanting to reach his farmstead before dark, but not before he made sure her mother knew of her behavior. Ulla, ever reserved and humble, politely agreed with him, and when he had gone, she confided in Kristianna and Noelle that she saw no harm in their activity, save the removal of their stockings. At that moment, Kristianna was filled with respect and love for Ulla. It was as if she had taken sides with Stone.

Kristianna's eyes were now accustomed to the dark shapes of the room, so she stood and found to her surprise she was hungry. She'd had nothing to eat since returning home from their outing. Along with the tarts they had brought, Liv had fed them tea and small slices of cardamom rusk, a rich coffee bread sliced and dried in the oven, then sprinkled with cinnamon and sugar. The fish they were to have caught for their supper . . . Well, the fish had been scared off by their swimming.

Kristianna felt her way along the edge of the trestle tabletop, then stretched her hand out to the wall and progressed to the opening of the new kitchen. Ulla had moved her sideboard into the small lean-to and on it was an old blue plate and the leftover rhubarb tarts. Picking one up, she bit into the flaky crust. While she ate, she looked out the new uncurtained picture window to see the wide closed doors of the haymow and slivered shafts of light illuminating from the cracks.

Stone was awake, too.

The thought of them both unable to sleep brought a light skip to her pulse. Was he as undecided as she, or was he still cross with her?

Then she realized that he had not eaten at all. Brushing the crumbs from her fingertips, she fetched a soft gingham napkin and placed two of the tarts in it. About to fold it up, she stopped, then added several biscuits Ulla had made and a handful of *potatis kakor*—potato cakes boiled in salted water. He was, after all, a big man. Satisfied, she neatly knotted the corners of the red-and-white napkin.

She replaced the beeswax candle in the stenciled lantern and stepped outside to light it. Striking a match and setting it to the wick, a flame came alive and she closed the hinged door, allowing the spiky rays to guide her way. Heeding the stumps, she crossed over the yard and to the barn with her offering securely in her hands.

The corral gate opened smoothly, no longer

sticking. She smiled inwardly, remembering the chastising she'd given him about fixing it. When she reached the barn, she set the lantern down and unlatched the heavy plank that kept the doors closed. Entering, the inside was bathed in a mellow light from the loft above allowing her to view the stalls. The familiar smells greeted her: leather, stock, manure, and hay. And now, very faintly, Bay Balm.

Looping the handle of the lantern to a nail in the rafter, she gazed at Brother Moon standing peacefully, not at all minding Jake and Tony, or even Dearie. She neared the horse, noticing a slight, crescent scar on its glossy, white hindquarter. For a fleeting moment, she wondered how the animal came by it. Its faintly gray mane and tail were silkily brushed and well cared for. Noelle was right, Stone's horse was prettier than Flicka and Fredrick.

Looking up at the haymow, she heard no noise from Stone. Had he dozed off with the lantern lit? Moving toward the ladder, she took in her surroundings, fondly caressing with her eyes her papa's things. His harrow and hoe. Scythes and cradles with blades and long wooden teeth to grab the wheat stalks. Then there were the hoof scrapers and picks. Curry comb, harness tack and leathers, and yokes. And in the midst of it all was Stone's saddle. Resting on its side, she was able to view the underpart and see that he'd scratched his initials into the wood. *S.A.B.* Just seeing his penmanship gave her a sense of intimate closeness with him. She reached out and traced his initials, his bold lettering sending a tingle through her. She wondered what the *A* stood for. There were so many things she didn't know about him, so many things that she wanted to know before he left.

She bunched her narrow, striped brown-and-black skirt and petticoat in her hand, as well as the napkin, then clutched onto the ladder's edge and began to climb. With each rung that brought her closer to him, her heart thrummed a little stronger. For now, this was his personal space, and she was invading his privacy. What if he were doing something private? As much as the thought made her want to turn back down, she continued. After all, what if he had fallen asleep with the lantern burning? She should extinguish it. God forbid he should accidently set the barn on fire.

As she neared, she still heard no sound. Should she call out? she wondered.

When at last she reached the step high enough up for her to peek her nose over the loft floor, she stopped for a moment. All around was bleached yellow hay, loose and in bundles. Many times, she had come up here to seek solace or fill the rafter with winter hay. But now, it had become transformed into one man's place. One man who brought a strange awakening in her. In the corner were his personal things: his shaving mug and brush, his clothing, various pouches, and split cowhide with leather thongs, his gun, powder horn, powder, measure, and rifle oil. And there, next to the shuttered window, was his pallet and covers. The quilt was a sunburst pattern she had made herself and the thought of him using it brought a warm flush to her face.

On the quilt, sitting with his back toward her, was Stone. She drank in his form, embedding it in her memory for when he was long gone. His wide shoulders were covered by the expanse of his green-blue calico shirt. The sides hung freely open, the buttons down the front unfastened. His glorious umber hair rested on his back, several inches below his collar. Legs, sleek, long, and muscular, were bent at the knee, Indian-style. His backside strained his denim trousers and it nearly unnerved her that a man's muscular bottom could cause such a helter-skelter flutter within her.

Oblivious to her presence, she could see him move his left arm, then reach down with his right hand to a small, rawhide box. Whatever he took out was so tiny, she could not make out what it was between his tanned fingers. He made a looping motion with his hand then he was digging in the box again.

She was about to speak, when he turned and she thought he was going to stare right at her. Instead, he grabbed a rectangular bottle. Leaning his dark head back, he took a pull, to drain what was left of the contents. When not another drop came forth, she heard him mutter a curse under his breath, then toss the bottle haphazardly. Right at her!

She ducked as it landed not an inch from her nose. The pungent smell of liquor stung her nostrils and almost made her sneeze. She peered at the label. Hudson's Bay rum!

He was drunk!

Having seen what the alcohol did to the trappers at the rendezvous, Kristianna decided to back down the ladder and let him starve. She had no desire to be the brunt of his wrath while he was under the influence of firewater. She'd barely moved when his husky, rum-laced voice called out to her.

"You may as well speak your peace, Miss Bergendahl."

Startled that he had known she was there all along, she halted for a moment. She could just leave the napkin and go or she could climb up and . . . and what? Make sure he ate it? He was not a little boy who needed to be fed. Far from it. Despite that fact, she moved upward.

"Why did you not tell me you knew I was here?" she asked, her foot on the final rung as she thrust herself up and stood. The ceiling was high, but for a woman of her height, she had to slightly dip her head. She thought of Stone, who must have to bend at the waist to get around, and she felt guilty for not having the insight to see that he was more comfortable.

"Why not, indeed? And interrupt yet another scrutiny of my body? How is it, that you like the man's form, and not the man himself?" His words were bitter, laced with a sarcastic edge as he turned to face her. Etched clearly in his face was the anger that she knew had been festering and building since Karl Thorson's visit. If she had any sense at all, she would just leave and let him boil over. After all, it really wasn't his business what she did, or how she explained herself to the elders of her community.

His open shirt revealed his expanse of hard chest and the dark patch of curly hair that covered his beating heart. She dared not linger over him, least he catch her again. "I brought you some supper. I thought you might be hungry." She chose to ignore his comment.

"I've had mine, thanks." He returned to whatever he was doing; she still could not fathom what it was.

"You cannot call Hudson's Bay rum, supper."

"I've gotten along fine for twenty-five years without you as my keeper, Miss Bergendahl."

Not at all miffed, she moved closer to him, the dry hay crackling under her clogs. "Do not think that I am concerned for your stomach, Mr. Boucher. I am only thinking of how useful you will be to us tomorrow if you do not eat. That is all." It was partially the truth. She tipped her head, trying to view what was in his hands.

He arched a slashed brow at her. "Curious, are you?"

A little embarrassed, she held out the aromatic red-and-white napkin as an offering. "I only meant to give you this and go."

When he did not reach for it, she laid it down behind him on the quilt. Standing for what felt like minutes, she realized he wasn't going to acknowledge her. Slightly irate now for having come this far, she turned to leave him to his spirits.

"Don't go."

His voice, low and with that fine, gravelly edge, called to her. At first she thought she didn't hear him correctly. She cast an inquisitive eye at him.

Stone's teal-blue eyes were bright in the light from the lantern. His tanned face was filled with a silent plea for a truce.

He hadn't meant to be so harsh toward her, but dammit all, she had goaded him. That old Swede deserved a fist in the meat basket for having made her feel humiliated. As if her being with him was like dirt. He'd been caught up in a silent rage ever since. The pint of rum had done little to soothe his ego; it would take a lot more than that to make him numb. Seeing her now made him almost forget he was mad. She had unplaited her hair and it tumbled down her back in a silky mass. Her iris-colored eyes, ever unique, were soft and glittery in the gentle light. She wore a simply striped skirt and a flaxen-colored blouse that hooked down the front and outlined her full breasts. How could he want to throttle her and kiss her at the same time?

The smoldering look Stone gave her made Kristianna powerless to resist. She found her way to him and sat, Indian-style, like him.

"What are you doing?" she asked, deciding for now, to keep the conversation on a neutral level.

He turned to the open rawhide box. "I'm beading."

She peeked inside to see a riot of colors and shapes. There were tufts of red horsehair trim, dentalium—tooth shells—green beads with white centers, tin cones, cobalt pony beads and glass beads of mustard-yellow and dark navy-blue. Just to look at the trinkets as they were, was awe-inspiring.

"Beading?" she parroted. A man sewing? It

was beyond her comprehension that such a brawny man who set iron traps with steel jaws, and lifted timber as if it were weightless, could even hold a sliver of a needle in his large hands.

Stone reached down to his lap and brought up two pieces of doeskin. He held them out for her inspection, pushing them into her hands. "You may as well see them now."

They were gloves. The most beautiful gloves she had ever seen. The part that would cover a person's palm was made of a strong rawhide and the top side was of the softest brain-tanned doeskin. Though she didn't know it, brain-tanned leather was far superior, for it was cool in the summer and warm in the winter, even when wet. One glove complete, and the other nearly finished, she examined the quillwork, a centered rosette in sawtooth embroidery with two contrasting colors of powder-blue and sunflower-yellow. Around the circles was intricate beading in black seed beads and pale rose glass beads.

"Oh, Stone, they are beautiful," she breathed sweetly.

"So you don't get blisters when you're shoveling," he said almost gruffly. Her innocent praise made him a trifle embarrassed, and now he was a little unsure he should have crafted her such a personal gift.

Genuine surprise filled her. "You made them for me?"

"Noelle told me it was your birthday next month." He knew he'd be long gone by then and he wanted her to have something from him, something of him that would burn in her memo-

174

ry every time she looked at them. Something that when it was against her skin, it was as if he were touching her, stroking her, caressing her. Something that would make her curse her damn Gunnar every time he took her into his reedy arms and wish it were him instead. And if for nothing else, to save her pure, satiny skin from being roughened and callused.

"I do not know what to say," she whispered, her eyes misting.

"You don't have to say anything. Just wear them." The thought of her crying over his offering ripped at his gut. Dammit all to blazes, but she was the most vulnerable female he'd ever come across. He took the gloves back, intent on finishing the beading on the remaining one.

"How did you know what size to cut?"

He gave her a knowing gaze, recalling the time he'd held her hand that day with the wild hog. "I remembered," was all he said and turned back to his handiwork.

She stared at him a long moment, watching with fascination as he continued. The veins on the backs of his hands were slightly prominent, and with fingers steady and sure, he strung five jet beads onto his needle and pushed it halfway through the skin so the thread would not be felt on the inside. The effect was a neat row of color called a lazy stitch. He repeated the process, slowly making his way around the rosette and varying the colors from black to pale rose. She noticed that his fingernails were clean and neatly cut short; the whites, small crescents. Not like Gunnar's, which were permanently stained from the soil he worked. Must she always compare them? They were not at all alike, for Gunnar had never given her a gift. Not even an engagement symbol. Stone's simple, sure movements brought a river of pride through her that he would do this for her, that his hands would create such a thing of splendor.

"Where did you learn how to bead?" she queried, moving just a fraction closer to him, telling herself that it was to view his work more closely.

"Jemmy Paquer," he said concentrating, then as an after thought, added, "and a Nez Percé squaw I knew."

Jealousy stabbed through Kristianna as if she were a bead on his needle and she fought it off but to no avail. Images of an Indian maiden floated in the recesses of her mind. She would no doubt have been beautiful and dark-skinned, with a honeyed smile and beckoning, velvet brown eyes. Kristianna had seen such women at the rendezvous, openly inviting the trappers into their tepees.

"That frown of yours is going to be permanent if you don't wipe it off," Stone tossed back with a slight chuckle.

"I was not frowning," she denied.

"Could have fooled me." The thought that she was remotely jealous brought a warm feeling to him. He needn't supply the fact that the Nez Percé woman was the old chief's gray-haired wife.

Kristianna watched him awhile longer, finding herself looking more and more at his full lips rather than the needle in his hand. The shadow of a beard on his square jaw intrigued her. Amidst the stubble were different shades of brown and black. She'd never noticed that before and she came close to reaching out to feel the rough, masculine texture of it.

"If I say boo to you, Kris, you'll be in my lap," he said without looking up.

She abruptly sat ramrod straight. She hadn't realized she'd been leaning so closely over him. "I—I am just interested in your technique."

Stone dropped the near-finished glove onto the edge of the quilt and faced her. "My technique of beading? Or my technique of kissing?"

The boldness of his question sent a bright stain of crimson across her face. Indignant, she scrambled to her feet. "You are so confident of yourself. Maybe I did not like the way you kissed me at all! Maybe I like the way Gunnar kisses me better." She spit the latter out, but was sorry the minute it came out of her mouth, knowing it was a bold-faced lie. Gunnar had never kissed her.

Stone lunged toward her, grabbed her by her slender waist, and yanked her down into the sweet-smelling hay. It rustled under the pressure of their bodies and several crushed blades floated over the side of the loft. She dropped to her knees, their faces only inches apart. Her breathing was ragged from the force Stone had used and by his nearness.

"You're a liar and you know it. You liked my kissing you and your damn Gunnar is much too self-centered to even think about putting his mouth on yours."

The fiery look in Stone's eyes swept her away and she felt as if she were drowning. "Do—do not talk to me about Gunnar . . ." She tried in vain to defend him.

"I'll talk about him all right. Or better yet, his old man. Why did you let him talk to you like that? I saw the look of humiliation in your eyes. Why is it, when you get around that stalk of wheat Gunnar or the like, you back down? Why not defend yourself? You've told me a thing or two."

"You are drunk," she accused.

"That's a weak excuse. Now answer me."

"I do not know." Her voice was mottled with emotions ranging from bewilderment to excitement. "You are confusing me. Before you came, I was never confused. I knew who I was and what I wanted to be. And now you have me thinking strange things all the time. I do not like it."

"Believe it or not, I've been a little confused myself." He was slightly startled by his own words. He'd never expected to tell her that.

"I—I find myself thinking about you. Wanting to . . . to touch you." Hot shame burned on her cheeks.

Her honest admission set fire to his loins. God, did she know how rare she was?

"I know it is wrong and sinful of me, but I cannot help it." She cast her eyes down, unable to meet his stare.

"Then don't help it," he commanded in a sensual whisper. He cupped her chin in his calloused hand and gently tilted it up. "Touch me."

For the briefest of moments, a flash of refusal coursed through her, but it was gone as quickly as it had come. Just this one time she would succumb to the feelings for him that had been haunting her. Shyly, her hands rose to his open calico shirt and she caught the material in her fingers. Her movements were slow and fragile, meshed with an uncertainty that couldn't have aroused him more if she had done it deliberately. The feel of hard, round metal buttons were cool, and she rolled one between her fingertips. The buttons were a warning to her that he was not her kind, but she chose to ignore the signal. Leaving the weave of the fabric, she gingerly slid her hands over his bare torso and felt his burning hot skin under her palms. Slowly, she moved over his flat abdomen, fingering the line of dark hair that guided her upward. She marked each rib with her fingers, moving to the slight rise of his solid chest, tracing the line of dark hair that guided her upward. He was all man. Strong and virile and without an ounce of unwanted flesh.

Stone's ragged breath caught in his chest. Never had he been so affected by a woman's caress. It was as if he'd never been touched by a woman before. Her hands grazed him with a blend of innocence and repressed sensuality. Without realizing it, she was taking him to heaven and hell at the same time. It was with great willpower he kept still, allowing her to roam his body freely, discovering what he was made of.

Kristianna moved up the tendons of his neck and buried her hands in his thick mane of umber hair. Coarse and silky at the same time, it

179

smelled of woodsmoke and clean air. He made no move to stop her as she felt his face as he had felt hers that day in the field. His forehead was smooth and bronze from the sun. She ran her thumbs over his eyebrows from where they were fully arched to the outer part where they tapered, making him look like he was scowling. He had closed his eyes, his lashes, surprisingly as soft and full as her own. She marveled at the strong, straight bone of his nose, so unlike the soft upturn of her own. As she tenderly caressed his face, she ran her fingertips over his full mouth and finally over the stubble of beard that had earlier intrigued her.

"Dammit, woman," Stone moaned. "Do you know what you do to me?" No longer able to restrain himself, he gently, but firmly, pushed her back into the hay. Its crackle was muffled by their weight, sending another light shower over the edge of the haymow.

His body on top of hers was a pleasant weight. Evidence of his desire strained in his denim trousers, and burned into the folds of her skirt and petticoat. He rested on his elbows and caught her face, then he took her mouth. This time, there was an urgency to his kiss as he pressed his lips to hers. She welcomed him, her coaxing lips eager to pleasure him as well. He tasted of mint and tobacco and the hard sweetness of rum. No longer timid, she moved her hands down the broad expanse of his shoulders and back, clutching his waist, and finally feeling the tight muscles of his backside. She quaked in his arms, jolts of passion radiating in every nerve ending of her body.

Stone's hands combed through her hair, absorbing the luxurious texture of the blonde locks and smelling the sweet cinnamon fragrance of her hair soap. He cupped her head in his wide, rough hands, kissing her as if there were no tomorrow. He traced the soft fullness of her lips, then changed the slant of his kiss. His tongue invaded the sweetness of her mouth and he was lost. She was not shocked by his aggressiveness, meeting his tongue with her own, sparring with him, drawing him deeper into her mouth. It was all he could do not to lift her skirt and press himself inside her velvet warmth. He was burning up and needed to be quenched. Without leaving her lips, he slid his hand down her neck and shoulder, kneading her with his fingers. He continued lower until he came to the mound of her firm breast. Moving slowly and artfully, he felt her fullness.

Kristianna's cry was lost on his lips as Stone gently stroked her breast. Her nipple sprang into a hard, tight bud against the thin material of her chemise and blouse. For a long moment, he caressed her over her blouse, kissing her with deep, drowning kisses. Only after she thought she would die if he did not touch her bare skin, did he lean on his elbow and deftly unhook the front of her blouse and part the fabric. With an easy pull, he untied the cotton ribbon that held the front of her *särken* together and pushed it aside. Her bare skin was exposed to the room, and he covered her breast with his hand. She burned from the contact, arching her back to him. The movement brought a groan from Stone who finally left her lips and moved to her earlobes. He traced the inner part of her ear, his breath moist and causing her breasts to pucker into hard pebbles. He worshiped her there for long moments, then ran his tongue across her cheek and then to her neck and the hollow in her collarbone. Lower and lower, he kissed and stroked her creamy satin skin until he at last reached her breast. With burning heat, he took the crest into his mouth and teased the peak with his tongue.

Kristianna felt herself falling into a sensual pool she never thought existed. He sucked on her nipple, causing her to dig her fingernails into his back, wanting, if it were possible, more. The sensitive place between her legs was moist with liquid heat and she instinctively pulled her legs apart, wanting to feel his hardness there.

Stone drank in her sweet-smelling skin, marveling at the feel of her in his mouth. He bathed and stroked her breasts, moving from one to the other, giving them equal attention. He felt as if he were going to burst from wanting her so much. She had gotten to him, and he was nearly powerless to stop. He wanted to yank her skirt and pantalets off and bury himself into that sweet soft glove of her womanhood. The image nearly made him go mad, but at the same time, cast a sobering picture. Jesus, he was no better than an animal. She was a virgin and she was going to marry someone else. He was no good for her. He wasn't even there in earnest. She thought he was honorable, wanting to help her family out, when the truth was, he was using them to hide from Granger. She trusted him and she was innocent. She didn't know what she was doing.

Abruptly, he moved off her and willed himself to sit up. A fine sheen of perspiration covered his brow, and his heart hammered frantically in his chest. He tugged the front of his shirt together, but didn't button it. "I think you'd better go." Stone's voice was hoarse and he didn't do a very good job of masking his emotions. He wanted her more than he had ever wanted a woman and it was tearing him in two.

Kristianna gazed at him with a painful question on her flushed face. Hurt and humiliation welled in her violet-blue eyes, threatening them with moisture. In the stark glow of the light, she became suddenly self-conscious of her nakedness and she moved to cover her bare breasts with her chemise. "I . . . I do not understand."

"No, you don't." Stone combed his fingers through his hair in a jerking motion. "You don't know what you're doing." He could barely look at her with those doe-like eyes on him and bits of hay in her tumbled hair. Her rosy lips were swollen from his kisses.

She sat up, holding back her tears with all her strength. "Is it because I am tall and awkward?"

"God, no!" he croaked. Her body had been made for his, unusually tall, graceful, and all woman.

"Then, what is it?" She retied the ribbon of her chemise and fastened the hooks of her blouse with shaky fingers.

"I'm no good for you. We're not alike. And this is wrong. I shouldn't have—"

"But you did not. I wanted to."

Her frankness almost made him back down and throw caution to the wind. But it was her vulnerability that kept him from doing so. He was a blackguard, a rogue and a bastard and he'd only hurt her. He'd be gone and she'd have nothing but grief and that goddamn Gunnar would shun her.

"I'm sorry."

She didn't realize how hard and rare it was for him to utter those words.

Kristianna's fragile facade was slowly crumbling, and she quickly swiped the gathering of tears at the corners of her eyes. "I am sorry, too." She rummaged to her feet and was backing down the ladder as the first flow of salty drops burned streaks down her cheeks.

Stone listened to her hurried exit from the barn, not bothering to take the lantern with her. The heavy doors rumbled shut, echoing down the walls. The animals nickered and snorted at the sudden disturbance.

"Goddamn!" he cursed under his breath and rammed his fist into the roughened timbers of the loft. A shooting stab jolted through his arm and his knuckles immediately began to redden.

He welcomed the sharp pain, so different from the sweet ecstasy that still seared his heart.

In her room, Kristianna clutched onto her pillow and buried her face into the soft down.

The white cotton coverlet was damp and cool against her warm cheek. She would cry no more. There was nothing more to cry about. She had gone to him and he had rejected her. He didn't care about her. How had she become so blind?

His face and body still danced before her tear-filled eyes. His mouth on hers, his lips on that intimate part of her body that she never expected to be so sensitive. It was as if her body had a will of its own, as if she was harboring a wanton nature deep inside of her that she never knew existed. Gunnar had never affected her in such a way. But Stone did. Why?

She touched her fingertip to her bruised lips, remembering the way he had kissed her. She felt as if she would die from wanting him. The afterglow still lingered inside her, dulling to a throbbing ache. She hugged the pillow tighter, but the softness was no substitute for Stone's rock-hard physique.

But it was more than his solid, muscular body and expert caresses that left her wanting him. It went beyond male and female bonding and touching. She was attracted to the way he walked with sure, easy steps in his moccasins. The way he told stories in that gravelly voice that she now knew came from when he smoked too many cigarettes. He had an easy-going manner and an aura surrounding him that didn't go unnoticed even by Noelle and her mother. He was not afraid to help her with simple things like milk buckets and fetching water. And what surprised her most of all was the way he could create beautiful gloves for her. That he would take such painstaking stitches to make a thing of beauty just for her.

Maybe it was because he was forbidden to her that she was drawn to him all the more. But she doubted it. That reserve about him had tumbled down tonight. It didn't matter to her that he was a woodsman any longer. He was Stone A. Boucher, a man who could make her do things she never dreamed about doing with anyone else.

Then it hit her with a force of such an intense undercurrent that it nearly swept her from her bed.

She was in love with him.

·12·

Stretching out his legs in front of him, Stone swayed the porch swing back and forth with the rounded curve of his heels. The hemp ropes that held the seat and that were strung to the eaves made a hair-raising screech with each rock, but Stone was oblivious to the irritating noise. He brought a rolled cigarette to his lips, drew in a breath burning what was left of the tobacco, then exhaled the smoke in a fine, thin curl. With the flick of his finger, he sent the butt into the yard. It landed in a small circle he'd drawn with an old twig.

Now the ring housed seven butts. If he kept this up much longer, he wouldn't have a voice left. It would be smoked over.

The yard was quiet, save for the low clucks of the chickens and the nickers and tail-swatting sounds coming from Brother Moon, whom he'd let out of the barn and into the corral. The sun was far up in the sky. Straight up. In just another minute or two, he wouldn't have the shade of the house on his back. It would almost be a welcome relief. The heat would snap him out of his self-pity. Damn, was that what he'd been doing? Pitying himself all morning? What for?

Ever since two nights ago in the haymow, he'd been itching with uneasiness and an undefinable feeling. If he were at the rendezvous, he'd have most likely started a fight. Anything to appease his frustration. He was like a bow, being pulled tighter and tighter by a string. He'd better get hold of himself before he snapped.

It all had to do with Kristianna. He cursed himself for going too far with her. What had he been thinking? That was just it, he hadn't thought. He'd only acted out of need and now that he'd tasted the fruit, he wanted the tree. So what was he supposed to do? Make love to her and leave her? He was still enough of a gentleman not to do that to her. But she would have had him; he saw it in her eyes. She wanted him as much as he wanted her.

Her casual indifference to him yesterday had irked him. She acted as if their night in the haymow had not even happened. She'd met him at the breakfast table completely withdrawn. He could tell she'd been crying and it tore at his insides. He wanted more than anything to reach out to her, to fold her into the protective web of his arms, but that would have only made matters worse.

After the meal was finished, he had followed her outside and handed her the gloves. She'd accepted them, offering her quiet thanks and was quickly gone into the forest. At least she'd taken them. Had she refused them, he didn't know what he would have done. He could never have given them to anyone else. They were made just for her, for her long, tapering fingers, her ivory hands, so soft and sweet.

She'd spent all day, from sunup to sundown, in that hot field, working herself ragged. By the time supper came, she was so physically exhausted, his limbs ached for her. She had quietly eaten her meal, barely touching her plate, and was off to her loft before Noelle. He'd watched her the entire time, trying to see what was in her head, what she was thinking. She had put up a facade that was unreadable. Before he had gone to bed, he'd taken a walk to the field to see what she'd done. It amazed him to see a long stretch of cleared land. Damn, but she was the most headstrong woman he'd ever met. What did she hope to accomplish? By the time she'd finished with it, she'd have to start over to weed out the grass and wildflowers again. She was fighting a losing battle, but she'd never admit to defeat. If she had a serviceable plow, she'd be a lot better off. He was no expert, but he'd walked over to assess the useless, wooden plow in the middle of the land. The share was broken down the middle, a clean cut through the blade. It looked bad. She would have a chance if he picked up a shovel and helped her. But as much as he felt for her, he would not do it. It went against everything he stood for.

A blue jay swooped down on the yard, its winged feathers a brilliant sapphire. It landed on the shallow track mark Gunnar's cart wheel had made earlier that morning, then flew off again with a gibberish cry. Stone's eyes rested on the indentation, remembering the smug look on the farmer's face when he'd come to get Kristianna for church. Cocksure of himself, Gunnar had lingered over Kristianna like a honeybee. And Kristianna allowed him full liberties, seemingly enjoying the man's attention.

"I see you are still here, Mr. Boucher," Gunnar had said to him while he pressed his soiled hand onto Kristianna's shoulder. His clothes, though neat, showed signs of wear and it was obvious he wore them to do his plowing. Didn't the man have the sense to dress up for his woman?

"That's right," Stone had drawled, his eyes filled with fury.

"After what my papa told me about your indiscretion in the creek, I thought you would have had the decency to leave. I know Kristianna would never have done such a thing unless she was provoked into it."

Kristianna had seemed more than eager to have Gunnar's arm around her. Stone had wanted nothing more than to pull her free of the farmer and wipe the man's face with his fist, but held himself back.

"Seems to me you could use a little dip in the creek yourself," he had tossed flippantly.

Gunnar's clear blue eyes had darkened to a threatening storm that Stone would gladly have challenged if the Swede had called him out.

Surprisingly, Kristianna had gently rested her fingers on Gunnar's narrow shoulders, urging him to let it go.

Stone had watched them ride off, gritting his teeth and swearing under his breath.

He really had no rights to Kristianna. She belonged to that stalk of wheat. But that thought was like a sharp blade, slicing through his chest. He envisioned her in the oaf's lean arms, kissing him, baring herself for him. The image nearly made him sick. He felt a fierce sense of possession toward her that he shouldn't have felt at all. What was happening to him?

There was no hope of a future for them. She would always be a sodbuster and he a woodsman. The two didn't go together at all. Maybe if they'd met under different circumstances there could have been something for them. For now, the best thing to do was keep his actions cordial toward her. That's what she was trying to do. There would be no more kisses, no more embraces. Even if it sapped all the willpower he had, he'd keep himself in line. He didn't know if he could stop himself next time.

From the distance came the sound of slow hoofbeats over the dry ground. Stone sat at attention and leaned down. He picked up his Hawken from where it rested against the porch post. The Bergendahls weren't due back for hours. Besides, this was the clop of a single animal, not a cart.

Stone slid back in the seat and laid the long rifle over his flat belly and waited. His eyes trained on the short piece of road that ended abruptly in the yard; he would be able to see who ever it was immediately. The rider would be at the disadvantage, having the sun in his eyes.

The hoofbeats became clearer and louder and then Stone saw a lone figure approach. The first thing he noticed was the billowing red plume on a felt slouch hat. The horse was a beautiful sorrel he'd recognize anywhere. A smile cracked his face.

"Where the hell'd you get that hat?" Stone called out, suppressing a laugh.

Jemmy reined his horse to a stop in the middle of the stump-lined road, and at the edge of the yard. "I won it. It's a fine piece of craftsmanship."

"Who says?"

"I do. Wipe that damn grin off your face." He swung his muscular leg over the saddle horn and dismounted. He was decked out in a ruffled, check calico shirt with silver ornaments dangling off the front. His long legs were encased in leggings, the seams fringed with colored loops, feathers, and hawk bells. Securing them at his knees were multicolored sashes. On his feet were neat moccasins, fashioned in the Seneca way.

"You find me okay?" Stone asked, meeting Jemmy halfway and gripping his hand.

"It were easy enough." Jemmy gave Stone's hand a firm squeeze before letting it go. "How you been, partner?"

"Better," Stone replied honestly. "You find out anything from Samuel Granger?"

Jemmy purposefully ignored the question. "Where are them Yellowheads? I didn't expect to ride in here to find you cooling your ass on a porch swing. Or have you been loafin' around here the whole time?"

"There's no work on the Lord's day—or so they tell me. The family's off to church."

"Damn, and I got all slicked up."

"The devil you say," Stone chuckled. "I didn't notice. You should be glad it wasn't Kristianna who greeted you. Looking the way you do now, she'd have shot your backside full of lead thinking you're some kind of savage."

"She full of spit and vinegar?"

"Could say so," Stone mused, more to himself, than to Jemmy. He didn't want to talk about Kristianna. For just a few hours, he wanted to think of something else.

"You competing with the chimney, Boucher?" Jemmy commented, taking notice of the small circle of burnt-out cigarettes.

"Nothing else to do." Stone turned toward the house. "You bring anything to drink?"

"No. I'm drier than a grasshopper on a griddle. You got anything?"

"Raspberry cordial."

Jemmy's dark brown eyes filled with wry amusement. "Raspberry cordial? That's flower water, Boucher. You going soft on me?

"That's all they drink around here."

"It'll do then."

Stone went into the house while Jemmy stayed outside. He gave the homestead a quick look around from where he stood, then took a seat in the porch swing. "You got any eats in there? I'm empty," he called over his shoulder.

Ulla had left Stone a meat dish similar to what he called red flannel hash. It was made with beets, potatoes, onions, and beef. In this case, she'd used what was left of her winter venison. He took down two wooden plates and dished them up. Grabbing the proper utensils, he snatched the raspberry cordial from its spot in the sideboard. It was nearly empty so he didn't bother with glasses, then he went back outside.

"Looks good," Jemmy said as he took his plate.

While they ate, they caught up on news mostly from Jemmy about the rendezvous and a little about Lawrence Taliaferro, the Indian agent. When at last they were finished, Stone uncorked the bottle of raspberry cordial and took a slow drink. He handed it to Jemmy who did likewise.

Jemmy stared out to the yard for a moment, as if he were gathering his words carefully. Before he spoke, a look crossed his finely planed face as if he changed his mind about what he was originally going to say. "I got us four dollars a pound for the beaver."

"Good. You got any of it left?"

Jemmy cast him a suspicious eye. "What the hell's that supposed to mean?"

"Just what I said."

"I got it. Hell, a man nowadays has to work himself to the bone to keep ahead. You know how much they sell a beaver hat for in Saint Lou? Ten dollars."

"I reckon things are changing."

"I reckon."

They were quiet for a long minute, then Jemmy

finally spoke up, "I found Samuel Granger."

"Yeah . . ."

"Your old man's had a heart attack."

Stone's face showed no emotion at the news. "Yeah," he said again.

"God A'mighty, Boucher. Your father's going to die or so Granger tells me. Alexandre wants you to go back to New York so he can see you."

Stone stood up and thrust his thumbs into his waistband. "To hell with him."

Jemmy rose. "You can't carry this hate with you to the orchard yard, brother. It's not right. Maybe you ought to go to Buffalo and see what he wants."

"He wants my hide," Stone spat out. "I'm no different than the beaver or coons. He wants to buy me so he'll have someone to run the New York Fur Company. Well, he can get somebody else. I'm not a city man."

"And you're not the kind of person to turn your back on a dying man."

"Maybe I am." He raked his fingers through his hair and sucked in his breath. He was having trouble knowing who he was lately. He had thought he was happy on the frontier trapping with Jemmy, but things were changing. The beaver and marten were fewer and farther between. They would have to go further west before fall set in, in the hopes of making a living. West, not east. He allowed himself the smallest bit of compassion for his father. He never pictured the old man feeble and broken. What would he look like now? Gray and with his skin slacking? Crippled and bedridden? He remembered a strong, virile, and volatile man whom he thought was powerfully handsome. What had that man become now? For the first time in nine years, a spark of regret flickered inside Stone, but he quickly stamped it out before it had a chance to grow.

Stone took a drink of the sweet liqueur. "I can't leave here until Sixten Bergendahl comes back." That was the truth and it gave him an excuse to stay put. He felt very committed to the family and would not leave them alone. It all revolved around that blasted plow which had sent Sixten Bergendahl to Saint Louis and made Ulla post the notice. In a way, the plow brought him here.

Suddenly an idea hit Stone. Maybe the plow would get him out. Away from Kristianna before . . . before he started thinking of things that could never be. If he could do this one thing . . . it could be his way of helping, without really helping at all. . . .

"I never seen you like this, partner. There something you're not telling me?" The red plume on Jemmy's hat bobbed in the afternoon breeze as he waited for Stone's answer.

"No. But there's something you can tell me."

"What's that?"

"You been up to the fort today?"

"I was on the slope at Monsieur Red's."

"You hear Murphy's hammer and anvil?"

Jemmy ran his bronzed hand over his jaw. "I reckon it was playing in the back of my head. Why?"

Stone was halfway across the yard when he

called over his broad shoulder. "I need you to help me lift something. We're paying the smithy a visit."

From the edge of the farmstead, a rider sat hunched over his horse. The roan was in sore need of attention, its coat dull and dusty, its hocks scarred and dry. The saddle leather and tack were neglected and old, and the man on the animal's back was no better off. His buckskins were ill-kept and greasy with food stains. Anchored at his waist was an old Hudson's Bay knife sheathed in rawhide and around his neck was a string of leather, with a turquoise nugget tied to it.

He watched Stone and Jemmy through watery blue eyes with pupils like two tiny lead dots, then a smile cracked his weathered face.

"I finally trapped you, you bastard," he said between his teeth, then jerked the reins of his tired animal and headed back the way he'd come.

·13·

Kristianna sat next to Gunnar in the cart as they passed by the familiar sights along the dense forest road that marked they were nearly home. She felt tired, more tired than she had been in her entire life. The shoveling of the sod and weeds was taking its toll on her. She'd attacked her task with vigor, anything to keep her away from Stone. Little good it did. All alone in the field, she had plenty of time to think about him. At least she'd made some good progress, though she was paying dearly for it now. Her shoulders ached and her feet were sore. Mostly her right one. She vaguely remembered stepping on the butternut shell that day at the creek, but had pushed the incident from her mind. Maybe she should soak her foot in some vinegar. And she'd ask Mama for some liniment for the rest of her body. There was no time to feel bad. There was too much to do.

If only Papa was home. How much longer would they have to wait for word from him? She was beginning to worry more than a little about him. It seemed as if he'd been gone for months, rather than weeks. When he returned, things could get back to normal. Stone would be gone. Though she'd tried not to dwell on him, she had.

The realization that she loved him had hit her with the force of a tornado and that forced her to have more romantic notions about Gunnar. If they were to have any life together, she had to convince herself it was Gunnar she was going to love for the rest of her years. This morning, she'd purposely touched him, rested her arm on his lean, narrow shoulders. She'd felt none of the excitement she had when she touched Stone's muscular body. Gunnar's form just wasn't solid. He was strong, but not tall, rugged, and brawny. Gunnar was, and would always be, a slender man no matter how hard he worked. Maybe in his later years, he would put on weight, most likely, right in his middle. The vision did little to encourage her.

At least Stone had taken notice of her attentions toward Gunnar. He acted almost . . . jealous? How could he be when he had turned her away? But then, he must feel something for her. He gave her the finished gloves. She had worn them for the first time yesterday. The soft leather was heaven next to her fingers and palms, and she imagined that the feel must be something akin to the bolts of velvet Mr. Bidwell kept behind his glass counter. The delicate beading and intricate quilling made her heart swell and her eyes moist at the edges. It was a good thing she was alone when she had slipped them on. She would have hated for Stone to see her so sentimental. He probably would have laughed at her.

It had been difficult to get through yesterday. To face him after their encounter in the loft. But she had squared her shoulders and pretended it hadn't happened. She was certain he had forgotten all about it, too. Surely, he'd been in that situation before and he would never be one to linger over something that he undoubtedly had experienced tenfold over. She would be civil toward him, nothing more. The opportunity would never arise again where they would be alone like that, so why dwell on it? But the memory of his mouth on hers still burned through her like a torch. . . .

"I see Steurn," Noelle called from behind Kristianna. Noelle and Ulla were sitting in the back of the cart on a bed of straw.

Kristianna looked up and saw Stone, too. He was currying his horse in the corral. The horse's white coat gleamed under the late-afternoon sun, its mane and tail combed out with not a single tangle. She felt that now familiar stirring spring forth inside her. Stone was so powerfully male that it sent her heart into a tailspin whenever she was near him. All her brave words of indifference went astray. She had never seen a more handsome man. Even when he was doing such a simple chore, she was drawn to him. The back of his faded, red shirt was slightly dampened from sweat, and he'd left the top two buttons unfastened to expose a small amount of the dark hair on his chest. He wore the brim of his hat over his eyes in a rakish angle which cast a band of shade across his teal-blue eyes, hiding his thoughts in those magnificent orbs. A slow, radiant heat made its way to her nape as she watched him.

She hadn't felt any giddy emotions in Gunnar's company all day. She had tried though. How she tried! She'd done everything possible to get him to kiss her, wanting to wipe the image of Stone Boucher from her mind. But Gunnar was not interested. He had spent the time after church talking with Hanna Lind's father. She didn't doubt Gunnar wanted to marry her. That was not the problem. Now, she was wondering why, if not for love? There had been only one other reason and it had been in the closed recesses of her mind, and now the door of suspicion was opening just a crack. She hated to even think it, but Gunnar's lack of affection only eased the door open further. Once they were married, his land and her papa's would share a common-law boundary. And when her papa passed on, it would all become Gunnar's. Was he marrying her for her land? The thought was so absurd, she quickly slammed the notion from her head, but it lingered and buzzed around her, nagging.

Stone looked up once, then continued manicuring Brother Moon. He seemed engrossed in what he was doing, and Kristianna was momentarily jealous of the horse's taking his attention.

Gunnar stopped Flicka and Fredrick in the yard. The horses stamped their hoofed feet and lifted their flaxen heads, the prickly hair on their noses twitching as they sniffed at Brother Moon. Gunnar jumped off his seat. He held the split reins in his hands as he moved to the corral post where Stone stood. Gunnar didn't like the fact that the trapper had stayed. He was a little intimidated by him and he could sense that the trapper didn't like him much either. A gnawing feeling hammered at him when he thought of Kristianna and Stone here together, but he brushed it off. Certainly Kristianna would never marry the likes of a woodsman. She was going to marry him, and once they were wed, he would have everything he wanted. But just in case, to show Kristianna he was the better man, Gunnar deliberately snubbed Stone as he tied the horses' reins. "My horses are descendants of Clydesdales, Mr. Boucher. Far superior to your own standard breed," Gunnar remarked snidely.

"I don't give a damn what kind of horse you put your ass on, Gutter," Stone said under his breath, not missing a stroke of his brush on Brother Moon's white coat.

"I heard that!" Gunnar yanked off his *kaskett* and rammed it into the waistband of his home-spun pants. His fine blond hair swayed with the effort, and he stroked it back with a dirt-stained hand. "Apologize for your language in front of the ladies!"

Stone ran his palm along his horse's flank, smoothing the glossy hair. "I wasn't speaking to the ladies."

Kristianna disembarked the cart, slightly favoring her foot as she landed on the ground. "Gunnar, please. I am not offended by anything Mr. Boucher says." Her arms and back sore, she was rather edgy and short-tempered. "Besides, you provoked him."

Intervening, Ulla helped Noelle down. "I think we should all go in and have supper. Gunnar, you are welcome to stay if you wish."

Gunnar narrowed his clear blue eyes at Stone, then looked to Kristianna who couldn't keep her eyes off the mountain man. "*Ja*, I think I will stay today."

The reply caught Kristianna a little off guard. Gunnar usually went right home after seeing them back to the farmstead. Why was he so intent on staying today? Could it be he was jealous of Stone? She had thought he merely disliked him for being a trapper. If he was jealous . . . Well, that cast a different light on the matter. Maybe he did love her after all.

"Kristianna, you sit and visit with Gunnar while Noelle and I cook the meal. You look positively worn."

"*Ja*, Mama," Kristianna agreed without hesitation. She made her way to the porch swing and sat down. Gunnar followed and sat beside her. She wished she could take off her clogs and let the air cool her stockinged feet.

There was an awkward moment of silence when neither of them spoke. Kristianna was remembering another time she sat on this very swing, next to a man who made her skin burn right through her clothes with his contact.

Gunnar's body was warm and smelled of hay and horses and dirt. Pleasant, but not exciting. She looked up to see Stone still grooming his horse. He pretended not to notice them. She tore her eyes from him and willed herself to concentrate on Gunnar. Oddly, she could think of nothing to say. Gunnar was quiet, too.

The creak of the swing ropes as Gunnar idly pushed them with his foot began to grate on her nerves.

"Would you like something cold to drink?" she fairly snapped at him.

He cast her a sideways glance. His long, pointed nose at the moment, seemed a little out of joint at her behavior. *"Ja,"* he huffed, "if it is not too much trouble."

Kristianna disappeared into the house, to return minutes later with glasses of mint tea. Handing Gunnar his, she sat down next to him again. Stone seemed to be taking longer than usual with Brother Moon. Occasionally, he would glance in their direction, but not obviously so. He made a pretense of checking his horse's teeth and eyes. Then he examined all four hooves. He moved to a pile of yellow straw and grabbed a fistful. Lifting one of the horse's legs, he rubbed the straw into the hoof to brush out any dirt he'd missed with the pick. Then he went to the second hoof, threw a brief glance across the yard, then repeated the process.

Creak, creak. Ths swing moved back and forth.

The third hoof was cleaned and an intermittent stare was tossed at the pair.

Creak, creak. Gunnar scooted next to Kristianna and rested his arm on the back of the swing.

The fourth hoof was done and a blatant show of daggers in the teal-blue eyes was aimed at the couple on the swing. The dry straw was crushed in his large hands and floated to the ground in splinters.

Creak, creak. Kristianna stiffened as Gunnar's hand moved off the back of the swing and rested heavily on her shoulder. Rather than feeling a tingle of pleasure, she wanted to shrug his clumsy weight off her. She suffered his touch though, hoping the show of affection would convince Stone Boucher she was indeed going to marry Gunnar Thorson and that Gunnar did love her.

Stone gathered his saddlery and retreated into the barn, slamming the two large doors. Well, let him have a burr under his skin! What was she supposed to do? Push Gunnar off the swing?

An hour later, they all sat at the pine trestle table eating *vitkalssoppa mit frikadeller*, Sunday soup, made from white cabbage simmered in stock, with sausage meat cut on the top. There was goat cheese as well as fresh garden vegetables.

"When is Papa coming home?" Noelle asked, looking up from her bowl. Even the little girl had felt a longing for her father that could no longer be put aside by her fascination over Stone Boucher.

Kristianna met her sister's round, green eyes and smiled softly. "He will be back soon." Then, more seriously, she added, "If we do not hear from him by Midsummer Day, I am going to Saint Louis to find him."

The statement brought a gasp from Ulla, a grunt from Gunnar, and a muted curse from Stone. She had spoken the words without really thinking and it was too late to take them back, but what was wrong with going to Saint Louis? She suddenly became conscious of the fact she'd been toying with the idea for nearly a week. Mama had a little money saved up, enough for steamboat fare. No one had even thought—or if they did, didn't say it—that maybe something had happened to her father. No one in Saint Louis would know how to reach them if there had been an accident. If he needed her, she had to try and find him. And she could do it, too!

"You cannot go to Saint Louis, Kristianna," Ulla informed her, clasping her white hands in front of her. She was nervous about Sixten's absence, too. Her face showed signs of stress. Dark smudges underlined her normally clear eyes, and tiny creases marked her mouth. Her light brown hair, usually tucked neatly underneath her *bindmössan*, frame cap, edged her oval face with small wisps. "You have taken on too much already. Turning over the field was one thing, but Saint Louis is quite another."

"I agree," Gunnar said, putting his two cents in, along with a mouthful of the cabbage soup. "You cannot do it." He talked while chewing. "You are a woman."

"I'm glad you've finally noticed," Stone hissed between straight, clenched teeth. He'd had just about enough of old Gutter. The man was a jackanapes, a rude, arrogant, dirt farmer with the manners of a worm. It had taken all of his self-control not to fling the man from the porch swing when he'd touched Kristianna.

"And what is that supposed to mean?" Gunnar snapped back. "It seems to me you had better quit noticing my fiancée or I will think something of it."

"Maybe you should." Stone's eyes hardened with anger, and he forced himself to sit still. He wanted to lunge across the table and pull the settler from his chair and beat him raw. The hypocrite. It was obvious Kristianna was nothing to him. Why he wanted to marry her, Stone didn't know—yet. Something did not add up and he aimed to find out just what the hell it was.

"Can I go to Saint Louis with you, too?" Noelle asked, ignoring the fact that her mother, Gunnar, and Stone had all been against the idea.

"She's not going," Stone interjected, pointedly staring at Kristianna.

Kristianna felt like a cauldron, ready to boil over. She met Stone's hot gaze with her own. How dare he tell her what to do! And Gunnar, too! "I can do what I want and I will not have either one of you telling me otherwise."

"Kristianna!" Ulla broke in. "What is the matter with you? You have not been yourself for days."

"*Ja*, I have noticed it as well." Gunnar's eyes remained fixed on Stone with malicious intent. "Ever since the man of the traps came."

"And just what the hell have I got to do with

it?" Stone gripped the edge of the table, his knuckles white from the pressure.

Noelle looked back and forth at both men, her wooden spoon clutched tightly in her cherubic fingers. She'd never seen a real fight. Were they fighting over Kristianna? One day, maybe a prince would fight for her.

"You have everything to do with it. I think you have done enough here. It is time you go packing, Mr. Boucher." Gunnar rose from the table and tossed his gingham napkin in his unfinished soup.

Stone scraped his chair back with such force, it nearly toppled.

Kristianna jumped up with Ulla.

Wide-eyed, Noelle almost clapped with anticipation. Would there be a bloody nose? She'd had one once when she tripped and landed into a tree trunk. Mama put a steel spoon under her nose to stop the bleeding.

"We are the ones who hired Mr. Boucher," Kristianna ground out. "We will be the ones to let him go!" She placed her hands on her hips and gave Gunnar a staring down that would have cowered a rattlesnake.

"Please," Ulla interceded, "let us not argue. I have not been myself, either, Gunnar. Sixten's absence has made us all rather jumpy. Please," she said again, "let us remember that today is the Lord's day."

There was a moment of silence as Ulla's words of wisdom were digested. Stone, not believing in a higher spirit, was quiet out of respect for Ulla.

Noelle, slightly disappointed that the grown-ups were not going to go into a battle of fisticuffs, resigned to finishing off her soup.

"Can you come to Midsummer with us, Steurn?" Noelle asked as she spooned her bowl clean.

Still seething with anger, Stone barely heard the child. "What? I don't know. What is it?"

Noelle's eyes grew large with disbelief. "You do not know what Midsummer is? It is nearly as grand as Christmas. And it will be here in four days! We can have candy and dance around the Maypole and everybody for miles will come."

Gunnar waited for Stone's reply with a scowl on his face. Kristianna was more than a little interested herself. She had known Midsummer was coming, but never thought that Stone would be the slightest bit interested in going. Midsummer was a time for young couples. A time to fall in love, to dance around the Maypole with the man you wanted to marry.

"I do not think Mr. Boucher would be welcome," Gunnar finally said, breaking the eggshell thin tension.

Kristianna gasped at her fiancé's rudeness. "I would like him to come." She said the words more as a way of getting back at Gunnar, but once out, she rather liked the idea. Why shouldn't Stone come?

Ulla wrung her hands together, not at all liking the way the men were vying for her daughter's attention. To break some of the hostility, she suggested, "Mr. Boucher, you are more than welcome to attend. Please think it over. But for now, would you grace us with your music playing?"

"He plays the fiddle?" Gunnar snorted.

"*Nej*," Noelle supplied. "He plays a harmonica. It is beautiful. It is shiny and I like to dance to it. Would you like to dance with me, Kristianna?"

Gunnar pulled Kristianna roughly toward him. *"Nej*, she will dance with me while he plays."

Stone clenched his jaw. He wouldn't deny the request, for Ulla's sake. But dammit all, he didn't like the idea of having to play music so Kristianna could dance with another man. Frowning, he reached into his shirt pocket and pulled out his reed. He brought it to his lips, conscious of Kristianna's eyes on him. He made a slow test of the notes by running his tongue along the chambers and blowing softly, the actions bringing the desired blush from Kristianna.

Ulla began clearing the table while Stone played an old ballad. Noelle got up and danced in a circle by herself. Gunnar gruffly took Kristianna's hand and pulled her to him, clasping her in a sloppy embrace. He guided her, moving in a box-like pattern, his clogs heavy on the planked floor. She followed his lead, trying to keep up with his clumsy steps. Her foot was tender and she did all she could not to put her weight on it. That only made her more dependent on Gunnar as she leaned into him, her breasts pressed into his chest. She noticed Stone hit a sharp note at her actions and she doubted it belonged in the song he was playing.

Stone watched Kristianna being subjected to Gunnar's excuse of a dance. The man was an ox. If it were him dancing with her, she'd be gliding on air, their bodies meshed together as one. Not pulling at each other like opposite ends of a magnet. What of this Midsummer? Dancing, Noelle had said.

Gunnar stepped on Kristianna's toe, and though she wore wooden shoes, she winced in pain.

Stone could barely finish the song much less concentrate on the melody. He longed to hold Kristianna in his arms and show her how a real man danced. And he would, dammit all! Before he left this farmstead, he would dance with her at Midsummer, or the devil take him!

When Stone was finished, Noelle clapped. Kristianna's heel bothered her so much, she didn't care to dance anymore. It was just as well Gunnar was a poor dancer, for he tired of it quickly.

"Gunnar, it is getting late. You want to be home before dark, do you not?" Kristianna hoped he took her suggestion, as she wanted to soak her foot in vinegar.

"*Ja*, I do have to tend to the stock." Gunnar shoved his visored hat on his head and bowed politely to Ulla Bergendahl. "My thanks for the meal, Mrs. Bergendahl. It was very good."

"*Tack själv*, Gunnar," she replied.

"Kristianna." Gunnar turned toward her. "I will see you next Sunday." Then he dug his fingers into the curve of her shoulders and pulled her to him and kissed her full on the mouth.

Kristianna didn't have time to react. The kiss was so sudden that she was stunned. Her lids flew open wide and the cry of surprise that escaped her lips was lost on Gunnar's mouth. The kiss was dry and emotionless and over before she knew it.

"Good day," he said nonchalantly as if he'd kissed her every Sunday of the year, then left.

Kristianna stood frozen.

Noelle squealed. "Oh! Gunnar has never done *that* before!"

Ulla tried to make light of the situation. "It is Gunnar's prerogative. He and Kristianna are going to be married."

Stone was rooted to the floor, the recent image of Gunnar and Kristianna slicing through his mind. He was having difficulty controlling his anger. He waited until he heard Gunnar's horses and cart roll down the road, afraid that if he moved now, he'd most likely stomp out the door and kill the man. Never had he been so all-fired consumed with fury. There was no explanation for it. No logical one, that is. The man was entitled to kiss his future wife, but the display burned through him hotter than Hades and he didn't like it one bit.

"I—I think I will go check—check the field." Kristianna thought of the first excuse that filled her head. She had to get out of the room away from all the prying eyes. Instead of being pleased with Gunnar's kiss, she was embarrassed and more than a little agitated. How dare he do such a thing to her? Then she wiped that thought from her mind as quickly as it had come. Well, that is what she'd wanted all afternoon, was it not? And now that he'd finally given her their first kiss, it was disappointing to say the least.

Stone moved in front of the door, blocking her exit. "I don't think you should go out. It's getting dark." He had to say something to keep her from that blasted field. If she found out that . . . Well, what he'd done with Jemmy's help, she'd surely let him have it and he was in no mood for that tonight. Tomorrow would come soon enough and then she'd find out. Hopefully things had worked out at Murphy's.

A frown etched Kristianna's delicate features. "I do not think I like the way you keep trying to boss me around!" she snapped, and reached for the latch string.

Stone's hand closed over hers, stopping her from pulling the door open. "Please," he whispered. "Trust me on this one."

Confusion welled deep inside her at his voice, at his warm hand on her own. Did she always have to melt at his touch? His gravelly voice? She glanced over to her mother to see her feigning casualness and concentrating on her dish-washing.

"All right," she sighed, not wanting to have words with him. "I will not go."

Stone gave her fingertips a light squeeze and released her. "Good." He spoke in a louder tone this time. "Tomorrow, I'd be beholden if you let me hitch up your wagon and go into Snelling."

"Can I come, too?" Noelle asked, eager for a trip to Mr. Bidwell's store.

"Sure. Your mother and Kristianna, too."
Stone's gaze rested unwaveringly on Kristianna.

Ulla looked up from her dishes. "I do not think
I should be far from home with Liv's time so
near. You take Kristianna and Noelle."

Kristianna wanted to protest. She was afraid to
be with Stone alone, but then Noelle would be
coming, as well. Certainly it would be safe with
all three of them together. And besides, it would
give her the opportunity to see if a letter had
come from Papa.

At first light the next morning, Stone had Jake
and Tony hitched up to the wagon, and they were
off to Fort Snelling. The day was clear and bright
with high wispy clouds and a sky that was an
endless azure. Towering green boughs and treetops provided a shaded canopy for their trip and
nature offered them a view of muskrats, deer,
grouse, and various other birds.

Once at the embankment of the fort where the
Mississippi and Minnesota Rivers met, all the
splendor changed. The sky was mottled with
gray, powder-burned puffs of smoke, and the
quiet melody of the forest turned to loud bangs
from rifles and whoops of drunken men.

Stone wound the team up the hill with ease,
not at all threatened by the goings-on. Kristianna
sat next to him on the bench seat, Noelle sandwiched in between them. There were several men
who greeted Stone with teasing words as to his
driving a wagon pulled by oxen, but Stone silenced them quickly by putting his hand on the

butt of his rifle that rested neatly in his lap. The men soon realized that Stone Boucher was a man to be reckoned with.

He guided the animals through the opening of the fort and into the throng. There were soldiers, other wagons, horses, and Indians. People milled about in all directions at none-too-slow a pace.

Kristianna straightened her five-pleated frame cap, holding tightly to the seat with her other hand. "When will this rendezvous be over?" she queried Stone who'd pulled up in front of the Sutler's Store. "I do not think I care to come here again until all of these men are gone."

"I'm one of these men," Stone said as he set the brake, tied the reins about the handle, and jumped down with an easy spring. He made his way toward Kristianna's side of the wagon and held out his arms. "You want me gone, too?"

She refused to reply, accepting his assistance. His hands were snug about her waist, and she felt a warm flush glowing deep within her. He lingered over her for just a brief minute, long enough for her to stare up into his rugged face, and at his tempting mouth. He'd worn his hat again, the brim low and rakish over his eyes. Before she could think further, he was removing his hands from her and lifting Noelle. It was just as well, she said to herself as she brushed the dust from her skirt. She had no business thinking anything about him.

"Do you want to buy some sugar hards, Kristianna?" Noelle asked hopefully. She loved candy and this was her only opportunity to enjoy store-bought sweets. Papa made maple candy in the spring from the melting snow, but this was real candy.

"I'll buy you some, Noelle." Stone reached into his parfleche and produced a small coin. "You buy what you want. Get Kristianna some, too."

"I am too old for candy, Mr. Boucher," she remarked.

He innocently brushed her jaw with his warm fingertips. "You're never too old for sweets, sweet one."

She fairly melted at the endearment and his touch. Why did he have to be so . . . so everything? So strong, so likeable, so masculine, so insightful!

"Do not let her fool you, Steurn. She likes peppermint sticks." Noelle smiled affectionately at her sister.

"I do not," Kristianna denied, but smiled as she was saying it.

"I've got to check on something. You two go into Bidwell's and I'll meet you back here."

Kristianna reached over the buckboard of the wagon and grabbed the baskets of eggs they were to trade with Mr. Bidwell.

"Don't wander," Stone said, looking directly at Kristianna. He thought of Newt Fraeb. Hopefully, he was dead drunk somewhere. "You get done before me, you wait right here."

"We will, Steurn," Noelle assured him, and clasped her sister's hand.

Stone watched them disappear into the store, only for a minute to make sure they were safely inside, then he turned and crossed the yard to the smithy's.

The ring of a hammer on an anvil cried out in a sharp staccato as he neared the brick building. Heat spilled from the double-door opening so intense it rained down on him and captured him in an invisible cloud. Alldredge Murphy, wearing a leather apron with a pocket for horseshoe nails, forged an iron wagon wheel rim. The well-proportioned smithy pumped the leather lung of the bellows, forcing air through the fire bed he was bent over, until the rim was hotter than red hot. Then he whacked the iron with his hammer, sending a spree of sparks to fly around him.

He wore an old coonskin hat to keep his sweat at bay, the striped tail at the nape of his full neck. His face with its muttonchops was ruddy from the intense heat of the fire and coals. His bushy brows were topped with lines of perspiration and a drop of moisture on the tip of his nose looked like a triangle. He absentmindedly wiped it off with the back of his dirty hand.

"Murphy!" Stone called over the noise of the hammer.

Alldredge Murphy inclined his head to his visitor, still holding his tool, the wagon rim cooling to a vivid scarlet on the anvil. "Boucher."

"You able to fix what I asked you?"

The dark-haired blacksmith put down what he was working on. "I did whut I could." He moved to a corner of the room. "It were a good thin' the break were clean. I cain't guarantee how long it'll hold though."

217

Stone followed him and they assessed the Bergendahl plow. The broken share had been taken off, heated, and the iron recast and put back on again. Stone ran his hand along the finished work. There was a slight ripple where the mend was, but other than that, it looked strong as new.

"Thanks, Murphy. It looks good."

Alldredge went to the ceramic jug he kept on his work bench. He uncorked it and took a long drink. Cocking a brow at Stone, he gave him a slow smile. "It's jist water, Boucher. I go without it in here, I'm liable to shrink up from the go'damn heat."

"I didn't say anything."

"Yeah, but you were thinkin' it. I did your plow without a drop of likker in me." He replaced the cork and scratched his head. "Seein's how the job's finished, jist whut the hell you need with a plow, anyway?"

"It's not mine," was all Stone offered and paid the smithy the designated amount they'd agreed on. "Thanks again. Help me load it, will you?"

"Yeah."

After they'd secured it in the wagon, Stone was on his way back to get Kristianna and Noelle. Amidst the sea of activity, he came across George Catlin painting an oil of the fort's interior. This time, he stopped to view the man's work. It was good. The colors were vivid—lots of red—the details fine and clear.

"Afternoon," Catlin said. Well into his fifties, with hollowed cheeks and clear gray eyes, the artist wore a well-scrubbed buckskin tunic with a white shirt underneath it.

"Catlin, isn't it?" Stone inquired. "George Catlin?"

"Yes, I am." He spoke with an Eastern accent. "Who might you be?" His words were enunciated perfectly with no trace of a slur of any kind, unlike the ruffians around him.

"I'm Boucher. Stone Boucher. You from the East?"

"Philadelphia. And you?"

"Buffalo."

"I've been there on several occasions." He continued his study of the interior, dabbing paint on his canvas.

"Nice picture. I've seen you paint Indians mostly."

"Yes, I do. They are a vanishing race."

Stone admired the man's insight. "I agree with you."

"They are men in the simplicity and loftiness of their nature."

Pushing back the brim of his hat, Stone reflected, "I guess you're right." He looked across the yard to see Kristianna standing under the awning of the Sutler's Store. She shaded her line of vision with a slim hand, as if scanning the crowd for someone . . . hopefully him. She was so beautiful. Her braided hair stood out even at a distance, its white blondeness brilliant under the early sun. Her eyes, though undistinguishable at this distance, were wide and searching. She'd worn a simple homespun gray dress that was dull and plain, but to him, looked perfect. It molded her tall, curving figure delicately. Over it was a clean white apron with violets embroidered on the hem's edge; he'd noticed that earlier on their way to the fort. A quiet ache filled him and he wished he could say she was his.

"Catlin," Stone began, rubbing his chin thoughtfully, "you think you could sketch someone without them sitting for you?"

George Catlin raised his head, a wooden pallet in his paint-stained hand. "I could."

Stone's heartbeat sped up. "See that girl on the veranda over there?" He pointed in the direction of Bidwell's.

Catlin tilted his chin. "The one with the white cap on her head?"

"Yes. You sketch her and I'll pay you anything you ask."

A short time later, Stone strode across the crowded yard toward the store. Next to his chest was Kristianna's picture. It rested there between the soft fold of his shirt and the warmth of his skin. True to his word, Catlin caught her image on paper. He'd had to walk past her once to get a close look at her, but Kristianna never noticed. He'd drawn her from the waist up, capturing the details that Stone had supplied so the artist could pencil them lighter and darker, shaded and outlined. Mostly Stone wanted him to mirror her unique violet-and-blue eyes and her dusky-rose lips, even though the sketch was done in black and white. Everything else, Catlin had done on his own. She would be his forever now even when she was someone else's.

"You girls ready to go?" he asked.

Kristianna was caught unaware. She'd been searching the crowd for him, surprised not to find his tall figure. But at the same time, she'd been thinking of her papa. No word yet. She refused to believe the worst and concentrated on Stone. His voice brought a warm rush through her that made her glad she was with him. His calling her a girl didn't bother her at all like the first time he'd done it. It seemed so long ago now, that first day she'd met him there.

"Where's our wagon, Steurn?" Noelle looked past Stone's broad shoulders.

"I've got it over by the blacksmith's." He reached up and took Noelle's hand and lifted her off the porch. "Come on. I've got a surprise for you."

"A surprise?" Noelle grinned from ear to ear, showing the gaping hole of her missing front tooth. It had at last come out the day before. "What is it?"

"You come with me and I'll show you."

He held out his hand for Kristianna, and though she was perfectly able to get down the steep steps by herself, she accepted his help. She would take any opportunity that presented itself to touch him, even if it was for a fleeting moment. His large, calloused hands were rough and strong in her own and all too soon, he released his hold.

As they approached the smithy's, Kristianna could see what was in the back of the wagon before they reached it.

The plow. How in heaven's name did it get

here? And what was it doing here?

She looked into the wagon bed and inspected the share. It wasn't broken anymore. "I do not understand." She ran her fingertip over the surface, noting the repair.

"Jemmy came by yesterday and we brought it here. I had Murphy fix it for you. Now you can send word to your father that he doesn't have to work anymore. He can come home."

Once again, she was amazed by Stone's generosity toward her and her family, and she was nearly at a loss for words of gratitude. "I do not know what to say. Thank you."

Stone could see tears glistening on her thick lashes and it was all he could do not to reach out with his finger, capture one, and bring it to his lips. Without his realizing it, she'd snuck into his heart and woven herself into the deepest recesses. For all of his strength and vigor, he was weak when it came to her. She had but to ask, and he would have done anything for her, but he couldn't be bound to her. He could not let it go further. They were on the verge of going their separate ways and to give into temptation would be the death of them both. Without pondering the impact of his words, he said, "Yeah, well, once he comes home, I can leave."

Her face immediately darkened. Gone were the promise of tears, brushed quickly away by her knuckles. "I see. You did it so you can be rid of us." All of her hopes that he did it because . . . maybe because he cared for her, vanished. He did it for himself, and no one else. "If that is the way you feel about it, you can leave now." She moved to climb onto the wagon bench. "Come along, Noelle."

"But isn't Steurn coming, too?" The child grabbed the side of the seat and pulled herself up.

"Yes, I am," Stone answered gruffly. He thrust his weight upward and bookended Noelle in between them again. "Give me those," he ordered Kristianna who was holding the reins. "I didn't mean it to sound like that."

"I am sure you did, Mr. Boucher. Why else would you have done it?"

His temper clouded his face as he glared at her. "You're putting words in my mouth. I did it so you wouldn't have to break your back over a goddamn shovel! Stubborn as you are, you may as well be digging your own grave out there for all the sense you've got."

Noelle tilted her head up, looking from her sister to Stone. Neither looked at each other, but stared straight ahead as Stone released the brake, set the team in motion, and headed out of the fort.

"So I am foolish. Is that what you think of me?"

"I didn't say that."

"But it is what you think of me. I am just a foolish sodbuster who is stupid and ignorant."

Stone jerked the reins, halting the oxen with a sharp tug. "Now you listen here, *Miss Bergendahl*. I never meant to imply any such thing. If you weren't so damn hellbent on putting words in my mouth, you wouldn't have taken it the wrong way."

Noelle looked up to see two pairs of flared

nostrils over her tiny head. Their faces were awfully close, their noses almost touching. She could feel each of them shaking on either side of her and she thought it kind of funny that Stone was that mad. Then, as they stared into each other's eyes, the shaking turned to trembling. They were leaning toward each other and smashing her in the process. "Are you going to kiss my sister, too, Steurn?"

They abruptly broke apart as if someone had put a firecracker between them. "I am not," Stone denied sharply, but he'd been thinking just that. How could he be hotter-than-a-pistol mad at her one minute and the next, wanting nothing more than to crush his lips over hers.

Kristianna put her hand to the neckline of her dress and pretended to adjust the gray collar. It was a good thing Noelle had spoke up when she did. Yes, she did want him to kiss her! What was the matter with her that she could forget her own sister was sitting right there? They were surrounded by hundreds of people and they were in the midst of an argument. And suddenly she felt herself being pulled to him like a bee to nectar. It was all too confusing to sort out.

"Let's go home." Stone's voice was hoarse and raw from yelling. He didn't know why she got the best of him, and he wasn't sure he wanted to know.

He moved the oxen through the gate and was turning down the hill when he heard his name.

"Boucher! Stop!"

Stone turned in his seat to see a bespectacled man huffing down the embankment. He held down the crown of his beaver stovepipe hat on his gray head, and in his other hand he waved a white handkerchief. Once he reached the wagon, he put the cloth to his brow. "Stone Boucher! I have been looking everywhere for you."

"Sam," Stone mumbled, "it's been a long time."

Samuel Granger removed his wire glasses and wiped his face with his handkerchief in a circular motion. When he was finished, he stuck the fabric into the sleeve of his burgundy waistcoat. Attired in Eastern finery, Granger stood out like a fox in a hen house. "Have you spoken to Jemmy Paquer?" he asked, catching his breath.

"I have."

"Then you know about your father." Samuel nodded briefly to Kristianna and Noelle, not taking the time to introduce himself or to wait until the proper introductions were instigated by Stone.

"I do."

"And you'll be coming back to Buffalo with me?"

"No."

"Good God, Stone, you're father is a very ill man."

Kristianna listened with more than casual interest. She'd never even thought about Stone having a family somewhere.

"He can go to hell."

"Stone!" Kristianna cried. "What an awful thing to say about your papa."

"My father's an awful man." His rugged face held no hint of his thoughts.

"Please, Stone, I beg you to come with me."
"I can't."
Kristianna, forgetting that she was angry with him, touched his sleeve. "Do not let us stand in your way. You must go to him."
"You're not holding me here." He looked Granger squarely in the eyes. "You tell my old man that I'm not for sale."
"But, Stone, you can't mean that," Granger countered.
"I sure as hell do." He slapped the oxen's rumps and the wagon lurched forward. "You're out of your element, Sam. You best watch yourself or you'll get robbed."
Over the ruckus of the rendezvous and the squeak and rumble of the wagon, Samuel Granger called out in the loudest voice he could muster, "I'll be at The Noble Arms in Saint Louis for three weeks on business for the New York Fur Company if you want to send a message!"
His words echoed and were drowned by the peppering of gunfire as he watched the humble wagon wind its way down the curving road.

·14·

Kristianna's neck and shoulders were stiff, and she tilted her head from side to side in an effort to stretch her tired muscles. She sat at the kitchen table, paring and coring apples to make a pie, her concentration constantly veering from the task at hand.

Her thoughts were in a jumble, ever since two days ago at Fort Snelling. So, she thought, cutting an apple into wafer-thin slices, Stone had a father he didn't want to see. That fact was disconcerting for her. She'd never considered the possibility of his having a family somewhere . . . maybe even a wife. She pushed the latter possibility from her mind. But even if he did have a wife, what concern was it of hers? In many ways, she didn't know him at all, but in many others, she knew him intimately.

She couldn't understand why he refused to see his father, especially since the man was ill. Stone was not the kind of man to turn his back on someone. There must be something deep in the recesses of his past, something that had hurt him terribly for him to be so indifferent. She wanted to go to him, to tell him it was all right to leave; and yet at the same time, she dreaded the day when he would. He'd become such a part of her life, she wasn't sure how she would go on living without him.

Kristianna drew her brows down in a soft frown and automatically grabbed another apple from the hickory basket and began the slow, methodical process of peeling it. She tried to push Stone from her thoughts. Forcing her attention on the apple, she tried to pare it without a break in the bright red ribbon of skin. For the briefest of moments, it worked.

She was alone in the house, Ulla and Noelle having gone to visit Liv Thorson. Liv had had the baby girl yesterday. Kristianna had declined to go, telling herself that there were too many things that needed baking for Midsummer tomorrow, that her foot was bothering her too much, but the honest truth was, she wanted to be alone with Stone. She hoped that maybe he would confide in her. Maybe he would trust her enough to tell her what was bothering him. And maybe, maybe he would kiss her again.

She'd sent her best wishes with her mother and watched them ride off earlier that morning.

The day had begun sunny, but now had cooled off with the onslaught of sweeping gray clouds.

The promise of a thunder shower was in the air, and the humidity had risen. Kristianna had removed her full petticoats for some comfort, but dared not remove her stockings. She'd been soaking her foot in vinegar for the past few days and even probed the area with a needle, but could find no trace of any butternut splinter. Since then, she'd applied a small poultice on her heel and it made her feel somewhat more comfortable.

Her own intense desire, more than any healing medicine, convinced her that her foot was getting better. She wanted to dance at Midsummer, and she wanted to dance with Stone. He hadn't said he'd come, but she had the impression that he would. She had sensed that he wanted to dance with her, too. Or was that just another heartfelt desire? No, she doubted it. She wasn't so innocent not to know that he wanted to be with her. He had liked her kissing him, only, maybe, he didn't realize it. Maybe he needed a little more coaxing on her part. Maybe . . .

The black enamel coffeepot on the iron spider sputtered and bubbled, signaling her water was hot. She detached herself from her wayward thoughts for the moment, and got up to brew herself a cup of herbal tea. She'd barely sat back down again, when she heard Stone outside. He was making a fence for the garden to keep the deer out. There was a grating sound as he passed over the wood with a sharp-toothed blade.

She thought she heard the sawing stop and with it, a growing sense of excitement fluttered inside her. Was he going to come into the house?

The expectation left as quickly as it came, for the sound of wood-cutting came to her ears again. She snatched another apple with growing vexation. Perhaps she'd sorted things out all wrong. He really wasn't attracted to her at all. Then why did he have to go and kiss her? To give her a taste of the firm sweetness of his chiseled lips, making her want to test the waters again and again?

She tapped her fingernails on the table with agitation, more at herself for sitting here dreamily thinking of a man who obviously didn't care an iota about her. At that, she huffed and hurled the half-peeled apple across the room, her missile hitting the wall with a sticky thud and bouncing to the floor. It was a childish thing to do, she knew, but it was too late to stop herself once she had released the apple. Intent on cleaning up the mess, she got up.

Stone had come to the house with the purpose of asking Kristianna about the length of the fence he was building. But that was only part of the truth. He had a good sense of what she wanted, and he needed to see her.

He hadn't been able to think of anything else but her lately. She'd filled his head so often, it was as if she lived there. Long after he'd gone to the haymow each night, he'd take out the sketch of her and stare at her image for hours. He had wished she were up there with him, their bodies pressed together for warmth and love.

He'd stopped short of the open doorway just in time to witness her hurl an apple at the wall. He watched Kristianna bend down, offering him an enticing view of her skirted backside to retrieve the bruised apple.

"What's the matter with you?" he asked firmly, crossing over the threshold and bending down next to her. Her eyes were paler than usual with a faint dark shadow underneath the rims. Her complexion was shallow, the pink blush on her cheeks dull. Even flushed and tired, she was still the most tempting woman he'd ever known.

"I am fine," she lied. The truth was, bending down so swiftly, had made her head swim with dizziness. She peered up at Stone to see honest concern washing over his chiseled face. His eyes were bright and filled with a tenderness she didn't think she was imagining. A fine bead of perspiration covered his slashing brows and around his forehead was a leather thong. Fine wisps of curly hair framed his face, and suddenly, she noticed that he was without a shirt. His tanned chest glistened with a moist sheen, and tiny pieces of golden wood shavings were trapped in his dark wiry chest hair.

She averted her eyes from his naked chest, and focused on her papa's leather apron wrapped around Stone's waist. Her heart began that flip-flop beating that occurred whenever she was near him. And to add to her embarrassment of him seeing her nearly faint, a blushing pink stain swept across her face.

"Why did you throw that apple?" he interrogated as he helped her to stand.

She swayed in his arms, first away from him then toward him as if there was an invisible string between them, pulling her into those powerful arms.

"I . . . I do not know." Her knees quivered, turning to jelly. She felt weak and breathless, her every nerve ending focused on the man who held her. His mouth was so tantalizingly close to hers.

Stone's dark brows drew down. "Don't know or won't say?"

Her eyes fastened on his wide, firm lips, and she leaned even closer into his embrace. "I . . . Why did you have to kiss me?" It was spoken aloud before she realized she'd said it.

Her question caught him off guard like a sudden blow, but with it his insides caught on fire. "What?"

She never even looked up into his eyes to see what was registering there after her bold question. And, without thinking of the consequences, or the fact that he might not share her desire, Kristianna lifted herself slightly on her toes, put her arms around his neck, and kissed him soundly on the mouth.

Stone was jolted by the moist warmth of her lips. It took him only a half second to comprehend her intentions and he didn't dwell on the reason—or lack of it—for the remaining fraction of that second. The flowery fragrance of her skin, and the texture of her soft, full lips aroused his ardor. With a low growl, he brought his own passion to the kiss, deepening it, stoking it with the desires he'd kept banked since that night in the loft. His hands traveled down her back, tracing her spine, and finally cupping her bottom, as he so recently wished to, in his large hands. He sucked in his breath as he realized she wasn't wearing anything under her skirt. What was she trying to do to him? He could only stand so much.

Kristianna angled her head to kiss him more deeply, to make his lips mold over her own. In the back of her head, she realized that she *did* hold a power over him. Not to be denied the heat of this newfound discovery, she gently parted his lips with her tongue, to trace it over his straight teeth. She heard his breath catch in his throat as she continued. His mouth opened to hers and he moved to cradle the back of her head with his hands. He wove his fingers into the silky tangle of her hair, drawing her face closer to him, pressing his lips harder onto hers, meeting her tongue with his own, teasing her, dueling with her.

Kristianna felt the hard contours of his bare chest pushing against her own. She marveled at his raw strength and her nipples strained against the thin material of her blouse. She wanted to be closer still to him, to be rid of any clothing between them, to bring back that night in the loft when she had felt him naked against her. She trailed her fingernails over his back, bringing the desired cry from his mouth onto her own. This untried wealth of fervor brought a sensual smile to her lips as she continued to run her hand down to the curve of his waist, all the while teasing him with her kisses.

She left the headiness of his lips momentarily to move her mouth over his square jaw, testing and feeling the rough texture of his beard. As she moved toward his ear, she left a trail of kisses in her wake. Once at the soft lobe, she recalled what he had done to her and tentatively brushed her lips there. He shuddered and she opened her mouth to flick her tongue over that sensitive part of his ear, lightly running the tip of it into the shelled cavern. Stone pressed her against him so tightly, she thought she'd break in two. She returned to his lips, once again receiving the pleasure they brought her.

A sizzling sound invaded her ears, faintly at first so she gave no thought to the intruding grate. She melded against Stone, running her hands up and over his muscled back, to the tops of his shoulders and up to his nape tousled and damp hair. The infernal noise kept on until she could ignore it no longer.

Not breaking the kiss, she eased her eyes open to find her senses slightly returning under a hazy cloud of passion. The sizzling sound came from the covered, black, cast-iron pot on the hearth.

Stone perceived that Kristianna was no longer giving her full attention to the kiss. He opened his eyes to find her staring intently at him. "What?" he spoke against her lips, grazing her flesh as he said it. "What, dammit all?"

"Something is burning."

"I know," he rumbled. He nipped at her lower lip with his teeth, alternately running his tongue over the sweet temptation.

The smell of char began to permeate the room causing Kristianna to jump back. "My corn fritters!"

Stone grasped at the air in front of him which Kristianna had so recently warmed with her body. "Let the blasted things burn! Come here."

Kristianna had turned sharply with the intention of removing the pot from the fire before it brought the house down. The action caused her head to spin like a top and she blindly grasped for the table's edge.

Stone was by her side in an instant. He pulled her back into his arms and smoothed her hair from her brow. This time, he wasn't met with desire in her eyes, but a vague expression that showed her confusion. He took it as a warning that she'd nearly fainted again. His passion somewhat cooled, but still blazing nevertheless, he momentarily admitted defeat to the infernal pot of corn fritters and to Kristianna's health. Locking his fingers onto her slender shoulders, he pushed her gently, but firmly, down onto a chair. "Sit down! I'll get them."

Grateful, she resigned to his command, but cautioned him. "Be careful, the oil is hot." She took the moment to collect herself. Her breath was ragged, her lips swollen, her heart thumping in her chest a hundred beats per minute. What had gotten in to her to make her behave so . . . so unlike herself?

Stone picked up a huck towel and folded it. "I know my way around a kitchen." His smoldering eyes passed over her briefly before he turned to the hearth.

His implication didn't go unnoticed by her as she watched him lift the lid and tilt it over the hot fritters. The steam moisture that had gathered on the underside dripped down into the hot oil causing the grease to splatter from the pan and onto his hand. "Dammit it all to Hades!" he cursed and dropped the lid unceremoniously. It landed on the floor and did a wobbly dance on its rim like a top, then slowly stopped, the thundering noise ebbing away quietly.

Kristianna stood up and turned, more carefully this time, on her good heel, ready to help him. He pivoted and yelled, "Sit down!"

"Quit bossing me!" she warned, but dropped back into the slat-backed chair.

Stone knelt on the floor and picked up the lid with the towel and set it on the table. He reached for the wooden spoon by the hearth.

"No! Not that one. Use the ladle with the holes in it," Kristianna instructed him briskly, trying her best to avoid looking at his fascinating, bare chest. "Hurry up before they all burn," she said more harshly than she had intended. She was still shaken by the tumultuous yearnings that always surfaced in her when she was around him.

He tossed the spoon and used the utensil she ordered him to. Putting the ladle into the pan, he caught one of the smoking fritters floating in the lard and plopped it onto the nearest plate. Kristianna leaned over the table to inspect the fritter. The topside was pale, the bottom black as pitch.

"I will have to start over now," she murmured with a pouting frown.

With the last fritter on the plate, Stone moved the pan from the coals and set it on the empty space of brick by the front of the hearth. He returned to the table, pulled out a chair, and straddled it to face her. "I had that thought in mind, too," he said huskily as he leaned forward to kiss her again.

She peered at him wide-eyed through thick-fringed lashes. "The fritters," she reiterated. "The kiss," it sounded so promiscuous to say it aloud, "was an—an accident," she finally concluded with the lack of a better excuse. The burning pan had been a token distraction, allowing her to put her feelings under control. Her pulse back to normal, she felt embarrassed for succumbing to such inexcusable behavior.

"An accident?" Stone arched a dark brow and gave her a brooding stare. "I highly doubt that. Accidents are unfortunate events resulting from carelessness. I'd say your kissing me was well thought out. Well thought out, indeed."

"I had forgotten how smug you can be, *Mr. Boucher.*" Why, oh why, was she being so tenacious? Why couldn't she just come out and say she'd commandeered the entire thing? That she wanted nothing better than to kiss him again?

"You're playing with fire, sweet one." He crossed his arms over his chest and this time Kristianna noticed that the majority of wood shavings were gone from the dark curls there. Involuntarily, she looked down to see them smattered on the front of her blouse. She immediately blushed and thrust her chin up to meet his heated gaze. "I guess it's my turn now to ask why *you* kissed me?" he mocked in a gravelly tone.

She carelessly flipped a stray lock of hair over her shoulder and took in a deep breath. "I told you, it was an accident."

He frowned and with the heels of his

moccasined feet, scrapped his chair closer toward her. His face was only inches from hers. She could smell the faint scent of Bay Balm and tobacco as she looked into the deep pools of his eyes. She held her breath, waiting for him to say something. And when he did, his words were so unexpected, she felt her heart trip. "Why don't we start being honest?"

"Yes . . ." she barely whispered. "Let us."

"We like kissing each other."

"Yes . . ." She couldn't believe they were openly discussing kissing as if it were an everyday occurrence between them.

"But nothing can come from it."

"No?"

"No." Stone leaned back and raked his hands through his long, thick hair. No? No! God almighty, she'd done it to him again. Made him forget who they were. Dammit all, he was sick and tired of pretending he wasn't attracted to her. What was wrong with kissing her? Everything. Nothing. "You keep forgetting that you're going to marry—" He couldn't bring himself to say the man's name aloud. It brought a bitter taste to his mouth. "You don't go around kissing men whom you're not going to marry."

Kristianna sat stiffly. "A fine time to tell me now after the fact. You did not seem so against it a minute ago."

"I never claimed to be a cavalier."

"What is that?"

"The type of man who," his words held a hint of exasperation as he grappled for the right explanation, "who Noelle would call a knight," he finally said for the lack of a better word.

"Oh." Kristianna straightened, a tiny crease on her smooth forehead. "So what are we to do now?"

Stone moved his hand over his stubbled chin. She was the most inquisitive woman he'd ever met. She truly didn't know the implications their kissing held. She stared at him so beautifully that it was all he could do not to reach out and press his lips to hers again. Her face was flushed, her eyes sparkling, her cheeks a little pale.

"Do?" he echoed in a deep, resonant voice. "We—we . . ." What was he supposed to say?

Kristianna gave him a soft smile. "Maybe if we knew each other better, our situation would take care of itself. We do not really know each other at all." A hundred questions plagued her mind. She wanted to know everything about him before he left, to keep his memory in a special place in her heart. She wanted to know more about where he was from. Why was he a trapper? Why did he hate his father? Did he have any brothers and sisters? She had always been afraid to ask such personal questions, but maybe now was a good time. Mostly, she wanted to know about his father. She sensed that underneath the hostility he carried, he truly cared.

She decided to broach the change of subject subtly. "Stone, what made you become a trapper?"

A slight flash of surprise caught his face in the sunny brilliance of the room. "Why do you ask?"

"I am curious. I have always been a farmer's daughter, but somehow, I doubt you were born a trapper." She tried to make light of her interrogation, coaxing him with a gentle smile.

"There's nothing you need to know, other than what you see in front of you." He easily sidestepped her question with a vague answer. He wasn't sure where she was leading with this. Why did she have to delve into his past? It was something he kept hidden, a secret part of him that was rarely exposed, even to Jemmy. How could he open that chapter of himself to her when he was confused with the present? He never thought he'd be one to allow his emotions to get the best of him, but whenever he was with Kristianna, nothing else seemed to matter. Only her. Maybe their kissing was safer than words. Her sweet voice broke through his thoughts.

"Please," she said softly. "I am interested in you."

Her voice weakened him, and he felt himself relenting. He searched her eyes as they roved over his face, waiting for him to speak. She was so beguiling, he responded without even thinking about it. "I don't like cities much. I've always wanted to explore new places, ever since I was little."

"Tell me," she urged gently. "Tell me about when you were little."

Christ, he hadn't thought about his childhood in years. Once he'd left Buffalo, he'd closed off that part of his life for good. It was not easy for him to talk about. There had been happy times, when his mother was living. But his old man had crushed the life out of her with his ambitions and she'd died when Stone was young. Most of his memories of Elaine had blurred over the years. "There's nothing more," he said tonelessly.

She wouldn't give up so easily. "You can tell me how you got your name. I have often wondered about it."

That was simple enough. "From my mother. Her name was Elaine Stone."

"I think that is nice." Kristianna smiled faintly at him and saw some of his resistance break down. "I am sure she misses you. Do you write to her?"

"She's dead."

A tide of regret washed over Kristianna. She didn't want to upset him. She only meant to free him of the painful burdens that he didn't know needed to be shed. "I am sorry," she whispered respectfully.

"It's all right. I have a new mother. Solange." His voice was tight and sarcastic. "The only problem is, she's more like a sister. She's only six years older than I am. My father remarried when I was ten and Solange was sixteen."

At the mention of his father, Kristianna saw the rage in his face. Sharp lines creased the edges of his clear eyes as he narrowed his lids in disdain. The corners of his full mouth drew into a scowl as if he were remembering . . . what? How much he hated the man! What could possibly have happened? "Tell me about your father." As soon as the words were out, she knew she'd overstepped her bounds.

He lifted his eyes and glared at her. "I don't want to talk about him. Wanting to know about me has nothing to do with him."

241

She leaned forward, closer to him, and rested her fingertips on his forearm. "I cannot imagine that you would dislike someone so much. You are so . . ." She applied light pressure to his warm skin and the contrasting crispness of the hair there. ". . . so easy to be with."

"My old man doesn't think so." He met her eyes and gave her no indication of his true feelings. Her fingers on his arm were like a feathery caress and he knew she was sincere. But he could not dig into his past. Not right now. Not when the most important part of his life was happening at this very moment—being with her. He knew that all the distance he would ever put between them would never be enough. He'd always know she was there, without him. He'd felt himself slowly allowing her to break down his wall of self-retribution since he'd first kissed her that day in the field. She'd been open to him then, exposing all of her inner self to him, allowing him to take what he wanted and asking nothing in return from him. Kristianna's sweet voice broke into his thoughts and he captured her inquisitive face with his eyes.

"Certainly if he is ill, he means to make amends."

As hard as he tried, he could not share her hopefulness; instead, his words were laced with a sardonic edge. "He wants to go to hell with a clear conscience."

She ignored his barb, knowing that he couldn't possibly mean it. He was not that kind of man. He was gentle, strong, and forgiving. She knew it. "Has it been a long time since you have seen

242

him? Was it in that Buffalo place the man—Sam —talked about?"

"Nine years." He pressed his fingertips to his temple as if remembering what course nine years had taken him on. Then, he said, "Buffalo is in New York."

"But after nine years, surely—"

He gave her a stormy glare that threatened her not to speak further of it.

Knowing his temperament, she wisely took the warning and withdrew her hand. He had already told her more than she had hoped, and that was a start. He didn't know it yet, but he needed to talk about his past. And she intended to be the one to help him do it.

"You tell me something." Stone's voice cut through her and she averted her concentration from her own musings to the man before her. "What made you almost faint?"

"W–what?" Her voice suddenly grew a little shaky, and she was reminded of the dull headache she'd had for the last several days.

"Earlier. You nearly dropped to the floor. Why?"

"I . . . There is nothing wrong." She should have known he'd detect her falter; he was the most perceptive person she knew. Discerning or not, she didn't want him knowing her weakness. Better he should think she was perfectly capable of running the farm without his assistance. "It is just the heat of the stove, is all."

"The hell it is. You've been working yourself sick. You're going to put a stop to it, too. No more working in that blasted field."

243

She'd been thinking that same thing, but she'd discontinue on her own terms. Attracted to him as she was, she would now allow him to make her decisions. "I will not!" she shot back. "Things do not get done by sitting back on your heels."

He slowly shook his head, then removed the thong around his forehead. "You are the most damned headstrong woman I've ever met. Don't you know when you're licked? You don't have a prayer in hell of finishing that field. Why do you do it?"

"Because no one else will." There was a slight cut to her remark. She knew good and well he could not help her do it, nor would she ask him to compromise himself. It wasn't that he lacked the brawn for the job, far from it. Inadvertently, she swept her eyes over the hard muscles of his taut body. *Far from it*, she repeated in her head. No, the reasons for him not helping her drew them back to where they started. In opposite corners, fighting over the land once again.

Stone must have sensed her implication because he gave a short, dry laugh. "*Touché.*"

There was a moment of awkward silence before Kristianna spoke. "I do not want to argue with you over things we cannot change." That was the truth. She had felt close to him this afternoon, despite his reluctance. They had shared a quiet understanding, a momentary truce, and she wasn't ready to give that up. She thought of tomorrow. She wanted Stone to see Midsummer with her, to see her heritage and all she stood for. To take part in the raising of the Maypole and dancing, to show him that he could be a part of it with her. She inhaled a wavering breath, gathering courage for her next words. "You have not said if you would come to Midsummer tomorrow. Will you?"

Stone looked into her upturned face, her dusky lips slightly parted. She was fresh and inviting and just looking at her made him want to enfold her in his arms. "Are you asking me?"

"Yes, I am," she replied shyly. It had been difficult enough to say it once, much less twice. He did not answer right away and her pulse grew rapid. She looked up and found his eyes held a glint of mischievousness. "Well? I will not ask again."

"There'll be people there who won't take kindly to my presence, nor I too kindly to them. You're asking for trouble, but I've never been one to turn away from it. Might be my only chance to dance with you."

He had said yes! But with a bitter note. She hastily tossed that last thought to the wind. He had said yes. Yes.

The rickety sound of a buckboard approaching grabbed their attention. Kristianna swiftly made order of the tabletop while Stone stood and crossed over the doorway to wait for Ulla and Noelle to pull up in front of the house. The oxen came to a halt beside the corral, and Stone watched as Noelle bounded over the seat and across the yard barely after Ulla had set the brake handle. She dashed into the house, sweeping past Stone and stopped, her cheeks flushed with excitement.

"I got to hold the baby, Kristianna!" Noelle

was breathless from running and her missing front tooth gave a slight whistle to her words as she spoke. "She is so soft. They named her Paulina after her name day." Noelle rushed on, switching easily from one subject to the next. She picked up a corn fritter, intent on biting into it, but when she saw the bottom black as tar, she dropped it on the plate and as easily as breeze changes directions, she chattered on. "I cannot wait for Midsummer tomorrow. Steurn can come, too. And next year, too."

"Noelle," Kristianna chided, "Stone will not be here next year." The words brought a small lump to her throat that she tried her best to swallow.

"I do not want Steurn to go." Noelle pouted. "I want him to stay right here and be with us. Even when Papa comes home. Then you can have a baby and I can hold it."

Kristianna's cheeks turned a deep crimson. "Noelle!"

"You like babies, do you, Steurn?" the child asked in innocence, not realizing how babies came about. She thought that fairies brought them, but knew enough that you had to have a mama and a papa to make the fairies come.

"I like babies." Stone's voice was deep and reverberating.

Kristianna had lowered her lashes to her lap and was fidgeting with the fold of her apron. She hadn't looked at him when he said that he liked babies and when she lifted her chin, she found Stone's eyes blazing down at her. The look on his engaging face was so intense, she wondered if he weren't thinking the very same thing as Noelle had suggested.

Much later that night, when everyone had retired for the evening, Kristianna hugged the bed covers to her chin. She was feeling much better now. After supper, Stone had gone to the barn and returned with a small pouch containing different herbs. He had inconspicuously pressed them into her hand so her mother wouldn't see. He had spoken softly when he told her to steep them and drink the hot broth. He said they would ease her dizziness and drive the stiffness from her body. The concoction had tasted bitter, but within an hour, her headache was gone, and so was most of the stiffness in her joints. The only thing that was still sore was her foot.

Kristianna rolled over, a sweet fragrance filling her nose as she did so. She smoothed her hand under the feathery down of her pillow and felt for the seven wildflowers she'd place there. It was on Midsummer's Eve that girls placed seven different flowers under their pillow to dream of the man they would marry, hoping that on Midsummer Day, when all the costumes were put on for dancing around the Maypole, they would meet him in the *ringdans*, ring dance, or perhaps in the *langdans*, long dance. Last summer, she'd logically dreamed of Gunnar. Tonight, she would dream of Stone.

Though there was no conceivable way they could ever marry, she wanted to have him. If not forever, then just for one time to see how it was supposed to be with the man you loved. Tomorrow, she was going to make him kiss her and not stop.

She closed her eyes and drifted off to sleep. It wasn't hard at all to dream about Stone. She'd done so since the first time he'd come to her rescue that day at the rendezvous.

· 15 ·

Midsummer Day was held at an open expanse of land that bordered the Mississippi River. Scandinavian settlers for miles around, and from both sides of the expansive water, gathered to celebrate the holiday, which in Sweden, was the longest day of the year when the sun never set. Here in America that fact of nature did not occur, but the festivities were observed and the tradition passed on from generation to generation.

The sky was endless and crystal-clear blue. Along the edge of the large clearing and scattered throughout were elm and hackberry trees. Bright sunlight dappled through the verdant canopies and dotted the colorful wildflowers that were strewn at the mighty rooted feet. Costumed immigrants spread blankets beneath these magnificent trees and brought out wicker baskets and hampers of food to be placed on long tables covered with painstakingly made quilts.

Kristianna sat next to Stone on the buckboard's bench. He drove the team with ease, the sights coming into view. They jostled along the weather-worn road, the wheels lurching, causing Kristianna periodically to bump her arm against his. His heat seeped through his shirt and her thin blouse, bringing with it a pleasant thump to her heart. She was secretly glad for the chance to touch him. Such an innocent graze made her want to melt against him, to absorb all of the warmth she knew he could offer.

She battled her inner turmoil, telling herself she would keep her eyes fixed on the road ahead, but her resolution fell short. With a will of their own, her eyes ventured a slow stare at the trapper beside her. Covering his broad shoulders and enveloping his taut chest, was a red, French calico shirt. The top two buttons at his neck were unfastened and her eyes were drawn to the strong pulse. He'd rolled the sleeves up to his elbows, exposing the dark sprinkling of hair on his tanned arms. He wore a pair of fancy buckskin trousers she'd never seen before. Fully quilled down the outer leg seams and decorated with fine blue-and-black glass beading, they fit him tightly, molding to the shape of his long legs. The bottoms of his skins were tucked into calf-high moccasins that were fringed and beaded as well.

Around his waist was his rawhide parafleche that contained his cigarette makings and other personal things, she knew. He took her breath away like no man had ever done, and no man ever would; she was fiercely proud to be sitting next to him. She only wished she could claim him as her own.

Stone stopped the wagon at a copse of willows and jumped down. He helped first Ulla, then Noelle, to alight over the buckboard. Noelle immediately scampered off, not giving a second thought to helping her mother with the baked goods. Ulla, too nervous and excited to notice her youngest's disappearance, was soon caught up in the goings-on as several gaily dressed ladies made their way toward her, expelling praises over her homeland costume of green brocade.

That left Kristianna on the wagon seat. Alone. Her heart thrummed and she was very conscious of his nearness, to the point of rendering her almost frozen to the spot in anticipation.

She didn't have time to ponder whether he would return to help her down as well. Stone moved around the wagon's side and rested a moccasined foot on the wheel hub. He looked up at her with open appreciation in his magnificent eyes. She met his silent compliment with a soft, and she hoped, inviting smile. She moistened her dry lips with her tongue, not realizing that the nervous action was far more sensual than she could have imagined.

The simple gesture made Stone's insides burn. It took all of the self-control he possessed not to reach out to her and fold her tightly in his arms. Her full lips were soft and shimmering, beckoning him to press his mouth over hers. Perfect. She was a flawless beauty. Her eyes drugged him with their depths. Never had he seen her look more beautiful than she looked today.

A little afraid of his raging emotions, he had held himself in check earlier that morning when he'd first seen her. But the resolve was bitter, leaving him empty, when he secretly wished nothing more than to gaze on her pure loveliness all morning. He didn't want to share her then, and he didn't want to share her now. He had wanted to take her away to a secret place and make slow love to her. Show her what pleasure he could give her and she him, to teach her ecstasy.

And now, her slow smile melted through the core of his heart and the sensation was something he'd never experienced before. It went beyond the physical. Heart-rending hunger came into play and it told him that he wanted more than her body. He wanted her love. It was growing harder and harder to think of leaving her, being away from her.

Stone sighed deeply. He gave in to the urge to rake his eyes over her body, to embed her image into his soul forever. He drank in every detail. So mesmerized by each feature of her face, he ached for her. She'd left her shimmering blonde hair loose, falling freely to her waist, crowned with a garland of wild violets, daisies, and pale pink sweet peas. Several long blue ribbons were attached to the floral headpiece and flowed over the light silky tresses.

Her blouse was white with a loose collar and embroidered with lavender cross-stitching. Around her slender waist was a sort of corset-looking contraption with laces and made from a type of muslin in the same lavender as her blouse trimming. The shade suited her perfectly, mirroring the color of her eyes that were fringed with long, thick lashes. Her skirt was checkered cotton in white, jade, and blue with a flowery cotton print apron over it. He swept his gaze over her, right down to her dark blue stockings and fine leather-topped clogs.

Feeling the intensity of Stone's eyes as he moved his smoldering assessment from the top of her head down to her toes, Kristianna blushed a fragile pink. She felt him on her skin as if he caressed her with his calloused fingers rather than his intense eyes. A little uncertain what to do next, she made a move to step down from the wagon. As she rose, Stone moved forward and outstretched his large hands.

She yielded to his offering embrace easily. His fingers, strong and warm, branded through the thin material of her blouse, causing a skitter of tingles to course around her waist as he grasped her there. With ease, he lifted her over the side and down onto the grassy ground as if she were nothing more than a butterfly. Gunnar, being thin as he was and the same height as she, never seemed to manage the task with an even fluidity of motion. She quickly banished all thoughts of her intended from her mind with a tiny frown. There would be no more comparisons, for there was no comparing fire and water.

"Is something the matter?"

Stone's deep, masculine voice tamed her wayward illusions, pulling her back to the present.

"No. Nothing." She smiled once again at his

chiseled face. His gentle caring made her beating heart ache with love. Why couldn't she feel this way about Gunnar?

Stone took notice of her fine, porcelain skin, somewhat paler than normal and a little flushed. "Are you still feeling dizzy?"

Yes, she was, but not because of any sickness. "No. The herbs made me feel better. I drank some more this morning."

Stone wanted to stroke her satiny cheek to test for himself if she had any signs of fever, but he held back. He was reluctant to remove his hands from her waist. He'd unrelentingly endured the sweet torture of her arm grazing against his throughout the journey there, and now, he had had a logical reason to take her into his arms. He lingered a moment, his fingers splaying her waist, drawing her closer, feeling the blazing heat of her skin beneath her clothing. Oblivious to his surroundings, he stepped a fraction closer, bringing her full breasts dangerously close to his chest. She was intoxicating with the fragrance of wildflowers.

He peered down on her upturned face and plainly saw her soft lips parted. It would be so easy to brush that pliable mouth with his own . . .

"Ho, man of the traps." Gunnar's accented sarcasm cut through the electrically charged air, dousing their intimate moment as if they'd been brandished with a bucket of ice water. "I did not think you would have the audacity to show yourself here."

Anger, swift and hard, swept through

Kristianna at Gunnar's intrusion. Her breathing labored in her chest as she tried to calm her nerve endings—each one focused on Stone. She should have been distressed to have her fiancé find her in another man's arms, instead, it was all she could do not to hurl an oath at him to go away, to leave them alone. Then a revelation sprang into life before she had a chance to analyze or even quell it. Had she come to love Stone so completely that she didn't care who knew it?

Stone did not release his hold. He eased one arm around her waist, and with his free hand, he automatically drew down the angle of his black hat with his forefinger. This afforded Gunnar no glimpse of his eyes and veiled the desire he knew blazed there.

The tilt of the brim offered him an unobstructed view of the farmer and Stone stifled a laugh. The man was dressed foppishly in yellow knee breeches with tassels, a blue, single-breasted vest of homespun linen, and over it, a black jacket with hooks.

As Gunnar continued to clop forward in his heavy wooden shoes, Stone stared at his hat. It was wide-brimmed with a straw band, and five small black woolen balls dangled from its edge. As Gunnar spoke his next words with vigor, the balls bounced under the brim in a riotous chorus, causing a slightly amused tilt to the corner of Stone's mouth.

"What have you, Kristianna? Taken leave of your senses? The man is not welcome here."

Kristianna straightened and squared her shoulders, feeling the weight of Stone's hand firmly at the small of her back, unflinching and steady. She tried to disguise her annoyance, but to no avail. "I invited him, and he is welcome in my company. If you prefer not to abide by my wishes, then you can go off without me." Had she really said that to Gunnar? She would have never dreamed of speaking out against him. This new attitude toward Gunnar brought a pleasant bit of confidence to her demeanor.

Gunnar was not quite sure what to do with the ultimatum Kristianna gave him. His line of vision narrowed fixedly on the trapper standing not a hair's breath from his fiancée. "Remove your hands from her." Then, seeing Kristianna's face redden with embarrassed anger, he hastily continued, a slight waver to his words. "If you insist on his presence, I will heed it. Though I will not tolerate his hands on you. Remember, *I*"—he brought a lanky finger to his chest and pointed— *"am your intended."*

Stone remained by Kristianna's side, and she felt the muscles in his arm tense as he drew himself from her. She knew he was boiling with fury and was doing his best not to unleash his temper at Gunnar for her sake and for the sake of causing undue attention to themselves. And for the simple reason that Gunnar had every right to insist Stone not touch her.

Nostrils flared, Stone moved around Kristianna. He reached under the seat of the buckboard and gripped a cool shaft of metal, then turned around. The heavy weight of his ornate Hawken rested in his hand at the stock, the barrel pointed casually toward the sky a fraction of an inch from Gunnar's ridiculous hat.

Gunnar's blue eyes widened with terror, and he blurted out in a stifled cough, "You have no need to come here seeking bloodshed, Mr. Boucher—"

"I came to dance with her," Stone drawled as if he hadn't an inkling as to what made the man quake in his boots. He'd had about all he could take of the stripling's cocky insolence. But under the circumstances, this time, Gunnar's demand had not been unfounded. It galled Stone far more than he cared to admit, that for once the farmer was right. Had Kristianna been his and he'd caught Gunnar with his arms around her, he would have rended him through with buckshot.

Gunnar appeared to recover quickly. His ashen face shaded to the hue of a ripe beet. He let the bold insinuation Stone offered go untouched. Surely, Kristianna would not dance with the man . . . would she?

Kristianna took no notice of Gunnar's blustering composure. Stone wanted to dance with her! She suddenly felt giddy, carefree, and girlish. Her heart leaped with anticipation over spending the festive day with him, of being in his arms again. The elation was short-lived. There was Gunnar to consider. Gunnar, from whom she'd have to tolerate a dance or two. More and more lately, the idea of spending time with Gunnar was not something she looked forward to. If anything, he'd grated on her nerves so fiercely it was all she could do to abide his presence, much less his touch.

Ulla came over to them, her face flushed with

nervous exhilaration. Her light brown hair was covered by a lace headrail with a fancy embroidered cap on top. She absentmindedly dashed a strand of hair that wasn't even there from her temple, then busily sorted through the various baskets in the back of the wagon. She paused momentarily, as if seeing Gunnar for the first time. "*God dag*, Gunnar!" Snatching a wicker hamper covered with a fine linen cloth, she exclaimed, "*Uffda*, but I do wish Sixten were here today to see it all!"

"*Ja*, Mama," Kristianna agreed, momentarily pushing away thoughts of dancing. A fleeting smile of melancholy traced her lips. She had hoped Papa would have been back for Midsummer Day as well. Now, more than ever, she was beginning to worry that something had happened to him. Her idle threat to go to Saint Louis was fast becoming a promise.

"You three go along and have fun." Ulla shooed them with an emphatic swish of her hand. "If you see Noelle, tell her to come help me. The child is such a wandering thing . . ." Her sentence trailed and she was preoccupied by another basket of foodstuffs.

The sound of *Svenska violiner*, Swedish violins, drifted to them on the scant afternoon breeze. The song brought memories to Kristianna of past Midsummer Days spent with Papa and happily with Gunnar. This day would, in years to come, bring forth images of a tall stranger who was hers for a whisper of a fervent moment. She pushed the future from her mind, vowing to concentrate on the present and what bliss the day would offer.

"You have no need to bring your weapon with you, Mr. Boucher." Gunnar's voice vented a little of his ire. "I can assure you, we are all quite tame."

Stone replaced his J & S Hawken under the front seat and draped a blanket over it. "Wasn't intending on carrying it with me. Just wanted you to see how it gleamed under the sun." There was heavy sarcasm in his words.

Gunnar's concave cheeks mottled, but he remained silent.

The trio set out to take in the festivities, and the numerous settlers who had gathered for the holiday took great interest in them as they strode by. Their trained eyes raked past Gunnar and Kristianna to fasten on Stone, and once they were out of hearing distance, disapproving whispers buzzed like wildfire.

Kristianna sidled a glance at Stone to see he'd pushed down his hat again. She sensed he was aware of the settlers interest in him. He did, after all, stick out like a carrot in a barrel of parsnips. Tall as he was, he naturally attracted attention, but in this case, it went beyond his extraordinary height. He just didn't look Scandinavian. Not wearing a traditional costume—though the garments he wore were much more preferable to Kristianna—he was being outright shunned. The fact shamed her to the core that her own kind could be so cruel.

Stone did feel the underlying hostility toward him. Well, what had he expected? He knew from the start he would not be accepted. And why should he be? Had the tables been turned, he doubted he would have given a cordial reception even to the most honorable farmer. He had nothing in common with these people, and with the exception of the Bergendahls, he didn't even like them. He felt as out of place as an Indian in full regalia would be at a fancy New York restaurant. He tolerated the blatant stares in his direction for one reason, and one reason only: Kristianna. Her beguiling innocence had beckoned him there.

It seemed natural for him to want to reach down and take up her hand, to weave his fingers lazily through hers, and spend the afternoon together as if they had all the time in the world. But they did not. And he did not reach out. He couldn't go on pretending there was a chance for them. His hand was forced to endure emptiness, a void that left him oddly cold and lonely.

He glimpsed her profile, etched with determination, as if she was daring anyone to question her walking with him. Her steps were intent, her chin high, and there was a defiant look in her eyes.

Unexpectedly, Gunnar stretched out his rangy hand and clumsily clasped Kristianna's. Stone's stomach clenched at the affectionate display that he was sure was more for his benefit than Kristianna's. He was fast losing his will to give her to the farmer. The logical reasons were dissolving by the minute.

The gesture was so sudden, Kristianna was taken aback. Gunnar's fingers were moist and clammy and not at all heart-rending. She wanted to pull away, but Gunnar squeezed and kneaded her hand, holding it possessively. She felt as if she were a lump of dough in his palm. He'd never shown her the slightest bit of affection in public, nor much in private for that matter. There had been a time she would have welcomed his attempt to court her, but now, she was trying her valiant best to abide his attempts.

The tantalizing aromas and colorful platters on the food tables caused them to stop for a closer inspection. Thankful for the opportunity to mill around the table for a moment, Kristianna slipped from Gunnar's grasp. She pointed out the various items for Stone to sample, such as the salt goose, cheeses, smoked meats, game, sausages, bacon, and fish. There were various vegetables and fruits, and watermelons. And even trays of golden honeycombs dripping with sweet nectar, and beside them, fresh-baked loaves of bread. Then she labeled the ethnic dishes, tutoring him first with the Swedish name, then the English translation. She translated *veteskorpor* to sweet biscuits; *surstek* to pickled joint of beef cooked in ale; and *knackebröd* to dill and fennel seed cakes.

"And this is," Gunnar mocked sourly, "*loytens alkavit*, potato spirits. It is strong and is not tolerated well by the body. A man has to gradually build up to it." Gunnar poured himself a liberal dose of the clear alcohol into a decorative stein. "I, of course, have the stomach for it." He raised one light blond brow and half-smiled. "Perhaps you would be better off with a glass of lemonade."

Stone nearly laughed. Gunnar's ploy showed through him like water pouring from a sieve; the alcohol could be no worse than Jemmy's Taos lightning. "Pour me one, Gutter."

"Gunnar," he corrected, grinding his teeth. "It is not wise—"

"Pour it."

"If you wish." Gunnar filled another tankard with the exact amount in his own.

Kristianna nibbled on a piece of goat cheese, not at all tasting the sharp flavor. She had thought this would be a calm distraction for the two. She watched Gunnar press the mug into Stone's strong hands.

"*Skål*," Gunnar toasted, his blue eyes devilishly smiling over the brim of the stein as he imbibed a portion of the spirits.

Stone brought the tankard to his lips and took a draught. The alcohol was nothing more than backwoods firewater; it went down smooth as silk and burned a hole in the pit of your stomach. He'd drank enough of this kind of liquor for it not to faze him. He gulped down not one, not two, but three long swallows before he lowered the mug and licked his lower lip with his tongue. An idea formed and Stone forced himself to cough, and even give a good wheeze. "Goddamn, Gutter. You're right. This stuff is liable to brand my insides."

A flash of victory settled over Gunnar's pale features. "I knew you could not stomach it. You have to build up to it—gradually." He emphasized the latter, though it was obvious the meaning behind it was anything but sincere.

"I don't know. I think I could get used to it mighty quick." Stone brought the tankard to his mouth and practically drained the contents in one gulp.

Gunnar nearly choked with glee. "If you say so. I will pour you another."

Somehow, Kristianna doubted the earnestness of Stone's words. She knew Gunnar was trying to trick him and she had the feeling that Stone was the one who was tricking Gunnar. She'd seen Stone drink a rum bottle empty and still be able to hold a needle and beads. A flash of white petticoats, blue dress, and a green apron skipped toward Kristianna, and she automatically reached out her hand. Noelle's cherubic face looked up as she halted under her big sister's fingers. "Mama is looking for you, little one."

Noelle frowned, her rosebud mouth stained by the sticky leavings of peppermint sweet hards. Her cap was askew on her curly hair, the ribbons trailing over her narrow shoulders. "I already saw her and helped." She moved her eyes up, way up, to Stone and gave him a beaming smile. "Hello, Steurn. Are you going to enter the shooting contest? I know you could win. Remember how you killed that wild hog—" She stopped short and clasped her tiny hand over her mouth. Gunnar could not be trusted with such privileged information.

"What is this about a wild hog?" Gunnar frowned.

"Never you mind, Gunnar Thorson." Noelle flippantly stuck her tongue out at him, displaying a very candy-reddened tongue at that.

"Noelle!" Kristianna chided. "Say you are sorry to Gunnar."

The child grew stubborn, finally grating out a mumbled apology. Then she smiled at Stone. "Are you going to enter?"

"Don't know if anyone will let me." That was the truth, though he wasn't sure he wanted to display his rifleman skills to a group of farmers. As needled as he was over Gunnar's pestering, he was liable to take a pot shot at the man.

"I do not think so, either," Gunnar berated quickly.

"Then you must play your mouthpiece while they raise the Maypole," Noelle insisted.

Stone stood at ease, the handle of the tankard held easily in his tanned fingers. "I reckon I could do that. That is if Gunnar"—he gave the man a mockly cordial, questioning look—"doesn't have any objections."

"*Nej*. On the contrary, I can accompany you on the fiddle." Gunnar had no doubt he was the better man musically. He'd heard the trapper play, and though Stone could carry a tune, Gunnar's talent for the fiddle was well known.

At a slight rise behind them, and at the edge of the clearing, the Maypole was being hoisted. Adorned with green foliage garlands and wildflowers, the pole was set in place; the top, crossbarred and decorated with vines and birch twigs, gave off a woodsy fragrance.

Gunnar left them, returning a moment later with a finely crafted *Svenska violin*. The violin, next to his draft horses, was his most prized possession. A Stradivarius, it was crafted of the finest maple and spruce. He brought the instrument to his chin, a deep line of concentration on his face. Cocking his ear, he passed the bow lightly over the four strings to see how the pitch sounded. He made a show of turning the tuning pegs at the head of his violin, tightening one string to raise the pitch, and loosening another to lower the pitch. After long minutes, he was satisfied and gave himself a confident nod. "Can you follow my lead, Mr. Boucher?"

Stone reached into his parafleche and drew out his shiny harmonica. "I can."

Gunnar settled the violin on his chin once again and struck up a Swedish folk tune. His thin fingers mastered the bar as his bow swept across the strings. He bobbed his head with the music, and the woolen balls on his hat jiggled under the rim. When he'd played the chorus through, he stopped and gave Stone a challenging smirk. While he waited, he poured himself another glass of spirits and daringly drained it with a slight shudder.

Stone, who had always played by ear, swallowed and brought his harmonica to his lips. He closed his eyes, tapped his moccasined foot, and repeated Gunnar's melody. The chords were a little off in places, but for the most part, Stone's rendition was every bit as good as Gunnar's. As he played, a small crowd had gathered to observe the pair.

Noelle brought her tiny hands together and clapped. Kristianna felt her insides go warm as Stone finished. She felt such a fierce pride toward him that it almost frightened her. Why hadn't she ever felt that way about Gunnar? Stone, with his tall, muscular form brought forth a rush of heated sparkles through her and she wanted to embrace him and kiss him leisurely on the lips, and brand him as her own.

The two dueled with several more songs before Stone took the lead in a feisty ballad. This time, it was Gunnar who had to follow along. Noelle jumped up and down as Stone wavered his tanned fingers over the edge of his reed and commandeered the notes. Gunnar, his temple sheened with perspiration, tripped over the tune, his bow taut in his fingers. He sawed furiously, his head shaking, his arm dipping. Finally, his bow could keep up no longer and the tightly strung horsehairs slowly frayed until one by one they snapped and grated to a sour note.

The contingent of onlookers, though they had no true affection for the outsider, clapped nonetheless at Stone's fine display. Gunnar relaxed his violin and mopped his dripping brow with the back of his jacket sleeve. Several men patted him on the back, but it did little to appease Gunnar's sense of dignity. He'd been bested, again.

Noelle ran to Stone and hugged his middle. She smiled up at him as he lowered his harmonica and pulled her up in his arms. She planted a big sticky kiss on his cheek. "I love you, Steurn!"

Kristianna's heart raced with an unsteady beat of joy in her chest. Tears threatened the corners of her eyes and she blinked them back with a quick flutter of her thick lashes. Oh, how she envied Noelle's innocent endearment! *She* loved

Stone, too, and she wanted to shout it to everyone. She had never felt such a strong emotion so threatening to everything she knew and was. At this moment, she cared not who she was, or what she would give up by loving Stone. She only knew that this power he held over her ran deep and was fiery, and at the same time, so fragile, it was barely a tangible thread between them. She loved him. She loved him so dearly she ached with the knowledge. How could she let him go?

The sun began its twilight descent, and the sky was bathed in a myriad of bright shades in scarlet and gold. Not a single cloud showed above the treetops that were slowly being silhouetted in front of the brilliant sunset.

Tarred torches were lit, and the glowing orbs of flames signaled it was time for the dancing to begin. One by one, couples formed, and entwined their hands and bowed their heads closely together to whisper endearments. It was a time to stroll arm and arm with the one you loved.

Kristianna automatically moved toward Stone, but a heavy hand on her shoulder caused her to turn with a start. Gunnar had put away his violin and his face was edged with a sullen frown. The fine, reddish-blond hair around his face was damp as were the creases on either side of his nose. "We dance the ring dance, Kristianna."

Before she could protest, Gunnar had trapped her into a clumsy embrace and was whirling her toward the Maypole. Her face was inches from his and she smelled the alcohol on his breath, mingled with the herring he'd eaten. The combination made her stomach churn. Only after he'd maneuvered her to the center of the dancers, did he drop his arms from her waist and join his hand to hers again. Numerous dancers made a hand-held circle around the Maypole, and Kristianna numbly took hold of the young man's hand next to her, not even taking notice of his face. All of her concentration was on Gunnar and the uncomfortable clamminess of his fingers on her own.

The music started, and he squeezed her palm tighter and tighter as the circle moved to the left to nimbly stepped movements of clogged feet. She did her best to look over her shoulder to search for Stone. The place where he and Gunnar had played was vacant. The dancers moved the circle faster, the music a lively celebration of age-old folk tunes. She scanned the onlookers once again. They whirled past in various hues of festive colors—blue, green, yellow, and red. Red. Stone's shirt was red. But before she could distinguish his face, she was spun away. Feeling somewhat lightheaded, she momentarily concentrated on the intricate dance steps. When she thought her equilibrium was returning, she looked up once more. Her eyes focused on the spot under an elm tree where she'd seen Stone. For a brief flash she was rewarded by the outline of his dark hat, a slight glimpse of his face and his French calico shirt.

She wasn't able to make out his features but sensed by the way he stood, that he was ill at ease. He stood ramrod straight, and his hat was pushed off his forehead to allow him full view of the dancing. Not paying attention to the music, she faltered and Gunnar practically yanked her arm from its socket to prevent her from falling. She winced and nearly jerked her hand free of his.

The *ringdans* finally ended, and resounding applause and merriment followed it. Couples paired off for more intimate dances as the melody of accordions and violins lightly and sweetly took up the tune of the *långdans*.

Kristianna snapped her hand free of Gunnar's and tried to catch her breath. He gave her a bold stare. "What is this, Kristianna? You used to like dancing the long dance with me."

"I am tired." She brushed off his inquiry with an answer that wasn't completely far from the truth.

"He is over there."

"W–what?"

"The man of the traps." Gunnar's voice was bitter. "I am not blind."

"I do not know what you are talking about." Her heart hammered in her chest as she denied his accusation, and was steered in the opposite direction from where she wanted to go.

Gunnar had manuevered them to the refreshment tables where he poured himself another tankard of the strong potato spirits. "Whatever you think of me—which I am beginning to wonder just what that may be—I am not a fool."

"I—I never said you were, and I did not mean to imply it."

269

The exertion from dancing made Gunnar's face ruddy. "Are you going to marry me, Kristianna?"

The question startled her and she was at a loss of words. "I . . ."

"Let's dance, Kristianna." Stone's gravelly voice broke into the answer she would have given Gunnar.

Kristianna found Stone's presence both unnerving and welcome. Given the jumble her emotions were in at the moment, she wasn't sure what she would have said to Gunnar. Stone's warm hand slipped over hers and he gently, but firmly, guided her toward the dancing arena. She gave Gunnar a brief look over her shoulder.

"If you go, Kristianna, do not come back to me." He raised his mug to his lips and drained it with a sharp jerk of his head. "Ever," he clarified with finality.

He was angry. Very angry. Kristianna had never seen Gunnar so angry. Suddenly, she felt a small twinge of guilt, but that guilt dissipated the moment Stone drew her into his arms and pressed his solid body against hers. She looked up into his eyes to see the silent question there. He was giving her the chance to go back. Back to Gunnar. There were a dozen reasons why she should, but only one reason why she should not. And that outweighed the lot. She loved Stone Boucher with all her heart.

She sighed and it seemed as if all of the tension flowed from her limbs. For tonight, she would put her life in Stone's hands and worry about tomorrow with the rising sun.

Stone was an excellent dancer, sure and steady on his feet, commanding, and exuding an air of confidence. Kristianna felt herself relax and melt against him. His chest was very close to her cheek, and when she looked at his open collar and the broad expanse of dark curly hair, it was all she could do not to lay her head there and listen to his heartbeat. Her own was erratic and unsteady.

She was afraid to raise her eyes to his, afraid he would see the power he held over her, and the undeniable tide of love there, too.

His large hands moved over her back and brought a light rush of warmth through her body. She felt giddy and confused at the same time, and that she couldn't press herself close enough to him. As it was, they danced closer than propriety allowed, but she didn't care. She loved the feel of his hardened muscles against her breasts and the heavy pressure of his sinewy legs against her thigh.

A blush found its way over her delicate face and she glanced down so he couldn't see it.

Stone's masculine voice broke through the moment. "Don't look at my feet," he commanded in a hushed tone.

"Where shall I look?" she whispered, meeting his bold stare. His eyes were compelling and she was lost in their wonderful depths.

"Look at me."

There was a slight glistening in her eyes as she did as he bade. A wayward lock of hair had made its way from under the brim of his hat to rest above his slashing brows and she had the strong-

271

est urge to touch it, to run her fingertip down over his nose and over his lips, caressing his face with her hands as she had done only once before.

"I like to look at you," she confided in a soft murmur.

Stone felt a shock of desire inside him, strong enough to send the air from his lungs. Her breath caressed his ear in innocent sensuality and sent a shooting river of fire through him to his loins that he tried his damnedest to repress. She smelled so sweetly of her cinnamon hair soap and fragrant flowers that he clenched down hard on his jaw to keep himself from turning his head and brushing more than a chaste kiss on her lips.

A strand of her hair fell over her shoulder and as she moved to look at him, it touched his chin lightly. He drew his hand up her back and wove his fingers into the depths of the silky cloud, toying with the blue ribbons of her floral garland. Her lips were parted and her cheeks flushed a soft carnation-pink. Being as tall as she was, she fit easily into his arms; her breasts burned him through the thin material of his shirt, branding him. Her hips made sporadic contact with his and he felt his loins tightening almost to the point of unbearable pain. He wished he were alone with her.

The song ended and Kristianna reluctantly backed away from him. Her legs felt as if they were made of liquid gold and she wanted nothing more than to abandon herself to Stone, to take him by the hand and lead him away . . . away from everyone . . . and kiss him.

She looked up and saw the intensity in Stone's eyes.

He wanted her.

Her pulse grew rapid and quivered. She glanced briefly to where they had left Gunnar standing at the refreshment table. He was coming toward them with a scowl set on his face. The potato spirits had obviously given him the boost to call Stone out and demand she return to him.

Kristianna licked her dry lips, her mind racing. Hastily, she snatched up Stone's strong, warm hand. "Come with me," she beckoned. Before he could react, she led him through the crowd, out of Gunnar's view and away. Away from prying eyes and to the inviting sweet fragrance of the woods where they could be alone.

·16·

Bright masses of light illuminated large portions of the heavens, and in other directions, nearly the entire expanse of the sky. The rays appeared to shoot upward, producing variegated tints among which the most beautiful pink and green and various indescribable shades were prominent. They constantly changed color, as did the form of the rays.

Kristianna led them, leaving the festive clearing behind. The folk music drowned to a faint hum, as she made her way toward the forest that was silhouetted against the backdrop of flickering light. Stone felt a queer tightening in his chest, knowing he should stop them from going farther —for surely this would do her reputation irreparable damage—but at the same time, blood pumped through his body with lightning speed.

The northern lights acted as a guide for Kristianna, and she kept walking toward them, their wavy dance a beacon. She had never ventured alone in the forest at night for fear of Indians, but now, with Stone by her side, she wasn't afraid of the ominous shadows the trees made. She was only afraid of the things she couldn't see: the expression in his eyes she couldn't read, the current of excitement that bubbled inside her, making her feel as if she were doing something wrong, but something that she had no will or desire to stop. She needed to be alone with Stone, whatever the cost.

Leaves and pine needles crunched under her heavy shoes as she moved through a grove of cottonwoods. Stone's hand tightened in hers, and she felt the tension in his fingers as they remained firmly grasped in her own. She hoped he wasn't having any doubts about coming with her.

She stepped on a small rock hidden under the thick ground covering and stumbled. Stone caught her immediately, his strong arm coming around her. He inadvertently skimmed her breast, and the contact fanned the growing fire within her. He settled his grasp on her waist, and his solid chest pressed against her back, scalded her through her blouse like a fiery brand. She leaned against him, fighting the urge to turn around in his embrace.

"Let me lead the way," Stone whispered huskily.

She was glad that he had taken command of the situation. Her courage was wavering, fighting a battle with her sense of responsibility.

She breathed deeply of the night filled with the scent of bark and pungent lichen moss and woodsy flowers. There was a crispness to the air, too, and bright stars. As Stone moved closer to a slight rise amid the trees, the wavering lights to the north became a clear display.

Stone stopped at an old fallen tree and with one smooth motion, straddled and crossed it without letting go of her hand. He turned around to help her over the decaying trunk. His hands slipped easily around her slender waist and he gently picked her up and deposited her on the other side.

A delightful shiver ran through her at his touch.

They'd reached a small, elevated clearing bordered with numerous felled trees that looked like a miniature fort made by nature's walls.

Stone lingered over her a moment, his senses slightly rattled. He peered down on her upturned oval face, soft and alabaster under the dazzling sky. "Do you want to stop here?"

"Yes." Her voice was honeyed and there was a slight waver to the single word.

He slid his hands down her waist, tracing the curves of her hips over the gathers of her skirt. Then he captured her dainty hands again in his as he lowered them to the leaf-strewn ground to sit.

The light chill in the air brought with it a cooling respite to Kristianna's burning lungs. She breathed in deeply, inhaling the night and the faint traces of the man beside her. Tobacco and leather.

Stone stretched out his buckskin-covered legs, took off his hat, and raked his fingers through his hair. He turned to her and trailed his forefinger over the soft curve of her cheek. "We shouldn't have come here."

"I wanted to." His intimate touch made Kristianna shudder.

"Wanting doesn't always mean doing." Reason was fast slipping from him. He should take her back; he should take her into his arms. "You don't know what you want."

"I want to be sitting here with you." She moistened her lips. "I . . . I want you to kiss me."

Her honest admission kindled Stone's emotions. She was so sweet and innocent, it nearly pained him. He leaned toward her and lifted her hair from her shoulder and wrapped it around his finger, luxuriating in the silken feel of it.

As Kristianna faced him, she felt as if she were floating on a cloud of uncertainty, of longing, of desire. She had never known desire before. There had never been anyone to evoke such a response from her. She stared into Stone's eyes as a flash of light bloomed across the sky and saw her feelings of desire mirrored there.

Without thinking, she pressed her palm to his cheek, and stroked him with her thumb. She marveled at the stubble, the roughened skin so unlike her own. The contrast made her pulse skitter. She ran her fingertip down over his mouth, to his square jaw. She felt him tense under her touch and she drew away thinking she'd angered him with her boldness. He captured her hand in mid-air and brought it back to his face.

"You keep doing that and I *am* going to kiss you. And once I start, I'm not going to stop."

"I do not want you to stop," she whispered, and framed his face with her other hand.

The strong barrier that Stone had tried to erect toppled with her words. He brought his lips down on hers with an urgency that nearly scared him senseless. She was soft and pliant, yielding to his mouth. He cupped the back of her head in his hands to draw her closer. She moaned under his ministrations and he deepened the kiss.

Kristianna caught fire, closed her eyes and blended against Stone. She moved her fingers over the muscles of his broad shoulders, playing with the fabric of his soft calico shirt. One kiss, long ago in a field, then another in a loft, had unleashed a passion she never knew existed within her. And those two kisses had haunted her until this moment. Now she knew she had to have whatever else kissing brought with it. This time, she would not let him back away, but continue forward to the unknown that surely was heaven. She wanted to feel every part of him.

Melting against his chest, she felt the erratic beating of his heart against hers. She kissed him with a need that brought tears to her eyes. She controlled the kiss, gently plying open his firm lips with the tip of her tongue. She sought the entrance to the cavern of his mouth where he tasted of tobacco and the lingering aftermath of *loytens alkavit*. Her actions inflamed him and he groaned, drawing her closer to him, digging his fingers into the soft slope of her shoulders and grinding his mouth harder on hers. She felt lost, dizzy and swirling in a wave of sensations that were building, demanding to be quenched.

"Please," she whispered on his lips. "Please . . ."

Her gentle plea brought a rush to his already-burning loins and he felt his heart wrench. That simple word made him feel as if he were the only man in her life, would be the only man in her life.

He removed the garland of wildflowers from her hair, breathing in the headiness of fresh fragrances. She smelled like no other woman he had ever known. Pressing the weight of his torso on top of her, he wove his fingers into her silky hair. He kissed her with light easy strokes, taking her lower lip into his mouth and running his tongue across the velvet sweetness. When he removed his mouth, it brought a cry of protest from her. He was almost afraid of the power he held over her, knowing that she was beyond stopping. But he was beyond any power to stop himself. Her cry was replaced by a whimper when his lips grazed the hollow of her throat and the satiny texture of her skin.

Wanting to taste and explore every part of her, he left a path of fervent kisses toward her eyes that fluttered closed under his touch. Her lashes were long and full, tasting faintly of tears; the knowledge that he could cause her to cry in unrestrained pleasure made his insides ache. He moved to her lobe and caught it in his teeth. Touching his lips there for a moment, he traced his tongue in the shell.

Kristianna dug her fingernails into his neck, feeling as if she'd been struck by a whirlwind of molten heat. He was doing things to her that should have shocked her but did not. She wanted him to do them; she wanted to feel his mouth on her body, and even more so on her naked skin.

The sensations Stone gave her made Kristianna's knees weak and radiated a warm torrent from the tips of her toes to the top of her head. It swirled and centered on that one place between her legs. She felt moist and wanting, needing him to touch her there.

He pulled away from her for only a moment. The look of loss in her eyes as the sky was lit by a flash from the northern lights made him brush a chaste kiss on her bruised lips to assure her he would return. He fumbled with the buttons of his shirt, cursing himself for his unsteady hands; then he deftly slipped out of the sleeves. Spreading the shirt on the grassy ground behind her, he gently pushed her down on to it.

Kristianna's hands unabashedly slid up Stone's chest and she reveled in the texture of the skin stretched taut over his muscles. It was hot and sleek, hard and tight. He was all male, so different from her. She fingered the line of coarse hair across his chest, and slowly outlined his nipples. Stone's breath caught in his throat as she circled each nipple with her finger. So, he liked it, too. This newfound discovery brought a quiver to her legs. She could drive him just as mad as he did her. She continued, grazing her fingertips over his shoulders and upward to the tendons of his neck and finally delving into the thick mane of his hair.

Stone was helpless to stop. He had to have her, whatever the cost. He ground his mouth on her passion-swollen lips while moving his hand up her waist. With his forefinger, he traced over the mound of her breast, and felt her nipple spring into a tight bud as he circled it through the thin fabric of her white blouse. She kissed him deeper, spurring him on and with ease, he unlaced the lavender strings of the corset around her waist. He unhooked the front of her blouse and swiftly pushed aside the soft folds of muslin. Quickly, he tugged at the ribbons of her chemise and pulled at the gauzy material. It rendered with a slight tear, but the reward was worth any damage she'd have to repair. He seared her smoldering flesh with his hands, when he cupped her and gently rolled her nipple between his calloused fingers.

Kristianna shuddered under his touch. The memory of his lips on her breast that night in the loft burned through her like wildfire and she wanted desperately to feel them there again. She arched her back and he lowered his head to take the offering into his hot mouth. He teased and bathed her for a long moment, and she felt as if she'd died a thousand deaths, for surely this must be heaven. Unable to stand the sweet pain any longer, she moved aside the rest of her *särken*, offering him her other breast.

Stone trailed his tongue down the valley of her breasts and fastened on the other pink crest. He spent equal attention there before he moved his hand down the length of her shapely hips. She was satin to his touch.

When Kristianna realized what he was doing, she instinctively parted her thighs for him. He bunched up the material of her skirt and petticoats, and she felt a rush of cool night air on her pantalet-covered legs. He slid his hand up across her abdomen, then down over the mound of her womanhood. The heated feel of his fingers over the material of her underpinnings was more than she could bear. She was breathless when he reached up to tug the ribbon free and slip his hand inside. At last, he made his way to the throbbing between her legs. She cried out as he slipped one finger inside and stroked her. A torrent of pleasure coursed through her and she trembled.

Stone raised himself up on one elbow and unfastened his buckskins. He was beyond undressing her or himself any further. He tugged down the waistband of his buckskins, freeing himself for her view.

Kristianna had never seen a man naked and had it been anyone else, she would have been frightened. But Stone was magnificent. His largeness intimidated her a little, but she trusted him, trusted him with her life. She had felt the contours of his back and buttocks, and now she wanted to reach out to that other male part of him.

She touched her fingers to the fiery shaft, surprised when he jerked from her touch. She was a little afraid she'd hurt him, but when he growled and moved forward, she circled the length of him with her hand and felt his velvet hardness. He was so different from her and this was what she had wanted from him.

Stone could stand it no longer. With a rendering tear, he slid the thin undergarment from her waist and moved his knee between her legs, but Kristianna had parted them already. A driving need soared in his chest as he lowered himself over her. Slowly, he probed her, burying himself inside her.

Kristianna had known that she wanted him, wanted more of the sweet ecstasy he had given her, but she was startled by the sharp pain that cut through her. She clutched onto his shoulders as he began to move deeper. Each time, he pushed farther into her until finally, she felt the pain ebb then die. Suddenly the emptiness that had been inside her was gone. This had been what she'd wanted. Stone moved slowly at first, the crisp hairs of his chest prickling her nipples as he moved faster and faster. Her heart thrummed in her chest and she clenched his tapered waist. Her ardor needing to be quenched just as urgently as his, she matched his rhythmic labors.

Just when she thought she could stand the sweet agony no longer, her body tingled and throbbed, exploding in a whirlwind of sparkles and hot tides. Stone thrust his hips once more and this time she felt the muscles in his back tighten and she clung to him, raking his damp skin with her fingernails.

Stone's ragged breath hotly caressed her ear

and she savored the glowing aftermath of their lovemaking, their bodies entwined and moist. She was afraid to move for fear of losing him. Burying her face in the soft wave of hair that fell over his shoulder, she breathed, "I love you so dearly."

Stone was lost and tried to regain control of his senses, his bearings. His breathing was labored and he pressed his mouth into the hollow of Kristianna's neck. He ran his tongue over her skin, tasting the sweet sheen of moisture there. Still cradled deep within her, he rose on his forearm and stroked back her damp hair from her temple.

She stared up at him with unmasked love shining in her beautiful eyes. His chest tightened and he spoke, his voice gravelly and hoarse with spent passion, "You're not marrying Gunnar. You're marrying me."

·17·

Kristianna was barely able to drag herself from bed. Her bones felt as if they were dough, her joints seemingly not even strong enough to hold her limbs together. There was an aching stiffness to her chest and shoulders that spread down to her toes. Her head ached as if she had been struck. And her heel . . . It hurt worse than it had in days, she decided, as she swung her legs over the side of her bed and put her weight on her foot. She slipped her arms into a gray muslin blouse and fastened the front hooks. Just that simple gesture was enough to make her want to climb back into bed.

Below her loft, she could hear her mother and Noelle preparing breakfast. She wished she could lay down for another minute, but there were too many things to do. There was the milking, and the plowing—now that the share was mended—and then there was the matter of her going to Saint Louis . . . Saint Louis. Away from Stone.

After last night, she was not sure what to say to him. They had shared such intimacy that under the cover of night she had abandoned herself to it, but during the stark reality of day, the memory of what she had done, made her cheeks burn with embarrassment. What did he think of her today? That she was wanton? She had almost begged him to kiss her. When he had, she was lost, lost to the rapture of it, wanting more, knowing she had to have more or she'd starve for it for the rest of her life. His body had been a strong, hard wall against hers, and she had reveled in every moment. And if that were not enough, Stone had asked her to marry him!

She felt like telling the world, and at the same time, she knew she could not tell anyone, for she had refused him, certain he had proposed for all the wrong reasons. He did not love her; he had never said it. She was not so blind as not to know he was asking out of mere duty. She would rather have no husband at all, than one who felt it was his obligation to marry her.

Kristianna moved slowly to her bureau and reached for her brush. She peered into the dim mirror and brought a finger to her lips. Hours ago, they had been bruised and swollen by Stone's kisses. Now, they were pale and trembling at her touch. There were dark smudges under her eyes, telltale signs she'd been crying. She hadn't cried over her lost virginity, but that what she and Stone had shared would never be repeated.

Deep inside, she would never be the same girl she once was, for now she was a woman. Would Mama be able to tell? Mama and Papa would be shamed to the core if they knew what she had done, but she had wanted to do it. At least when she was old and alone, she would know what it was to be loved by a man. Even if that man did not love her in return, he had given her something that he could never take back. The feeling was so indescribable that she would not have understood if Mama had tried to tell her about it.

She lifted the brush to her tumbled hair, the simple task nearly sapping all of her strength. Her scalp hurt when the bristles touched it, and her aching fingers could not plait her long hair. She let it hang loose and pinched her cheeks to bring some color to her face. She needed to drink another cup of Stone's herbs which would make her feel better, as it had before.

With deliberate movements, she made the descent down the ladder and into the heart of the house where the shifting of pots and utensils and the sweet smells of breakfast awaited her. Drawing in a deep breath, she forced a cheerful smile to her pale, pink lips.

"Good morning, Mama." She found when she spoke, there was a tightness to her jaw. She swallowed hard, testing to see if she had a sore throat, but she did not.

Ulla, busy with a skillet of eggs, barely looked up at her daughter. "Good morning, Kristianna.

Midsummer must have worn you out. It is after six." She moved to the coffeepot that was sputtering on its spider. "Dearie has been bawling for nearly an hour now. Tend to her, please."

"*Ja*, Mama." She walked carefully, avoiding putting any hard pressure on her right foot.

Noelle looked up from setting the table. "Steurn is not up yet, either." There was a mischievous gleam in her eyes. "Did you dance all night with him?"

Kristianna raised her arm to the milking buckets on their wall pegs and continued toward the door, afraid that if she stopped, she wouldn't be able to make her legs move again. "*Ja*, I danced with him."

"And is he a much better dancer than Gunnar?" Noelle asked with an impish grin.

Forcing herself to smile back at her sister's upturned face, Kristianna said, "*Ja*, he is."

"I knew he would be," she replied, and went back to her chores, a knowing smile lighting her face.

Kristianna pulled the latch string on the door, surprised at how difficult this simple act was. She managed to free the leather thong and open the door.

Once outside, she transferred the empty pails to one hand, while with the other she shielded her eyes from the sun. It seemed brighter than normal this morning. Peering under her forearm, she noticed there wasn't a hint of clouds in the sky, nor a single breath of a breeze. The evergreen trees stood motionless and majestic in the early hues of orange and yellow. Making her way along the path to the barn, she wondered if Noelle had been right about Stone not being up. Most mornings, he would have been sitting at the kitchen table when she came in from milking the cow.

She dreaded facing him; she was not up to confronting him. She recalled the look of astonishment in his eyes last night and the way he had stared down at her as if his proposal had been something she should have accepted without a doubt. That she should have tossed caution to the wind and welcomed him with open arms. Well, it wasn't that easy. There was still the matter of him being a woodsman and she a farmer. Even if he did love her, where did that leave them in life? Wandering in the woods with the changing seasons? That was Stone's life, not hers. She could not forget about farming. She'd been born to it. As much as she loved him, she could not cast aside her personal beliefs for his.

After he had asked her to marry him and she'd refused, he'd jerked on his clothes, barely sparing her a glance. She had turned her back and slipped into her garments as well, blinking back threatening tears. She'd been dreadfully confused and fulfilled at the same time. Soon after returning to the dancing area, they helped Ulla pack up for home. They hadn't had a moment alone since.

Before Stone came into her life, she was dead set on who she was and what she wanted out of life. Now, an uncertainty larger than she could have ever imagined overtook her and was pushing at her, telling her to go to him, to say yes, but she could not. To say yes would be unreasonable and illogical for them both and in time, Stone would come to regret his asking her.

A songster's morning chirp brought her to the present. Reaching the barn, she was relieved to see she didn't have to unlatch the heavy doors. One already stood open. Brother Moon was in the open corral, along with the oxen. From the interior, she heard Dearie bawling, and felt sorry for the cow. Poor thing was uncomfortable because Kristianna hadn't dragged herself from bed on time. Then she wondered, since Stone had obviously opened the door, was he inside or out?

She didn't have to wait for an answer. She was barely inside the barn when he strode from the stalls, holding a rake in his powerful hands. She grazed him with her eyes, taking in as many details as she could in one swift glance. His hair was disheveled, as if he'd frequently run his fingers through it; his eyes were not their usual magnificent teal-blue, but rather a softer shade; his lips were tightly set and there was a day's growth of beard on his chin. He'd rolled up the sleeves of his calcutta shirt and wore tight-fitting denim trousers and his moccasins. He set the rake on its teeth and balanced his arm over the handle.

"Mornin'," he greeted, but there wasn't the normal warmth to his voice.

"Good morning," she said softly, trying to ignore the swell in her chest, the racing of her pulse. She never tired of looking at him, or the way he made her feel. There was a lightheadedness to her that she knew had nothing to do with her illness.

Stone watched her as she set down the buckets and went to fetch the three-legged stool. She reached down for it from its spot in the corner, but as she grasped the seat, Stone's hand came around her wrist like a vise. She rose, too quickly, for all of a sudden she was dizzy and swayed back toward the wall. Stone steadied her with a strong grasp on her upper arms.

"Don't shrink away from me," he said, misconstruing her actions.

"I am not," she denied. In fact, she wanted nothing more than to relax into his embrace. He smelled so good, that familiar scent of Bay Balm and even a little hay.

"Look at me," he commanded. When she met his intense gaze, he went on. "I see you're not up to the day yet, either." Her cheeks lacked the usual pink blush, her eyes were shallow and dull. And if he wasn't mistaken, she was favoring the way she walked. "I reckon you slept about as much as I did."

She wasn't given the opportunity to speak, for they were interrupted by Dearie's bleating cry.

"What I still can't understand, is after you told me you loved me, you refused to marry me."

"I thought we had closed this discussion." She tried hard not to look him in the eyes.

"You did. I didn't."

"I have a cow to milk." Kristianna tried to break free from him, but his grip was like iron. Her heart hammered in her chest and she felt herself weakening toward him. Even now, she wanted to kiss him, to feel his lips on hers one more time.

Stone was not easily appeased. "Do you deny saying that you loved me?"

"My telling you that I love you does not mean you have to marry me." A spark of fire danced its way into her violet-blue eyes. For a quick moment, she felt strong enough to resist him. "Did you ever think that maybe I loved what you were doing to me, and not you?"

There was a silent fury on his chiseled face. "You told me you loved me and it was from your heart."

"I am sorry if you misunderstood what I said."

Stone's fingers crushed into the soft flesh of her arms before he realized he was on the edge of hurting her. He loosened his hold, wanting nothing more than to shake some sense into her. Why was she doing this? She had said she loved him as if she meant it. Was she angry because he hadn't repeated the words? How could he when he wasn't sure what love was? He'd never had it at any age as far as he could recall. Love was something totally foreign to him. It was not something that came easily to him, nor did he know how to go about attaining it.

He had stayed up all night, trying to sort out his feelings for her. He had never felt so complete with a woman, had given so much, and received so much in return.

The cow cried once again, and Kristianna shrugged from his embrace. This time, he let her go.

"You're not making this easy." He moved toward her as she retrieved the stool and set it next to Dearie.

She cast him a weary glare as she lowered herself onto the stool. "Easy for whom? You owe me nothing. I am not holding you here. You are not obligated to me." She was breaking in two.

Resting her cheek against the cow's right flank, she began the milking. She was glad for a moment to sit down, to lean onto the animal's soft side for support. Had Stone not held her when he did, she would have fallen. What was wrong with her?

"Christ, is that what you think? That I asked because I felt obligated?"

"Do you not?"

There was a long silence between them, the only sound in the barn the sloshing of Dearie's milk as it hit the bucket.

"No, it's not that," he finally said as if he'd needed the time to reassure himself. "I asked because I thought that's what you wanted."

Kristianna nearly reeled. She stopped milking and stared at him. "What I wanted? How noble of you not to think of yourself at all. What a generous sacrifice!"

"I didn't mean it to sound—"

"I think you meant exactly what you said." She cut through his explanation with a voice that was as cool as a steel-edged dagger.

Tears pooled in her eyes. Her brave front was on the verge of shattering. How could she have fallen in love with him? He was stubborn and arrogant and he was a trapper. He was everything she disliked, but he was the one who'd crept into her heart and made himself at home. Well, she'd shoo him out!

293

She rose in haste, snatching up the half-full bucket with the intention of leaving. The room spun with her quick action and she stumbled.

Stone instantly crossed the distance between them and was almost at her side when she reached out to hold herself up next to the planked wall.

Do not touch me, she thought. *Please.* She would dissolve into his arms and forget everything. She had to fight him, to fight herself from surrendering to him.

She took a deep breath and squared her shoulders. "There will be no more need of you here, Mr. Boucher." As the spinning room somewhat subsided, she let go of her support. She staggered past him, forcing her steps to remain even and straight. "I will be going to Saint Louis to find Papa. He will come home with me and we will not need you." The icy words fairly stuck in her throat. "My mama will pay you after breakfast."

Stone blocked her exit, his strong arms crossed over his broad chest. "You're not going to Saint Louis. No woman in her right mind would travel there alone."

"You have no right to tell me what to do." Her jaw tightened as if she had no control over it, and she was afraid she was going to cry. Hot tears flooded her eyes, and the bucket in her hand seemed to be slipping away. The barn began to cartwheel again.

"I have . . ."

His words were lost on her. The room tumbled as if it were hit by a cyclone. Colors ran together in a dim funnel of brown for the wooden timbers,

294

black for the tack wall, yellow for the straw and finally, the cool white of Stone's shirt as he caught her. The last thing she remembered before she fell into darkness was the pail sliding effortlessly from her fingers.

"What happened?" Ulla spun away from the hearth as Stone carried Kristianna in his arms over the threshold.

"I don't know." Stone made no hesitation as he moved across the planked floor and through the curtained partition to lay Kristianna on Ulla's quilted bed. He quickly assessed her pale face, pushing a stray lock of hair from her brow. Her forehead was hot as an oven. "I don't know," he repeated, noting that her eyelids appeared to be translucent, the sandy crescents of her lashes a stark contrast. "She fainted."

"Fainted?" Ulla echoed as Noelle came to her side. "Kristianna has never fainted."

"Is she sick, Steurn?" Noelle asked, her lower lip trembling.

Stone did not answer as he tried to rouse her. Her breathing was raspy and panic filled him.

Without looking over his shoulder, he directed Ulla to bring him a basin of water and a cloth. She whisked away, leaving Noelle by his side.

"Take off her shoes, Noelle," Stone said while unhooking the top fasteners of Kristianna's blouse. As his knuckles brushed over her burning skin, he cursed himself for not noticing the signs earlier. Once the material parted, he untied the ribbon of her chemise and folded the soft fabric open to create a vee just above her breasts. He didn't even question the propriety in the gesture or what Ulla would think of him doing it. It was something that needed to be done.

"Her stockings, too, Steurn?" Noelle's voice was on the brink of cracking, but she managed to keep her lower lip stiff.

Stone barely comprehended the words as he tilted Kristianna's head back. It seemed logical to open her breathing passages as much as possible. "Yes," he finally said as Ulla returned with the water.

He dipped the cloth into the tepid basin and wrung it out, then put it to Kristianna's temple. Stroking the hair from her face, Stone tenderly ran his fingertip down her cheek, then rested his palm there. He'd barely removed his hand when Noelle cried out.

"*Titta*, Mama! Look at Kristianna's foot!"

Stone followed Ulla's wide-eyed stare, his heart thundering in his chest as he viewed the bright, swollen red spot on Kristianna's heel. He felt his chest tighten and the blood leave his hands. A slow tide of recognition flooded through him. He'd seen something like this once before a long time ago. If this was what he thought it was . . ."Sweet Jesus," he choked, then turned toward Kristianna's white face. He took her head in his hands and slightly shook her. "Come on, sweetheart. Wake up."

He shook a little harder, a little sharper and when she did not respond, he slapped her cheeks wishing Jemmy were here. Jemmy had tried to treat this once before, though Stone refused to believe Kristianna would succumb to the same malady.

"What is it, Mr. Boucher?" Ulla's voice was full of distress. "Why is she not waking up?"

Stone did not answer. He did not hear the words. All of his concentration was centered on one person: Kristianna. He snatched up the cloth from her forehead and dipped it into the basin again. With a firm squeeze, he let the water trickle over Kristianna's brow. She moaned and he felt himself breathe again as her eyelids fluttered open a fraction.

"Is she going to be better, Steurn?" Noelle's mouth was arched in a worried frown.

He repeated the process of dousing Kristianna's face with the water, not acknowledging Noelle's hopeful inquiry. "Mrs. Bergendahl, I want you to drive out to Snelling and send word to a friend of mine, Jemmy Paquer. I'll give you a message to leave with Bidwell. He'll find him. Then I want you to get a room at the fort and stay there until I send for you. Bring that cow with you."

"But, Mr. Boucher, surely my daughter only—"

Stone gazed sharply at Ulla. "Do what I say." His words were unflinching. He had to get them out of the house. They wouldn't be strong enough to endure the days ahead, and it would kill Ulla to feel so helpless.

"*Ja.*" She straightened from the bedside and reached down for Noelle.

"Can you manage hitching up the team?" he asked, hoping she could. He didn't want to leave

Kristianna even for the few minutes it took to harness the oxen.

"I can manage," Ulla replied shakily.

"Good. I want you to climb up into the hay-mow and get me my small leather pouch. It's by my split hide."

"I will." Ulla's face was flushed, her forehead creased with panic, as she and Noelle quickly exited the room.

Stone hovered over Kristianna. She hadn't regained full consciousness, but she was breathing easier. He continued to swab her hot face until finally her fringed lashes opened. She seemed to be confused, and he brushed a kiss on her cheek, grasping her hand in his own. Her fingers were fragile, reminding him of rose petals. He barely applied pressure for fear of hurting her, but he squeezed just enough to let her know that he was there.

"What . . . what happened to me?" Her voice was weak and distant.

He leaned closer, trying to read the dullness in her eyes. "You fainted."

"I . . . did . . .?"

"Yes. Kristianna, tell me about your foot. How long has it been like this? Is this why you've been dizzy?"

"Foot . . . ? It hurts."

"I know, sweetheart. I want to help you. Tell me how it happened."

"It hurts my jaw to talk . . ."

"Take it slow. Don't breath so deep."

"I stepped on a . . ."—she licked her dry lips—". . . shell. A butternut shell."

"When?"

"Swimming . . ." She closed her eyes and he knew she was drifting off.

Stone captured her other hand in his. "The day at the creek?"

She was quiet, her breathing labored and wheezing again.

"The day at the creek?" Stone asked again, his resonant voice louder and commanding an answer.

"Yes," came the soft reply.

Stone did some quick calculating in his head. A week ago. Seven days. He hung his dark head and cursed under his breath. *Seven days*. He swallowed hard and forced the awful images from his mind. The other case he'd seen had surfaced within four days and by the fifth day, the man had died. Not Kristianna. It would not be too late for her. Ulla would find Jemmy and Jemmy would know what to do.

"Why didn't you tell anyone you were hurting?" There was a quiet agony in his tone, an underlying dread of the days to come.

Kristianna's eyes barely seemed to focus on him, but she answered back clear as day, "Because I wanted to dance with you." Then she slipped away into a faint again and he was left with an ache in the pit of his belly.

Later that afternoon, the shaking began.

With a quick sweep of his arm, Stone cleared the contents off the kitchen table. The bowls Ulla had set out for the morning's breakfast skittered to the floor, along with spoons and cups and the tiny Delft sugar bowl with its missing handle. It shattered on impact. Moving intently, he ransacked Ulla's cabinet for a clean blanket and with a snap of his wrist, spread it over the pine table. He returned to the bedroom to get Kristianna.

She lay on the bed with only her thin chemise to cover her trembling body. He'd divested her of her clothing to keep her fever down. So far, she'd drank next to nothing of the herbs he'd steeped for her. He'd tried to spoon the broth between her tight lips, but her jaw was stiff and unyielding. She'd begun to shake so badly, it was all he could do to keep her on the bed. That was when he decided to move her to the kitchen table.

Scooping her up in his arms, he held her tightly to his chest, trying in vain to cease her shivering. Once at the trestle table, he deposited her on its covered top. Draping an arm over her middle, he reached down for the pieces of sheets he'd ripped in strips and tied them around her middle, her shoulders, her arms and legs. He felt sick, binding her down, tying her as if she were a rabid animal. He felt the bile rise in his throat, but knew of no other way. Jemmy's words came back to haunt him from that night long ago. "The shaking can get so bad, a person's bones start breaking in two." Stone shrugged off the omen, refusing to believe it would happen to his Kristianna.

Once Kristianna had been fastened securely to the table, she was not able to move as much, and he felt a slight sense of accomplishment.

The room was stiflingly hot, and even though

he had the windows pushed open, the air outside was no cooler. The small room was permeated by the strong odor of mustard seed and snakeroot. He'd had no choice but to keep adding fuel to the fire in order to make a plaster. Moving to the hearth, he stirred the thick, spicy concoction which bubbled over a slow flame. He grabbed the cooking tongs and removed the pot from the iron spider.

The light in the kitchen area was dim in the lingering traces of afternoon. He fetched a lantern from the sideboard. After wiping his sweaty fingers on his thighs, he picked up the box of matches, lit the lantern, then reached for his Green River knife.

The handle was heavy in his hand as he whetted the blade across a thick leather strop, honing the edge to absolute sharpness. Upon finishing, he made his way to the hearth again, sticking the blade into the red-hot coals. Once the steel edge was cherry-red, he removed it. Swallowing hard at the lump in his throat, he walked steadily to Kristianna.

He thanked her God she was unconscious as he moved the lantern to the end of the table near her foot. Sitting, he clenched his teeth and moved the tin lamp closer to her heel. Beads of perspiration rolled down the sides of his face and he absentmindedly swiped at them with the sleeve of his shirt. The blade had cooled to ashen, but was still hotter than a smoking gun barrel. Inhaling a ragged breath, he clutched onto her ankle and steadied the knife in his hand.

The crackling of the fire was deafening in his

ears as he drew the tip down, cutting into the infected skin of her heel.

Stone thought he was prepared to hear her cry but the anguished sounds brought stinging tears to his eyes and he wished it were him lying there instead of her. He bit down hard, tasting the blood in his mouth, forcing himself to continue, telling himself that he had to do it. She writhed under his ministrations as he made another shallow cut to relieve the pressure of the reddened area. Her scream made him want to die for her. It was almost more than he could take.

He murmured softly to her as he cleansed the wound with warm water, probing for any traces of the shell. Each time he gently moved the tip of knife, she cried out. Christ, how could she have walked on it? Why hadn't he detected any sign of her limping sooner? When he was beginning to think he would find nothing left of the shell, he saw a tiny fragment no bigger than a fine piece of thread. He tenderly pulled it from her heel.

Quickly now, he reached for the pot he'd removed from the fire and applied the thick mustard plaster to her heel. After wrapping her foot with strips of sheets secured at the top of her ankle, he stood.

He leaned over her face, stroking the damp tendrils from her brow. Her cheeks were searing hot and flushed scarlet.

"I'm finished now, sweetness." He knew she couldn't hear him, but he had to reassure her.

She looked so defenseless that his heart swelled in his chest. It was then he realized how much he loved her with all of his heart. For he would gladly give up his life for hers, to take the pain from her. Love had found its way to him at last and had been staring him in the face, but he'd been too blind and unsure to see it. So simple. So sweet. His Kristianna.

A feeling of helplessness overwhelmed him. He wanted to tell her, to have her look into his eyes when he proclaimed the vows.

"I love you, Kristianna." His voice was hoarse and broken. "I love you . . ."

The revelation renewed his strength and he brought a chair to her side.

Now the difficult part began. He had to sit and wait. Wait and hope. And believe in Jemmy's Great Spirit deeply enough to ask for a miracle.

·18·

Three days passed and still Jemmy had not come. Keeping a tireless vigil over Kristianna, Stone refused to give way to the exhaustion that plagued him after the first day. She'd been fitful and barely responsive as he'd forced a tincture of snakeroot in the guise of tea between her lips. She'd drank enough to keep her fever down as well as quelling some of her muscle spasms but she was far from recovery.

He'd spent the better part of last night alternately lying across her on the table top to keep her from shaking, and the other part banking the ashes to keep the coals alive to heat batches of mustard plaster and herb broths. This morning he'd awoke at dawn, his body stiff and sore, from spending the last few hours of the night in the hard ladder-backed chair.

Stone's head felt heavy on his crossed arms. For a brief moment, he was disoriented, not realizing he'd fallen asleep. Kristianna's soft cry jolted him awake. He raised his head and reached out to place a hand on her brow. To his relief, the dry skin felt somewhat cooler. He peered at her wan complexion, noting the dark blue smudges under her eyes. It tore him to see her this way. Her hair, a mass of white-blonde tangles around her face, fell in a soft cascade over the blanket. He smoothed away a lock from her temple, and after the strands were gone, he continued stroking her lovingly.

Still clad in her chemise, her alabaster skin was mostly exposed to his view. He remembered Midsummer and the touch of her naked body next to his. The feel of her pliant lips against his mouth and the exquisite passion they'd shared. Such fulfillment would not be quickly taken from him, he vowed. Their last words would not be spoken in anger; she would wake up to have that moment again. She would recover and she would marry him.

Rising to his feet, Stone went to the sideboard and found the water pitcher nearly empty. He settled his hat on his tousled hair and picked up the water bucket.

"Back in a minute, sweetness," he said to Kristianna who still slept deeply. Then he pulled the latch string and went out into the beginnings of dawn.

Newt Fraeb tethered his roan to an old tamarack branch. Smearing his hands on his oily buckskins, he then wiped away the remnants of his hastily eaten breakfast of donkey meat. He'd had to eat on the run, so to speak.

Seemed he'd angered a few of the boys over a game of faro and they weren't too amused by the fact he'd cheated. Damn that firewater, but it made him addlepated. He shouldn't drink so much of it at rendezvous, but with whores aplenty and his pockets full of money, it just seemed right that it all go down together. Now, he had to lay low for a few days until the boys blew off some steam.

He'd left Fort Snelling in the dead of night and made camp at the edge of the Mississippi. As the first rays of daybreak came through the pines, he'd up and packed his gear and headed north— toward Stone Boucher.

He hadn't forgotten about Boucher and his smartass airs. No, sir. He'd been meaning to pay a call on that good-for-nothing trapper, only he got a mite sidetracked with the whiskey and squaws and all. But now he was ready for revenge and it seemed all the sweeter to him since he'd found out that Mama Yellowhead and her little one were staying at the fort.

That information he'd had the good fortune to stumble across standing at the counter in Bidwell's Sutler's Store waiting for some chaw. Seemed Boucher needed that half-breed Seneca of his for something urgent, urgent enough to keep old Mama away from the house till Paquer got there. That meant that that pretty piece of yard goods and Boucher were all by their lonesome. Well, shit and spit, he'd pay a little social call and get the party rolling.

Newt's horse snorted and jerked its head. "Keep quiet, you sorry excuse for horseflesh. We don't want to announce we're here"—he paused with a smirk on his lips—"yet."

Stepping around the horse's hind legs, Newt retrieved his rifle. It got his ire up even more as he grasped the weapon in his hands. He missed his old flintlock trading rifle. The gal done shot that one up and he'd had to pay out good money for this years old Kentucky that had a left pull to it, always making his aim a little off.

After pouring powder down the shaft and packing the wading, he replaced the ramrod under the barrel in its thimble. He'd added a little more powder this time, just in case. He wasn't about to be shot at again.

Traversing the short distance through the heavily wooded area, he came upon the small, log cabin. A faint curl of smoke came from the chimney, signalling someone had stoked up the morning fire. Newt slowly left the cover of the thick brush and made his way to the back of the house.

The windows were shuttered, and he cocked an ear but didn't hear any sounds within. Easing himself around the side of the house, he steadied his walk with a hand on the rough, chinked wall. He cautiously came to the front closed door. Stopping, he listened again.

At first he wasn't sure if he heard right. Then he pressed his face up against the planks of the door. Hot damn, if that wasn't a woman's moan. There it was again—plain as day! That dog

Boucher was laying with her right now!

Newt almost laughed out loud. That scum wouldn't let anyone else have her, but he sure as hell was willing to do the job himself. Well, he wasn't about to be left out in the cold. He cocked the hammer back on his rifle with a slow click and raised it to eye level. Then with a sharp and swift kick of his booted foot, he sent the door crashing open.

Whatever carnal delights he'd envisioned were suddenly sapped from his mind. There on the table was the woman—tied down. She was wearing her underwear and nothing else. He'd had some wild nights of his own, but this was something else.

Newt lowered the barrel of his rifle and scratched his greasy black head, scanning the interior of the room. Boucher was no where to be seen. "What the hell?"

He moved toward the table and squinted a look at the woman bound there. Yup, it was her all right. There was no mistaking that hair. Lowering his gaze a little, he instinctively sniffed. She smelled like a medicine box. Hell-fire and shit, what had he stumbled onto?

She whimpered again and Newt jumped back. Whatever she had, he didn't want. He clutched at the turquoise nugget around his neck and chanted to an old Indian spirit, then turned on his heel with the intention of hightailing it out of the house.

He'd taken one step and was met smack in the jaw by a stone wall. Funny, he thought as his head snapped with a sprinkling shower of bright stars, there weren't no stone walls when he came in. Before he blacked out, he got a brief look of the Stone he'd run into, then he thudded to the floor unconscious, his unfired rifle clattering down next to him.

Stone had just left the copse of trees behind him when he noticed the front door was open. He'd dropped the water bucket in the yard and cursed himself for his carelessness in forgetting to take his Hawken with him. His only other weapon was his Green River utility knife, and that was in the kitchen, too. There was no strategy in charging full blazes into the cabin since there was no telling what he was up against.

He'd soundlessly snuck up to the side of the cabin. Whoever had opened the door was quiet. Stone wasn't sure if that was a good sign or not. He felt his way along the outside wall, progressing toward the front door that was gaping open. When he'd reached the entrance, he jutted his neck into the house for a quick second, then pulled back.

He'd seen a fleeting blur of a man in buckskins and a rifle. There was something faintly recognizable about the man's slouching posture. Before he had time to question who it was, he heard the intruder shuffle over the puncheons. Stone didn't take the time to think, but acted out of the need to protect Kristianna.

Leaping over the threshold, he came down on the man, catching him off guard. Just as he gave vent to a slamming blow to the buckskinner's face, he was met with a pair of startled, watery blue eyes.

Newt Fraeb. The split-second recognition gave him time to put a biting edge to the sweep of his fist as it crashed into a fleshy jaw.

Newt fell like an old, stuffed burlap sack at his feet. Without stopping to assess the damage he'd done, Stone crossed the remaining distance to Kristianna. Still under the affects of the drugs he'd been administering to her, she wasn't aware of what had happened.

Stone breathed a quick sigh of relief, then took a long stare at Newt, wondering what to do with him. He hadn't pondered the question long when the sound of hoofbeats came rumbling down the path toward the homestead.

Automatically, Stone slammed the door shut and secured the leather latch string. He briskly snatched up his Hawken from the corner and readied it to fire, wondering what other lice Newt could have brought with him.

The hoofbeats stopped short in the yard. Stone heard a lone rider dismount and tread toward the door with a jingling of hawkbells. Newt frequented with the blackest of the Dakotas, damn his soul, and Stone debated whether he should open one of the window shutters. The slightest movement on his part could alert the savage.

Wishing he'd had more time to devise a plan of defense, Stone swiftly concluded that surprise would be his best element. He whipped to the side of the door's path when it would be opened, and pressed himself against the wall. Whoever it was would enter and Stone could spring himself on the man.

A fist pounded on the door that creaked open a fraction. "You in here—" The words were cut short as Stone reached around the door's edge with a roundhouse swing.

He clutched onto a man's red collar and yanked him into the room. "What's your business here you son-of-a—" The rest of Stone's sentence was silenced by a pair of gleaming obsidian eyes and a head full of shining jet hair braided down the back in a queue. "Goddamn, why didn't you call out?"

Jemmy Paquer shrugged off Stone's ham-like fists from the material of his shirt. "You crazy, brother?"

"Hell, no! I just had a visit from our friend Newt"—he pointed at Newt's prostrate form—"and wasn't sure who else he had invited over for fun."

Jemmy stared down at the grizzled trapper sprawled at his feet. "You kill 'im?"

"No. I should have though. Damn snake."

Kristianna's soft cry brought Jemmy's black head up.

Stone stepped over Newt as if he were nothing more than a sack of flour in his way. "She's bad, Jem. It's her foot."

For the moment, Newt Fraeb was forgotten.

Jemmy moved over to Kristianna, the motion setting off the small bells that were sewn on the outer seams of his buckskins. He removed a long, fringed leather pouch from his shoulder and laid it on the table. "What'd she step on?"

311

"Butternut shell."

"You cut her?"

"Yes. I got it all out."

"Mustard plaster?" Jemmy queried, looking at the bandage on Kristianna's foot. He unwrapped it, and using a water-soaked cloth, cleansed the poultice away to assess the wound.

"Yes."

"What else you done?"

"Snakeroot."

"Got to have quinine. Lots of it. And alcohol. I was able to get a quart of whiskey, that's all. Things are drying up at the rendezvous. What you got?"

Stone was halfway to the sideboard and opening the door. "A little raspberry cordial. Not much."

"Then we'll make something up." Jemmy untied the whangs on his leather pouch and sorted through various tiny rawhide purses.

The house was filled by the different aromas of herbs and spices, leaves and barks. As Jemmy gathered the medicines he needed, Stone spoke quietly, "Where the hell you been?"

Jemmy worked while he talked, putting out a carrot of tobacco and a gnarled root of wild ginger. "Down to Traverse des Sioux with Lawrence Taliaferro."

Stone was angry with himself and the helpless feeling that hung over him. If Jemmy had been here sooner, maybe . . . "Well, you sure picked a fine time to go."

Casting him a brooding glare, Jemmy retorted, "That ain't you talkin', brother, so I ain't taking offense. Don't know if my being here sooner would've made things different. It ain't too late."

"It's what Will Taverns had, isn't it?"

Jemmy gave a short nod. "Looks like it."

Though Stone had thought the worst, deep in his heart, he'd hoped it wasn't. His massive shoulders slumped and he suddenly grew tired again. In a voice barely audible, Stone sighed. "Will Taverns died."

"She ain't Taverns, Boucher. She's strong." He moved over Kristianna's listless form and with a vigorous flick of his wrist, he ripped her chemise down the middle. "Boil some water. She's takin' a hot bath."

During the next several days Stone and Jemmy took turns tending to Kristianna. Jemmy showed Stone how to mix a concoction of wild ginger. The root caused her to empty her stomach and rid her body of the poisons. But Stone wasn't so sure it was good for her. Kristianna looked so thin, and she hadn't eaten anything in nearly a week, only small mixtures of herbs. She dozed in and out of drugged sleep. Stone was almost thankful for the time she lost consciousness so she wouldn't have to suffer.

They'd poured as much of the homemade quinine down her as she could take, alternating it with whiskey. Jemmy said the alcohol would numb her quaking muscles. They also submerged her in very warm baths in the half barrel Stone had fetched from the side of the house. The baths relaxed her limbs even more. So far, she seemed to be responding slightly to the treatment.

Jemmy had continued to change the poultice on her heel three times a day, as well as an application of wet tobacco leaves on her abdomen. The leaves' potent strength penetrated through her skin, making her stomach lurch even worse than the ginger.

With the combined effort, on the sixth day, the color began to return to her face. Stone moved her from the table and back to Ulla's bed. He'd dressed her in a clean night rail he'd found in Ulla's bureau and lightly wrapped a sheet around her thinning waist. For the first time, she rested peacefully throughout the night.

The next morning, Stone was at the kitchen table milling coffee beans in the grinder when Jemmy came in from outside. He'd been sleeping in the haymow while Stone slept on the floor on a pallet near Kristianna's bed.

"How's she?" Jem asked, stepping over to the hearth. He added a small amount of kindling to the crackling fire.

"She slept the night." Some of the edge was off Stone's weary voice, and he finally allowed himself to think the worst was over.

"Good sign, Boucher. I called to the Zephyr and he answered." Jem brushed the silky, ebony hair from his coppery-skinned brow. He'd changed into a red tunic and navy leggings with a wide sash around his middle. And wearing a small brass earring with a short feather in his pierced earlobe, he looked much more like a full-blooded Seneca, than half.

"Zephyr a Great Spirit, Jem?" Stone asked without a trace of disrespect in his words. Once, he might have ribbed his friend over tribal ghosts and gods, now, he accepted what he could not see.

"Zephyr is the god of healing. I called to him and he answered."

"Thanks, Jem." He paused for a moment. "Thanks for everything." Rising to his feet, he reached over the table and grasped his partner's hand firmly in his.

"She means something to you, this wooden shoe girl." Jemmy's words were not questioning, they were a statement.

"Yes, she does." Stone's reply was unflinching. He saw no point in denying it; he'd denied it to himself for too long.

"What are you going to do about it?"

"I'm going to marry her."

"You asked her?"

"Yes. She turned me down, but she'll change her mind."

Jemmy was thoughtful for a brief time. "Where's that going to leave us?"

"I honestly don't know, partner."

The Seneca brushed off the admission with a shrug. "I expect we better see what the lady says afore we make any plans. Now, are you going to brew that coffee, or what?"

"I reckon."

The slight banter between the men eased some of the tension they'd undergone in the past few days.

"Wonder what old Fraeb's up to?" Jemmy grated a chair across the floor and straddled it.

Stone stifled a rumbling laugh in his chest. "I

don't suppose he'll be back here in the near future."

"Nope. I hog-tied his ass, but good. Slung him over that poor beast of a horse of his and sent him on his way. Horse had any sense, would've gone back to Snelling. Though that animal of his looks 'bout smart as a flea. Could've ended up in the middle of hostiles."

"Serve him right."

"You see how godawful kept his sticker was? Fur and dried blood on it. Disgusting. A man that don't keep his essentials clean, ain't ought to have 'em." There was a sly smile on Jemmy's lips as he drew out a newly cleaned Hudson's Bay Co. knife from his belt. "Nope. Ain't ought to have 'em."

Stone chuckled, poured the coffee grounds in the enamel pot and set it on the iron spider. "Chip pan's low. I'll go cut some."

"You do that."

Stone had barely slashed through a piece of dry timber when Kristianna's feeble attempt at a scream reached him. He dropped the ax from his hand and sprinted from the back of the house. While he ran, he jerked the Green River knife from his belt, raising the ominously sharp blade. He'd kept it secured around his middle ever since that day with Newt. He wouldn't be caught unawares again.

Pushing the door open with a splintering crash, he crossed the room in one fell swoop to where he'd left Kristianna.

She was sitting up on her elbows, but the effort

was fast sapping her strength. She peered terrifyingly at Jemmy who stood over her.

Stone lowered the knife in his hand and replaced it in its sheath. "What the hell happened?"

Jemmy backed away. "She woke up."

"I can see that." Stone knelt down beside the bed and took Kristianna's cold hand in his. "Kris?"

Her long hair was in a wild disarray around her oval face, her cheeks flushed pink from the small exertion. Violet-blue eyes stared unflinchingly past Stone to rest on Jemmy. She blinked them once, then twice, as if trying to focus clearly. When at last she found her voice, it was as weak as a lamb's. "There's an Indian in here, Stone. Get him."

Stone felt a tide of relief wash through him, and with it came a wide grin. "Welcome back, sweetness."

·19·

Kristianna felt like she'd been dragged through the mud and back and was sure she looked about the same. She'd lost all track of time and was astounded when Stone told her she'd been sick for over a week. The last thing she remembered was quarreling with him in the barn. . . .

Stone. He looked so tired as if he hadn't had a moment's sleep during her illness. There were weary creases at the corners of his eyes and he hadn't shaved, his chin and cheeks shadowed with heavy beard. His sleek brown hair looked longer, more jumbled, over his wide shoulders, but beholding his haggard face brought her strength.

After getting over her initial shock at seeing Jemmy Paquer, she'd drifted off into a light doze. She'd heard every sound in the house—the scrape of a chair, the creak of the door, the crackling from the cook fire.

As the sun rode low in the sky and twilight descended, Stone came into her room with a food tray. She'd hazily come awake moments before, staring thoughtfully at the rafters in the ceiling above her. Detecting Stone, she diverted her eyes and fastened them on the giant of a man she'd come to love.

"Hello." She smiled a tranquil greeting.

He moved soundlessly across the planked floor and set the tray on the bureau. Pulling up a chair, he sat and faced her. "You been awake long?"

"No." Kristianna pushed herself up a little to press her back higher into the feather tick pillow.

"How you feel?"

"Better than I did this morning. I must look a fright." She tried to smile at the latter.

"You look beautiful." Stone's eyes swept over her disheveled hair, exquisite face, and the alabaster arch of her neck. "I missed you."

"I missed you, too." The honest admission brought a sensation to her empty stomach like the caress of a dozen butterflies' wings. "I truly did." She had thought she could go on living without him. But during the days of her illness, when she'd faded in and out of delirium with violent pain, her will to live had come from Stone. She'd sensed him by her side, come to know how gently coaxing his touch could be.

Kristianna licked her dry lips. "I do not remember much. My head feels like cotton."

"It's the drugs we gave you. Jem said that will pass."

"Your Seneca." She recalled the first time Stone had mentioned him long ago when he'd come for the hired man's job. She'd put him through an inquisition because of the Indian and now she was indebted to him. "Who put me in my night clothes?" Kristianna had been pondering that question when Stone had walked into the room.

"I did. After your baths."

"Baths?"

"Jemmy said to put you in a tub of hot water to relax your muscles, so we did."

"We?" She felt a strange pumping in her chest. Had the Indian seen her naked, too?

"Jem's seen it all before." Stone confirmed her worst horror. Then he added on a teasing note, "But he did find you rather unique. If he wasn't my friend—"

"Stop it!" Kristianna lamented weakly with utter embarrassment and brought her hands to cover her ears. Her face flushed. How could she ever face the man? Then she winced, the sudden movement feeling like a thousand needles were marching over her skin.

Stone's deep laugh inflamed her temper.

"What else should I know?" she groaned in resignation.

"Nothing. Honestly."

"At times, it sounded as if you were reading to me and the words were vaguely familiar."

"I read you passages from your Bible." Stone rested his elbows on his knees and knit his fingers together. "I thought you might like it."

"That was considerate of you, seeing how you feel about the Good Book."

"Yeah, well, I did a lot of thinking while . . . while I watched you."

Kristianna waited for him to elaborate, and when he didn't, she prodded him on. "Yes?"

"I came to realize something." Stone leaned forward and brushed her flushed cheek with his fingers, drawing them slowly over her mouth. "I love you, you know. I've been waiting a long time to tell you that."

His touch was dreamlike, only this time she was very cognizant of the reality behind it. A pleasant tingle prickled her skin and she fought back tears of joy. "Are you sure?"

"Never more." He moved closer and pressed his lips on hers. The kiss was given in tenderness, soft and intimate.

His mouth on hers stoked the banked fires within her. At the gentle pressure, her eyelids fluttered closed and she savored the warm, sensual graze of his lips, the light taste of his tobacco. The kiss was brief, but heart-searing. When he lifted his head, she looked into his rugged face and saw his eyes were dark and smoldering.

"You gave me a scare, Kristianna. Why didn't you say something about your foot?"

"Because I did not think it was important. I thought it would go away."

"Christ, you could've died. You almost did. Don't ever do that again—hide something from me." Now that he knew she would recover, his voice held a sharp edge.

"I will not."

"See to it." He straightened, his emotions running together in a disorganized manner that was not at all like his usual levelheadedness. He was so fiercely in love with this woman that it shook him to the core to think that he had almost lost her.

"When will I be able to get up?"

"If you continue to improve quickly, a week far as I can tell."

Kristianna sighed. What newborn strength she'd had was slowly waning. She settled further into the softness of the bed. "Good. As soon as I am able to travel, I am leaving for Saint Louis."

Stone's dark brows shot up like rockets. "What did you say?"

"I am going to Saint Louis to find my papa," she reaffirmed. "My being ill has not changed my mind; it has only set me back."

"The hell you're going to Saint Louis!" Stone pushed back the chair, stood, and turned away from her. He wildly combed back his hair with his hand and pivoted. His eyes were stormy and full of disbelief. He met her feigned innocence head on. "I thought—Well, I . . . Doesn't my telling you I love you mean anything?"

"It means everything to me, Stone." Her words were soft and loving. "But I cannot turn my back on my papa."

"How do you intend on getting there? It'd take you a good month on horseback. A woman alone in the woods—you'd never make it. That leaves coach or steamship, both of which don't come free. You have any money?"

She felt belittled and foolish by the way he was talking to her, especially since most everything he said was true. "I have a little."

"A little? You better have a lot, because that's what it's going to cost you, sweetheart." He ground out the endearment with a sarcastic bite.

Kristianna was about to defend herself when he spoke up again. "And once you reach St. Louis, where are you going to look?" He paced up and down the length of the bedstead, pausing once to point a lean finger at her. "That town is no mud puddle. It's big, Kristianna. Bigger than you'll ever know."

"I will manage, Mr. Boucher," she answered in a vexed tone. "I did think for myself before you came along."

"There's no talking to you. You're stubborn as Uncle Mary gets when—"

"You yellin' at the patient?" Jemmy's dry words broke through the room.

Kristianna automatically drew the bedcovers over her chest at his unexpected intrusion. She still wasn't all that sure about Jemmy Paquer. He'd given her quite a fright when she'd first awakened to see his face hovering above hers. She hadn't really remembered him clearly from the rendezvous that day with Newt Fraeb, and to view him standing there, she had thought the worst. And now that she knew he'd seen her—all of her—she blushed down to her toes.

"I'm just giving her a talking to, Jem. She's got a hide on her thicker than a griz. Come on in and I'll introduce you proper."

Jemmy's sinewy form crossed to the bed, his

323

stride light and easy. He'd removed his feather earring and was dressed more like Stone. He looked less intimidating to Kristianna this way and she wondered if he'd done so for her sake.

"This is my partner, Jemmy Paquer. He's responsible for your recovery."

Jemmy shrugged. "If Stone hadn't done what he did before I got here, you would've been in the bone orchard sure. He's bein' generous."

Kristianna alternated her gaze from one man to the other and observed the evident respect between the two. Happy as she was about Stone's admission of love, she wondered where and if she would fit into their lives.

"I'm glad you're back with us. Stone here went through all his tobacco and half a mine. I ain't never seen a man smoke so much. Like a damn chimney."

"A man's got to do something," Stone said, defending himself.

"Yeah, and I've got to get back to some unfinished business at Snelling. I can see now you'll be all right on your own. I told Stone what to do. You best take it slow next couple of days and favor that foot a yours. It was cut."

"I will," Kristianna obliged. She was fast coming to like the man in the short span of time she'd spoken with him. Underneath his gruff exterior, she felt he was a man of genuine caring.

"You can tell Mrs. Bergendahl it's all right to come home now," Stone said as Jemmy was leaving the room.

"I'll do that."

Kristianna turned her attention to Stone.

"Why did you send my mother and Noelle away? I vaguely remember you telling me that yesterday."

Stone never wanted Kristianna to know how horrendous her illness had been. "It seemed the right thing to do at the time. No sense in all of us getting under each other's feet."

She accepted his reason, but sensed he wasn't telling her the whole truth.

"You up to eating something?" Stone's line of questioning moved to a safe subject—for the moment. "You're too thin." He brought the tray to her lap. He'd made her a cup of vegetable broth and a baked potato.

"I am hungry, but my jaw is so stiff. What did you do to me? Hit me in the mouth?" She laughed weakly, attempting to lift his foul mood.

"No. Maybe I should have rattled your head though. Knock some sense into you."

She'd taken a small spoon of the broth when Stone sat down on the chair again and crossed his arms over his chest. "There is one way you can go to Saint Louis that I'd approve of."

"Oh?" She set the utensil down and peered questioningly into his eyes. "And what way is that?"

"I'll take you."

Her heartbeat quickened a beat at the prospect, but she was wary at the same time. "As my guide? My protector?"

"Your husband."

It took her a minute to swallow. "Oh."

"Is that all you can say? This is the second time I've asked you. Don't turn me down again."

"Do not boss me," she tossed back. "The first time you asked, it was out of duty. If I am not mistaken, the second time is asked for the same reason. I said it before, and I will say it again, you are not obligated to me."

"Dammit, woman!" Stone ground out, and leaned over her and put his hands on her shoulders. "I'm asking you because I love you. I want you. I want to spend my life with you."

"Really?" she whispered hopefully.

"Hell, yes." Then he bent down to kiss her again. This time, there was more need in his kiss. His mouth slashed across hers, bringing with it exquisite delight throughout her body. She melted against his strong chest, feeling a wave of pure headiness at being so close to him. The tray on her lap teetered and crashed to the floor.

"Stone," Kristianna spoke on his lips, giving him tiny kisses in between her words. "You spilled the soup."

"I'll clean it later," he answered with his mouth on hers, flicking his tongue over the soft contour of her lower lip. "I've got more important things to do now."

Kristianna relaxed as he circled his arms around her neck and drew her closer. Abandoning herself to him, she wouldn't think about the future and where it would lead them. For now, this was where she wanted to be.

"Say it, Kris," he murmured, moving his lips down the column of her neck. "Say it . . ."

Kristianna tilted her head back and parted her lips. She clung to his broad back and moved her

hands up his spine to the muscles in his neck.
"*Ja* . . . I will marry you."

Later the next morning, Ulla and Noelle returned home. The reunion was tearful and in the days that followed, Kristianna flourished under her mother's constant ministrations, along with herbs Jemmy had left Stone to give her. By the end of the week, she was ready to get out of bed; and three days after that, she was able to manage climbing the ladder rungs up to her loft to pack for Saint Louis.

"I do not see why Stone Boucher has to rush things, *dotter*," Ulla clucked as she handed Kristianna the flaxen blouse she'd just folded. "You should take things slowly."

Kristianna took the blouse and placed it with several others already stacked in her valise. "He is not the one rushing things, Mama. I am. The sooner we are married, the sooner we can go to Saint Louis. Stone said there is a paddle boat leaving this afternoon."

Ulla sat on the bed, pondering for a moment. "Is that the only reason you are marrying him? So that he will take you to Saint Louis? I, too, am worried about Sixten, but we must be sensible. Marriage is forever."

Kristianna snatched up her brush and hand mirror from her bureau and tossed them into her case. "I know it is." She opened one of her bureau drawers and took out her chemises and stockings. In the far corner was a neatly wrapped tissue bundle. Moving her undergarments aside, she reached for the fragile wrapper. She slipped her fingers into the edge of the paper, feeling the cool texture of fine silk. The fabric was to have been made into Gunnar's bridal shirt. She sighed and pushed it aside to continue her packing. Her wedding would not be as she had often pictured it.

There would be no church, nor family and friends other than her mother and Noelle. No Swedish service, but rather a military chaplain at Fort Snelling. There would be no folk music and dancing. No traditionally costumed groom. And she hadn't had the time to outfit herself properly. Because of her need to have something of her heritage at her wedding, Kristianna had donned her lavender folk costume to wear as her gown. At least that would be right today. And Stone as the groom.

"Do you love Stone?" Ulla's face was filled with compassion.

"*Ja*, I do." Kristianna turned to her mother and suppressed any remorse over their hasty departure and pending nuptials. "With all my heart."

"Then it is right that you marry him. I had only hoped Sixten would be witness to your wedding ceremony when the day came."

Kristianna rose and took down several skirts from the wooden dowels that stretched across the rafters. "I did, too."

"Have you thought of waiting to marry until after you return?" Grateful as she was for Stone Boucher, Ulla was still uncertain about the union. Things were coming together too fast. She had known there was an attraction between her daughter and the trapper long ago. Such a marriage would be put to the test and she hoped their love was strong enough to endure it.

"Stone will not take me to Saint Louis unless we are married."

Ulla sighed heavily. "I suppose he is right."

There was a quiet pause as Ulla fingered the ribbons on one of Kristianna's frame caps, then she spoke softly, "Do you really think you can find Sixten?"

The words made Kristianna stop folding the skirts over her arm. "Oh, Mama. I know we will."

Tears misted in the older woman's eyes as she rested the cap on her lap. "I have tried to be strong but now I am frightened for him."

Kristianna's heart welled and she dropped to her knees, resting her head in her mother's lap. "Do not worry, Mama. Stone will help me find him, I know it. And we will bring him home and everything will be as it was." Not quite, she added silently. Now there would be Stone.

Ulla stroked back Kristianna's cascading hair, allowing silent tears to course down her cheeks. "I pray you are right."

"Steurn is ready, Kristianna," Noelle called up to the loft.

Kristianna reluctantly straightened and wiped at her tears with the hem of her floral apron. "Oh, and I am not even half packed." She tried her best to control her faltering composure and put a smile on her lips.

Between the two of them, they managed to

complete the task and were down below just as Stone crossed over the threshold, a scowl darkening his face. "Chaplain said he'd meet us at noon, Kris. We're going to be late if you don't hurry it up."

"I am ready." She handed him her stuffed-to-the-hilt valise. "Let me make sure I have everything."

"By the feel of this, I'd say you did." He moved his gaze over her, affording himself a pleasant review of her face. No longer was her complexion pale and shallow, now her skin bloomed with color. Her iris-colored eyes were alive, reflecting the color of her lavender blouse; her cheeks blushed a soft pink; and her mouth was a rosy hue. He had the sudden urge to kiss her, to affirm that her recovery wasn't too good to be true.

Acting on impulse, he reached out with one hand and drew her into an embrace and pressed his mouth over hers.

Kristianna was startled, but pleasantly so. Their surroundings didn't afford her the time or the privacy to continue the kiss for a longer time. And it appeared Stone was aware of that fact as well, for he lifted his lips from hers with a little more noise than was proper in front of Ulla.

"Couldn't help myself, Mrs. Bergendahl." He grinned lazily at Ulla and went outside.

The contact, though fleeting, quickened Kristianna's pulse and she smiled a shy, silent excuse to her mother.

It was time to go and she took a moment to scan the room. Everything was neat. The trestle table had been scrubbed clean with sand and resting on its top was a lace doily and a fresh bouquet of wildflowers. Noelle had picked them for her the day before. The chairs were on their pegs on the wall and the window shutters were thrown open allowing the sun to cast its bright rays over the entire setting. She would deeply miss this house.

She wished she and Stone could have their own house and that Stone would settle down. But they had yet to have that discussion and Kristianna refused to speak of it now. For the moment, she was just happy being with him wherever they were; whatever they were doing. And after Saint Louis . . . Well, then they would talk about it.

Kristianna caught one last glimpse of the room and started out the door. Her steps were marred by only a slight limp, other than that, there were no traces left of her illness.

Once outside, she marveled at the bright colors of the landscape. The sky overhead was powder-blue with scant wisps of clouds that looked as though an artist had painted them with fleeting strokes of his brush. The mossy green pine boughs and elms provided a shaded canopy over the porch, alternating with that of the bright sun. She lifted her chin, closed her eyes and allowed the gentle heat to rain down on her face.

"Kristianna, Steurn said I could ride Brother Moon to the fort."

Kristianna opened her eyes to see her sister coming out of the barn astride the big white horse, Stone leading them with a rope. The child's face was alight with a wide grin. "Mind you hold on tight, Noelle," Kristianna warned her.

Moving from the porch, Kristianna slowly made her way toward them. She'd barely reached the wagon when the easy trot of hoofs from the road caught her attention. She looked up to see a lone horseman coming down the path. There was no mistaking the stocky build of the animal, nor the reed-thin outline of its rider.

It was Gunnar Thorson.

A queer tightening settled over her muscles. She hadn't seen Gunnar since Midsummer Day. There had been times when she'd thought of him, wondering if he knew of her illness, for he had not come to inquire about her. But then, why should he after the way she had treated him?

Stone tethered his horse to the back of the wagon and moved next to Kristianna as Gunnar reined Flicka to a stop. Noelle knew to stay quiet, and Ulla only nodded a polite greeting, her face showing the uncomfortableness of the situation.

The visor of Gunnar's *kaskett* was tugged over his pale brow and his clear blue eyes were set with an unfathomable edge. He was outfitted in his work clothes and there were still spots of perspiration marking the weave of his homespun shirt. "*Hej*, Kristianna."

"*Hej*, Gunnar." Kristianna's voice was faint.

Not acknowledging Stone, Gunnar glanced briefly to Ulla and gave her a courteous wave of his hand. He swept past Noelle and fastened his gaze on Kristianna again. "If I could have a moment with you," he said in Swedish.

She looked fleetingly at Stone, who obviously didn't understand Gunnar's question. Repeating it in English, she saw Stone's face grow skeptical under the wide brim of his black hat.

"What does he want to talk to you about?"

"I do not know. But I owe him that much. Please, Stone." She would have spoken to Gunnar whether Stone liked it or not, but having his understanding would make it easier.

Stone's jaw tightened, but he conceded to her wish. "I reckon you do." His line of vision was unwaveringly locked on the blond man, and he remained rooted to the spot. He'd be damned if he would walk away to leave them alone. "We're on our way to get married, Gutter. You'd better make it quick."

Gunnar's facade was visibly shaken with the announcement. "Does he speak the truth?"

Kristianna could have killed Stone with a look. She had wanted to tell Gunnar herself, but hadn't had the opportunity. No, that was not the entire truth. She had wanted to tell him, she just didn't know how. She had never intended to hurt him.

"*Ja*, Gunnar. We are to be married."

"And when were you planning on telling me?"

"I do not think this is something we should talk about . . ." She paused and glanced hastily at Ulla and Noelle, then at Stone and added, "Here." She began to walk toward him.

Gunnar dismounted and stuffed his hands into the pockets of his buff breeches. His steps were strong and steady as he met Kristianna halfway. "Had you told me you were to wed another of our own, I would have been angry, true. But you tell me you are to take vows with this—this man of the traps. An outsider, a man who condemns us and pilfers our fields. I find it hard to forgive you."

Stone ground his teeth, his rugged face filled with rage. He took an ominous step forward and balled his fists. "You'd better watch yourself, stripling. I haven't taken a fist to you yet, but the day's not over."

"Stone, please," Kristianna pleaded.

"It is all right, Kristianna," Gunnar intervened. "He does not scare me with his bully ways. You see, I have nothing to lose. I have already lost what was mine."

"Maybe if you'd treated her better than you do your goddamn horses, you wouldn't have." Stone was close to coming to blows with the man.

Kristianna stepped between the two and shot Stone an admonishing glare. "Please, Stone, you are not making this any easier for me. I owe Gunnar an explanation and he will have it."

Stone was deathly quiet for a moment, as if pondering the circumstance. Then he raised his hand and pointed a finger at Gunnar in warning. "You've got one minute to speak your piece, farmer."

Gunnar brushed off the half-threat and stared at Kristianna. "May we go someplace private?"

She gave Stone a hasty glance over her shoulder, then returned her attention to Gunnar. "*Ja.* Come into the house."

Once inside the cabin, Kristianna left the door open. She nervously smoothed down her blouse and skirt, self-conscious under Gunnar's scrutinizing gaze. When after a short time he didn't speak, she finally did. "Gunnar . . . I meant to talk to you, but I did not know what to say."

"Say the truth," he berated. "That you do not love me and you never did."

She cast soft, pleading eyes at him, hoping he would understand. "I cared for you, Gunnar, but you are right, I did not love you. And I am not all together sure you loved me, either."

He expelled a disgruntled huff and shrugged off his hat. "Do not go placing the blame on me. I did love you."

"With all of your heart? That you would have done anything for me?" There was a brief pause and she continued, "Did you know that I was ill?"

Gunnar shuffled his feet over the floorboards and stared down at his mud-stained boots. "I heard of it some two weeks back from your mama when I was at the fort."

"And you did not come to see me?"

"Your mama said you were being taken care of and that we were all supposed to stay away. I see now the mistake of my actions."

"Oh, Gunnar. Do you not understand? If you loved me as much as you say, you would have done anything to be with me."

"I wanted to but I have been having trouble on the farm. There was the west field and Fredrick lost a shoe . . . and . . ." He grappled for significant excuses. "I am here now. That is all that

335

matters, is it not? You do not have to marry him. I will forget all of what has happened. We can marry now. We do not have to wait until after I have established myself."

Kristianna pressed a conciliatory hand on his arm. "Please do not be bitter, Gunnar. I think this is for the best. You will find someone who truly loves you and shares your interests and enthusiasm."

"I do not want your pity," he fairly snapped, and jerked his hat back on. "I should have known this is how you would have it. Do you love this man?"

"*Ja*," she answered softly.

"Then I break our engagement."

"I am sorry."

"*Ja*, well, as it so happens, I have been calling on someone of late. Hanna Lind. Her papa's farm is very efficient."

"I am glad, Gunnar. Truly I am. She has always been fond of you."

"I have liked her, too. It was out of respect for you and our parents that I did not pursue her sooner. If you must know, I think you are too pretty for your own good. A farmer's wife has to be strong and able."

Kristianna allowed him to justify the situation which ever way most pacified him. "I wish you well."

He was quiet a moment, as if pondering an inner dilemma. Finally, he dug into his shirt pocket and produced a folded parchment. "Since we have no further business together and you have made your feelings clear, I will leave you with this. Mr. Bidwell gave me this to bring you. It is from your papa."

Kristianna's heart leapt to her throat. "Papa?" She reached for the letter from Gunnar. Once in her hands the paper brought a wash of relief throughout her as she scanned over the outside and the familiar penmanship of Sixten Bergendahl. Papa had written at last! "How long have you had this?"

"I only received it yesterday."

Yesterday? He'd had it for an entire day and hadn't brought it to her until now. She didn't know whether she wanted to box his ears for waiting so long, or hug him for finally delivering it.

"I am certainly glad you saw fit to bring it today," she said curtly, deciding she was angry with him. He knew how much the letter meant to her. "Stone and I are on our way to Saint Louis to look for him."

"I see then I delivered it just in time," he caustically returned. "I would not want you and your new husband to make an undue journey. I bid you good day, Miss Bergendahl." He gave her a curt nod.

Kristianna watched him depart, feeling a sense of relief at having finally confronted him, no matter how bitter the exchange had been. Then she quickly diverted her attention to the letter in her hand. Swiftly, she broke the wax seal and unfolded the paper and read the words she'd been starved for, for so long.

11 June, 1836
My beloved family,
All is fine in this city of great opportunity. I have acquired a very honorable position. The salary is one I cannot complain. I hope that you all are well. I miss you and have faith in God that I will return home to you soon.

My
love,
Papa

Kristianna read it through once more, slowly this time, assessing every word. She quickly came to the conclusion that something was wrong. Terribly wrong. This was not at all like her papa. He was not a man who . . .

"Are you all right, sweetness? I saw Gunnar leave." Stone had come up behind her and slipped his arms around her waist. "Did he upset you? I'll yank him off his horse and whip his hide—"

"No . . ." she answered vaguely, then turned in his arms and showed him the letter. "It is from Papa. Gunnar gave it to me."

Stone took the paper and scanned the scant lines. "You'll have to tell me what it says, it's written in Swedish."

"Oh." She hadn't even realized that. Quickly, she translated the brief words.

Stone lifted his brows questioningly. "What's the matter? I would have thought you'd be elated to finally hear from him."

"No." She shook her head and took the letter back. "You do not know Papa. He is a man to boast and brag. This letter is not like him at all. It says nothing. It does not say where he is working and for how much. My papa is a proud man, but even working for someone else, he has always been one to state what a day's work has earned him, no matter how small the wage may be. He is not a man to lie, and when he cannot tell the truth, he will not speak at all. And then there is Mama. Mama whom he loves dearly, and not even a single, special message to her." Kristianna paced over the floorboards. "No, there is something wrong, Stone. I feel it."

Stone took the letter from her once more, to check the stationery head. He hadn't paid it any mind at first, and now, it stuck out at him like a ripe berry. The Sovereign House.

If the man had gone to Saint Louis, supposedly to make enough money to keep the family from starving, then what the hell was he doing staying at the most plush hotel in all of the city?

"I do not want Mama to know of this, Stone. Not until we find Papa."

His concentration broke, and he looked up from the letter and into Kristianna's worried face. There was no point in adding another burden to her basket now. "All right," he finally said, his face shielding his thoughts. "I won't say anything."

It seemed as if for the time being, all three of them would be harboring secrets of their own. Stone brushed an assuring kiss on Kristianna's temple, then ushered her toward the door. "We'd better head out if we want to make that steamboat as man and wife."

·20·

The modest ceremony took place at Fort Snelling on the high banks overlooking the Mississippi River. Kristianna held onto a garland of wheat, listening intently to the simple vows the cleric recited. The service was brief and soon after the chaplain had opened his Bible, he was asking Stone to give her a ring. She gazed down at her hand in his as he slipped a filigreed marcasite band on her fourth finger. The tiny grayish-black stones twinkled luminously one moment like a firefly, and the next, they flicked back to the flat shade of night. Long ago he'd given her a firefly ring. Today he gave her another that was exactly like it, only this one would last forever.

Kristianna looked up at her new husband with a silent question in her eyes which he answered with a slow, secret smile she understood. Then, he lowered his head over hers and gave her a sealing kiss. It was six weeks ago to the day since she'd met Stone Boucher and if someone had told her then that she'd be married to him, she never would have believed it. Now, she was proud and honored to be his wife.

When they were pronounced husband and wife, Noelle, who'd been holding a tiny bandbox lifted the lid and released two golden butterflies. They flitted on the breeze as if getting their bearings from being confined in the small box, then were gone on the current.

"For you and Steurn," the child proclaimed with the utmost seriousness.

"Oh, Noelle, they were lovely." Kristianna picked up the hem of her skirt, turned and kneeled down next to Noelle. "You caught them by yourself?"

"*Ja*, I did. I did have three, but one got away."

"I love you, Noelle." Kristianna hugged the child and pressed her close to her bosom. So many times she'd snapped at Noelle when she was underfoot, but she was such a special little sister that it made Kristianna sorry she'd ever thought her bothersome. She blinked back tears and rose to her feet, vowing she would find Papa and bring him back for Noelle.

Stone had commissioned Noelle and Ulla a room at the fort while he and Kristianna were away. Kristianna understood her mother's reluctance to leave the farm again after being gone so long already, but Stone had convinced her it was for her own safety. A woman alone was an open invitation to renegades. There had been two recent Indian incidents involving settlers, and in both cases, the farms had been completely ravaged. And as for Ulla and Noelle staying with Swedish neighbors, her marriage to Stone had not only segregated her, but also her family. They would not be as readily accepted now.

When Kristianna rose and turned around, she found Jemmy Paquer standing beside Stone and her mother. His long, ebony hair, caught by the light wind, streaked in wisps across his face. Absentmindedly, he pushed them away and tucked them into the collar of his bright red tunic. His fancy earrings, now exposed, shone in the afternoon sun. "I expect congratulations are in order."

Kristianna smiled warmly at him, hoping he was sincerely happy for his partner. She knew, from what Stone had told her and from what she'd detected from Jemmy himself, that he was not overly fond of the settlers.

Stone extended his arm and grasped Jemmy's hand in his, giving it a firm shake. "Thanks, brother."

Kristianna stepped forward. "Mama, do you remember Jemmy Paquer, the man Stone sent you to find for him?"

Ulla Bergendahl was slightly taken aback by the man's formidable Indian attire, but managed to overlook it, knowing her daughter owed her life to him. "Of course, I do. God bless you, Mr. Paquer, for coming to help my daughter."

"Wasn't any great deed. Stone asked me, so I came." Jemmy's expression was aloof and without a hint of gallantry.

343

Noelle stared in awe at Jemmy, her mouth gaping open. "Steurn told us about you. Kristianna did not believe him, but I did. Have you killed many white men with your arrows?"

"Noelle!" Ulla reprimanded. "I am sorry, Mr. Paquer."

For a single flash of a second, the Indian's lips held a suggestion of a smile; but it was gone quickly as he turned to Stone. "Is she serious?"

Stone gave a soft chuckle. "Yes. She doesn't know you're a peaceful, city-born Indian. She's just fascinated by tall tales."

"Oh." Jemmy scowled at the inquiring child whose white cap on her head was slightly askew. "*Wush haw ne was haw.*"

Noelle's green eyes grew wide as saucers. "How many is that, Steurn?"

"One hundred, but don't believe a word of it. He's a might winded. Only thing he's ever arrowed he's eaten for supper."

"Oh!" Noelle cried.

The steamboat whistle blew steady and strong.

"You'd better say your good-byes now, Kristianna. We have to go." Stone had already seen to it that their luggage was taken on board.

Though she knew the time would come when they would have to depart, Kristianna dreaded leaving her mother and Noelle. Everything was changing so fast. She'd just become a bride and not a quarter hour later, she was embarking on an uncertain journey. Despite wanting to be joyously happy at being a newlywed, her nerves were stretched taut as she thought of the days to

344

come. She'd never ventured beyond the Mississippi and Missouri River fork that she could remember, much less left her home and family. She hoped everything would be the same when she returned.

Anxiously, she straightened the ribbon to her waxy, black lace hat. "This is good-bye, Mama." She hugged Ulla and handed her her wheat stalk bouquet, then she whispered, "We will find him. I promise."

Backing away, Ulla's eyes shimmered with unshed tears. "God be with you." She looked up to Stone and added, "Keep her safe, Mr. Boucher."

"I'll do that." Stone put his hand at the small of Kristianna's back. "We'll be back before you have a chance to miss us." He said the latter hoping he was right. He wasn't quite sure what they'd stumble upon in Saint Louis after Kristianna had read him Sixten Bergendahl's letter.

"I'll walk you to the paddle boat." Jemmy started down the embankment, leaving the sentimental farewells for the family.

Noelle ran up to Stone and gave his leg a squeeze. "I will miss you, Steurn. Kristianna, too."

"We'll bring you something." Stone reached out to straighten her cap.

Kristianna waved as Stone led her down the dirt trail. *Hej då!*" she called, leaving them on the embankment.

She and Stone took the narrow trail down to

the makeshift dock and soon caught up with Jemmy who'd stopped to wait for them.

Stone hadn't approached Jemmy with plans for the future since he didn't even know himself what they might be. They hadn't talked anymore of heading further west for possibles, nor for the fall trapping. He knew Jem was sorely disappointed with the entire situation, but for the first time in his life, Stone Alexandre Boucher had followed his heart and it had led him to Kristianna. He couldn't give her up, not for all the beaver, open land, or even the friendship of his long-time partner.

"How long you figure you'll be gone?" Jemmy asked.

"Hard to say."

Jemmy kicked a stone from the path. "I'm takin' on a little venture of my own. You know how I've been talkin' with Taliaferro? Seems he's taken on the notion to head north and scout out the Indian regions for the Bureau of Indian Affairs. Invited a couple of Frenchies to survey the terrain."

"Sounds interesting."

"I'm supposed to act as a guide, though I've never been that far north myself."

Kristianna had been listening with concern. "Do you think it is safe to travel so far up the Mississippi, Mr. Paquer? Is there not the threat of hostile Chippewas?"

"I'd still be in Buffalo, New York if I wanted to lead a safe life, Miss Bergen—er, Mrs. Boucher."

At the reference to her married name, Kristianna found she rather liked it. Suddenly, the entire morning seemed real. She really was Mrs. Stone A. Boucher.

They'd come down to the flat stretch of sandy beach, a crude harbor for the many water vessels of birchbark canoes, bullboats, and rafts. In the midst of them was a white side-wheeler with painted red trim, the *Missouri Grand*. She was nosed up to the bank and made fast to the stumps that littered the mock dock. Kristianna had viewed the mighty paddle boats at a distance, but this was the first time she'd ever seen one close enough to take in the details. The upper deck and part of the lower was surrounded by a red railing. Toward the back of the boat, there were two spiring black stacks topped with crowns, spewing long plumes of jet smoke. Smaller stacks behind them billowed clouds of misty gray steam. At the front of the boat, were two long wooden planks on either side for the passengers to board her.

While staring so intently at the boat, Kristianna hadn't realized they'd been joined by several other men. She shifted her attention from the *Missouri Grand* to the three men before her, noting one was dressed in military uniform and the other two were anchored down with an array of equipment she'd never seen before.

Stone nodded a greeting to Lawrence Taliaferro. "Major." Then he introduced Kristianna as his wife for the first time. "Jem tells me you're going beyond the Falls of Saint Anthony."

"With the help of these two men," Taliaferro said after nodding his head politely to Kristianna, then he gestured to the strangely garbèd men at his side. "Jean Nicollet and Fronchet. Paquer, they're going to map out the region."

Jemmy eyed them skeptically. "What the hell you Frenchies packin'? I never seen the likes of this here tack."

The one named Jean Nicollet looked down at the gear that Jemmy thought was such a spectacle. "Zees are my tools, Paquer." His French accent was thick and strongly baritone. "I carry my sextant on my back, my barometer against zee sextant, a portfolio under my arm, and"—he patted the leather case in his hand—"in here ees my thermometer, chronometer, pocket compass, and spyglass. And of course at my right side ees my powder flask and shot bag."

Jemmy's black eyes had narrowed unbelievingly. "How the hell you going to paddle a canoe and walk with all that foofaraw?"

Fronchet, who was outfitted in much the same manner, stepped forward. "We are astronomers, *Monsieur.* Paquer. Eet ees our business to be at home weeth all of this. Do not worry, *mon ami*, we shall carry the load—literally! *N'est-ce pas*, Nicollet?"

"*Oui.*"

The *Missouri Grand's* whistle gave vent to another screech of vaporizing steam.

"The Bureau could use a man like you, Boucher." Taliaferro crossed his arms over his chest. "They say beaver are coming far and few between. Depending what we find up at Lake Itasca, there could be treaty talks. Paquer here says you know the Dakota tongue."

"We'll see, Major. I'm not a man to sit idle in one place." As soon as the words were issued, Stone instantly regretted them when he saw the look on Kristianna's face. He hadn't meant to hurt her, he'd spoken out of habit. To reassure her, he took up her hand and gave it a gentle squeeze. Then to direct the conversation in a different line, he tossed to Jemmy, "Jem, don't go getting yourself killed on me."

"Sure, brother." Jemmy was undaunted.

"Major. Gentlemen. I'll bid you good luck. I've got a honeymoon to attend to."

The Major respectfully tipped his hat and wished them Godspeed.

Stone led Kristianna up the long gang plank and aboard the *Missouri Grand*. The crew took in the wide board and set free the anchoring ropes. A few seconds later, the boat began to vibrate as the large, red side-wheeler churned up the muddy water and backed into the flow of the Mississippi River. Black soot clouded the sky, filling the air with eye-stinging smoke.

Kristianna shaded her tearing eyes and watched as the shoreline and the bank where Fort Snelling stood gradually disappeared. Her heartbeat picked up speed and she clutched onto the edge of the railing. For a little while, she didn't want to think about what lay ahead in Saint Louis. This was her first steamboat trip and she felt a quiet rush of giddiness at the prospect of seeing new trees and river towns and all of the colorful people that went with them.

Stone pressed his body against her and she

leaned into him for support. "Scared, sweetness?" he whispered in her ear.

"A little."

Stroking back her long hair, he placed a light kiss on the slender column of her neck. "Come on, I want to show you our room. I've got a wedding present for you."

She turned to face him and gave him a yielding pout. "Oh, Stone, I did not think to get you anything. With everything such a rush and—"

He silenced her with his finger, trailing it over her full, lower lip. "No frowning on our wedding day. You're my present." He placed a slow kiss on her mouth and she automatically drew her arms up his broad back. "Maybe," he spoke warmly, lingering over her lips. "I should unwrap you . . ."

"Do not tease me."

"I'm not."

Stone lifted his face from hers, passion blazing in his teal-blue eyes. She knew that, indeed, he was not teasing. A maddening tingle rushed through her and Kristianna slowly lowered her hands from him, feeling every sinewy muscle, every rib, and plane of his back. "Which way is our room?"

He gave her a dazzling, white smile and offered her the crook of his arm. "This way."

They passed several other passengers and exchanged polite greetings. The deck was a scurry of activity as the pilot called, "Mark twain," signaling safe water ahead. Then the crew went into action, singing as they worked.

"No one can do as the boatman can,
The boatman dance and the boatman sing,
The boatman is up to everything."

Kristianna was fascinated by the goings-on as Stone took her through a narrow portal and into the dim interior where the staterooms were. He moved down the confined hallway and stopped at the second red door from the end, opening it with a key.

Inside, the stateroom was spartan with a single built-in bunk, washstand, a few hooks for clothes, and a small oval mirror over the basin. Their luggage was piled in the far corner underneath a tiny, square window covered by sunfaded, red velvet curtains.

Stone ushered her farther into the room and closed the door behind him. He faced her, took her into his arms, and kissed her. Kristianna melted in his embrace, reveling in the fire of his kiss. He swept her breath away as his searing lips grazed over hers. He parted her mouth with a single thrust of his tongue, invading the warm recesses and offering his pleasant taste she'd come to recognize. She kissed him back with a hunger of her own, sparring with him and drawing him deeper into her mouth.

She slid her arms over the breadth of his wide, shoulders and traced her fingernails over the back of his calcutta shirt. Moving up to his neck, she sank her fingers into the soft waves of his lustrous hair, tugging free the leather piece he'd used to tie it back. She felt her limbs grow weak and it occurred to her with stunning force that this was the man she'd be kissing for all eternity. He was hers.

Stone changed the slant of the kiss, framing the soft curves of her face in his calloused hands. He gently nipped at her bottom lip, alternatingly sliding his tongue over it. "I love you," he spoke on her lips. "Damn, but I love you."

There was shimmering love in Kristianna's eyes as he raised his head to search her face. He wove his fingers in her silken hair as she spoke the words he longed to hear.

"I love you, too." She reached out and tenderly touched his clean-shaven cheek as tears filled her eyes. Her voice was but a whisper, her words trembling. "More than you could ever imagine."

Shaken over the intensity of his emotions, Stone cleared his throat and placed one more kiss on her mouth, then regretfully moved away from her. "You better open your wedding present so I can open mine."

A curious smile found its way to Kristianna's lips, and along with it, a pretty pink blush. "*Ja.* Where is it?" Though she suffered the loss of Stone's kisses, she was very interested to see what her husband had for her. It would be the second gift he'd given her. The first, and one she'd cherish forever, were her doeskin gloves.

She waited in anticipation as Stone moved toward his split hide and satchel, reaching down below and behind them. When he turned to her, he was holding a long, brown paper package tied with a string, narrow at one end and the other ballooned like a flower bulb.

"Happy wedding day, wife." He handed her the present.

Despite its odd shape, the parcel was not heavy. Kristianna untied the string and tore the paper away. When the gift was revealed, she gasped. "Oh! Oh my, Stone! It is the red parasol from Mr. Bidwell's."

"Now you don't have to be afraid to touch it, sweetheart. It's yours."

Gone was any guilt over it being red and an evil color that she should be denied. She ran her fingers through the faded tassels, making them dance. She smiled at the slight coolness their jiggling caused and sunk her hand down into one of the folds.

"How do you open it, Stone? Show me." She stifled a girlish giggle as she anxiously thrust the parasol at him.

Stone smiled at her carefree innocence and showed her how to shake it open. The folded scarlet web sprang to life with a slight puff of dust. Having been kept in the Sutler's Store corner for such a long time, the satin dome was streaked with bright, then dull shades of red. Kristianna didn't care as she drew the carved, wooden handle over her shoulder. The tassels dangled above her brow and she smiled demurely.

"How do I look? Like a Yankee wife?"

Leaning back on his heels, Stone assessed her. She was garbed in Swedish attire with her silly black lace hat, the one that she'd been wearing the first time he'd set eyes on her. He'd thought it ridiculous then and he still did. And above it all was an old parasol that no Eastern-bred woman would dare leave the house with. But she was more lovely with her hodgepodge attire and sparkling violet-blue eyes than any woman had a right to be. And she was his.

"You look grand." He came to her and placed his hands over hers, easing the parasol away. Depositing it on the floor, he faced her and brushed his palm over the outline of her high cheekbone.

She rested against his hand. "I wish I could have made you a wedding shirt. That is our Swedish custom. The bride always makes the groom the shirt he will be married in."

"Maybe you can teach me Swedish, instead."

His voice was gravelly and husky sending a delightful shiver down her spine.

"Swedish? What do you want to know how to say?"

Stone plucked off her stiff, black hat with its starched lace edge and tossed it to the floor. "What's that called?"

"*Bindmössan.*" Her stomach filled with butterflies as she came to understand what he was doing.

Next, he reached around behind her and tugged at the bow of her floral, cotton apron. Slowly, he slid it from her waist and it too was dropped to the floor.

"And this?" he queried with a seductive arch to his dark, slashing brow.

"*Skimpa.*" Her heart caught in her throat and she found she was having trouble breathing normally.

With one long, lean finger, he traced the lacing rings to her lavender bodice and unfastened the ties. "This?"

"*Livkjol.*" She closed her eyes, fighting the urge to sway toward him.

Then he moved his hands up and over her shoulders, massaging her and stroking her nape. Finally, he unfastened the row of hooks down the front of her white blouse. As his burning fingers brushed the thin material of her chemise, she trembled and gasped softly. "This?" he growled, his voice showing his self-restraint.

"*Overdel,*" she murmured as the blouse slid down her arms and floated to the floor. A chill ran over her bare skin as she was left standing in only her chemise and skirt.

Once again, he reached behind her to remove another piece of clothing. This time, there was more urgency in his fingers. He fumbled with the hooks that led down the back of her checkered cotton skirt, freeing them one by one with gently, but firm tugs. At last, the garment slipped over her hips and billowed around her trim ankles. She stepped out of the circle of fabric and kicked off her clogs in the process.

"That?" Stone's voice cracked to a moan as he viewed her alabaster skin as she was clad only in her delicate underpinnings. His heart rumbled in his chest and he forced himself to keep the erratic beats from becoming deafening in the small room.

"*Kjol,*" she whispered, lifting her chin. She met the full force of his eyes, daring him, wanting him, to continue.

Stone stepped forward and pulled free her pantalets, then in the same fluid motion, yanked the ribbons of her chemise. "And this?" He parted the soft, intimate fabric and exposed her high, proud breasts. The pink nipples were puckered and begging him to reach for them.

"I . . ." Kristianna found she could not think of the proper word to tell him. She was drowning, dying for his touch, his kiss.

"Dammit," Stone groaned. "Who the hell cares?" With that, he ripped the chemise down the middle and drew her into his arms. He kissed her deeply and with uncontrollable desire. Her mouth was like fire, her lips hot and moist. She kissed him back with an intensity of her own and he was unwilling to wait any longer.

Breaking free for a split second, he shucked his moccasins and shed his shirt and trousers. She stood before him trembling, still wearing her dark blue stockings and delicate garters. That excited him more than if she'd been completely nude. Everything else was exposed to his view— her quivering breasts, her slender waist, her hips, and the pale triangle of her womanhood. He caught her eyes and found she was appraising him as well.

Kristianna went to Stone and blended into his sinewy arms, delighting in the rouch texture of his chest hair against her taut nipples. The feel of him, strong and hard against her thighs made her knees weak. Then he was kissing her again, gently bending her back onto the narrow bed.

The mattress cushioned them as Stone put his weight on top of her. She kissed him back, basking in the glory of it all, parting her thighs for him. He moaned against her lips and entered that private part of her that was ready for him.

She received and gave herself, thrusting back and meeting him until she felt she was going to die from pure ecstasy. When at last she thought she could endure no more, a warm wave swept through her, causing her to shudder against him as she cried out his name. Only then did Stone move one last time. His back muscles tensed and he cradled his full weight on her. She clung to him, holding him as tightly as she could.

The stateroom was quiet save for the mingling of spent breaths and fleeting, sweet kisses, murmurs of love and soft caresses.

Outside, the world floated by on the current of the Mississippi River, and through the tiny room the lulling call of the water and the steady churn of the paddles drifted through the curtained window.

". . . boatman dance and the boatman sing,
The boatman is up to everything . . ."

·21·

"Saaaiint Louie!"

The pilot's cry echoed down to where Kristianna and Stone stood at the railing on the upper deck. As the *Missouri Grand* manuevered its way into the harbor, Kristianna scanned the congested area with interest. She had never expected the city to be so large. Stone had warned her, but having spent nearly all her life in Wisconsin Territory, she wasn't prepared to face such an intimidating place.

The wharf was a conglomeration of stern-wheelers, keelboats, barges, pirogues, canoes, Mackinaws, and side-wheelers, their smoke-stacks dispatching dark streams of sooty clouds.

Several boatmen converged at the bow and uncoiled the heavy ropes that would anchor them to their berth. It was only a matter of minutes before the side-wheeler gracefully slid into her spot and the passengers were given the go-ahead to disembark.

Kristianna took in a deep breath and declared, "I think we should go directly to The Sovereign House, Stone."

Stone had placed his hand at the small of her back and was guiding her down the wide flight of stairs to the main deck. "I thought we already discussed this."

"We did not. We argued about it." Kristianna's delicate face was set with determination as she slid her hand down the railing. She scanned the city's rooftopped horizon, her heartbeat picking up speed. Somewhere in the midst of it all was Papa. "I do not want to wait until you have checked into it yourself. He is my papa."

"And I told you that as your husband, I'll handle it." Stone steered them around the chaotic deck, dodging porters carrying departing luggage, as well as the crew who were already "wooding up" fresh stores of fuel timbers for the boilers.

Kristianna held onto the stiff top of her black velvet hat and the handle of her red parasol for fear of losing them in the commotion. Leaving the boat behind them, they blended into the crowd on the levee. She spoke as she veered out of the path of an intent dock worker. "But it seems so simple that we go to the place on the letter."

"We'll talk about it when we reach the hotel." The expression in Stone's eyes cautioned her and rather than go into a full-blown argument in the heart of all the bustle, Kristianna sighed and let the matter drop, but vowed to take it up as soon as they were settled. Resignedly, she absorbed the scene around her.

The levee was scattered with brightly dressed voyageurs, traders and colorfully attired men and women. Indians—Stone had told her they were from the Osage tribe—roamed freely. Cargo, stacked mounds of long timbers used as steamboat fuel, bundles of pelts, barrels, and sacks were scattered everywhere. And surprisingly, in the midst of it all, grew trees with blossoming pink-petaled flowers.

Stone had secured a buggy and was instructing the driver where to pick up their luggage when she turned her attention back to him. He blended in perfectly with the setting in his full buckskins and low-crowned hat. She was in awe at how confidently he handled himself and she had to admit that she was glad he'd insisted on coming. He had taken over the situation with an easy command that put her at ease. He turned and lifted her up into the black buggy and gently deposited her on the tufted red leather seat. The cushion was soft and comfortable, not at all like anything she'd ever ridden in back home.

After Stone pulled himself up next to her, he said, "*Château de Saint Louis*, driver." Stone put his arm around Kristianna's back and settled in. "Keep your hem away from the wheel, Kris. City hacks are hell-bent on getting as many rides as they can."

She wasn't exactly sure what he meant, but

didn't want to argue with him on the point. Better not to test his words with her striped prairie-brown-and-black skirt so she gathered the full folds in her hand.

The hackney threaded its way through the maze of pilots and seamen, crates and freight, finally turning away from the levee and onto the narrow streets of the waterfront. The poorly constructed dirt roads were a disaster both in the winter and summer. During the rains, the city's inhabitants joked that the streets were a navigable waterway through the city, and in the dry season, the dust was an overabundant, choking cloud. As a result of Nature's torture, the roads were pocked and pitted, giving every passenger who traveled them a spine-shaking journey.

Though the thoroughfares were horrendous, they were lined with flourishing boat shops, taverns, and grogshops with numerous men milling outside their doors. Kristianna wrinkled her nose at the pungent odors of hard ale and heavy spirits that came from the establishments. She guessed most of their patrons to be trappers, rivermen, and wagoners. Colorful signs on various enterprises hinted they were gambling houses, and more than once as they drove by, she could hear the boisterous men within.

Soon they were turning up a quieter street where hawthorn trees clustered with blossoms were well kept and storefronts gleamed. There, the clean, fresh air was scented with a light, pleasant odor from the blossoms. Several of the shop signs were written in French, and she recalled Stone telling her that two men, Pierre

Laclède Liguest and Auguste Chouteau, had founded the city; their ancestral heritage was evident above the levee, retaining the sophisticated behavior of the original French settlers.

The hackman pulled up next to a three-story limestone building with windows curtained in emerald velvet. Kristianna shaded her eyes against the late-afternoon sun to read the brass sign over the front door—*Château de Saint Louis*.

"We are staying here?" She couldn't believe her eyes. The hotel looked like a mansion, far grander than anything she'd ever beheld.

Stone had swung his legs over and gave her a hand down. "You like it?" His eyes were on her, smiling and reflecting her enthusiasm as he waited for her answer.

"I have never seen anything to compare," she breathed, looking at the elegant entryway that was covered by an emerald canopy.

Lifting the corner of his mouth into a grin, Stone paid the driver and took Kristianna's hand in his. "Wait until you see the inside."

For a brief moment, Kristianna wondered when Stone had been at the hotel and more importantly—with whom? Deciding not to let anything dampen her hopeful spirits, she brushed off her insecurities. He was married to her now and that was all that mattered. She couldn't believe that she was now here herself. So much had transpired in the last several months, that it was beginning to overwhelm her. Her life had changed beyond anything she could have ever imagined. She was more than a little nervous as they stepped through the wide double doors with beveled glass, and crossed the threshold.

The foyer was magnificent. The tiled black-and-white floor shone from many coats of wax. Above her head was a three-tiered chandelier dripping with crystal prisms. The walls were elegantly papered in forest green flock and complemented by several landscape paintings of the frontier.

Reaching the front desk, Stone swiveled the registry to face him and picked up a feathered quill. As he scratched his name on the paper, he spoke to the desk clerk, announcing their arrival, and the dapper man nodded curtly.

Kristianna watched with fascination as Stone turned the book toward him. It had to have been on some sort of disk to do that. Imagine, it just turned back and forth without ever having to be picked up. She peeked over Stone's shoulder and watched him sign their name. Their name—*Mr. and Mrs. Stone Boucher*. Seeing it for the first time made her feel very proud, as if a thousand stars were dazzling inside her. She stood back again and toyed with the handle of her parasol, nervously twirling the red web. The clerk gave her a quick perusal and she self-consciously stopped her fidgeting. She was anxious to be in their room to plan the next course of events that would lead them to Papa.

The desk clerk rang for an attendant to show them to their room. Soon after, they were led up the stairs and given a spacious suite on the third floor that offered a view of the many differently shaped rooftops below, and beyond that a sliver of the Mississippi River. Stone paid the attendant several coins and bid him to bring up their luggage when it arrived.

Kristianna removed her hat and parasol and set them on the four-poster, royal-green canopy bed that graced the room, then she walked over to the window. Stone had pushed aside the white lace curtains and was looking intently out the glass. Kristianna broached the subject that weighed on her mind. "I want to go with you. I know we have been through this already, but you have not been listening to me." She put her hand on his taut biceps and applied slight pressure. "Please. He is out there somewhere and I have to find him."

"I'll find him for you."

"No." She relaxed her hand and gave him a disapproving stare that furrowed her delicate brows. "I do not want you to. I want to be the one to see him first. He will not know you, he will want to see me."

Stone left the window and Kristianna followed him, not giving up. The dark look on his face showed he was in a foul mood and she decided to let him ponder her words for a moment before she resumed her argument.

Stone didn't want her to accompany him to The Sovereign House; it was as simple as that. Especially since he didn't know what he'd find. There could be a dozen reasons why the man was staying at such a fine hotel and one of them burned hot within him. He'd heard of country men leaving their wives to come to the city and set up a different way of life. Gambling and drinking were often a man's downfall; the Missouri and Mississippi Rivers were like whores and they lured men everyday with such prospects. He'd be damned if he'd let Kristianna walk in and see her father with another woman. Though he could very well be wrong, he didn't want to take that chance.

"No." His refusal was strong and unwavering. He moved toward her. "You're staying here and that's the end of it."

Kristianna stamped her clogged foot and balled her fists at her side. She placed her arms akimbo and huffed, "I did not realize I married such a bully!"

Stone gave her an easy grin, thinking she looked especially pretty when she was fired up. He cupped her pert chin between his fingers and pressed a soft kiss to her sulking lips.

Despite herself, Kristianna felt her anger subsiding and she allowed Stone to kiss her. He grazed her mouth sweetly and she responded by putting her arms around his waist, pressing herself close to him. "You cannot sway me so easily," she murmured against his mouth.

"I'm not trying to." Stone lifted his head and caressed her chin lightly before releasing it. "If it will make you any happier, I'll go to The Sovereign House right now."

"You will?" Kristianna's eyes lit up.

"Yes. Only you stay here." There was a sternness in his rugged face which she secretly dismissed, but she pretended to take seriously.

"*Ja*, I will," she replied dutifully.

"You do that, Kristianna," he warned, and settled his hat farther on his forehead. "I'll be back in a little while. Wait here for the luggage and you can unpack it."

"*Ja*, I will do that." Unpack, indeed!

"I'm trusting you." He pointed a finger at her as he opened the door.

"Good-bye," she called to him as the portal closed behind him.

She counted to ten in Swedish very slowly, then snatched up her hat from the coverlet and plopped it on her head. Well, he never should have trusted her when it came to Papa! Papa needed her, not Stone.

For a minute, Kristianna thought she'd lost him. But as she scanned the street in front of the *Château de Saint Louis*, she glimpsed Stone's hat and broad back as he sat in an open carriage headed in the direction they'd just come. She hadn't counted on him riding in a buggy! She had thought she would follow him on foot.

Quickly, she looked for an empty carriage amid the milling coaches that filled the street. When she finally found one, she dashed to it, hoping she wasn't too late to follow Stone.

"Please, Mister, I need to ride in your buggy. It is of the utmost urgency."

The rather stout man snorted and nodded his head. "Come on up then, gal. Pitney will take you. Alone are you?"

"*Ja*." Then seeing a glimmer appear in his robust face, she stammered, "*Nej*! No. I am following a man, but he must not know I am following him."

He cocked a bushy brow. "Are you now?"

"Yes, and if you do not hurry, we will lose sight of him for sure! Please, drive on."

"Where is the fellow?" Pitney asked as he clicked the horse into action and snapped his leather whip.

"Down there, that way." Kristianna pointed.

The driver slouched down in his worn seat and glanced over his shoulder to Kristianna. "Married, is he?"

"Yes," she answered, though she wasn't sure at all what that had to do with anything.

"Pity. You suspect he's gone back to his wife, do you?"

"What?" Kristianna was trying her best to listen to the driver and crane her neck at the same time. She could not see any signs of Stone at all. He'd disappeared around a corner.

"Married men. Never trust 'em, I always say. And so does me wife!" With that, Pitney laughed, his rotund belly jiggling with the effort.

"I am married to him!" Kristianna clarified his misinterpretation. "Oh, there he is! That way, driver! To the left."

Pitney pulled around the corner, the carriage wheels clattering over the street. "That him, gal? The big one with the frontier hat?"

"Yes. That is my husband."

"You suspect he's off to meet with his paramour, eh?"

Kristianna hadn't the faintest idea what a

"paramour" was and at the moment, the defini-
tion was the farthest thing from her mind.
"Look, they are turning down there."

"I see, gal. I have two eyes." Pitney
manuevered the horse around a slow-moving
barouche and veered in the direction Stone's
carriage had taken. They followed Stone down
two more blocks and turned to the left once
more, finally stopping. "There they are. They're
reining up now in front of The Sovereign
House."

"Thank you, Pitney," Kristianna called as she
disembarked and started toward the hotel doors
Stone had slipped inside.

"Come back, gal! I didn't give you a ride for me
fancy!"

His words were drowned out and lost as a four
horse-drawn rig rattled down the street.

Kristianna strode purposefully to The Sovereign House and opened the double door. She was
barely inside when a heavy hand came crashing
down on her arm. Swiveling with surprise, she
peered into Pitney's ruddy face. "Comely as you
are, gal, you still owe me fare."

"What?" Kristianna was momentarily
stunned. "But I thought you—"

"Don't know what you thought, but the fact of
the matter is I've got me a brood at home and a
wife to feed and it don't get done giving gals free
rides. Now pay up."

"I do not have any money." Tears threatened
in Kristianna's eyes as she shrugged off his iron
grasp. She hadn't realized she was supposed to

pay the man! But then, come to think of it, Stone had and he'd also paid the attendant at the hotel, too. Stone was right, she didn't know city ways and now was not the time to be learning them, either. Biting her lower lip, she searched the lobby for Stone. What did it matter if he saw her now? Now she needed him!

"No money, eh?"

She ruefully shook her head.

"Then you better come with me—to the law. Poor as it is in this river town, they don't take too kindly to filchers!"

Pitney extended a fleshy hand and was about to snake it around her slender wrist when he was stopped by a resonant voice.

"I wouldn't do that if I were you."

Stone!

Kristianna let out a visible sigh of relief.

The ironlike weight on Pitney's shoulder was cause enough for him to back down. He cussed under his breath and turned around to face his assailant. "Gad! You are a big one! No sense in getting yourself in a lather, fellow. The lady owes me fare. You pay it and I'll be on me way."

Stone hadn't given Kristianna a single look and she knew that underneath his scowling facade, he was boiling with anger. And could she blame him? She'd defied him and now she'd caused a spectacle of herself.

Reaching into his parfleche, Stone drew out several coins which Pitney eyed hungrily. "For your trouble. But I don't ever want to pay you for it again. You understand?"

369

"Sure, fellow. Sure. I'll be on me way then."
He touched the brim of his shabby top hat and
disappeared out the door.

Kristianna swallowed, waiting for the tirade
she was sure would follow, but when it did not
come, she looked up into Stone's teal-blue eyes.
They were cool as spring water, though his lips
were set in a grim line. "Seems you've come
down here for nothing."

Not quite sure she understood him properly,
she questioned him with her eyes.

"He's not here. There never has been, nor is
there now, a Sixten Bergendahl at this hotel."

Kristianna's shoulders drooped and she stifled
a defeated cry. "Oh . . . Papa . . ."

Two days later, they were no closer to finding
Sixten Bergendahl than if they'd been sitting on
the porch swing at the farmstead. Kristianna was
out of her mind with worry, and after Stone's
stern lecture about her venturing out on her own,
she'd resigned herself to waiting for him at the
Château de Saint Louis while he made inquiries
as to her papa's whereabouts. However, on the
morning of the third day, her patience was almost gone.

"I cannot stand another day of doing nothing,
Stone." Kristianna sat at the vanity in her wrapper, brushing her hair. She turned around to see
Stone still lying in bed. "If I do not get out of this
room, I think I will go mad."

Stone propped himself up and rested his tousled head on a fluffy pillow. "I thought you liked

it when I drove you mad. Why don't you come back here and we can go mad together."

Beside herself, Kristianna blushed at his suggestion. Her eyes roved over her husband's bare torso, reveling in the hard contours of his chest and the dark triangle of hair there. His shoulders were tight with muscles, the exposed tanned skin contrasting with the starched white of the bedclothes. It didn't matter that they'd already made love that morning. Just the mere suggestion from the man and she wanted more of him! How could she had turned into such a wanton? "You know what I mean," she finally said, ignoring his allusion.

"All right, sweetness. Then let's get you out of here for the day. I'll take you shopping for a fine city dress and later we can go out to dinner."

"Stone, I really don't think—"

Stone rose from the bed and walked to the bureau. Kristianna caught her breath as she viewed his naked body. He wasn't even aware of the effect he had on her—or was he? His body looked as if it had been sculpted by the finest of artists, his torso solid and fluid with tautness. His legs were long and lean and sprinkled with a fine dusting of dark hair. And that hair tapered to . . . She blushed again as she viewed him in the stark daylight. Since she'd married Stone, her modesty had changed. She was no longer intimidated by his nakedness. She liked seeing him without his clothes. As he turned to open the drawer, she was given a tempting picture of his firm buttocks.

"Maybe we should stay here . . ." Kristianna's voice was unsteady and it cracked an octave higher than normal.

Stone slipped into his denim trousers and faced her as he buttoned them. Her eyes were drawn to his lean fingers as they deftly fastened his waistband. He strode barefoot toward her over the plush carpet and she had a hard time swallowing. He rested his hands on her delicate, sloping shoulders. "We've been here for three days and you haven't even seen much of the city, much less eaten a decent meal."

"But I have. I've eaten two boxes of those trifle candies you gave me."

"Truffles," he corrected, a flash of humor on his face.

"Truffles, then. I know you meant well, buying them for me, seeing how I've never had any before, but I fear they've settled right onto my hips."

Stone laughed, a deep and effortless sound. "Your hips are still as lush as they were the day we were married." He swooped down and kissed her parted lips. "I meant we should have a real meal in the dining room. Not what we've had sent up to us. You've not seen anything of Saint Louis, save for your friend Pitney."

Kristianna frowned. Would she ever live that down?

"I want to buy you a fancy dress and take you to dinner."

"It is a lovely idea, Stone, but I would not feel right about it because of Papa."

"Kris, you've got to have patience. We'll find

him. You can't expect to waltz into town and find
him right under your nose? The address on the
letter was a strong possibility, but it turned out to
be a flash in the pan. Why should we sit around
idle when we can enjoy the city while we're
here?"

"I thought you did not like cities."

"I don't like living in them, but the comforts
they offer are something to be desired."

Kristianna sighed.

"Come on. I'm going to buy you a dress that
will be the envy of every female in the Wisconsin
Territory. Right down to the lace pantaloons."

"Lace pantaloons?"

"So soft and sheer, you'll feel like you don't
have a thing on at all." Stone brushed his finger
along her thigh where her dressing gown had
parted.

"Stone, you are wicked." His·touch made her
tingle way down to her toes.

"Never claimed to be anything else."

Later that evening, Kristianna slipped on the
lace pantaloons with the help of the ladies' maid
Stone had insisted on hiring.

"Are you sure I have to wear—*that*?"
Kristianna asked the young girl.

"Of course, madame. Every lady wears one."
Ivy picked up the cotton-glazed, boned corset
Stone had purchased for Kristianna that after-
noon.

"That is what the shopkeeper declared."
Kristianna stood in the middle of the room,
wearing a new batiste chemise of fine lace and

ribbons that was transparent and light. At first, she'd been embarrassed in front of Ivy, but the young girl hadn't given her a second glance so some of Kristianna's inhibitions had vanished.

With Ivy's help, the corset was fitted around Kristianna's slender waist. Ivy adjusted the stiff bone stays in the seams and began to tug on the laces.

Kristianna winced and held onto the bedpost as Ivy pulled until Kristianna thought she'd snap in two. Finally, Ivy fastened the laces and moved to reach into one of the packages on the coverlet. She produced two flannel petticoats and a heavy crinoline that was stiff with compressed horsehair and a padded frame. Next came three percale underskirts.

Still as fascinated as she'd been in the dress shop, Kristianna looked at everything with awe. She hadn't questioned Stone when he'd commanded the shopkeeper, telling her to bring out this and that. A tiny finger of jealousy had pricked at her as she had wondered how he knew so much about ladies clothing. When he'd picked out her dress, she'd protested, for surely its expense was far more than he could afford, but he'd placated her with a rakish smile and she forgot about everything else.

Now, as she withstood Ivy's ministrations, she was nervous as a canary cornered by a cat. What if he found her lacking in the city finery he'd bought her? She sucked in her breath as Ivy slipped her dress over her head, careful not to damage her neatly arranged hair.

Somehow in the midst of it all, she thought of

Papa. She felt guilty getting dressed up to have a good time when he was yet to be found. But Stone had reasoned that they should have this one night of fun and she vowed she would enjoy it.

"You're ready, madame."

Ivy broke through Kristianna's thoughts and she smiled faintly at the young girl. Giving herself a quick once-over in the mirror, Kristianna couldn't believe her eyes. Just as she'd imagined many times, she was now outfitted like a true Yankee woman.

Ivy gave her handiwork a sweeping glance up and down and nodded with confidence over the results. "You look beautiful, madame."

"Thank you, Ivy, for everything. I hope my husband thinks so, too." With that, she slipped out of the room to meet Stone in the lobby.

Stone sat in an ornately upholstered wing chair staring up at the landing. He'd been waiting for what seemed like hours. He was on the verge of marching up the steps and seeing for himself what was taking Kristianna so long, when suddenly she appeared.

He inhaled sharply, feeling as if someone had just socked him in the gut. His unwavering eyes blazed over Kristianna with appreciation.

She was a vision. An angel. He knew he'd married a beautiful woman, but he had never guessed that her beauty would be enhanced beyond compare by a mere dress.

She smiled shyly at him as she raised her hand to the banister and made a slow descent to where he sat. Remembering himself, Stone stood and moved to the bottom of the stairs. He leaned onto the balustrade for fear of rushing up to meet her, to touch her to see if indeed she was real.

Stone's gaze lingered on her face, noting the soft hue of her eyes and her full mouth. Her long, blonde hair had been curled with irons and artfully arranged at the back of her head. Her face was framed with tiny wisps that had been coaxed to soft tendrils. As she neared, he heard the seductive whisper of her petticoats and the thought of her scantily clad legs in lace pantaloons drove him mad. He controlled himself as he looked at her gown. He'd picked it himself, choosing it for its unique color. It was a crisp, deep amethyst silk evening dress with short sleeves puffed by pleats. The neckline was low, draped, and pleated. He stopped for a moment to appreciate the enticing swell of her breasts and the alabaster skin that was revealed. As she came closer, he took in the fluid motion of her steps and smiled inwardly as he gazed at her shoes.

She had agreed to everything but the shoes. He'd wanted to buy her fine satin slippers, but she would have none of that. Her eyes had fixed on a pair of Prunellas and she had to have them. Why, he could not—still did not—understand. They were the color of prunes with square toes and long, thin throats. She'd claimed she had seen a picture of them once in a catalogue and she'd secretly wished she owned a pair. Well, now she did, and regardless of how silly they looked, she walked in them with grace and ease and he was damn proud of her.

"Am I terribly late, Stone?" Her voice was faintly breathless.

Any impatience he'd had was gone. She'd been well worth the wait. He sensed she was nervous, as if awaiting his approval. "No. Not at all. You look like an angel."

Somewhat relieved, Kristianna sighed away some of her apprehension. "I am glad." She didn't know why she felt so giddy, so wanting to please him. She suffered his long assessment of her on the stairs, and was elated that he approved of her appearance. Now she had her own chance to assess him.

Stone was attired in city finery, too. She had never seen him in a suit before. He appeared comfortable in his new black double-breasted coat with a padded, velvet collar and an embroidered, dark blue silk waistcoat. His long trousers were held taut by leather straps underneath his shoes. He'd combed his long umber hair away from his face and she marveled in the handsome contours of his nose and square jaw. He was, she decided, suited very well for fancy clothes.

"You ready to eat?" he asked, though suddenly, eating was the farthest thing from Stone's mind.

"*J–ja*, I am." She had the overwhelming need to be next to him, to touch him, and she was glad when he offered her his arm. She slipped her hand over the coarse fabric of his jacket and allowed him to guide her into the fancy dining room of the *Château de Saint Louis*.

Conscious of every step she took, Kristianna felt that if she moved the wrong way, she'd unravel like a wayward ball of yarn. As she took another careful step, she heard a faint noise and pull at her side. Then as they continued, it came again. She held back momentarily and Stone looked at her with a question in his eyes.

"I—I cannot go in here."

"Why not?"

"Because I am creaking," she whispered, utterly horrified.

Stone gave her a disarming smile and looked down into her upturned face which was filled with dread. "I don't hear anything. Besides, we'll be sitting down and then no one will hear you."

"I do not know why I let you and everyone else talk me into this—this corset. I do not like it. My stomach hurts."

They were shown to a table with a fine linen cloth and centerpiece of beautiful roses. Stone helped her sit, his fingers brushing like brands on her exposed shoulders. She felt a burning tide wash over her and she involuntarily shivered with delight.

"Would you care for a bottle of our best wine, sir?" the waiter queried.

Stone glanced briefly at the menu and closed it. "I'll let you choose it. Have the chef prepare us his finest dish. This is my wife's first city restaurant."

Kristianna blushed under the admission as the waiter scurried off. "You did not have to say that."

"Why not? This is your first time in a fine restaurant and I want you to have the best it can offer."

378

"I am not sure how much I can eat," she muttered under her breath, and leaned a little closer over the table. Unbeknownst to Kristianna, Stone was offered a very tempting view of cleavage. "I did not want to say anything earlier, but I am trussed up so tightly, Stone, I do not think I can swallow more than two bites without bursting from this contraption."

Stone's mouth curved into a captivating smile. "Then we'll eat slowly and later when we're upstairs, I'll have to help you out of it."

She was about to reply when they were interrupted by the *mâitre d'hôtel.*

"Your pardon, Mr. Boucher, but there is a Mr. Heacock in the lobby who would like to speak with you."

Kristianna's gaze flickered to Stone. "Is it about Papa, Stone?" she inquired anxiously.

Stone was curt as he pushed back his chair and stood. "No, sweetness. This is business of another matter. I'll be back in a minute."

"Oh . . ." Her voice trailed after him. She watched his tall form disappear out the fringed and draped curtains that led into the lobby. There, she could barely make out another man as Stone met him and they walked away from her view.

Maybe Mr. Heacock did have to do with Papa and Stone didn't want her to know. Maybe he'd come upon some news and . . . The *mâitre d'hôtel* passed by once again and she gestured him to the table.

"Please, can you tell me the nature of business Mr. Heacock is in?"

"I believe Mr. Heacock is the agent for the New York Fur Company, madame."

Kristianna was suddenly baffled. What would Stone have to talk to a fur company about? How could that possibly connect with her papa? "If I can ask you further . . ."—she bit her lower lip, almost afraid of the man's answer—"if a man is a trapper, what interest would he have in a fur company?"

"I'm not much of an expert, madame, but it has been my assumption that a fur company hires trappers to trap for them. I suggest you take the matter up with your husband."

"Oh, yes, I will do that, thank you." Kristianna gazed vaguely at the empty lobby, her heart sinking. Of course, fur companies hired trappers. Stone was a trapper, that was what he did. Why had she ever thought he would do otherwise? Why had she even considered that he might settle down and build a life with her? Just because he'd married her didn't mean he would change. He would continue on with his way of life. He would leave her every fall and winter and maybe one season he would not come home at all.

The revelation was swift and hard and hit her like a gust of wind. What lingering appetite that hadn't been cinched off by her constricting corset vanished.

It seemed as if her man of the traps was still a wisp of smoke, after all.

·22·

"I won't be gone more than an hour."

Stone's back was to Kristianna as he gathered his parafleche and tied it around his waist. She watched him from her perch on the mattress, her cheek resting against the tall bedpost. She'd had a fitful night's sleep and had awakened with a dull headache. "More business?"

"In a way. It may concern your father." Stone faced her now and she gave him a fleeting glance. He'd discarded his fancy city clothes for his old trapping garb and low-crowned hat. She couldn't read the expression in his eyes, but she doubted his sincerity. He was, no doubt, off to see the man from the New York Fur Company to make further arrangements for the buying of his pelts or whatever it was that trappers did.

He moved toward her and she fought back

tears. How could he act so casual, as if what he was doing didn't concern her in the slightest? Didn't he love her enough to tell her the truth? She could try and accept his decision; after all, she'd known from the start where his heart was. She only wished it didn't hurt so much.

Stone came to the bed and stood before her. "Still feeling bad because of dinner?"

For a scant second, she thought he was reading her thoughts and she wasn't able to speak.

"If I had known what the specialty of the house was, I'd never had ordered it." Stone smiled as if thinking of it.

"Oh, yes . . ." He was talking about the meal, not Mr. Heacock. She briefly recalled the "specialty of the house," snails to be exact. She'd been horrified to find the garden creatures floating on her plate in a saffron sauce. The smell, along with the tightness of her corset, had given her ample excuse to dismiss herself from the table. She hadn't been up to eating anyway after Stone had returned from his meeting with Mr. Heacock.

Stone reached out and brushed her jaw with his finger. "You feeling all right, sweetness? You look a little pale. How's your foot?"

"My foot is fine," she mumbled, and turned away so he could not touch her. His fingers on her skin were warm and sparked an attraction that she tried hard to deny. "I think I will lay down and rest while you are gone."

"I'll be back soon and then I can tell you—"

"Fine," Kristianna cut him off, not wanting him to say anything more, knowing that his words would no doubt be excuses. She looked down at the folds of her skirt, waiting for him to leave. Finally, she heard the click of the door as it closed behind him. Only then, did she allow the tears to flow freely.

Kristianna spread out on the coverlet and wept the tears she'd held in since the previous night. She felt such a loss, she ached. How could he claim to love her when all the time he wasn't planning on staying with her? She should have known from the start she couldn't pin him down. He was, and always would be, a wandering man and nothing she could do could change that.

Sitting up, she wiped her stained cheeks with the back of her hand and took in a deep breath. Well, she wouldn't sit here and wait for him to come back. She'd find her papa herself and then she'd go home where she belonged. If she had stood by her convictions, none of this would have happened at all. She should have known that farmers and trappers didn't go together. But it was too late now; she was hopelessly in love with him.

Kristianna went to the bureau and patted her eyes dry with a handkerchief. She sniffed and tucked a wayward strand of hair back into her long braid, then she gave herself a quick inspection. She was attired in the day dress Stone had bought her yesterday. He'd insisted she have two new frocks, one for special occasions, and one for everyday. Though what purpose the day dress would serve on the farm was beyond her. The material was a delicate floral-printed cotton in lilac, green, and orange. Its ruched, piped bodice accentuated her breasts and slimmed her waist. It was very pretty, but even so, she felt as if she didn't belong in it. She was no city girl and she had no right to act like one.

But rather than take the time to change, she kept it on and refastened the laces of her Prunella shoes. Those, she liked. Those, she would wear at home. They were of the softest woolen material and it felt as if she were wearing no shoes at all. Her steps were carefree without the heavy burden of her clogs.

Straightening the gathers of her full skirt, Kristianna swallowed and left the room.

The hallway was quiet, and she descended the stairs unnoticed and made her way to the street. Outside, the sky was dull and gray, giving off a faint drizzle. She debated going back for her red parasol, then changed her mind. The parasol reminded her of Stone.

She walked down the tree-lined street with no real sense of direction. It really didn't matter where she went. Even she knew it was futile to expect to find her papa this way. As Stone had said, she couldn't waltz into the big city and find her father right under her nose. But to appease herself, and to get a much-needed breath of fresh air, Kristianna continued to walk.

She passed the best parts of Saint Louis where the early French settlers had left their marks in the graceful architecture. The houses and shops were well manicured and clean. There were quaint storefronts with lovely trinkets and as she strode by each one, she stepped inside to inquire if they'd heard of Sixten Bergendahl. To her frustration, they had not.

The day wore on and she lost all sense of time and direction. The well-kept stores were becoming few and far between, and, sandwiched between were the grogshops and taverns she'd noted on the day of their arrival. The heavy smells of ale and liquors assaulted her nose as she passed by them. Boisterous calls from within slapped at her ears, making her blush hotly at the freely given curses and rabble-rousing. There was no sense in inquiring for Papa in one of those dens of iniquity.

When at last she inhaled the musty scent of river and smoke from the steamboats, Kristianna realized she'd come upon the levee. She hadn't intended on going so far and suddenly she was more than a little afraid. It was one thing to view the wharves and ships in Stone's company, but alone, she felt vulnerable and lost.

As the day had deepened to pending night, gone were the prettily dressed women she'd admired before. Now the streets were filled with drifters and men intent on filling the saloons. Wagons and carriages careened down the street and had she not been quick on her toes, she would have been struck down by a freight cart laden with timber.

With her heart pounding in her chest, Kristianna decided to turn around and find her way back to the *Château de Saint Louis* before darkness came. But to her surprise, she wasn't quite sure which way to go. She'd been so intent on making queries about Papa, she hadn't paid attention to where she was going.

The loud notes of a fiddle and an accordion floated to her on the breeze across the waterfront, and Kristianna followed them. She vaguely recalled passing an establishment that had seemed less disorderly than the rest. From there, she would get her directions back to the hotel.

Her steps were light and swift as she neared the tavern, its narrow, double doors opening and closing quickly, to admit what seemed like an endless stream of rivermen, wagoners, and trappers. Through the bawdy tunes came the peel of a different instrument she'd never heard before. It was tinny and quite bold. For a flicker of a second, her own curiosity was peaked and she wondered if that was the reason the men were so eager to get inside.

She was at the saloon now and held back just for an instant as a grizzled man, who completely ignored her, opened the door and stepped inside without closing it behind him. Without thinking, Kristianna peered into the opening to see what was making the music.

The interior was dim and at first she could barely see through the haze of smoke. She blinked and focused, scanning the room with wide, disbelieving eyes. It was filled with raucous men, all seemingly drunk, holding heavy glasses in their hands. And there were women, too! They were all dressed in white pinafores and were talking and laughing with the men and . . .

"You one of Kelley's new dance girls?"

A rowdy voice behind her startled her, and she

twirled to face a heavily, red-bearded man with a wild disarray of filthy hair.

"M–me?" She was struck by his overwhelming smell which fleetingly reminded her of Newt Fraeb with his odorous scent of bear grease.

"I'd pay you fine, girl, for one dance." He winked at her and she jumped back.

"I am not a dance girl." She saw in his cold gray eyes that he did not believe her.

"Sure you are, sweet pea. What else you be doin' down these parts?" He reached out and gave her bottom a fierce pinch.

Totally taken aback, she automatically swung her arm and delivered an air-cracking slap on his crusty face. "You listen here, Mister. I am no dance girl and you had better keep your hands off me."

"Hot damn, but I likes 'em feisty." He came at her again, completely undaunted by her attack.

Kristianna screamed and stumbled backward into the tavern. Her frantic voice was unnoticed by the loud calls of drunken men and the wild choruses of music. The bearded man swooped down on her and encircled her waist and she frantically pushed at his barrel-like chest. He crushed her to him and she kicked at his shins with all of the strength she could muster, but her thin shoes were no protection. Her attempts were ineffectual and she was filled with unequivocal terror.

"Kelley's sure got his lot in with the likes of you, sweet pea. Come now, give ol' Tom a kiss."

Kristianna struggled as Tom's head hovered over hers and with a final gathering of nerve, she slammed her fist on his hairy, red jaw. When Tom shook his head, she reasoned she'd hit him hard enough to rattle him a bit. She seized the opportunity and ran for the door.

She'd barely made it two feet when an arm caught her by the middle and she was toppled to the dirty floor. She let out her breath with a whoosh as Tom's heavy body fell on top of her back.

Kristianna cried out in pain and scratched at the floor, trying to scramble away. It was hopeless; no one noticed her, or if they did, they didn't care. She screamed once again as loud as she possibly could and when she thought her voice no longer capable of uttering a sound, Tom's weight was mercifully removed from her. Finding no one was trying to stop her, she weakly tried to crawl away. Able to rise, she turned to see Tom's sour collar in the ham-like fist of an exceedingly tall man's hand whose back was toward her. He was blond and built like a barn with wide shoulders and girth. She backed away with the intention of letting the two men fight it out amongst themselves, when the tall man spoke. Through the loud noise and ruckus came words hauntingly familiar and she was once again drawn to him.

His back was still turned and the smoke-filled room didn't allow her to study him further, but she strained her ears to hear him again.

"*Nej då*! Kelley runs a clean place, Tom Finnigan, and he will not be bothered by the likes of you." The brawny man moved and scooted Tom toward the door. She was now able to see his face and examined the shape of his forehead, cheeks, and mouth.

Pressing a hand to her lips to keep from crying out, Kristianna pushed herself against the wall. She blinked her eyes as burning tears welled from the acrid smoke and the absurdity of the entire situation. The voice, the hair, the build, the face belonged to none other than . . . A sob caught in her throat.

When at last Tom was dispatched from the tavern, the tall, blond man moved toward her and she had to hold herself against the planks of the wall for fear of tumbling down.

"Are you all right, Mistress?" He was above her now and looking into her face, not recognizing her in her city clothes. "Old Tom can be a cur with the women and Kelley does not allow it, nor do I."

Kristianna's pulse soared wildly and she allowed the tears to slip free freely from her eyes. "Papa . . . ? Papa, do you not know me?"

His pale eyes narrowed as if what she was saying was not the truth. When at last he really studied her face, he spoke in a pained voice. "My Lord, Kristianna . . ."

"Papa. Oh, Papa." She fell against his wide chest and clung to him as if she'd never let him go.

Sixten Bergendahl stiffly clutched his daughter and breathed into her hair. "My Lord," he repeated. "What are you doing here?" He put her at arm's length and examined her with a keen eye. "And dressed like a Yankee woman?"

Kristianna blinked back the tears. "I am with

my husband, Papa. We came here to find you."

"Gunnar Thorson is here, too? Where is he?" Sixten quickly scanned the doorway.

"*Nej*, Papa. I am not married to Gunnar. I married a man named Stone Boucher." She didn't want to dwell on Stone or the reasons for her hasty marriage. At the moment, the only thing of concern was that she had at last found her papa and he was safe!

"Stone Boucher?" Sixten's words were cut by the shattering sound of broken glass behind the busy long bar.

"*Ja*," she answered over the confusion.

"Come. Let us go some place where it is quiet. Mr. Kelley's office is this way." He snatched her hand and threaded them through the throng of uproarious men. Making his way toward the rear of the tavern, he veered to the left and down a narrow hallway to the end where a small office was located.

Once inside, he closed the door behind him and some of the deafening noise was cut off.

Kristianna approached him to give him another hug, but he held her back and took a seat in the rickety chair by the desk.

Sixten appeared oddly nervous as he ran a shaky hand through his thick, white blond hair. Drawing in a deep breath, he exhaled slowly. "Do you mind telling me what you are doing here without your husband—whoever he may be?"

"I . . ." She was at a loss for words. To go into detail would take forever and she wasn't exactly keen on the idea of telling her papa that Stone was a mountain man and not a farmer. "Are you not glad to see me, Papa?" She truly didn't understand his aloofness. "Mama and I and Noelle, too, have been worried sick about you. You did not write—"

"I did," Sixten interjected. He nervously fingered one of the hooks on his homespun shirt. "I did write."

Kristianna looked at him quickly, noticing that he had not given up his farmer's attire. He was dressed in the linen shirt Mama had made him and his woolen pants, and knee-high boots. He'd even kept his leather suspenders to crisscross over his wide shoulders. "We got your letter the day Stone and I left for Saint Louis. Really, Papa, you did not expect me to be satisfied by your scant words. I did not even tell Mama of them."

Sixten hung his head in shame. "I could not tell Ulla . . ."

"About this place?" she inquired softly. "Is this why you did not write sooner? Have you been here all this time?"

He stood and rubbed his finger across his straight nose. "*Ja*, I have been here." There was embarrassed pain in his words.

"Why, Papa?" she coaxed, resting her hand gently on his shoulder.

Sixten stared at a hole in the shabby wallpaper and spoke in a far-off voice. "When I left you and your mama, I thought I could come into Saint Louis and find a job right away. Me, a big Swede with a talent for craftsmanship. But no one wanted to hire me to build things. I got work on

391

the docks, but was let go when the boss's nephew wanted a place on the payroll."

Kristianna listened compassionately to him while he continued. "I tried to get a decent job, but I could not. As time went on, I worried about leaving your mama so long, that I took what job I could find. Mr. Kelley needed a big man to keep order in the place, and that I can do. I keep the riffraff like Tom out and he pays me a fair wage."

"But what about The Sovereign House? Your letter was on that stationery."

He looked puzzled for a moment, as if trying to recall what he had done. "Mr. Kelley took me to dinner there once after I had broken up a particularly bad fight. I thought the writing looked so fancy on the menu that I asked them for a piece of hotel paper on which to write you a letter. I never thought anything of it."

"Oh . . ."

"I have saved quite a sum of money, but I could not tell Ulla. She would be shamed and disappointed in me. She would want to know how I came by it and I could not lie in a letter. I have nearly enough to buy a new plow."

"Mama would not be shamed," she assured him, and applied gentle pressure to his arm. "She would understand, Papa. And, besides, we do not need a new plow now. Stone had our old one fixed."

"Who is this Stone, Kristianna?" Sixten frowned. "He does not sound Swedish. And where is he?"

"He is not Swedish," she admitted. "He is a trapper and he is no doubt at our hotel seething with anger at my disappearance."

"A trapper?" Sixten's blond brows drew down in a deep curve. "I believe you owe me an explanation as well, daughter. I want to know how you came by this man and what in God's name happened to Gunnar?"

For the next thirty minutes, she told him everything. From the time Stone rescued her from Newt Fraeb, to his being their hired man, and his tending to her during her illness. By the time she was finished, Sixten's face was filled with a scowl.

"And are you sure he plans to continue his trapping ways?"

"*Ja*, Papa, I am sure. Why else would he be talking to that man from the fur company?" Tears threatened and she blinked them away.

"And you still love him?"

"*Ja*." The single word was barely a whisper.

Sixten balled his meaty fists. "Why you got mixed up with a trapping man is beyond me, Kristianna. But married to him you are, and I will see to it he not leave you to grow old alone. Like it or not, the man will farm."

"Papa!" Kristianna exclaimed. "You cannot pin a man like Stone Boucher down. You do not know him."

"Then it is high time that I do."

393

·23·

Stone slung his rain-soaked Mackinaw blanket over his broad shoulders, ready to go out to search for Kristianna again. He grabbed his wet hat and his J & S Hawken and left the suite at the *Château de Saint Louis*. He'd been out three times already, and three times he'd returned hoping she'd be in the room. Thrice, he'd been disappointed. No, disappointed wasn't a strong enough word. Frantic was more like it. Where the hell had she gone?

There was only one theory that made any sense and that was that she'd gone in search of her father on her own.

Stone clenched his jaw and stomped down the stairs into the lobby. He'd told her to wait, to have patience. If she had any sense at all, she would have listened to him. After the stint with

Pitney, he should have known she'd try again.

If she'd waited until he returned, he would have been able to tell her that he had a lead on her father. But no, she had to be her usual headstrong self and thrust smack into the middle of everything. At least in the big woods, he knew what he was up against. Here in the city, there were so many places she could have gotten into, it was like searching for powder in sand.

He'd already looked up and down Main Street, but by the time he'd been able to inquire at Broadway, all of the shops had been closed for the evening. The afternoon's drizzle had turned into a rainstorm as darkness overtook the city and he'd had to search in the dimly lit streets for signs of her. He thought surely this last check at the hotel would have found her safely in their room and out of the rain, and now he was filled with panic which threatened his common sense.

Stone crossed the shining lobby floor, now strewn with throw rugs, and put his hand on the door to yank it open and slip into the night again. The door was being pushed in at the same time he was pulling it. He took a quick step back to allow whoever it was to pass through quickly so he could be on his way. As he moved aside, he brushed arms with the insistent patron and was met by a pair of violet-blue eyes. He sucked in his breath, let out an oath, and snatched Kristianna by the shoulders.

"Dammit all to Hades, woman! Where the hell have you been?" he yelled at her, digging his fingers into her tender flesh. She was soaked to the bone, her hair messily braided with wisps plastered to her face.

Kristianna was shocked to her toes to find Stone on the other side of the door. "I was—"

"You do not have to answer him," Sixten Bergendahl spoke from behind her, his massive frame filling the closed doorway.

Stone stared beyond Kristianna and to the brawny man behind her. "Who in damnation are you?" Stone didn't give the man a chance to answer. He didn't even give him more than a fleeting glimpse before he railed on. "What the hell is going on, Kristianna? What were you doing out in the rain, out in the middle of the damn night—with him?" Automatically, Stone gently pushed Kristianna aside and out of the way. He raised the barrel of his Hawken at the blond man's wide chest.

"You are the upstart Kristianna has told me about." His brows knit suspiciously. "I can see it in your eyes, young one. You point that gun at me and I will see your hide stretched out on my supper table."

"The devil you will, whoever you are." Out of habit, Stone raised the Hawken at a threatening angle at the man in front of him. Before he had a chance to cock his weapon, Sixten Bergendahl took a swing at him, landing his meaty fist square on Stone's jaw.

Stone stumbled several steps back on his moccasined feet, his rifle lowering to his side. He rubbed his chin in disbelief and shook his head to clear it. "Goddammit, you—"

"Stone! Stop it!" Kristianna intervened and

stepped between them. "You, too!" she called over her shoulder.

"Do not use the Lord's name in vain unless you want another taste of my hand." Sixten stepped around Kristianna and stood tall and straight, nearly the same height as Stone, save for a fraction shorter.

"Goddamn . . ." Stone mumbled as the realization struck him just as hard as if he'd been given another blow. There was only one other person who had been so hell-fired mad at him when he used undue profanity. And now with Kristianna standing next to the man, there was no mistaking where she learned the lesson from.

"He does not listen, your trapper. I warned you not to take the Lord's name in vain." Sixten took a step forward, and Kristianna put her hands out to halt him.

"Please, he never listens," she said in rapid Swedish.

"I know who you are." Stone practically laughed with a slightly hysterical edge.

"*Ja*, you had better know, upstart. I am her papa." Sixten pointed to himself. His shirt was soaked to the skin outlining the rigid contours of his chest as he puffed proudly. "Do not forget you are talking to your elder."

"Well, I can see now where she gets her temper from." Stone moved his jaw back and forth, snapping out the kinks. "Where did you find him?"

Before she had a chance to answer—not that she would have given him the satisfaction of one—the front desk clerk huffed his way to them from behind the counter, his face ruddy from the effort. "I will not tolerate altercations in the lobby. Take your leave at once." He pulled an impeccable, white linen handkerchief from his coat pocket and dabbed at his brow. "I should have known when you showed up in the hides of animals you were nothing but the same. I'll have your bags sent down posthaste!"

Kristianna, who was still in shock over the past hour's events, stood wide-eyed with embarrassment.

"You had better not be calling my daughter an animal, sir," Sixten threatened the clerk.

Stone cut in. "If she needs defending, I'm the one to do it. I'm her husband."

"And I am her papa!"

They were nose to nose now, each with eyes blazing a passionate rage. Kristianna choked back a squeal of helplessness. The situation had gone from bad to worse to hopeless. She'd always envisioned a joyous reunion with her papa and now it had turned into a complete disaster.

Stone and Sixten were arguing again and Kristianna raised her hands to cover her ears. "Stop it! Both of you," she shouted, on the verge of tears. "You, Papa!" she called. "Leave him alone."

Sixten seemed to back down a bit, but added nevertheless, pointing his finger, "I will not have you going off and leaving my daughter."

Stone's brows crashed down in dark slashes as he tried to decipher exactly what his father-in-law meant.

Kristianna was embarrassed to the core! How

could Papa humiliate her so? She'd hoped Stone would confront her about his plans himself and they could discuss them in private—not in the middle of a hotel lobby!

"What is he talking about, Kristianna?"

Sixten crossed his arms over his chest and snorted. "As if you did not know."

"Now is not the—" Her sentence was cut short as the clerk tossed their baggage at their feet.

"Out with you now!" he rebuked them. "Before I send for the law to do it!"

Kristianna sniffed back a tear. "Oh, why bother to discuss it when you have already made up your mind, Stone." She snatched up her valise and parasol, and trudged toward the door.

"Where are you going?" came from Stone and Sixten.

She ignored them and pressed through the double doors and out into the cold, damp night. She'd had enough of both of them. Papa being stubborn and pigheaded, not even bothering to tell her he was sorry for causing her such worry. And Stone, for caring for her, but not enough to want to stay with her.

Blindly, she walked up the street.

She hadn't gotten more than one building's length away when her father reached for the luggage in her hand, and Stone, holding onto his own gear and rifle, managed to drape the end of his Mackinaw blanket over her shoulders.

"I don't know what the hell is going on here," Stone reflected tightly, "but I do know that we're going to have it out. And not in the damn rain. You're coming with me, Kristianna. Now."

He steered her down a narrow street, as Sixten trailed along. "You," Stone called over his shoulder, "might as well come along."

"I have every intention of doing just that, Stone Boucher. And watch your cussing! It is not mannerly in front of your wife."

Kristianna knew it was futile to argue with the two of them and at the moment, she was anxious to be out of the rain. She was soaked clear down to her lace pantalets and the prospect of a warm, dry room outweighed her sodden pride. After she'd warmed up a bit, then she could think straight again. For now, she'd let Stone take her wherever he was going. She'd had ample taste of venturing through the city alone for one day. Besides, with Papa along to keep the peace, there could be no harm.

Stone came to another hotel and took the two short steps leading up to the front entrance. As she glanced at the sign above her head, The Noble Arms, she was filled with an odd sense of recognition at the name. But quickly, she dismissed it. She hadn't inquired in this part of town today; perhaps the name just sounded like one of the many other establishments she'd visited.

As Stone crossed over the lavishly appointed lobby floor, he didn't bother stopping at the front desk. The clerk looked up once from his books and gave Stone a nod. "Good evening, Mr. Boucher."

Kristianna gave Stone a quick, puzzling glance. He didn't acknowledge her questioning eyes. Instead, he climbed the plush, red-carpeted steps leading to the second floor. She held back a minute, slipping out of her end of his Mackinaw blanket. Scanning her surroundings, she noted that the hotel was elegant and more richly decorated than the *Chateau de Saint Louis*.

She looked fleetingly at her father who was gazing at the furnishings as well. Then she followed Stone, and Sixten came up behind her.

Stone strode to the end of the hall and opened the last door on the right without the help of a key. He entered and stood aside, allowing her and her papa to pass through.

Kristianna was surprised to see two men already in the hotel room—if a hotel room is what she could call it. There was no bed, clothing armoires, or washstands. There were two large oak desks with numerous ledgers and papers scattered about, and there were several wing chairs and on the far wall was a territorial map. She moved her gaze to the two men again and immediately remembered one of the men. Mr. Heacock, the man Stone had spoken to last night. And the other man . . . As she concentrated on his face, his identity struck her; he was Samuel Granger. There was no mistaking his wire glasses and Eastern finery. He'd told Stone that day long ago at Fort Snelling he'd be at The Noble Arms. Now she knew why the name had sounded familiar to her.

"I . . . do not understand." Kristianna found her voice, then hesitated, her eyes blinking with confusion.

Stone deposited his belongings on one of the chairs and slipped out of the blanket. He took off his hat, slapped it against his thigh to get some of the droplets off it, then slung it on the hat tree in the corner. "I believe you know Sam, Kris."

She mutely nodded at Samuel who in turn gave her a formal bow from the waist.

"And this is Heacock."

Mr. Heacock nodded curtly.

"Gentlemen," Stone declared in a resonant voice, "this is my wife, Kristianna, and her father, Mr. Bergendahl."

Sixten stayed back, not stepping forward to offer his hand. His pale eyes were filled with more than a little mistrust.

"I still do not understand." Kristianna smoothed her damp hair away from her brow. "How is it that Mr. Granger and Mr. Heacock know each other? Did you not say Mr. Granger worked for your papa?"

"If you would permit me, Stone," Sam spoke up. "I work for Alexandre Boucher, indeed. And Alexandre Boucher is the New York Fur Company. You see, Heacock here, is the agent, and I am Mr. Boucher's solicitor."

Kristianna looked at Stone who shrugged and raked his hands through his damp, dark brown hair. "As much as I hate to admit it, I'm the New York Fur Company, too."

Her confusion was worse than ever. "But why did you not tell me?"

"It's a long story." Stone moved to Kristianna who had begun to shiver. "First, I want you to get into some dry clothes. Then I'll explain it to you. I'll tell you everything."

Kristianna wanted desperately to hear his explanations. She wanted to believe that somehow she'd come to understand him and hoped that maybe, just maybe, she was wrong about him, that her thinking he was going to go off trapping had been a mistake. She gave her papa an appeasing look. "I need to listen to him, Papa."

Sixten shifted his feet and hooked his thumbs into the straps of his suspenders. "I am not sure I trust the upstart."

"Let me decide, Papa," she said softly.

Stone met Sixten's glare. "I can assure you, whatever you may think of me, I love your daughter. She's the most important thing in my life and I'll be damned if I'll let you influence her before I've had my say."

A warm rush leaped from Kristianna's heart. Did he really mean it? She was the most important thing in his life?

"May I put you up in a room tonight, Mr. Bergendahl?" Stone had taken a step closer to Kristianna and put his arm around her waist. His closeness sent a shiver down to her knees that she knew was not from the chilly clothes covering her skin.

"*Nej.* I stay in a room at Mr. Kelley's." He gave Kristianna a questioning frown. "Are you sure you will be all right with him tonight, daughter? I can find us another place."

"I will be fine," she barely whispered her assurance. "Please do not disappear again, Papa. I want to see you tomorrow."

"*Ja,* you will."

"Oh, Papa . . ." Tears filled her eyes and she left Stone's arms. She met her father's open embrace and she cried against his chest and this time he did not pull away in shame. Sixten stroked back her damp hair, talking comforting words in Swedish. Finally, he lifted his chin from her head and looked into her face. "*Jag är så glad ni är här i Saint Louis, dotter.* I am glad you are here in Saint Louis, daughter."

He then said to Stone in a sure tone, "I will see you tomorrow, Stone Boucher. You can be certain of it."

"I'm sure you will."

"*God natt*, then." Sixten left, giving his daughter a final nod before closing the door behind him.

Kristianna wiped the tearstains from her cheeks and sniffed.

"Come on, Kris. Let's get you into a hot bath."

For once, she didn't argue with Stone. That was exactly what she wanted.

Kristianna slipped deeper into the hot, rosewater-scented tub and sighed away her weariness. She lifted a handful of fragrant bubbles on her palm and blew them away, delighting in the scattered white shapes they made in the air before landing in the water.

The small room Stone had ushered her into was a separate bathing room, equipped with an ornate bathtub, carved oak washstand, and numerous towel racks holding opulent towels in navy and gold. The entire room was of those colors as well. Wallpaper, richly flocked, lined the walls and the single, small window was draped in heavy, gold velvet.

Kristianna thought the room looked masculine and wondered how many times Stone had taken a bath in this very tub. A tiny frown marred the corners of her mouth. Thinking of him in these richly appointed rooms was oddly disconcerting. She'd never pictured him as anything but a woodsman. To know that he'd always had this excellence at his disposal was hard to imagine since he did not seem to readily accept his city surroundings. So why . . .

"Feeling better?"

Stone's gravelly voice startled her and she snapped her head in his direction. He had donned a royal blue satin dressing robe that stopped at his muscular calves. With a will of their own, her eyes grazed over him, noting the way the tightly cinched cord around his waist emphasized the breadth of his chest and the narrowness of his hips. His feet were bare and he seemed at ease as he stood on the elegant throw rug in front of the tub. She suddenly wondered if he was naked underneath the robe and the image brought forth a tinge of pink to her cheeks.

He'd come in the second door that led into the small bathing room. The first door was connected to the office area, the second was attached to the private bedroom suite.

The close confines of the room and image of a naked Stone made her a little giddy. She was glad for the cover of the frothy bubbles so Stone could not see her trembling. "I am warmer, yes."

Stone kneeled beside the tub. She was tempting with her long hair partly flowing over the edge of the tub and floating in the water. Her breasts were hidden from his view, but he could see where the lush curves began. The alabaster skin inflamed him and he stopped himself from reaching out to her. Instead, he ran his finger across the water and he saw Kristianna shiver even though he hadn't touched her. "Mind if I join you?"

"No," she blurted, then quickly rescinded her answer, "*ja*, I do mind. You have not told me what all this is about and I could not think with you . . . with you in here with me." Beside herself, she blushed profusely.

Kristianna was surprised when Stone suppressed a laugh. "It's nice to know you still find me desirable, even though you're mad at me. Which I think is strange. If one of us is mad, it's me. You haven't excused yourself from running out on me to go find your father."

She frowned, her ire rising. "I found him, did I not? If I had waited for you, I might never have."

"That's a lie and you know it. I would've found him for you. I promised."

"You were too busy making arrangements with your fur company." She couldn't let him see the hurt in her eyes.

"That's right."

He didn't deny it and that enraged her.

She barely heard him when he continued, "I asked Heacock to help me. He's got quite a few connections in the city and I thought that maybe he'd be able to locate your father quicker than I could. I was mad as hell he showed up at the hotel. But as it so happens, he had a lead this morning."

Kristianna wasn't sure whether to believe him or not. As hard as she tried to stay angry at him, his words made perfect sense. "Then why did you not tell me?"

Stone leaned forward and rested his forearms on the edge of the tub. His eyes were mesmerizing and she stared into their unflinching, teal-blue depths. "Because I didn't want to get your hopes up until I had tangible information."

She sighed, supposing his story could be true, but still weighed other possibilities in her mind.

"Where did you find him?" Stone asked.

"I . . ." She didn't want him knowing about Tom Finnigan and Kelley's tavern. He'd surely go into a rage if he knew she'd been accosted. "I found him right under my nose." That was the truth.

"Under your nose," he repeated, his tone implying he needed more of an answer.

Nervously, she slipped deeper into the cooling water. "*Ja.* I just walked around and I ran into him on the street." Well, Kelley's tavern was next to the street.

"Ran into him?"

"Quit repeating everything I say."

"Quit talking in circles."

Kristianna resigned to telling him, knowing that he wouldn't give up until he was satisfied with her answer. "Very well. I got lost after walking up and down the streets. I ended up at the levee and stumbled into a tavern and found him."

Stone's eyes slightly narrowed, his jaw clenched. "What do you mean a tavern? Were you inside?"

"*Ja*, silly. How do you think I came to find him? He was working at a place called Kelley's and he did not want my mama or me knowing. He was ashamed."

Stone's temper soared, his lips tightening into a thin line. "I ought to tan your hide! You could've been hurt, or worse. I thought after your encounter with Pitney, you'd had enough of the city."

"Do not start yelling at me again!" she snapped. "He has been found, he is safe and that is all that matters."

Stone raked his hand through his shoulder-length hair and she caught herself staring at his face. He truly was concerned for her. He hadn't shaved since last night and there was a dark shadow of stubble across his rugged chin. She was quiet for a moment, promising herself to be more civil toward him.

"You had me crazed, you know." Stone picked off a bubble from the water's surface with his fingertip. His hand skimmed over the top, toward her. "I didn't know where you'd gone or what had happened to you. I kept thinking I'd die if I lost you."

Her pulse tripped a beat at his soulful admission. "Truly?"

"Christ, what do you think I am? Made of steel?" He fastened his hands on her bare shoulders. "I love you, dammit."

Kristianna quivered under his touch, lost in

the unyielding desire in which he given it. He leaned forward and she knew he was going to kiss her. She wanted him to, more than anything, but there were still unanswered questions. Regretfully, she placed her palms on his chest, the feel of his bare skin and soft curly hair sending a thousand tingles through her. "No . . ." Her voice cracked and she licked her dry lips. "No. Not yet."

Stone didn't let go of her, but he lifted his head. "What?"

Her heart was thundering wildly in her chest, and she forced herself to remain calm and to keep her thoughts off Stone and what he was doing to her—what she wanted him to do to her. "I have to tell you . . . when I saw you with Mr. Heacock, I thought you were planning on trapping this fall and leaving me. We have never talked about it, Stone, but what of the future? Will you stay with me, or will you leave me alone?"

Stone removed his hands and straightened. "Can't we discuss this later?"

"I think we have put it off long enough." Her voice was barely a whisper. She was deathly afraid of his answer. She believed he loved her, but she was uncertain he would sacrifice his livelihood for her. She had to know if her doubts and fears were for naught.

"I'm not a farmer, Kristianna. You knew that when you married me."

"I do not expect you to farm," she answered. "But you must understand that it is just as hard for me to give up what I believe in, as it is for you.

Just as you cannot farm, I cannot live the life of a trapper."

"I never asked you to," he replied quickly.

There was a long pause and Kristianna was afraid to meet his eyes. Finally, she lifted her head and tried to read the expression on his face. "Then what do we do?"

Stone leaned forward again and caught a piece of her wet hair between his tanned fingers. "I think Jemmy might have the solution."

"Jemmy?"

"Yeah. He's been discussing this Indian Affairs business with Lawrence Taliaferro. At first, I didn't like the idea, but I've been doing some talking with Heacock about it. The Bureau's going to be big in the territory. There's already talk about peace settlements with the Chippewa as early as next spring."

"What would you do?" Her interest had been kindled, and with it, her hope.

"I'm not sure. Heacock says some of the duties are dangerous, especially if the Indians don't trust me."

"Stone, I do not think I like this." Her earlier enthusiasm was quickly dashed with the thought of him endangering his life.

"There are other duties as well, Kris. One of them"—his face took on the start of a smile—"is to teach the Indians to farm. And we both know how much I know about that."

"Really?" Her brows lifted in question.

"I'm not saying that you could march right in the midst of a village and tell them how to use a shovel, but I think you could show me a few things that I could pass along."

Her hopes were lifting at the prospect and she smiled softly at him. "*Ja*, I could do that."

"Good. Now are you a little happier?"

"I am." Though she knew the solution sounded easier than it was going to be, his plan did make perfect sense. For the time being, she was satisfied. "Now you can kiss me." She gave him an inviting curve of her lips.

"You can bet I'm going to do more than that." Stone rose and pulled at the cord of his robe, letting it fall off his wide shoulders and into a heap at his feet.

Kristianna's breath caught in her throat as she looked at his naked body and watched as he put his foot into the water. His tightly muscled body tensed as he came into contact with the bath. "Damn, the water's cold."

She lowered her lashes sensually and extended her arms to him. "Then you will have to heat it up . . ."

Much later when the sun barely etched the sky to greet the new day, Stone and Kristianna lay entwined in the large bed of the New York Fur Company's suite. They'd spent most of the night making love and discussing plans for the future. Kristianna had never felt more content or fulfilled. She had everything she could ever want or need in life. She'd found her papa and he would be going home, and she had a husband who would stay by her side and live his life with her. She only wished Stone could say the same thing. Though they had not brought the matter up, she sensed Stone was thinking about his father. It was not hard to do, since they were staying in a room that was part of Alexandre Boucher. She'd gotten Stone to finally say his father's name and she recalled her earlier musings over Stone's middle initial, *A*, and now she knew that he'd inherited it. Her earlier questions came back to her and she wondered why Stone had had a falling out with his father, one that was serious enough for Stone not to want to see him even though he was sick.

Since she'd lost and found her own papa, she couldn't understand how Stone could be so cold. He was not that type of person at all.

Kristianna snuggled deeper against the man at her side, reveling in the warmth his body offered her. He drew his arm around her shoulder and held her tightly against his chest. She slid her hand over his torso and fingered the hair on his chest. For a long time, she was quiet, thinking of a subtle way to broach the subject. She knew he was not asleep, but deep in his own thoughts.

Stroking his firm neck, and moving to his thick hair, she finally spoke, "I think there is something else we need to talk about . . . that you need to talk about." She held her breath, waiting for him to reply.

"Alexandre Baptiste Boucher." She felt Stone's voice rumble faintly in his chest and on her cheek as he spoke.

"You have been thinking about him, too?"

"Christ, how can I not with Granger hounding me every chance he gets." He idly stroked her bare arm with his fingers.

"Are you still angry with him?"

Stone gave a short, deep laugh. "My old man and I will always be mad at each other. We don't like each other."

Kristianna was thoughtful for a moment. "I think you should give him a chance. It has been a long time. Surely whatever it was that you had a disagreement about is long forgotten."

Stone's silence gave her cause to think he was considering her words. "Maybe . . ."

"I think we should go see him."

Stone shifted and moved on his side to face her. He reached out and touched the tip of her nose with his finger. "You do, do you?"

"*Ja*, I do."

"You don't know what you're letting yourself in for. He's a barracuda. He'll snap you up with his sharp teeth."

"Then I will bite him back."

Stone chuckled and kissed her playfully on the lips. "I believe you would, sweetness."

"Good, then it is settled. We will go to see your papa and you can make up with him."

Backing away, Stone scowled. "I never said I'd make up with the man. I only consented to see the old cuss."

"Whatever you say." Kristianna gave him a knowing smile.

"We better tell your father that we're not going back with him." Stone settled his head back on the pillow and stared at the ceiling. "I'll book him fare on the next paddle boat."

"I do not think he would like that," she answered, toying with a lock of his hair.

"Why the hell not?" He cocked a questioning brow at her.

"Because he is a proud man. He will pay for it himself."

"I should have figured that." He took in her beautiful face, her large, luminescent eyes. "Now come here so I can kiss you proper."

She melted into his arms and allowed his firm lips to cover hers. His body pressed closely, burning like fire on her skin, searing her down to her toes. She deepened the kiss with a need of her own, blending with him, tasting him.

From the distance came an insistent pounding that she discounted as being her beating heart. The steady rap continued until Stone uttered an oath and lifted his head.

"What the hell?"

Muffled on the other side of the hallway door came a heavily accented voice. "*Dotter*? Are you in there? I said I would be back and here I am. Where is that upstart?"

Kristianna stifled back a giggle.

"Well, isn't this a flash in the pan!" Stone grumbled as he twisted the sheets from his long legs.

Sixten Bergendahl pounded on the door again. "Shall I kill you, Boucher? Where is my daughter?"

Kristianna laughed and sat up, her long hair in a tumbled web around her oval face. "What should I say to him?"

"Tell him he's the one who's going to be killed."

·24·

Buffalo, New York was different, yet the same. Stone looked out the carriage window at the many new buildings that lined Court Street. Scanning the new facades, he spotted a familiar establishment. The Eagle Tavern. He recalled the many times he'd sat in Benjamin Rathbun's pub, talking with the proprietor who had big goals. Now, as Stone took in the altered street, he experienced a strange part of his childhood that he'd thought—at the time—was in his past. But seeing everything once again, he realized that Buffalo was still very much a part of him.

There was an imposing three-story building with five double doors next to the tavern. The sign stated it was the Eagle Street Theatre. So, Benjamin had finally done it. He'd always talked about a grand theatre.

The carriage turned down Delaware Street and Stone felt his muscles tense and his heart speed up with apprehension. He wondered what his old man would say to him. He wondered what he would say to the old man. He hadn't written to say they were coming. There had been no point to it. Chances were, he and Kristianna would have arrived before any letter.

Inhaling deeply, Stone told himself it was too late to turn back, too late to change his mind. Instead, he gazed out the window and absorbed his surroundings. When he'd last walked down this road, it was nothing but chestnut groves and hemlock trees, and a single lumber mill. Now, it was gone and in its place, stately mansions. The road had been paved, no longer at the hands of the elements. Each house was painstakingly cared for with finely manicured lawns that encircled the massive dwellings. Stone fleetingly wondered what Alexandre thought of it all. The Terrace was no longer alone in all its majesty.

Stone settled back into the leather cushion and willed himself to accept his fate. He put his arm around Kristianna and gave her a brief smile. She smiled back at him and rested a reassuring hand on his thigh and he was once again in complete awe of her.

She'd weathered the harsh trip wonderfully, from the many coaches and bone-rattling roads, to the packet that took them across Lake Erie and into the Buffalo harbor. The harbor where he'd so often sat and stared and thought of what lay beyond the cry of the gulls and the oily smells of the wharves. Now he knew. Kristianna lay beyond it all and she'd been his strength, his resolve in coming home.

Her delicate fingers on his leg were a soft caress and he wished he could surrender himself to his true desires. Instead, he settled for a long glance at her. She was more lovely than any city-bred women they'd come across in their journey, wearing a new dress of navy-blue silk taffeta with a wide collar of cream lace and a single ribbon around her waist. The full skirts complemented her lush figure. She'd blossomed in the last weeks, her face taking on an almost constant flush that he found quite becoming. She'd arranged her long hair in a simple braid down her back, but accented it with a navy ribbon to match her gown. Her cheeks were blushed a soft pink, her lips full and dusky rose. Her eyes, which now turned to gaze at him, were a unique mix of violet and blue.

His heart ached for her with a love he never thought possible.

"You have been quiet." Her sweet voice carried softly to him.

"So have you," he answered, and captured her hand in his.

"I have been admiring our coach. I have never seen one with wallpaper in it before." Though the statement was true, she had been preoccupied by thoughts of Alexandre Boucher. But she didn't want Stone to know she was a little nervous.

Stone took the carriage for granted; he hadn't

even noticed the ruby-red wallpaper until now. "Rathbun owns it. His name is on the side of the door."

"Someone you know?"

"Used to know. Seems he's changed since I last talked with him. And for the better, I'd guess."

The steady clop of the horses turned to a slow walk as the carriage pulled up to its destination. The driver called down from his perch on top of the covered coach. "The Terrace, sir. As you requested."

Kristianna gave Stone's lean fingers a gentle squeeze and leaned forward to place a light kiss on his lips. "It will be all right. You will see."

Stone grazed his knuckles over her smooth cheek. She was like a fragrant flower and he'd be damned if he'd let his father crush her. He would go to the door prepared and at any sign of disrespect toward his wife, he'd be gone—this time, for good.

"Come on then." Stone reached around and pulled the leather door latch and swung it open. He disembarked and turned to help Kristianna down. After paying the driver, he sent him on his way; then it was just the expanse of lawn that kept them from The Terrace of Alexandre Baptiste Boucher.

The house was as he remembered it. A verdant carpet of manicured grass and flowering lilac clovers made up the grounds as well as wide branching sycamore trees. Lush woodland still encompassed the side rear of the house and Stone held back a single, hard laugh wondering if the old man still had his pond stocked with fish.

Stone unlatched the white picket fence and stepped aside for Kristianna to enter the long, pebbled walkway. He shut the gate behind him and closed his eyes, conjuring the image of the boy who'd slammed it in fury nine years ago. The boy was gone, the gate was still here.

When he opened his eyes, Stone examined the house before him. It was still a work of art, he had to grant his father that. A stately Georgian mansion rooted on a solid foundation of terracotta brick. He observed the many bright colors of shrubs and plants that lined the path to the house and thought of Solange. She had always had a fondness for her garden. The August weather had produced lemony buttercups, pastel roses, and cadmium touch-me-nots that emitted a heady fragrance.

From the side of the house a distant yowl became clearer as several peacocks with rich blue heads and resplendent trains of iridescent gold and green, dragged their tails and caught dew from the damp lawn.

Kristianna jumped back on seeing the odd birds and Stone put his arm around her waist. "Peacocks. They're harmless."

"I have never seen the like." She turned her head as the birds moved lazily under the late-afternoon sun. "Do they fly?"

"If they were smart, they would." The barb was lost on Kristianna as they approached the clean, charcoal gray steps that led up to the long veranda with slatted porch railings.

Kristianna grew expectant, knowing that in a few short minutes she was to meet her father-in-

law. If the manner of his house was any indication what type of man he was, she could not see
why Stone was so apprehensive. The house was
beautiful, the gardens well cared for. Surely the
man was just set in his ways and Stone had
misconstrued the seriousness of their falling out.

As she took the steps, Kristianna raised the
hem of her dress a little, still not used to the
longer lengths of the Yankee gowns Stone had
bought her. She looked at the white awning posts
and the hanging baskets of flaming azaleas with
small, parchment butterflies flitting over them.
She thought of Mama who would be more than a
little appreciative of the splendor.

She lifted her gaze; the house was a clapboard,
extending two stories in height with twelve paned
windows that were accented by malachite-
louvered shutters. Massive double doors
matched the color of the shutters and held heavy
twin brass ring knockers. On either side of the
doors were glass-enclosed wrought iron lanterns,
cold and dark in the morning hour.

Stone lifted one of the rings in his hand and
released it with a single rap.

Kristianna held her breath, knowing that this
was the moment they had come for. She didn't
have to wonder any further what would meet
them for soon they would be inside.

A single door swung inward and a dignified
butler stood before them. The expression on his
well-worn face showed he was rather perplexed
by the appearance of a well-dressed couple on the
threshold. Deliveries were usually made in the
rear and respectable callers had the good grace to

nnounce their visits in advance.

"Yes?" His full brow rose a fraction with more han a little hesitation attached to it.

Stone was not at all surprised to find he didn't now the butler. The way Alexandre's temperament was with servants, it was a wonder he could old onto any at all. "We're here to see Alexandre Boucher. Is he in?"

"Yes. But he cannot be disturbed. He is recovring from an illness."

"I know. That's what I'm here to see him bout. I'm his son."

"Yes?"

So far, the butler had said yes three times and ach time it held a different inflection; the last vas by far the more suspicious.

"Never mind." Stone pushed aside the door nd entered, stopping once to take Kristianna's and in his. "I'll tell him myself."

"Sir! This is highly irregular," the butler ar;ued, racing ahead of Stone and trying to stop im.

"My visit is irregular."

Kristianna helplessly followed Stone into the oyer of the grand house without a single pause as 1e strode purposefully to a pair of inlaid, heavy :losed doors.

Stone balled his fist as he stopped at the barrier vhich had closed him out before. This time, he vould not knock with intimidation. He gave a ;hort rap and pushed open one of the doors.

The butler dashed passed him, his face red vith agitation at the prospect of a severe reprinand from the master. "Mr. Boucher," he stammered, "I can assure you I tried to stop them!"

Alexandre Boucher sat behind his massiv desk, his fine linen shirt open at the neck. H stared up in surprise and his nostrils flared "Blakely, what the hell—" He stopped himsel short, his faded eyes narrowing on the tall man before him. A glimmer of life danced in thos eyes for a split second, then was quickly doused His eyes hardened to cold blue and he raised hi hand to his chin to rub it over his squared jaw "*Sacré bleu*, the wilderness son returns."

Stone locked his gaze on his father, his throa constricting. The old man had aged, but in a powerful manner. His hair, once a dark brown was now streaked with lustrous waves of gray His burnt honey skin had begun to show signs o his years, especially at the corners of his eye where the creases were prominent. Other than that, he did not look like he was at death's doo as Samuel Granger had implied. "*Monsieur*, it i good to see you, too." The gibe was cold and demanding a retort, but Stone could not contro himself.

Alexandre steepled his fingertips and sat back in his chair. "What would you have me say to son who renounced me nine years ago?" H looked beyond Stone to Kristianna who had remained silently at his side. Blakely still stood in the center of the room, his mouth agape at the revelations. Alexandre thoughtfully crossed hi arms over his chest and gestured to his butler "That will be all, Blakely."

"Very good, Mr. Boucher." There was still an undercurrent of mistrust in the servant's voice a he took his leave quite slowly. After a drawn-out glance over his dark-coated shoulder, he was gone from the room.

Kristianna watched Blakely go and when he had disappeared, returned her gaze to Alexandre. He was almost a mirror image of Stone. Quite handsome in a refined way. She swallowed hard, wondering when Stone would get around to introducing her or if she would have to do it herself. She didn't have to wonder long.

"You"—Alexandre pointed at her—"who are you?"

She licked her dry lips and answered before Stone could intervene. "I am your daughter-in-law, Kristianna."

Alexandre's brows spired. "So you've taken a wife? You're not French. What are you? Scandinavian?"

Kristianna felt the muscles tense in Stone's arm and she gave him a pleading glare for him to allow her to answer for herself. He relented, but not without her coaxing him with a gentle, confident smile. She turned away from her husband and directed her attention to Alexandre once again. "I am Swedish. Is there anything else you would like to know?"

"Why did my son come back after nine years?" The question was icy and cruel and Kristianna fought to control her composure. Stone applied pressure to her wrist and she was sure he was going to whisk her from the room.

"You self-righteous bastard. You haven't changed at all." Stone knew he was on the verge of a tirade, but it was too late to stop. "We came here because Granger said you were dying. I should have known I'd find nothing but a bitter old man who was still locked away in his fortress, looking out his goddamn picture window. What'd you do, send Granger off on a whim to find me and lure me back? If that's the case, you sure as hell have gone to a lot of trouble for nothing."

"I never sent Sam looking for you." Alexandre lifted the lid to a crystal decanter of gold brandy and poured himself a liberal draught. "Whatever he said or did, he took it upon himself, boy."

"I'm not a boy," Stone ground out. "Don't call me that again."

Raising the glass to his lips, Alexandre took a full swallow. He didn't counter Stone's allegation. "So you've come to see for yourself what happened to me? I can assure you I am still on this earth, though not enjoying it as much." He fumbled with the latch to his tobacco box and searched for a cigar. Finding the box empty, he cursed and bellowed out in a resonant voice, "Blakely! Dammit all, man! Where are my cigars?" He snapped the lid closed with resounding force and muttered, "The rake sides against me with that quacksalver Doctor Johnson. Blakely!" his words reverberated again. "My cigars!"

For a brief instant, Stone felt something akin to compassion toward his father. The older man hid it well, but he was not the same man he once was. For a flicker of a moment, he'd let down his guard and his face showed signs of the attack he had succumbed to. Suddenly, Stone felt as if he were years older than his father and it was his turn to be the domineering one.

"Maybe you should not have a cigar." Kristianna had spoken up, daring to address the issue. "If the doctor said not to, you should listen to him if you want to get better."

"*Mon Dieu, femme,* but you have nerve." His hooded eyes assessed her as if truly seeing her for the first time. Then to Kristianna's amazement, he added, "I like that."

Kristianna gave him a heartwarming smile that was not lost on him. His spindly composure was rattled and he picked up a stack of papers from his desk and shuffled through them. "Sit down, dammit."

With some resignation, Stone led Kristianna to the two New England wing chairs in front of the desk and helped her take a seat. Then he ensconced himself as well, knitting his fingers together and resting them over his broad chest.

"You don't look like a trapper," Alexandre observed without raising his head.

Glancing down to his tailored burgundy coat and tight-fitting trousers, Stone commented, "My buckskins are with our belongings down at the harbor."

"Where are you staying?" The graying head remained down.

"Haven't decided yet."

"You'll stay here."

"You ask me and maybe we will."

Alexandre's chin lifted. "I'm not asking for myself, I'm asking for Solange. She'll be happy to see you."

Stone wondered about the truth of that statement. He'd never really considered Solange anything but a timid woman who'd had the misfortune of marrying his father when she was too young. "How has she been?"

"She's been with me." There was an insinuation to the reply that Stone didn't bother with. Alexandre cleared his throat and tapped his finger on the edge of his desk. There was a moment's hesitation before he took the initiative to speak again. "Have you done well for yourself?"

Stone knew the question had cost his old man his pride, and didn't give him a rhetorical reply. "I have. Jemmy Paquer and I put in good seasons, enough to see us comfortable in the spring and summer."

Alexandre didn't comment on Jemmy Paquer. Stone knew that his father harbored an intense dislike for the Seneca, thinking Jem had come between them. Little did his father know that he would have gone west with or without Jemmy.

"And you," Alexandre directed his line of questioning to Kristianna. "What have you to say about all of this? I'm sure my son told you what a bastard I am."

At first she sought to rebuke him for his language, then she thought better of it and ignored his ill manners. "He warned me, *ja*. But I think you are more of a rainstorm than thunder."

"What is that you say?"

Stone allowed himself a slight smile. "She has a way with words like no one else."

Just then Blakely peeked his head through the double doors. "Yes, Mr. Boucher?"

Alexandre's attention was swayed and he bellowed, "Where the hell are my cigars?"

"I didn't take them, Mr. Boucher. I believe you should inquire of your wife about that matter."

"Dammit all then, where is she?"

"She's gone out, sir."

"Then go and buy me a box! And while you're gone, see to it my son's luggage is picked up and brought here."

"Yes, Mr. Boucher." Blakely slipped his head from view and shut the door once again.

Kristianna stared at Alexandre. "I thought you said you were not going to have a cigar."

"You suggested it, I did not agree to it."

A grain of irritation pricked Kristianna. "I can see now why Stone talks about you the way he does. You are not an easy person to reason with."

Alexandre took another drink of his brandy and narrowed his eyes. "I'd be interested in hearing more of this at dinner. You'll stay, of course. I want to know about you, madame. What kind of stock has my son married?"

Kristianna felt her anger rising to a threatening degree. "I am not cattle, Mr. Boucher."

"*Touché*," Stone said at her side. "I don't know why I doubted you could handle yourself with my father."

"I misjudged you." Alexandre ran his finger over the edge of his inkwell holder. "You are stronger than you look. Tall, too. I've never seen a woman with your height. It suits you."

Kristianna wasn't sure if she had just been given a compliment or not. She took in a slow, deep breath, suddenly feeling the stifling heat of the room. She hadn't noticed it until now, but the window was closed. "If you do not mind, Mr. Boucher, I would like to rest before the evening meal. Could you please show us our room?"

Stone's brows drew downward in a frown. He'd never known Kristianna to be so tired. During the last week of their journey, it seemed as if her energy had been sapped by noon. At first, he attributed it to the fast recovery she'd had with her foot and the pace of their travel, but now, he wasn't sure. He worried there could be something else. Maybe an after effect from one of the drugs he and Jemmy had given her.

Standing, Stone extended his hand to Kristianna. He pulled her into his arms and gazed questioningly into her eyes. She reassured him with a smile that didn't necessarily appease him.

"You know where to go, Stone," Alexandre suggested, not bothering to rise himself in the presence of a lady. That lack of etiquette grated on Stone's nerves, but he wasn't about to go into it now. His first concern was seeing Kristianna comfortable. "Your old room is as you left it."

It was oddly surprising to Stone that the old man had left his room intact. He'd have thought his father would have taken it down piece by piece, just as he had wanted to do with his son.

"We shall see you at dinner, Mr. Boucher," Kristianna confirmed, allowing Stone to lead her out of the room.

"*Oui, oui*." Alexandre once again focused his attention on the pile of papers on his desk, not bothering to look up. Only when the click of the door closing echoed in the room did he look up.

In that moment, his face relaxed and he lifted his fingers to his firm lips. He stared pensively at the door for a long time, his teal-blue eyes holding an expression of vagueness and faraway thoughts. Only after the clock outside the door chimed in its soprano "ting-ting," did he blink his lids as if to clear his head. He sat back in his large, leather chair and looked down at the gold-headed cane by his knee.

The next morning, Kristianna felt more refreshed than she had in weeks. A good night's rest on a bed secured to a solid floor and not a ship's planks had done her good. She wished she could say the same for Stone. He'd tossed and turned the entire night, his movements periodically waking her.

Dinner had gone reasonably well. She'd met Solange, who was not at all what she'd expected. She was quiet and reserved, allowing her husband to take full reign of the conversation. Somehow though, Kristianna found she liked the woman. Kristianna sensed that underneath her passive demeanor, there was a woman with great strength and fortitude. She'd had to have a strong will to have lived with Alexandre Boucher all these years.

Kristianna was fast discovering the truth to Stone's words. Alexandre was an unflinching man; a man who wanted things done his way, or no way at all. He was unpredictable, a factor that she had a hard time dealing with. At least the topics had remained on a fairly courteous basis. Mostly, there was talk on how much Buffalo had changed in Stone's absence.

She hoped breakfast would go peaceably also. Stone had already gone downstairs and she made her way down to the dining room table where she'd sat last night. The room was airy and sunny with a resplendent view through two French windows that opened onto a terrace brimming with riotous flower pots and baskets. Solange, Alexandre, and Stone were already seated and she felt a little embarrassed at being late. But she'd been hard-pressed to pull herself from the comforts of the bedclothes.

"I am sorry," she muttered a quick apology and took her seat across from Stone.

Stone gave her a quick appraisal, noting her color was much improved from the day before. Her complexion was white with a faint blush to her cheeks. She'd worn one of his favorite gowns, a simple day dress of rose muslin that accented her fair coloring perfectly. She'd left her long white-blonde hair loose to cascade down her back in shimmering waves.

The table had been covered by green baize and in the middle was an ornate floral arrangement of lavender roses, white daisies, and orange tree leaves, and Kristianna wondered if Solange had arranged them. She was struck once again by the contrast between the couple. Alexandre was dressed in a gilt-buttoned dress coat, ruffled white shirt, and flowing white cravat, while Solange was attired in a blue-black gown of silk, her black hair pulled severely from her face. Solange was truly pretty, Kristianna thought. The woman's skin was the color of magnolia petals, her eyes bluer than a robin's egg, and lips a natural ruby red. She reminded Kristianna of one of the China dolls Mr. Bidwell kept behind the glass counter of the Sutler's Store. And in a way, she thought Solange was also behind a wall of glass, so pretty, but just sitting there waiting for someone to pay her attention.

Kristianna broke from her musings and returned her mind to the present. "Your centerpiece is quite lovely, Mrs. Boucher." She decided that maybe all Solange needed was a little encouragement.

Solange's eyes glittered and she appeared surprised by the kind words. "*Merci*," came the soft thank you.

"Solange is always poking around in the dirt," Alexandre remarked as he took up the silver platter of pastries.

"I think her flowers are beyond compare. My mama would enjoy seeing them." Kristianna wished Alexandre wouldn't always have to put a cloud over everything.

"*Bon*. She will then." Alexandre continued to fill his dish. "Since my son has returned home, you will be living here."

Stone's fork clattered to his china. His eyes were steel-edged daggers of rage and the veins in his hands were prominent as he clutched the side of the table. "I knew you hadn't changed. I'm not here one day and already you're trying to run my life, dammit. Can't you understand that I make my own decisions?"

Alexandre's nostrils flared and he tossed his utensil down as well. "I thought *you* had changed. You are still the same foolish boy who left here nine years ago. Look at what you are throwing away again. You could have it all. The New York Fur Company can make you a wealthy man."

"I don't want your damn money! I never did. That's not what this is all about. It's about me and who I am. I'm not a city man. I'm *not* for sale and I never will be."

Kristianna stared helplessly, knowing that this time there would be no restraining Stone. He'd have it out, once and for all.

Stone scraped his chair back with vigor. He raked his fingers through his hair and pointed to his father. "The trouble with you is, you've never been out of this goddamn house. You don't know what's out there and you're afraid as all hell to see it. Open your eyes, *père*, there's life beyond The Terrace. It's expansive. A green wilderness full of nature and freedom. It's alive"—Stone balled his fist and shook it at his father—"and it's what I am." Stone caught his breath, trying to control the heavy heaves in his chest. "I'm sorry, Kristianna. I tried, I really did. I can't stay here. We're leaving."

Alexandre watched his son leave the dining room, his expression clouded. He fought his own internal battle and it showed on his face. Depositing his crisp linen napkin on top of his unfinished plate, he pushed back his chair. Without a word, he stood, gripped the edge of the table for support, and shuffled across the floor. He used the marble top of the sideboard for help with his stiff steps, then grabbed onto the doorpost as a crutch.

Kristianna watched in horror the obvious effort Alexandre put into walking and the pain that

t must have caused him. She turned her head
harply to Solange. "What happened?"

Solange sat straight in her chair, her dainty
vhite hands in her lap. "It is a result of the
ittack. He needs a cane to walk, but refused to
ise it in front of Stone. He says it makes him look
veak."

Her mind racing, Kristianna tried to think
back on their brief encounters with Alexandre.
When they'd arrived, he'd been sitting behind his
desk. Last night and this morning he'd been
sitting at the dining table before them, or at least
before her. And after dinner he'd insisted they
retire to the parlor before him . . . something
about him having a word with the cook. Now, it
made perfect sense.

"It may not be my place to speak . . ."
Solange's words were softly whispered. "But
Alexandre's heart was broken long before his
attack."

"Please," Kristianna urged the other woman,
"go on."

Solange stared out the window at the multi-
tude of flowers there. "When Stone left here nine
years ago, I should have said something then, but
remained silent. I feel that I am somehow a part
of their falling out as well. Alexandre is a very
headstrong man. I knew that when I married
him. But he is a good man, in spite of his faults.
He wanted so much for Stone to come into
business with him that maybe he did not handle
it in the right way."

"You cannot always please your parents.
Sometimes their decision is wrong." She thought
back to Gunnar and the mistake she would have

made in marrying him when her heart was with
Stone.

"Alexandre has been a broken man since his
son left him. He feared he would die never seeing
him again. I think it was pure stubbornness that
made him recover." Solange toyed with the hem
of her napkin and gave Kristianna a placating
smile. "Do not be angry with Alexandre. He only
wants what's best for Stone."

"I have to disagree with you, Mrs. Boucher.
think he wants what is best for him. And that is
not always the answer." Kristianna pushed away
from the table. "If you will excuse me, I think
will speak with Mr. Boucher myself."

Solange acquiesced with a nod of her coiffured
head, her blue eyes coming to rest evenly on
Kristianna.

Alexandre was sitting in his oversized chair at
his desk, staring out the large picture window
when Kristianna entered the study. He didn'
turn in her direction, but she sensed he knew she
was there. She moistened her lips and clasped her
hands in front of her rose dress.

"I will not speak long, but enough to tell you
how unfair you are being to your son."

There was no answer from Alexandre, not even
a flicker of movement. She dared to continue
"When I first met your son, I never thought
would marry him. He has different beliefs than
do and we constantly bickered over them. But
came to love him and he me and we have
compromised our situation." She took a step
forward to see if she could read any expression

on her father-in-law's face. She was only granted a fraction of his profile as he stared intently over the treetops and the distant Lake Erie. "Maybe if you would be willing to compromise yourself, you could see Stone's side of it. Come to Wisconsin Territory and at least view the land Stone loves. You do not have to agree with his opinion. Just come."

The silence was nearly deafening to her and she sighed heavily. "I am going to have a baby. Your grandchild." The chair creaked as Alexandre shifted his weight; still, he did not face her. "I have not told Stone yet and I am sure once he knows, he will want to get home as soon as possible. I will write to you and tell you when the baby arrives." She took a shaky breath, glad to have said her peace. "That is all I have to say."

Turning on the heels of her Prunella shoes, she left the room.

Alexandre's hands trembled as he held onto the arms of his chair. He looked beyond the sycamore trees of his magnificent home and to the horizon, his eyes reflecting he wasn't really seeing anything at all. Swiveling the chair to his desk, he examined the desk, absently shuffling the many ledgers, papers, and documents that belonged to the New York Fur Company, the company he had lived and breathed for for most of his fifty-three years. Finally, he could control the quaking of his fingers no longer. He rested his head in his hands and squeezed his eyelids shut.

·EPILOGUE·

July 12, 1837
Wisconsin Territory
Minnesota Country

"**W**hy does she have to wiggle so much?" Stone asked, struggling to dress his baby daughter. "I can't get the blasted hooks fastened."

Kristianna turned away from the oversized stone hearth. Her hands were laden with hucks and a cake pan that was still steaming with fragrant vanilla sweetness. She set the finished cake on a cooling rack resting on the pine table-top and laughed at Stone. "You have to tell her who is boss. Otherwise, she will try and roll over on her back."

"I've realized that."

Moving across the puncheoned floor of the small log cabin, Kristianna stood next to her husband. He was sitting on their bed in the corner with Anna on the sunburst-patterned comforter. The baby was dressed in a cloth diaper with one arm in her dress and one arm out. Kristianna placed her hands at her aproned waist and scowled at the rosy-faced baby. The infant's pale downy hair was in wispy disarray, evidence of her struggle. Seeing her mother's face, she ceased her wiggling and stared up at her with large, deep blue eyes. *"Anna, ni bli en bra icka för Papa."*

"I think she's listening to you," Stone commented, his hands still holding onto the ruffled dress that was askew. "What did you say?"

"I told her to be a good girl for you. She will now." And true to Kristianna's words, the baby settled long enough for Stone to slip her other arm into the tiny, snowy gown.

"Thanks, sweetness." She moved away from him, but he caught her by the fold of her full skirt. "Come back here so I can thank you proper."

She giggled and bent down to receive his kiss. His lips were warm and hard and evoked a dazzling disorder to her every nerve ending. She would never tire of his kisses, no matter how fleeting they were.

"Wish we had more time . . ." Stone playfully tugged on the end of her apron, slowly untying the bow.

"You are impossible." But she smiled with a twinkle in her eye and she retied her bow. Going back to the table, she forced her heartbeat to slow down and inspected the cooling cake. She frowned as she looked at it. "It is crooked again. When are you going to fix my iron spider?"

"I'll bring it into Murphy first chance I get. You

437

know I've been busy with the Bureau now tha
the Chippewa Treaty is being signed in tw
weeks." He picked up his daughter, held h
under her arms, and swung her around in a circl

"She will spit up her milk on your shirt if yo
spin her hard."

"No, she won't. She likes me."

Kristianna smiled at her husband. He pam
pered the child. She couldn't have asked for
better and more giving father for their baby.

Sighing with a soft breath, she recalled th
transitions their lives had taken over the las
year. They'd returned home from Buffalo, Nev
York and Stone had accepted Major Lawrenc
Taliaferro's job with the Bureau of Indian A
fairs. Stone had thrust himself into the ne
position with vigor. She knew part of his enthus
asm had stemmed from the fact that he'd give
up his trapping ways. He still met with Jemm
Paquer and they went off on hunting trips fc
days at a time. She allowed him his freedon
knowing what price he'd paid for it. Since the
were just outside of Fort Snelling, she was give
ample time to spend with her parents while h
was away.

Stone had built a fine, strong cabin and it wa
here that they spent most of their time. Th
furnishings were simple and sturdy, made wit
Stone's own hands. He was a fine craftsman an
she'd decorated the one large room as warm an
comfortably as she could. There were trinket
representing Sweden as well as Stone's French
Canadian heritage. But the most prized posses
sion of all was the framed sketch on the wa

above their bed. It was her picture, drawn by George Catlin. She'd come across it in Stone's belongings and he told her how he'd paid to have it done that day at Fort Snelling. She valued it above everything else.

Kristianna was snapped from her musings by the approaching sound of horses and the rattle of a buckboard's harness. She dashed to the gingham-curtained window to see who it was. "I do not have the cake frosted yet! And my dress. It is a mess." She quickly swiped at the flour imprints from her dark, prairie-brown skirt. "Mama, Papa, and Noelle must be early."

Stone stood beside her at the window. "So what if they're early? We don't have an anniversary party every day."

Looking at the dusty path that cut through the evergreen pines, Kristianna saw the horse-drawn vehicle come into view. The driver definitely was not Papa and was no one she recognized at this distance. "I wonder who it is?" She smoothed back the wayward strands of her hair that had escaped from her braid.

"Don't know." Stone handed her Anna and reached above the door for his J & S Hawken. He pulled the latch string and stepped outside into the bright afternoon sun. Kristianna followed and stood next to Stone. Shading her eyes against the glare, she tried to make out the driver and his companion, who at this point, was obviously a woman.

As they neared, it was apparent the man knew nothing of driving a rig. The horses tugged and pulled, colliding against their harnesses. Almost at the cabin now, recognition hit Kristianna full force. It must have came to Stone at that exact moment, too, for she noted the way his lips compressed into a thin line.

The man, dressed in a fine coat of emerald velvet and a black, silk top hat covering his lustrous gray hair, drew back on the reins. He attempted to set the brake handle of the weathered and ill-repaired wagon. "Dammit!" he cursed, and tried to pull back the steel lever again. "I've never driven such a piece of rubbish. Solange, get down before we fall through this contraption right on our asses."

Solange Boucher gave Kristianna an apologetic smile and tried to get out of the buckboard with a fair amount of dignity.

Kristianna nudged Stone to go help her. Still clutching his rifle, his face was tight and filled with shock. His eyes were dark and mistrustingly on his father as he moved to give Solange a hand. He gave her a feeble smile to put her at ease.

"No one at that infernal outpost you call a fort would consent to drive us out here." With effort, Alexandre swung his legs down, his hands gripping the iron-rod back of the hard seat. "I had to rent this abominable contraption for three times its value." He reached over the floorboard and grabbed a gold-handled cane, then hobbled around the stomping horses to where his son stood.

Stone swallowed hard. He knew Kristianna had written to his father several times in the past year, but had refused to ask her what she had said and if his father had ever written back.

"Well, aren't you going to say anything, Stone?" Alexandre resounded, putting his weight on his cane.

"What would you have me say?" His voice was deep and flat, masking his emotions.

"You could start with hello," Alexandre offered. "Then you can tell me what an ignorant bastard I've been."

Stone lifted his dark brows incredulously.

"I've come to see this Godforsaken land you love so much." He briefly assessed his surroundings. "There's too many damn trees and rivers. No decent roads."

"Time will change that."

Alexandre's nostrils flared slightly and he cleared his throat as if his next words were stuck in his vocal chords. "I don't have time." He moved his cane from his right hand to his left, then outstretched his arm.

Stone looked at the hand his father was offering. His father had never shook his hand, had never even signified that Stone had become a man. Silently, he accepted the gesture, his fingers firm in his father's. Alexandre's grasp was strong and steady, not at all hinting at any weakness.

Moisture filled Kristianna's eyes at the reunion. There may have not been startling vows of love and overt apologies, but it was a beginning. A new beginning. "Well," she sniffed, blinking her eyes to keep the tears from slipping down her cheeks. "Come into the house. We are having a party today and my parents should be along shortly."

"First, give me my granddaughter," Alexandre

insisted. He handed his cane to Solange and stretched out his arms for the child. Kristianna willingly gave Anna to him.

Anna studied the man holding her with curious eyes. When she realized he was no one she was familiar with, her tiny face screwed up and her rosebud lips curled into a whimper. Alexandre gruffly patted her back. "Don't you cry for *Grandpère, ma petite.*"

Not having accustomed himself with the gentle handling of babies, his brusque tapping paid off with a milky spot of spit on the lapel of his finely tailored jacket. Alexandre looked down at the stain and gave vent to a loud, resonant laugh. "She's got nerve. I like that. She'll do well with the New York Fur Company."

Stone gave his father a warning glare, but there was not much force in it. "You'll never give up, will you?"

"I still haven't given up on you." Alexandre gave his son what Kristianna could have sworn was a wink of his hooded eye, then his face darkened to a grimace as he tugged at his lapel. "Solange, for Christ's sake, give me your handkerchief so I can wipe this off!"